W9-BBV-188

THE ASCENT

THE ASCENT

ADAM PLANTINGA

This book is a work of fiction. Names, characters, places, and incidents are the product of the author's imagination or are used fictitiously. Any resemblance to actual events, locales, or persons, living or dead, is coincidental.

Grand Central Publishing
Hachette Book Group
1290 Avenue of the Americas, New York, NY 10104
grandcentralpublishing.com
twitter.com/grandcentralpub

First Edition: January 2024

Print book interior design by Jeff Stiefel

Library of Congress Cataloging-in-Publication Data

Names: Plantinga, Adam, author.
Title: The ascent / Adam Plantinga.
Description: First edition. | New York : GCP, 2024.
Identifiers: LCCN 2023036564 | ISBN 9781538739877 (hardcover) | ISBN 9781538739891 (ebook)
Subjects: LCGFT: Thrillers (Fiction). | Novels.
Classification: LCC PS3616.L366 A94 2024 | DDC 813/.6--dc23/eng/20230804
LC record available at https://lccn.loc.gov/2023036564

ISBNs: 978-1-5387-3987-7 (hardcover), 978-1-5387-3989-1 (ebook)

Printed in the United States of America

LSC-C

Printing 1, 2023

For my big brother Nate,
who's always been in my corner.

THE ASCENT

I did not die,
yet nothing of life remained.

—*Dante*

The best way out is always through.

—*Robert Frost*

CHAPTER 1

Officer Kurt Argento parked in the station lot of Precinct Nine and hoisted his off-duty bag over his shoulder as he walked to the back entrance. Someone had snapped the antennas off two of the parked patrol cars and scrawled red graffiti on a third that read *Fuk Police*. The fact that the *c* in *Fuck* was missing made it more insulting somehow. It was par for the course at the Ninth Precinct, which was an outpost deep in hostile territory. Last week, someone had taken a wet shit on the roof of the lieutenant's personal SUV, although Argento wouldn't have been surprised if the culprit been another cop—station morale had been ebbing for some time.

When Argento got to the locker room, he took hold of his padlock before he realized he couldn't remember the combination. It wasn't a new lock. He'd had it for years. But the numbers to open it were lost in the fog. He stared at his locker. The bumper sticker that said *Sig Sauer Firearms: To Hell and Back Reliability*. The takeout menu for a local Italian joint on red-and-white paper. A photo of a thirty-five-pound Chinook salmon he'd caught on a fishing trip in Canada years back, during better times. Giving up, he went downstairs to the station keeper's office and grabbed a pair of bolt cutters. Like his gun, the tool felt right in his hands. The keeper was asleep in a chair, a TV remote on his chest. Argento slammed the cutters on the counter and the keeper jolted awake.

"Morning," Argento said.

The keeper pinched his forehead, irritated at being woken. "Make sure you sign those out," he said. He was a fleshy guy named Sweeney, with a pronounced chin and a sprig of hair plastered across his forehead like a mollusk, working inside because he was no good for the street. Seemed to be more and more of those types these days. Some were on a deserved reprieve from an injury or a traumatic incident in the field. Others were just wasting space. They didn't quit, they didn't get fired, they just lingered, cops in name only, doing the same job a civilian could do for less pay. Argento stared at Sweeney until the other man looked away and busied himself with paperwork.

Back upstairs, Argento snipped his lock off. He opened his locker and removed his boots from the top shelf. He hadn't polished them in a while and it showed. But no one in the department, other than the command staff, polished their boots. No one would give him any grief about it. It was a hotter-than-normal summer in inner-city Detroit, which meant the shootings and street rips were stacking; the bosses were just happy you showed up to work at all.

He ran through his gear: handgun with two mags, knife, pepper spray, radio, backup piece, flashlight, collapsible baton, badge, two pairs of cuffs because not all criminals traveled solo, leather gloves to guard against razors and syringes, a vial of Narcan to revive junkies, and a police whistle that he had never once found cause to use. He had been a cop for twenty-one years and had done this inventory thousands of times, but he ran through it again, just to be sure. If he couldn't remember his locker combination, he could easily forget something else. Wander into the field with no cuffs and a fucking turkey sandwich jammed into the ring where his nightstick should be.

He held his duty gun in his hand. A Glock .40 with rubber grips and night sights. He hefted the weight. It felt right. Guns made sense. They were something he could count on. If he squeezed the trigger, a bullet would come out. He pictured going somewhere quiet and still, pushing the barrel into his mouth, angling it up, and shooting himself through the brain. Pictured the finality of it. The relief it would bring. He'd be leaving a world he was no longer at home in. But it was an idle thought. He knew he wouldn't do it. Suicide was quitting, and he wasn't much for quitting. The cleanup and aftermath would be a headache for his coworkers. Plus, he wasn't going to kill himself today because he hadn't killed himself yesterday. It was habit, nothing more. He was in the habit of living. He holstered up, the gun settling in with a familiar metallic whisper.

He allowed himself a look at her photo before he closed the locker. Long, tangled brown hair. Slightly crooked grin. Oversized Red Wings T-shirt, even though she had never shared Argento's interest in hockey. *I want to look tough*, she said. Something bottomless opened in the center of his chest and the weight of it made him want to take a knee. Last night he had eaten dinner alone at home and used the good plates, the ceramic ones they'd gotten as a wedding gift a decade before. When he was done, he dropped them one by one until the floor was covered in shards.

Downstairs, he walked past officers without a word. He checked the daily lineup on the bulletin board. He was assigned to work with a patrol sergeant instead of another officer, which was unusual. Meant the lieutenant wanted to check up on him and was sending a sergeant to be his eyes. Maybe the lieutenant had heard things about Argento's recent work performance. His trouble focusing. His anger issues. Multiple citizen complaints of excessive force, although those boiled down to suspects starting fights with Argento and then immediately wishing they hadn't. The sergeant's name was Pendelton, a rawboned guy on his second Filipino wife. He was halfway competent but had a reputation for playing it too safe.

"I'm sorry about Emily," Pendelton said when they got in the squad car.

Argento nodded and stayed silent. It had been two months and he still didn't know how to respond to condolences. He was still trying to come up with his locker combination. If he could retrieve it from the fog, then maybe he could build off that. He'd have more clarity.

Their first assignment was a cold burglary at a new condo complex that had sprung up on the edge of gangland turf. A laptop and a bicycle had been stolen. The condo carried the odor of lemon and weed. The homeowner, a young guy with bro-stubble and shiny track pants, followed them around the house like he thought they were going to steal something themselves.

"The bike was a Cervelo R5, fifty-four centimeters, with Dura-Ace 9000 brakes and a Quark Elsa crankset power meter. It had a zero-setback seat post."

"Okay," Argento said. He had a mountain bike of his own, and neighborhood kids would come to him when their bikes broke down because he liked to tinker, but none of them had Quark meters. They had whatever they could find at garage sales or from shops going out of business. One of the kids, a scrawny fifth grader with big ears, wouldn't tell Argento his real name, going only by "Tincan." He was loud and funny, insisting that the only thing he knew about white people was they had the money to ride horses, and not even on a ranch, but for fun. Tincan was prone to asking hard questions about the job and why cops were the way they were. Sometimes Argento had the answer. Sometimes he didn't. Regardless, Tincan was easily Argento's favorite out of the bunch.

"It had a Fizik Antares saddle. Are you writing all this down?"

"You're describing a bicycle, right?" Pendelton asked. "Sounds like a spaceship."

"Yeah, it's a bike. Bike that probably costs more than you make in a year."

The radio crackled with a report of a fight in progress. Six to eight male suspects, dark skin, late teens to early twenties, were jumping on the hoods of cars and trying to pull out the occupants at an intersection three blocks from the burglary. They left the condo without a word. Pendelton hit the lights and siren and pulled up short of the scene. Argento activated the body camera mounted on his chest plate by pressing the center button twice in rapid succession.

He saw the problem numbered more like twelve. A local street gang called Tre-9 had claimed the turf, and it didn't take much to set them off. It looked like their regular crew: tattooed young men, white T-shirts, low-slung pants, the usual. They had taken over the intersection and were trampolining parked cars and throwing glass bottles at passing motorists. Next to a Volvo with its driver's side door open, three men huddled over a fourth man, who was prone on the ground. One of the men reared back and kicked the fourth man in the head. His body twitched. The Volvo had a Wayne State University bumper sticker. Maybe the guy took a wrong turn after visiting his kid on campus. Now he was being beaten half to death in public by strangers.

Summer in Motown.

"There's too fucking many. We'll wait for some more cars to clear them out," Pendelton said.

It didn't take long for them to be spotted. Half the pack broke and ran toward them. Pendelton tried to throw the squad in reverse, but he wasn't fast enough. The pack surrounded them and Pendelton locked the doors. One of the bangers stood on their hood.

"Come out, bitches," the guy on the hood said.

"Stay in the car, Kurt," Pendelton said. "We ain't gonna win this one."

Argento took his baton out. It was heavy and he was strong. In his hands, it did more damage than most men could do with a sledgehammer. Argento was good at fighting. He liked to fight. And now with Emily gone, there was nothing to hold him back. Nothing at all.

"Kurt, stay in the car. I ain't trying to...that's an order." Sweat had popped on Pendelton's brow, and his eyes darted as he looked for an escape route. Tactically, he was probably right. But he was weak. They were all weak.

The three men were still standing around the fourth man, who was still motionless. One of them stomped on his head, which made the man's toupee fall off. The group found this funny. One of them scooped up the hairpiece and put it on his own head at a jaunty angle. The guy on the hood was now pissing on the windshield. Argento hit the wipers, looking for guns in waistbands. He didn't see any, but that didn't mean they weren't out there. He unlocked his door.

"Goddamn it, Kurt, stay in the . . . What are you doing?"

What was he doing? When he signed on to be a cop, he agreed to put himself in harm's way. He agreed to protect the good people of Detroit from violent predators without delay. It was insulting that the bangers thought they could beat a man near death in front of his marked squad car without reprisal. And he was looking for a brawl. There were twelve-odd suspects. Argento wanted more. Forty. Four hundred. Send the whole city.

"Stay in the fucking car!" Pendelton rasped.

Argento got out of the car.

CHAPTER 2

His Ford F-350 pickup had a hundred thousand miles on it, and he figured it had another hundred thousand left before it was through. He drove west, through the flatlands until the skies darkened. Their cinnamon-colored Chow-Shepherd mix, named Hudson after Argento's favorite character in *Aliens*, occupied the back seat. Argento reached back and scratched his head occasionally as they drove. He stopped at a rundown place with a sign that read *Gas & Food*. He liked that. Anonymous, just like him. He ordered coffee and two burgers, fed Hudson from a bag of gourmet dog food, and looked at a discarded newspaper as he ate. The Detroit Tigers were languishing in last place. They couldn't get any runs. "All slumber, no lumber," the columnist wrote. The front page had an article on a cyberterrorism group that had hacked into state government mainframes nationwide and stolen Social Security numbers and building blueprints. Argento didn't know anything about cybercrime and didn't care to; he'd take a meat-and-potatoes violent felony any day. The paper's entertainment section ran a picture of a famous model who was celebrating her nine-month anniversary with her boyfriend. "Turning Heads in Thigh-High Boots," the headline said. In the photo, the boyfriend had complicated hair and wore a smirk on his face like he'd won something. Argento tilted his coffee cup toward the picture and let the drops spatter the newsprint until the couple's faces disappeared in a wet blur.

After dinner, he drove a few more hours in darkness until he crossed the Missouri state line, finding a roadside motel that looked in his price range. Emily was far from a debutante, but she preferred to stay in places that were three stars and up. This place looked like a solid one star; the lobby carpet was patchy and stained, and Argento could smell the booze on the night clerk's breath.

"What's the name of this town?" Argento asked.

"Rocker."

"How is it here?"

"It sucks, dude," the clerk said. He had shoulder-length hair and a pierced nose, which made Argento resent him for no particularly good reason. The clerk handed him his room key.

Argento didn't ask about the pet policy. Hudson was a welcome addition to any motel no matter what the rules said. He walked to his truck, liberated Hudson from the back seat, and the two of them went to the room, which smelled like cigarettes and feet. He sat on the edge of the bed and rubbed his unshaven jaw. He didn't have to follow department grooming protocol anymore and could grow a beard down to the floor now if he wanted. He had noticed a liquor store a block down the street, but he wasn't going to drink, not tonight. He had cut down markedly on the booze after he married Emily, and he hadn't been drunk in years. And he knew if he started now, he'd never stop. He'd be well on his way to becoming one of the alley rummies from his old patrol sector, the ones with grimy faces and plastic cups they rattled in the hope that you'd put coins in them. The bottle killed more cops than bullets ever would.

"Just the two of us now, Hud," he said.

Hudson padded over and lay down next to him, making a sound that almost seemed like a sigh. Hudson keyed into emotions as much as any human, and he knew Emily was gone. It made him sad, and it made him sad that Argento was sad. Argento once had a court case where an eleven-year-old girl named Isabela had been severely beaten by her father and was terrified to testify against him. Argento formed a bond with the girl and had subsequently gotten the judge's approval to bring Hudson to the stand with her. She testified, with a low voice that picked up strength as she went, looking directly at her father, one hand rubbing Hudson's thick cinnamon coat. When it was over, Isabela gave Hudson a kiss and held him tight.

"I'm sorry," Argento said. "I miss her, too." He rubbed Hudson's head, then closed his eyes and thought back to how it had all ended a week before. He'd disobeyed a direct order from his sergeant, and it had led to four broken bones and three concussions. None of the injuries were his, but one of the concussions was Pendelton's, who had reluctantly followed Argento out of the car and promptly taken a glass bottle to the dome. It had also resulted in multiple felony arrests, including the man that assaulted Pendelton. The motorist with the toupee had survived.

But the police commission hadn't cared about any of that. They cared about Argento's insubordination. They cared about his recent history of unlawful force complaints, which meant he was on a short leash. They cared about what it looked like to the public to have a white cop free-swinging a baton at multiple young males of color in a department with a long history of racism that was under federal consent decree and supposedly focusing on de-escalation. They thought he should have stayed in the car, too.

He was given a choice. Resign from the only job he was fit for or face a termination hearing on multiple administrative charges, including insubordination. The man presenting him with this choice was a doughy police commander who had a habit of looking away when he talked to you. Argento knew from a credible source that this man had once abandoned his partner and fled from a bar fight when he was two years into his career and had been called Captain Cluck behind his back ever since.

"I'll resign," Argento said. "But not to you. Send a real cop in here."

They did, calling in a deputy chief whom Argento had worked with before and respected. And then that was the end of it, after twenty-one years on the job. No gold watch, no plaque, just a plastic bin to put his uniforms and equipment in, some paperwork to sign, and a partial pension. Twenty-one years of running toward screaming and gunfire, a few thousand arrests, a stint on SWAT and Street Crimes, and three commendations for valor. He had been in two shootings, one of them fatal, and had once safely caught a baby that a man with orange hair high on bath salts had flung off a roof. He hadn't always gotten the job right, but he never took a cheap shot at a suspect or lied on the stand.

Last Christmas, he had given a shivering seventeen-year-old prostitute a few hundred dollars and put her on a bus home to Chicago. Then he had found the girl's pimp, a gap-toothed parolee with the street name of Muppet, and broke his jaw when he resisted arrest. Twenty-one years. It was the family business, law enforcement. His uncle had been on the job in Detroit, as had his father, who once came face-to-face with a convenience store robber, with a gun in hand. Argento's father let loose with the shotgun at close range, spattering the man's brain and skin all over his own face and mouth. He'd cemented his legend when, after he'd wiped off some of the gore, he'd casually asked the clerk if he had a toothpick to get out the rest.

Argento could have tried to stay on the force. Could have gotten a lawyer from the police union, appealed to an arbitrator. But times were changing on the job, and he wasn't changing along with them. They wanted guidance counselors these days, not lawmen. They wanted the police to take resisting felons into custody using only soothing words, although the viral videos of cops roughing up compliant suspects had left him disgusted at their lack of honor. Even if he won and stayed employed, they would have made him wish he hadn't, by shipping him off to some meaningless assignment processing parking permit requests or tracking shoplifting complaints on a digital map.

Argento was in Rocker, Missouri, for no better reason than he had to be somewhere. He had an affinity for Detroit, even with all its problems, but at the moment there was nothing to hold him there. His parents had passed, and he had a sister who lived out of state that he didn't speak to after she'd put a series of ACAB and "abolish the police" posts on social media. Emily's family had never taken to him. They had always thought Emily could have done far better than a street cop with only a high school education. They had been quiet and bewildered at her funeral, looking at him as if he'd somehow brought this hell down on their only daughter. He had friends from the job, mostly hunting and fishing buddies, but the ones he'd been closest to had retired or moved away. When anyone else called him, he didn't answer. He had been alone before he met her and now she was gone and he was returning to his natural state. He needed to be away from the things that reminded him of her, so he'd left home, gotten in his truck, and driven west. He'd never seen the Pacific Ocean. Neither had Hudson. Maybe they'd start there.

He liked the idea of being somewhere calm and warm. He'd oiled and stored his tools in the garage but left his cell phone on his nightstand because there was no one he wanted to talk to. He hadn't bothered to put a stop to his mail or newspaper. He imagined both piling up in yellowing mounds.

He fell asleep on top of the bed still dressed, Hudson at his side.

He woke in the morning saying her name. He looked around the room and checked his watch. He had slept late. Hudson was awake, watching him serenely. The pain of her absence was inescapable. One more moment with her. That was all he asked for. One more moment, to hold, absorb, live in. He closed his eyes. He heard rustlings in the adjacent hotel room. The indeterminate hum of pipes and appliances. Faint sounds of traffic outside. He was a sinking ship, he thought. And when the ship is going down, you seal off the damaged compartment so the craft can stay afloat.

But the seal doesn't always hold.

He opened the drawer next to his bed, where Gideons had placed a Bible. He took it out but didn't open it. There were passages inside that he knew would help him, but he wasn't in a place where he could hear them. For now, it was enough just to hold it. After Emily died, his lieutenant had observed somberly that God was dropping rocks on his head. But he wasn't angry at God. He had suffered a crushing loss, but worse things had happened to better people than him. He needed whatever help he could get from above, for today and for whatever was to come.

He got back on the road but stopped when he saw a bright sign with an arrow advertising the Rocker Summer Festival. It seemed as dumb a place as any to get a late breakfast. It was midmorning but the temperature was already on its way to eighty. Maybe they'd have apple cider. Argento turned off the feeder road and parked his truck in a dirt lot, where it joined several others. He leashed Hudson and rubbed his head.

"Could be fun," he told Hudson. "We'll leave before you get too hot."

The festival wasn't much. There were a few farm exhibits, one of which described the varying qualities of hay. Games of chance and fried foods on sticks. A few carnie-operated rides, but no Ferris wheel. Some prize-winning pigs, although the fourth-place pig looked about the same as the first-place to him. He sat at a wooden table far enough away from the smell of animal dung and watched the crowd. Some middle schoolers walked by, chattering. A chubby girl of about twelve in glasses and a sequined shirt too tight for her brought up the rear of the group but stopped as the others kept going. She was sweating heavily as she eyed a frozen lemonade stand. She dug into her pocket for change. Argento could see her lips move as she counted it. There was a slowness about her.

A thin man with a widow's peak and a sharp jaw was leaning

against a tree nearby watching the girl. He wore a jean jacket and his pants were streaked with mud. He saw the girl look at the price of the lemonade, look at the few coins in her hand, and then put the money away. He waited a beat and then strode up to her. Something extra in his step. Something Argento didn't like.

"You want one of those lemonades?"

The girl nodded.

"There's another place nearby, sells 'em cheaper. I'll take you there. Then I'll take you back to your friends." He began walking toward the edge of the fairgrounds and motioned for the girl to follow. She hesitated for just a moment.

"You know me, right? You've seen me around?"

The girl nodded again.

"Then let's go."

She fell in beside the man, who put one hand lightly on her shoulder to guide her off the fairgrounds. He looked behind him to see if anyone was following. Then the two of them disappeared from view around the back of a thick grove of trees.

Argento was in a bumfuck town where he didn't know anyone, much less this girl. He wasn't a cop anymore. He was an unemployed transient with a dead wife and few prospects.

But there were some things you don't walk away from. His father had taught him that, long ago, when he was a boy. Shown him, too, on a few occasions, young Kurt watching from the safety of a doorway in awe as his father interrupted a strong-armed street robbery of an elderly man by tossing both twentysomething suspects into a dumpster and locking the lid.

When he found them behind a rusted trailer, the man in the jean jacket was unbuckling his pants with one hand and was using the other hand to force the girl to her knees. She looked at Argento, her eyes shot through with confusion.

"This isn't what summer festivals are for," Argento said. He tied Hudson to a tree, giving a sharp pull on the leash to make sure it would hold. The man sniffed, rubbed his mouth, and let the girl go.

He took a buck knife out of a sheath on his belt. Hudson barked, seventy pounds of muscle straining at the leash.

"I got people," the man said. "Let me walk."

"If I do that," Argento said, "you'll just keep doing this."

The man flipped the knife blade open. "Have it your way."

Argento felt it then, the hum of physical expectation that shot through his arms and torso like an inflamed nerve. He peeled off his shirt and twisted it into a rope good for warding off a blade. It was bad business walking into a knife fight unarmed, but Argento didn't mind. He had been here before. He walked toward the man, who seemed startled, but just for a second. He raised the knife.

"This is gonna hurt," the man said.

You got that right, Argento thought.

CHAPTER 3

Two Rocker County deputies arrived at about the same time the ambulance did. The first was a young, broad guy in sunglasses with a sunburned face and a name tag that said *Ferraez*. He looked at the girl, who was sitting on the grass with her legs crossed, eyes focused on nothing. He looked at the man in the jean jacket who was flat on his back, very still, his arms and legs at unnatural angles.

"Jesus," Ferraez said. "Was this a car accident?"

"That's Donny Rokus," the second deputy said. He was an older man with long sideburns and a name tag that said *Wells*.

Ferraez tilted his sunglasses up off his face and surveyed the still form. "Sure is."

The ambulance crew was a private contractor; the side of their rig was marked *MedStar*. They checked Rokus's vitals. His breathing was shallow.

Wells turned to Argento. "What happened here?"

"He took the girl back here to sexually assault her. I stepped in. He drew a knife and we got to fighting."

"And?"

"I'm better at fighting than he is," Argento said. He turned to the ambulance crew. "You should C-spine him. He's gonna have head injuries."

"Where's the knife?"

"I gave it back to him. It's in his leg."

"Check for that," Ferraez told the ambulance crew. One of the EMTs stabilized Rokus's head. Then they rolled Rokus to the side on a three-count, which revealed a streak of crimson and the hilt of a knife protruding from the meat of his upper thigh. "Yep," the EMT said as he cut away Rokus's pants leg with medical scissors to get a better look at the wound. "He's gonna be a transport."

"You need to get out of here," Wells said.

"You want to take my statement at the station?"

Wells looked at Ferraez, who shook his head.

"Take my advice," Wells said slowly. "Leave town as soon as you can. We'll call you if we need you."

"I'm a witness in an attempted sex crime against a minor. I stabbed this guy with his own knife and then I hit him in places that did some damage. Pretty sure you'll need me."

"Partner, let's get this young lady reunited with the group she came with," Wells said.

Ferraez nodded and took the girl by the hand. "C'mon, sweetheart." She followed obediently, just as she had followed Rokus before. She cast a backward glance at Argento.

"Bye," she said brightly.

Argento gave her a wave. "Get her a lemonade," he told Ferraez. Then he turned to Wells. "You gonna interview her? Ask to see my ID? Take any pictures? Look for more witnesses? Do any cop stuff?"

"We got what we need."

"Something special about Donny Rokus?"

Wells's face grew tight, which was as much as a yes.

"This is the worst felony investigation that I've ever seen," Argento said.

"Special circumstances. I'm trying to look out for you."

The ambulance crew immobilized Rokus with a hard backboard and cervical collar, and secured his head to the board with tape and foam blocks. "We gotta go," one of the EMTs said. "Right now. He might have a brain bleed."

"I'll follow you," Wells said. He took his sunglasses off and perched them on top of his head. Then he looked Argento up and down. "You one of those martial arts guys?"

Argento gave a noncommittal shrug. He had been a regular in the Police-Fire boxing league and won not because he had an overly refined technique, but because he was a merciless hitter and could absorb blows himself without losing his moorings. A few years back, he had been unofficially banned from the circuit after he'd been in the ring with a preening fire lieutenant and punched the glory boy so hard in the abdomen that he put one of his ribs through a lung.

"Pretty sure you did what you had to," Wells said. "But remember what I said. Go get yourself out of town." He leaned forward and scratched Hudson's head, who was still patiently waiting by the tree. Hudson let him. The deputy was wearing a uniform, and Hudson liked cops. "That's a good boy," he said. And got in his squad car and followed the ambulance off the fairgrounds. When they reached the feeder road, the two vehicles hit their lights and sirens and sped off.

Argento stood there for a time. A small crowd had gathered but thinned once the police and ambulance departed. An old-timer with a white beard and a hat that made him look like a train conductor peered at Argento through thick glasses.

"Chow Shepherd?" he asked, pointing to Hudson.

Argento nodded.

"Fine animal."

"The best."

"Looks like you hit that fellow real good. Knocked his block off."

Argento hadn't heard anyone say *knock his block* off since the eighties.

We'll call you if we need you, Wells had said, but he hadn't asked for a phone number.

"This place got apple cider?" Argento asked the older-timer.

"Nope."

Argento looked at his hands. His knuckles were red and raw from hitting Rokus. Argento's wedding ring had always been a little loose, and the fight had pushed it up almost over the second knuckle. He cinched it back down. Taking out Donny Rokus had gotten his blood pumping. It was a welcome change of pace to feel something other than sorrow and inertia. But it was time to pack up shop. The brawl had attracted too much attention.

He walked Hudson back to the truck and drove through what Rocker called downtown. The highlights seemed to be a gun store and a supermarket with a red, white, and blue sign that said *Hometown Proud* and was advertising a two-for-one special on nightcrawlers. He followed a sign pointing to the freeway. He had the on-ramp in sight when he saw the red and blue lights of a deputy sheriff's car behind him. He pulled to the shoulder. Maybe they had changed their mind about needing him as a witness. Or maybe this was all about to turn into something else.

"Driver," a crackly voice came from the PA. "Go straight a block and take your first right."

Argento was a law-abiding type and did as he was told, finding himself in a dead-end alley sandwiched between two abandoned buildings. Not where he would have picked to make a stop. If things went bad for the officer, no one could see you. Maybe the sheriff's department had their own down-home traffic stop procedures he was too big-city to understand. He killed his engine and put his hands on the steering wheel, just as he'd ordered motorists to do when he was working. Then something told him to take his wallet out of his back pocket. He turned his radio to 88.5 and pressed the rear defrost button at the same time, causing a small compartment to open up underneath the dash. He'd taken a drug interdiction class once where the Highway Patrol instructors had demonstrated how dealers rig their cars with traps and crevices to hide contraband. He'd been so impressed, he'd built one for himself, just for fun. He dropped his wallet in the compartment and closed it. Just in case.

It wasn't a deputy who approached him on the driver's side of the truck. It was the sheriff himself, based on the amount of pins and bars on his uniform. He was a gaunt man of about fifty with white hair near the temples and a sour face. Argento caught a whiff of sunscreen and tobacco. Another officer, this one a deputy, posted up near the passenger side of Argento's truck. He was a hefty guy with thick forearms and wraparound shades. He had his game face on, but it softened upon seeing Hudson.

The sheriff's face didn't soften. He looked at Argento. Argento looked at him back.

"Keys," the sheriff said.

Argento handed them over. The sheriff put them in his left shirt pocket just underneath his name tag, which said *Rokus*.

And Argento understood.

"You got ID?"

"I'm sure it's in here somewhere," Argento said.

"Get out," Rokus said.

Argento looked at Hudson. Hudson whined.

"Be right back," Argento told his dog and got out.

Rokus motioned toward the back of the car. Argento went there and the deputy thoroughly patted him down. Argento wasn't armed. He had turned in his service gun and hadn't brought any of his own firearms with him. He owned eleven of them, a mix of pistols and long guns, and they were locked up at home in a Kodiak gun safe that had a swing-out rifle rack. He figured if he needed a weapon on this road trip, he'd just borrow one from somebody, like he'd done with Donny Rokus and his buck knife.

"So," the sheriff said, his right hand resting on his holster, "we got a report from the fair that a hard-looking fella in a Ford truck with Michigan license plates and a dog busted up my little brother. Hurt him bad. Fella matching your description. And here's your Ford truck with those Michigan plates. And there's your dog."

"Your brother was forcing himself on a sixth grader. Then he came at me with a knife. Didn't leave me a lot of options."

"Donny," the sheriff said, "he ain't wired right. But that don't mean you can do him the way you did. Family, you know?"

Family. *No, I don't know*, Argento thought. *Not anymore*. He took a look around. No one else in line of sight, just the three of them. No witnesses. He sized up the two lawmen. The deputy was silent, maybe even a little uncertain. Just following the sheriff's play. Both were wearing body cameras, the same kind used when he was in uniform. They were on, but neither of them bore the steady red light to indicate they were recording. Not an encouraging sign.

The sheriff saw Argento looking at the camera. A faint smile creased his face. "State said we had to get 'em on account of police reform. But sometimes we forget to hit all the right buttons."

"I stayed at the scene, tried to give a statement to your boys," Argento said. "They weren't having it. You want to take me in, take me in. But make a decision."

"Oh, you're coming with us," the sheriff said. "That's for damn sure. But you shouldn't have resisted arrest."

Argento pushed back the familiar white cone of anger in his chest. He had to play this smart. Two rednecks policing like it was 1950s Alabama weren't going to goad him into a fight.

"This bell you're thinking about ringing," he told both men, "you can't unring it." He turned around and put his hands behind his back. Compliant. Going with the program. That was when the sheriff shoved him with a strength that belied his age and frame. Argento was propelled into the deputy's chest, one of his hands landing on the deputy's badge and the other on his body camera.

"Lookie there," the sheriff said. "You just assaulted a deputy. Tried to rip his badge off. Tried to take his camera."

Argento saw the deputy's nightstick clear the ring and he hunched and pivoted to absorb the blow on his thigh. He took the second swing higher up on the same leg before he went down, hands over his head, legs drawn in to protect his vitals. The Sheriff joined in and both men rained blows on Argento's back, his arms, his lower torso. Argento stayed hunched in on himself, his face bunched in pain and baking on the hot asphalt. Hudson barked, a few sharp retorts at first and then sustained fury.

"That bell you were talking about," the sheriff huffed between blows. "Think we ringing it."

"Okay," the deputy said, equally out of breath. "He's had enough. We gotta stop."

"I say when we stop," the sheriff grunted.

"Don't hurt my dog," Argento managed. "Don't..."

A baton rose and fell and a balloon burst in his head. He tasted blood on his tongue. Heard a staticky hum. Then nothing.

CHAPTER 4

"Height?"

"Five nine," Argento said.

"Weight?"

"Two ten."

"Race?"

"White."

"You look kinda mixed."

Argento's mother was German, his father Italian, and he had inherited the latter's olive skin. He did not feel like explaining this. He'd woken not in a hospital but at a police station, although given how he felt, a hospital would have been far more appropriate. He was handcuffed to a bench, and another deputy he hadn't seen before was filling out his booking card in a sally port. Argento's head throbbed and he knew he was or would be black and blue from head to foot, but he didn't think he had any broken bones. Still hurt like a mother. He took short breaths, a sour taste caking the inside of his mouth, and tried to compartmentalize the pain. He ran his tongue over his teeth. Felt like he still had them all. That was a win.

"I'd like an ambulance."

"For what?"

"Got hit in the head with a nightstick. A doctor should look at me."

"How 'bout you stop being a pussy," the deputy said. "What's your name?"

"Chris Spielman."

"Spell it."

Argento did.

"Address?"

Argento thought about that. He wasn't sure when he'd be going back to his house. "Transient."

"Where'd you live last?"

"Detroit."

"Negrotown," the deputy said automatically. He was a slight man with a bad complexion and although he was young, his hair was already thinning and formed a crescent moon on the top of his scalp. His uniform was too big for him and billowed at the sides.

"Plenty of white trash," Argento said. "You'd fit right in."

"You got a smart mouth. Maybe we'll take you back to beat-down alley." He gestured up toward the ceiling where a bubble camera was trained down on them. "You're lucky there's cameras."

"Lucky," Argento said.

"Occupation?"

"Unemployed. What are my charges?"

"The sheriff will be along shortly to explain all that."

"Someone gonna explain where my dog is?"

"Sure," the deputy said. "You bet."

After a while, the first deputy was joined by a second, the meaty one who had been at Argento's traffic stop. Argento stared at him, and the deputy held his gaze for a moment before looking away. He had seemed ambivalent at the scene of the beating. His heart wasn't in this. That didn't give him much credit with Argento. He couldn't remember his locker combination, but he was going to remember this deputy.

Argento was escorted to a cell that smelled of piss and was

single-cuffed to a metal hook. The door shut behind him. He took inventory of his surroundings. Sink, toilet, bench. Several people had scratched their initials into the wall across from him. Someone had carved the words DO FLUSH in all caps. Shitty search, letting a prisoner take anything with an edge into the cell. Argento was less than impressed with the Rocker County Sheriff's Department. They had room for growth.

Kurt Argento had never laid down for a beating before. He loathed how it felt, physically and mentally. Prior to today, he wasn't sure he'd ever lost a fight. Even at the academy in the RedMan training scenario, where recruits were put in full pads and PT'd to exhaustion in the mat room, then pitted against the hardest instructors the department could muster, he'd prevailed. Hurled the 230-pound SWAT sergeant off the mat and then kicked him through a set of double doors into the hallway. They were still talking about that one at the Detroit Police Department. Long after he graduated the academy, he still worked out every day. The most committed cops all did. Sprints, jump box, weights, and mat work. If some con tried to wrestle his gun away, he was too strong for them to get it. If someone ran, he'd catch them, even with an extra fifteen to twenty pounds of equipment on his belt.

But none of his experience or fitness mattered back in the alley. There was no utility in taking on two cops on their own turf without friendlies to back him.

Argento had seen police corruption before. A plainclothes unit at his station had been indicted for filing false police reports in an effort to shore up their gun cases against violent felons. A few guys had gotten pinched for turning in inflated overtime cards. An officer or two had been busted for soliciting sex on the job or committing domestic violence. But he hadn't seen anything like this. Unprovoked beating, denial of medical care, arrest on what would undoubtedly be some trumped-up charges, all to protect the pedophile brother of the local law boss. Where was the American Civil Liberties Union when he needed them?

He stretched out on the cement bench as best he could. It was his first go-around in jail. It didn't bother him much. Whether he was behind bars or not, Emily was still gone and he was still out of work and the Pacific Ocean wasn't going anywhere. He tried to put himself in the head of the Rocker Sheriff's Department. What would be their next move? Right now they thought he was just a bum who'd wandered into town, but if they knew he was a recently retired member of the Detroit PD, that would present them with a problem. It was one thing to thump a drifter. Quite another to do it to an ex-member of a major metropolitan police force, someone who could take the witness stand and be credible and convincing. So they'd probably consider suiciding him in his cell.

That was why Argento had given them the name Chris Spielman, a former linebacker for the Detroit Lions. Spielman's name combined with a random date of birth wouldn't come back with any positive hits, so they'd have to wait for fingerprints because he highly doubted anyone would find the trap in his vehicle that held his wallet and driver's license. Argento knew his prints were in the system because all police recruits were printed prior to being accepted to the academy. But he didn't know how long it would take Detroit's computers to talk to Rocker's. A few hours? Better part of a day? Argento was thinking this over like he cared, but all he really wanted was to go a few rounds with the sheriff and his lackey to square what they'd done to him at the traffic stop. Then he'd call it a draw, and he and Hudson would keep pushing west. He was no crusader. If the good people of Rocker wanted to rise up against their rotten sheriff's department, that was on them.

Argento turned onto his side on the bench. He moved slowly but the motion still hurt. Before Emily had left this world, he'd slept about five hours a night. Now, he slept as long as he could. Ten hours, twelve, sixteen. He would come home from work, exercise, eat dinner, and go to bed. On his off days, he'd rarely leave the house except to go to the gym or take Hudson for a walk. There was nothing out there for him. But he couldn't sleep now, not without knowing that Hud was okay. He concentrated on the ceiling. Thought about sports. His mind drifted to baseball and the '84 Detroit Tigers. He ran through the starting lineup. Trammell, Whitaker, Gibson, Parrish. His father had pulled him out of school once when he was a kid and taken him to a day game at Tiger Stadium, the grandest place Kurt had ever seen. Jack Morris had struck out the side, and when the ball rolled past him, Morris had deftly flipped it up with his feet into his waiting glove. Argento always remembered that.

Then his thoughts turned, as they always did, to his wife. The timbre of her voice. The way she looked when she was sad. She was gentle, patient, forgiving. She had faults but he couldn't remember them. He only remembered the good. Maybe that was how it was supposed to go. Maybe that was how God kept people from going crazy. As a cop, he had always worked a tough beat. They had talked about what if something happened to him. They never talked about what if something happened to her. When she was first diagnosed, there had been tears and anxiety and endless calls to doctors and insurance companies, but then she had settled into a preternatural calm that sometimes, late at night, Argento had coveted.

An hour later, there was a sharp rap on the door and it opened. The sheriff stood at the doorway chewing on some sunflower seeds.

"The man himself," Argento said.

"That's right," Rokus said. "So how'd you like our summer fair?"

"Learned the difference between straw and hay."

"And what's that?"

"Hay is dried grass. Straw is the dried stalks of already harvested cereals, like wheat or oats."

Rokus spat a seed near Argento's feet. "Fucking fascinating."

"What am I being charged with?"

"Two counts of resisting arrest. Two counts of attempting to disarm a peace officer. Two counts of aggravated assault on a peace officer."

Nothing about the festival or Donny Rokus, Argento noted. He figured there was no way they could cover that up without revealing the assault on the girl. "What's the bail?"

"More than you got. And we don't got no bail bondsman in this state so there's no help for you there. Hell, you're not even going to be able to afford the tow fees on your truck."

"I asked your deputy for an ambulance, but he didn't seem to know how to get one."

"They got nurses at the jail. They'll take good care of you. Why? How's your head?"

"It's okay," Argento said. "Helped that you and your deputy are weak and out of shape."

The sheriff's expression didn't change. "And here I was starting to feel a little sorry for you."

"You run me up yet?"

"Your name's not coming back. That's usually what happens when fellas have warrants they want to hide. We'll wait on fingerprints. People lie, but fingerprints don't. And I had them expedited so we'll get the results by the end of the workday. Your truck is listed to an Emily Vasquez. She your side piece or just some poor gal you stole it from?"

Emily had kept her maiden name. Argento tried to ignore the question even as it sent a hot spike of anger up his center. Rokus spat another seed on the floor with seasoned nonchalance. His complexion looked sallow under the yellow industrial light of the booking hallway. His eyes were deep-set. There was nothing behind them. Maybe he'd always been a bad cop. Maybe he'd started out right but something along the way had turned him. It didn't matter to Argento. He was going to settle this with the sheriff. Whatever it took.

It was time for Argento to ask the question that he'd saved for last. The one he really didn't want to ask, but the only one that still mattered. "What happened to my dog?"

"It got mean when you started fighting us," Rokus said. Jaw working the sunflower seeds. Face expressionless.

Argento's hands tightened into fists so tight he thought his fingers might burst through the skin.

"Had to put him down."

Argento looked down at the floor as the hot spike morphed into a red squall. He closed his eyes. Everything that was good was gone. When the storm subsided and he could talk again, he said, "Gonna make you wish you hadn't."

"You got other problems on your plate. Prison bus is taking you to the state penitentiary. We got some sewage issues in the county jail, so we've been shuttling a select number of folks straight to the Whitehall Correctional Institute. I get to say who. You got arrested here on a Friday, and Monday is the July Fourth holiday, so you won't be seeing a judge until Tuesday. Makes you a good candidate for the pen. As for me, I'm gonna go see my brother in the hospital where you better pray he makes a full recovery. After that, I'll be on my way to Louie's Smoke House. Every Friday night they got two for one ribs. I'm gonna eat my ribs and drink my beers while you get sodomized by some fellas who probably won't even be polite enough to introduce themselves first."

Argento thought about that. Then he said, "You always been this way?"

"Which way is that?"

"Clown dressed up like a cop."

"You," Rokus said, wagging his little finger at Argento. "You're one of them guys. Billy Badass. Joe Cool. Folks who try to make all the things they say sound tough or funny. Well, I run into that type all the time. And when I'm done with 'em, they ain't so tough. And they for sure ain't laughing. So what do you think of me now?"

"About the same," Argento said.

Rokus was about to reply when a voice came over the the PA.

"Transport bus is here, Sheriff."

Rokus nodded. He spread his hands toward Argento, as if in invitation. "Welcome to hell, shitbird."

CHAPTER 5

Julie

Julie Wakefield blinked the sweat out of her eyes and checked her watch. Ten miles down, two to go. She was running a race called Centurion, a dozen miles of rough terrain and thirty-odd obstacles from start to twisty finish. It was her fourth such event, and she was on pace for a personal best. She was staying in Jefferson City for the summer taking classes and had some friends in town, but they weren't up for the rigors of the Centurion, and the most athletic thing her fiancé, Eric, did was take out the recycling. Eric was a quiet, considerate man who would rather watch a political debate than a ball game, and she loved him for it. They were getting married in a little over a month, and the race was a welcome break from the endless wedding tasks like seating charts and cake choices.

Julie was twenty-five years old and in the best shape of her life. She was pushing hard and it hurt. In lieu of her coursework, she'd been reading a book called *War* by a journalist named Sebastian Junger, about U.S. soldiers fighting in Afghanistan. In the book, Junger described pain as being at the edge of a dark valley. At the bottom of the valley was true incapacitation, but it might take hours of misery to get there. Julie remembered the exact quote that followed: "If you don't panic at the first agonies, there's much, much more of yourself to give."

It hurt, Julie thought as she surged forward, but she had more to give. Much more. She took in the next obstacle ahead, a thirty-foot-high wall canted toward her at a sixty-degree angle with irregularly placed studs for handgrips. It was called The Mammoth. No problem. Her breathing was labored but she felt strong. No, screw strong. She felt *mighty*. It was a glorious early July day in central Missouri, and the sun was warming her bones. She squirted an energy gel into her mouth for the boost and kept her legs churning, which were coated in brown sludge from the course's mud. She headed right for the center of the The Mammoth, sidestepping a runner who was blocking her path. He was leaning forward, hands on his knees in the classic tripod position, his mouth hanging open as he looked up at the thirty feet of woe the wall represented. Defeat was etched on his face. Julie had seen him that morning in line at registration, gussied up in a headband, designer athletic gear, and two gold rope necklaces.

"Let's do this!" he shouted to no one in particular. Then he'd noticed her, puffed his chest out, and leered at her.

"Baby," he'd said. "See you at the finish line."

Julie noted that the man's headband had now slipped over one eye and he was missing a shoe.

"Let's do this," she said as she surged past him and attacked the wall. She wasn't a gloater by nature, but there was an exception to every rule.

He looked up at her, bleary-eyed, and coughed wetly. Julie didn't even try to suppress the grin.

A few hours later, she was showered, changed, and in her father's office, feeling the oxygenated repose that followed a hard workout.

"How's the wedding stuff going?"

"Not bad. Mom is helping me with the heavy lifting."

"Believe me," her father said, "she loves it. How's Eric?"

"Working nonstop on his dissertation. I could tell you the title of it, something about chemical matrixes and free ions, but neither of us would know what it means. How's tricks in the statehouse?"

"Let's not talk about me," he said. "Let's talk about you. Specifically, your future."

"And I was in such a good mood."

"Jules."

"I know. I'm not mad. It's your parental duty."

Governor Christopher Wakefield looked like the celluloid stereotype of a politician. Strong jaw, good hair, crisp dresser. He was fit from a combination of swimming and tennis and stood around six foot two but seemed taller because of good posture. He had ably served as the governor of Missouri for the past six years, six years of strong leadership and sensible legislation. The closest thing he'd come to a scandal was when he'd blanked on the name of the St. Louis hockey team during a press conference after the Blues had made the playoffs; he later confessed to Julie he'd never watched a hockey game in his life. There were whispers of a presidential run, but Wakefield hadn't made any formal announcements.

"My future," Julie echoed.

"You don't seem all that invested in your master's degree. You don't talk about it much or where you're hoping it'll lead you. I know you killed it on the course this morning. You gonna be a professional obstacle course runner?"

"I don't know. One thing at a time. I'm going to prison tomorrow. Then I'm going to spend the Fourth of July with Eric. Beyond that, I haven't planned much."

The governor grimaced at the mention of the word *prison*.

"It's fine, Dad. I need to do a field visit for my summer class in Corrections. It's going to be a quick tour."

"I don't like the sound of it. Why can't you tour a courthouse or somewhere more pleasant? It's a Corrections class. Judges correct people. I know a bunch of judges. I could arrange for lunch afterward. Let me make some calls."

Julie was already shaking her head before her father was finished talking.

"Damn it," her father said.

"What?"

"I made a tactical error."

"Was it forgetting that I despise special treatment as the governor's daughter? So you saying you can make some calls on my behalf just makes me want to double down on going anyway?"

"That's the one."

"It's fine, Dad. This place is close. Besides, I like to see how the other half lives."

"That's what documentaries are for."

"I'm paying for my own grad school, which means you aren't allowed to meddle."

"And after grad school?"

"Well," Julie said, "that's where we're in sort of a gray area."

"All right, how gray?"

"Charcoal," she said and smiled. It was one of their favorite exchanges from the movie *Fletch*, which they had watched together umpteen times when she was growing up.

"Which prison are you going to?"

"Whitehall."

"That's a private prison. Maximum security. I've heard some things about it I don't like. They have a state inspection coming up and there's some rumblings they're not going to exactly shine."

"This isn't an immersion tour. I'm not going in a cell with a bunkmate."

"I'm sending two of my guys with you."

"Not necessary."

"Politics," the governor said, "is the art of compromise. I learned that at Governor Camp. I don't want you to go on this tour but you're going anyway, so the compromise is you allow two of my security team to accompany you."

"Governor Camp," Julie snorted. "Do your constituents know how goofy you are?"

"Let's hope not," Wakefield said. "I think I'm supposed to be regal."

"How will the taxpayers feel about paying for security for my school trip?"

"I don't travel much, which means I'm way under budget on security costs, plus this falls under the basic protective duties the first family is entitled to. Even if it didn't, I don't care about the taxpayers. I care about you."

"I don't think, as governor, you're allowed to say that."

"Julie, you'll do it. You'll do it because you love me, because you're my only child, and because you're getting married soon, which means I'm officially losing you. And because your mother wants you to. That's like seven reasons right there."

"So dramatic."

The governor turned a framed photo around on his desk so it was facing Julie. Unlike some politicians' offices, her father's was not adorned with diplomas, glad-handing shots with celebrities, and framed articles about himself. Other than a mounted sheet of rare stamps, a hobby her father readily acknowledged as dorky, the office just had pictures of family. This shot was of the two of them on a hiking trip last year in Glacier National Park, the snow-capped mountains providing a majestic backdrop. "There's going to be fewer and fewer of these. Now it's going to be you and Eric doing these kinds of things together. Eric is a good man, and that is as it should be. But it makes me melancholy."

Julie thought this over, but didn't take long. "I agree to your terms."

"Love you, kiddo."

They both stood and hugged. Julie looked up at her dad. "Are you crying?"

"Not technically," he said. "Just a middle-aged guy getting a little misty."

The voice of her father's secretary came over the intercom. "Your call is waiting, Governor."

Wakefield looked skyward as if soliciting help from above. "Corn lobby's kicking my ass. See you for dinner on Thursday?"

"You bet." Julie headed toward the door.

"Julie."

She turned.

"Bad guys are in there," her father said. "I know they'll be behind steel doors, but watch yourself."

"You know I will."

"One of the guys I'm sending is Coates. He'll keep you out of the mix."

"Coates could guard a prison by himself."

"And I don't care what the prison regs say, keep your phone on you. Give me a call when the tour's over so I know you're out. Call the other number if you need to."

He liked to remind her about the other number from time to time. It was the number to his second cell phone, the one he kept only for family and state emergencies. He had pledged to always have the phone on him, always charged, the phone he would always answer no matter what the hour, no matter who he was meeting with, no matter what he was doing.

"I've got your number," Julie said. "See you Thursday. Ask Mom if she'll make her scallops."

As Julie left, she caught a glimpse of her father seated at his desk, looking at the photo of the two of them hiking, an unreadable expression on his face.

The next morning, she was picked up at her front door in an unmarked Crown Vic by Missouri state troopers Derrick Coates and Maxwell Jamerson. Both wore navy suits, but where Coates's was tailored and immaculate, Jamerson's was wrinkled and flecked with lint. Coates drove, Jamerson sat in front, and Julie sat in back. Jamerson had a plug of dip in his cheek, which didn't seem to go with the suit. He spat the brown juice into a paper coffee cup. Julie knew and liked Coates. He had worked with the first family since her father was elected. He was a Black man of about forty-five, a little thick around the middle, with a no-nonsense haircut just starting to silver and a calm demeanor. She had never met Jamerson. He was pale, in his late thirties, half a head taller than Coates, with a cocky swagger and a ridiculous droopy mustache that combined to make him look like a cowboy dropout. She took an instant dislike to him.

"What up," Jamerson said. "Don't get used to me. I work Narcotics Task Force. I'm just filling in for the day because I'm a big supporter of the first family. Also, the overtime."

Julie cast a questioning look at Coates, who saw her expression through the rearview mirror.

"He's from the reserve pool. Couldn't get anyone else on this short notice on the holiday. But we came up through the academy together and did some highway time. He's an acquired taste, but he'll do."

Getting a trooper from the reserve pool was uncommon, and Julie knew her father didn't care for it. He liked the regular rotation guarding his family because he knew and trusted them. But if Coates vouched for Jamerson, it would be good enough for the governor.

"Narcotics Task Force, huh?" Julie asked.

"Yuh," Jamerson said.

"How's that drug war coming."

"We're fucking winning," Jamerson said with a trace of annoyance in his voice. "Be winning more if the Democrats would let us off the leash."

"Language," Coates said.

"It's okay," Julie said. "I'm a big girl. Is your mustache within department regulations?"

"The hell?" Jamerson twisted around in the seat and looked at her.

"She's like that," Coates said, smiling widely as he drove.

Jamerson turned back around and spat into his cup.

Julie tugged absently on the sleeves of her plain gray sweatshirt. She had read up on the visitor regulations and knew she couldn't wear anything that resembled what prisoners wore, particularly anything orange, red, or purple. She was also not to wear anything tight or revealing, which wasn't a problem—she wasn't some showgirl. She lost track of time as they drove. She had her mind on her studies, Eric, her wedding, her father, her next job. This prison tour was just one last thing to check off her list for her Corrections class, which was one of the final courses she needed to complete her grad school degree in public administration with a concentration in criminal justice. Once she had her masters, she'd be off to...

Off to what, exactly?

She had no idea. Most of her classmates were a lock for DC to work for the government or nonprofits. They'd become advocates and immigration officers, join congressional staffs, and find work with lobbyists. But she wasn't sold on that scene. She had taken a bridge year after college and done Teach for America, working at an inner-city high school in Philly—the hardest year of her life. One bridge year had turned to three. She'd finally decided on public admin because she admired her father and his career in public service. She'd focused on criminal justice because issues of crime and punishment had always resonated with her, fueled by long family dinner conversations about race, drug laws, and public safety. But her summer internships at an immigration advocacy group and a health policy think tank had left her unsatisfied, and she wondered, not infrequently, if she had missed the boat. If law or med school might have been a better fit. Her father had taken the lighter touch when it came to career counseling. He didn't care if she selected a career field that wasn't a moneymaker, and at times he seemed amused she'd elected to roam. Her mother was a Princeton-educated pediatrician and expressed more exasperation at her wanderings.

She caught patches of the conversation in the front of the car.

Jamerson was bragging about some drug raid he orchestrated. How he was first through the door, geared up with a heavy vest and a boot knife, the way the place smelled like carne asada, how he'd smashed the butt of his gun in some Puerto Rican's face when the guy wouldn't show his hands. Julie felt like he was talking loudly for her benefit. He wanted her to know how tough he was.

"We gonna have to check all our weapons at the door, I take it," Jamerson said.

"For sure," Coates said.

"Maybe they'll let you keep your boot knife," Julie said.

Jamerson slowly turned around in the seat again. He stared at Julie. Julie held it. Jamerson was the first to look away.

She smiled. "It is a privilege to protect members of the first family."

Coates chuckled in the driver's seat. Jamerson threw his hands up in defeat. "Gnarly," he said and spat into his cup for good measure.

They passed a sign that warned against picking up hitchhikers followed by the sign for Whitehall Correctional Institute. Julie assumed there was a relationship between the two. They took the prison exit, a narrow road that led to the wide front gates. Whitehall was institutional ugly surrounded by long swaths of barbed wire that reached at least fifteen feet. Its bulk was taken up by a seven-story structure that looked like a grim warehouse and was spattered with bird shit, flanked by a handful of drab outbuildings. Through the gates, Julie could see a patch of grass and earth in the courtyard that looked like it might have once been a garden but had reverted to yellow weeds. Julie didn't think most prisons budgeted much for aesthetics, but even given that, this place looked god-awful. They checked in with a uniformed guard.

"Tour?"

"Yep," Coates said.

The guard found their names on a clipboard. He looked at Julie a few seconds longer than was comfortable, his mouth halfway open.

His teeth were the color of the weeds behind him. "You sure?" he asked.

Julie waited for him to smile, or make a follow-up joke. He didn't.

"Something we should know?" Coates asked.

"Nah," the guard said. "I say the same thing to everybody." He hit a button that opened the exterior gates for them to pass through.

"Here we are," Coates said. "The cradle of civilization."

"Shee-it," Jamerson said, tossing his cup out the car window.

CHAPTER 6

Sheriff Rokus

Hours after the bus departed, Sheriff Rokus was still finishing up the paperwork on the vagrant who assaulted his brother Donny. As sheriff, it was rare for him to write a police report himself, but he had been actively involved in the arrest, and the report needed a little finesse here and there so it would read the right way. He'd leave for the hospital soon. Visiting hours were over but he was the sheriff of Rocker County. Visiting hours for him were whenever he showed up until whenever he decided to leave. He wouldn't stay long. He'd defend Donny if he had to, because family was family, but he didn't want to spend much time with him. His brother was sick and weak and lately had only served to cause him headaches. But their doddering mother would demand an update on his condition so, as the responsible older son, he'd provide one.

He'd already transitioned to thinking about the beer he was going to put down at Louie's when his office computer made a digital chirp. The prisoner's prints had come back. His name wasn't Chris Spielman. It was Kurt Argento. Rokus smiled thinly. Liar, liar. Big surprise there. Another charge to slap on the hobo from Michigan who had called him a clown, knowingly providing false information to an officer during an official investigation. He ran a warrant check on Argento, expecting to see a felony or two. There was nothing. In fact, there was no offense record whatsoever. All Argento had in the interstate system was a noncriminal reference number. That didn't make sense. This shitbag, with no priors? Rokus rolled his chair over to his bookshelf, found his thick National Crime Information Center guidebook, slapped it down on the desk, and looked up the code.

The reference number was for law enforcement.

Argento was a cop.

In the municipality of Detroit, Michigan.

Rokus wanted to say *fuck* in response to this revelation, but it took him a second to find the word in the hornet's nest that his brain had become. When he was able to speak, it came out slowly in three syllables.

"F-ah-ukkkk."

He got online, typing furiously now, "Kurt Argento" and "Detroit police." There were several entries, mostly from the *Detroit Free Press*. Rokus read them as fast as he could. One was accompanied by a photo featuring Officer Argento being presented with a Medal of Valor for heroism in the line of duty. A second, also with a photo, concerned Argento being cleared by the DA's office for an on-duty shooting of a kidnapping suspect who'd held a woman hostage. Rokus scanned the photos. This was the same guy, all right. In full police blues. He looked severe.

So he and his deputy had tuned up a cop good and then slapped some made-up charges on him. And why? Because the guy made Rokus mad because he hurt his brother while stopping that same brother from sexually abusing a minor. And they didn't do this to just any cop. They did it to some kind of hero cop.

Rokus had to think fast. Faster than he was used to. He had to unfuck this. He ran through the options. An apology wouldn't quite cut it, even if it was cop-to-cop. If this thing unraveled, if the truth saw the light of day...he didn't even want to think about what that would look like. And it wasn't just this case he was worried about.

There had been others. If the spotlight of the state DOJ or, God help him, the feds fell on the Rocker County Sheriff's Department...

It was simple, in the end.

Kurt Argento could not see the inside of a courtroom. He'd need to disappear. Rokus had done it before. Trickier to do with a white cop than a hood rat from the projects. But not impossible.

The place Argento was going, Whitehall Correctional Institute, was more of a pit than a prison. Rokus knew it to be a poorly run facility, with shitty staffing and worse morale, that housed the most dangerous offenders in the state, bar none. He and his deputies tried to stay out of Whitehall at all costs. If they had to take a custody there, drop and go was their mantra. Screech the tires and get out ASAP, return to home base. Odds were Argento could easily meet his fate at the hands of any one of the stone-evil inmates inside Whitehall who didn't know how to play nice. But Rokus couldn't count on chance here. He had to be sure.

There was a man he used when messes needed to be tidied. A man he could count on. And because this man sometimes found himself on the wrong side of the law, he was currently incarcerated on a two-year drug trafficking beef. His current place of confinement was Whitehall. He didn't have a cell phone, this man, and even if he did, Whitehall had a cell net that shut down wireless calls. But Rokus had a go-between he used that could get a message to him.

So Rokus found his burner phone and put in the call for Micah. He delivered the instructions.

"How will Micah know the target?" the go-between asked.

"He'll be booked under the name Chris Spielman but his real name is Kurt Argento. Looks like that guy from the *Transporter* movies, except angrier. He assaulted me and one of my deputies, so they'll probably put him on the second floor after intake. Standard fee."

A pause on the other end of the line. It lasted too long for Rokus's liking.

"Do we have a problem?"

"No," the voice on the other end said. "I'll get him the message."

Rokus hung up. He understood the gravity of the call he'd just made. He was sending a fellow lawman to his death. But he'd already moved past it. He had neither the time nor the inclination for hand-wringing. After all, it was a basic matter of survival. If he was to survive, Argento could not. The hard case from Detroit had picked the wrong town. It was just how things worked. Rokus had seen that time and time again in his fifty years, both on and off the job. Awful things happened to people. Murder. Car wrecks. Natural disasters.

Sometimes it wasn't anyone's fault.

Sometimes it was everyone's fault.

Sheriff Rokus wasn't a particularly introspective man, but at some level, he knew everything he was thinking now was just a tissue-thin justification for doing whatever the hell he wanted. But he was the sheriff. He'd earned that title and everything that came with it. And even if he was lying to himself, there was something he'd learned about making up your own lies.

If you tried hard enough, you could choose to believe them.

CHAPTER 7

Argento rode on a prison bus to Whitehall along with forty other shackled cons. The guy in the seat next to him was wide-shouldered with bristly red hair, and his BO smelled like fish.

"Don't fucking say shit to me," the man with red hair said.

"Sure," Argento said. "I'm just here for the weekend."

Argento had taken plenty of prisoners to the county jail over the years but hadn't had occasion to be at the state pen much. Once prisoners were sentenced and ended up there, the police were pretty much done with them. He had seen *Cool Hand Luke* several times. Maybe he could use that as a guide.

Cool Hand Luke was the movie he and Emily saw on their first date. They had met at a work party of one of Argento's district attorney friends. Argento had noticed Emily come in alone, as he had. She was a trim brunette with hair down to her waist dressed in a sweatshirt and blue jeans. Far from Look-at-Me clothes. If she was wearing any makeup, it was understated. That was fine by Argento. He didn't think much of flash. She took a drink from a cooler of ice. Leinenkugel's Red. That was fine by Argento, too. He was walking her way when a drunk party boy Argento didn't know had clapped a hand on Argento's shoulder, slopping some of his drink on Argento's shirt without noticing.

"So I hear you're a cop."

"Yep," Argento said, stepping back from the guy's eighty proof breath.

"What do you like about that?"

"I like arresting violent predators and taking their firearms away."

"Hey, you ever shot anybody?" The party boy made a gun with both hands and wiggled them up and down.

"Yeah, I shot the last annoying drunk who asked me that question."

Sensing trouble, one of the other guests near Emily guided the man away from Argento with an apologetic shrug.

"That was a little harsh," Emily said.

"Who, me or him?"

"You."

"Bad form to ask a complete stranger at a party about a police shooting. Maybe I was in one and my partner got killed. Or I shot the suspect, but a ricochet killed a civilian walking by. Am I supposed to talk about that with this guy and then go get some more crab dip?"

She looked at him intently. "Good point."

He extended his hand. "Kurt Argento."

"Emily Vasquez," she said, taking it. "Please know that's the only time I've ever been wrong."

"Only time I've ever been right," he said and she smiled. Her smile, Argento noticed, was just a shade crooked.

They fell into a natural conversational rhythm that was unusual for Argento, whose social leanings tended toward the monastic. She was a physical therapist who lived in the city proper along with a dented car and a stack of student loans. She favored Michigan State over Michigan, which was a problem, but not an unworkable one. He made a joke and she laughed and the sound of that laughter, the way it rose and then tapered off with a sigh, made something jump in his gut. At the end of the night, he asked her out and she said yes.

Their first date was a showing of *Cool Hand Luke* at an old Detroit movie house that still played the classics on Sunday nights and served draft beer. They held hands walking out of the theater. He had never met anyone quite like her. She was smart and funny, kind and resilient. And when she returned his good-night kiss outside her front door, he felt certain he'd never be able to explain to anyone how electric it felt without sounding like a moony teenager.

The prison bus passed a water tower with the words *Town of Rocker* painted on it above a large smiley face. Argento looked up at the tower. The desk clerk had warned him. "This place sucks," he'd said.

Whitehall's anchor structure was a seven-story dull-colored building with barred windows ringed with guard towers and a high fence with spiraled barb wire lining the top. The bus stopped at the entry gate to await clearance. Alongside the gate was a large sign that said *Whitehall Correctional Institute, Department of Corrections & Rehabilitation, State of Missouri, Warden Ian Stroster*. Next to it was another sign that said *Turn Off Lights Show ID* and warned that it was a felony to bring tobacco, firearms, or alcohol inside.

The gate guard and bus driver were talking. "You sure you want to come in?" Argento heard the guard say. "The natives are running hot."

"It's Whitehall. They're just restless, Pete," the driver said as the gates parted with an electronic hum.

Once inside, the prisoners were stripped, searched, and disinfected. Argento was given an orange shirt stamped *MDC* for Missouri Department of Corrections, orange drawstring pants, and shoddy orange sandals to put on before he was routed to New Bookings. He went through a medical screening, answering yes to the question about whether he'd recently been injured, and his pictures and prints were taken digitally on a computer. It didn't matter that they'd already been done at the police station. State prison was its own entity, and redundancy was common in law enforcement.

The correctional officer processing him was a trim Hispanic guy with gelled hair whose name tag said *Aguilar*. He seemed friendly, at least as friendly as possible inside a state penal institution. He was a young guy, early twenties at most, so maybe his positive outlook was only because he was new. His badge was sewn on his shirt; Argento figured that was because the pins on physical badges could be used as stabbing instruments. Everything in prison was a potential weapon.

"Scars, marks, tattoos?" Aguilar asked.

Argento didn't have any tattoos, but he showed Aguilar the wallet-size patch of burned skin on his left shoulder from when a female crack addict tried to set him on fire during a search warrant. The addict had the matronly name of Gertrude, which Argento had thought was funny, although not at the time. Gertrude sounds like the woman who politely teaches a sewing class, not the wild-haired druggie who tries to burn your skin off.

"What's that from?"

"Woman trouble," Argento said.

Aguilar took a photo. "You want to declare a religion?"

"Lutheran."

"What is that, like Catholic?"

"Sure," Argento said. "What's my bail?"

Aguilar scanned Argento's paperwork. "Resisting arrest, two counts, that's five thousand each, but those are just the misdemeanors. You got two counts of attempting to disarm a peace officer and another two counts of aggravated assault on a peace officer. Add that all up and you're looking at about three hundred thousand. You had yourself quite a day."

"Good thing I'm innocent," Argento said.

Aguilar nodded, as if weighing this information. "Just so you know, we hear that a lot in here."

Argento didn't have three hundred thousand dollars. Even if he did, he probably wouldn't post it. He wasn't sure a weekend in prison would bother him. He'd been in worse places, like Detroit for the last two decades. And staying in Whitehall meant Rokus couldn't fabricate any more charges against him.

"You affiliated with any gang? We gotta separate gang members."

"No," Argento said. He wasn't sure which prison gang his German and Italian lineage qualified him for.

A small box attached to the fingerprint computer whirred and produced an orange plastic band with Argento's booking photo on it. Aguilar attached the band to Argento's wrist with plastic tabs. "You're done at my station. You're gonna be in Intake for a while until we can assign you a floor, but based on your medical, you're going to need to see the nurse." Aguilar called over another correctional officer with corporal's insignia whose name tag said *Spentz*. Spentz motioned Argento down an adjoining hallway. He was a tall guy with bad teeth who fixed Argento with an *I don't give a shit* stare. They reached a brightly lit office with a sign outside that said *Infirmary*.

"Sit," Spentz said, pointing toward a chair. It had been a short walk but the guard was already sweating. The hallmark of a heavy drinker.

"You'll get better results if you don't talk to people like dogs."

"We gonna have a problem, convict?"

"Haven't been convicted of anything yet. I'm overflow from the county jail."

"Well," Spentz said, opening his mouth wide to better showcase his browning gumline. "Aren't you something. Now you sit the fuck there and keep those eyes off me."

Argento was already tired of the conversation. He sat and turned to look inside the infirmary. There were two staffers, both in scrubs, a spectacled Asian man in white and a woman in green writing in a chart. The woman turned toward Argento, and he saw *RN* stitched on her top. She was a woman in her forties, broad through the shoulders but in an athletic way, like maybe she had played college softball. She looked exhausted. Argento couldn't imagine that being on the medical staff in a correctional facility was a highly coveted position. He wondered why someone would opt to work in such a place where your patients ranged from meth-heads to murderers.

Maybe they got the equivalent of combat pay or forgiveness on school loans.

He reflected on his own situation. He was in jail, but what was this preventing him from doing? He was going to be surrounded by career criminals, by metal and clatter, but that was what life had been before his ten years with Emily and it was what it was after her. Noise. Violence. Pain. Here, there just weren't any barriers to hide it. He didn't know what would happen with his case. He wasn't sure he cared. He had no wife. No job. No dog. No truck.

He had run out of things people could take from him.

Argento had once responded to a report of an armed robbery where the sixty-year-old victim hadn't given up his wallet and had been pistol-whipped as a result. He still lost the wallet as well as most of his teeth. Argento asked him why he hadn't complied. "My wife left me for my best friend, I just got laid off from my job, and my daughter won't talk to me" he said matter-of-factly. "I got nothing to lose, man."

Argento knew how he felt.

"You're up, Rover," Spentz said. He wiped his sweaty forehead on his sleeve, pressed the ID card on his neck lanyard to a digital pad by the double doors to the infirmary, and then pushed the doors open. As long as the guard didn't sweat on him, Argento was willing to let the dog comment be. He entered. The door chimed like it did at a dry cleaner.

"Dr. Lau," Spentz said.

"Good day," the spectacled man replied. He was an older fellow with a beakish nose and a prominent paunch out of step with his slim frame.

"You want me in or out?" Spentz asked. Lau looked at the nurse to make the call.

"Out is fine, thank you." She turned to Argento and checked his name on his jail bracelet. "What brings you here, Mr. Spielman?"

"Got hit in the head with some police batons."

"You get treated at county?"

"I asked for an ambulance but they took a pass."

The nurse didn't seem surprised by this. Maybe it was commonplace, or maybe she assumed Argento was lying. Argento had experience with plenty of prisoners falsely claiming mistreatment. It was something to do to both pass the time and make life harder for their captors.

The nurse took his vitals and started a chart. She had long black hair tied back and a beaded necklace. The lines around her mouth and her just off-color teeth told him she was a smoker but she smelled good, or maybe it was just that she didn't smell bad, like the rest of the pen, which carried a stench that combined body funk with Lysol.

"I've had a concussion before," Argento said. "Feels like the same thing." He wasn't an EMT but had taken a series of tactical lifesaving courses through Detroit SWAT and was used to self-diagnosis and treatment. He once had an ingrown toenail that got so entrenched and inflamed that it prevented him from walking. He borrowed some Lidocaine from a med rig, stripped the nail down to the bed, dressed it, and soaked it overnight. He came back to work the next day good to go.

The nurse didn't respond to Argento. She wasn't looking at him. She was looking past him, through the window to the hallway where Spentz was posted up. Argento followed her gaze. Spentz wasn't alone anymore. He was ringed in by three men in red prison garb. Spentz backpedaled, fast enough to where the back of his head thudded against the glass and made a sweaty smear.

"Sit," Spentz said to the men, his words muffled outside the nurse's station. No one sat. Two of the men held Spentz by the arms. One of them ripped his handheld radio from its holster and pounded it against the wall until it came apart. Then the third stabbed him through the throat with a thin metal shank, once, twice, four times, twelve times, quick powerful thrusts that turned into a bloody blur. Spentz folded, and fell. One of the men pulled Spentz's ID badge from his neck and used it on the digital door lock.

And just like that, the three men in red were inside the infirmary, the doors announcing their arrival with a soft chime.

"Jesus," Lau said, his voice cracking, and then he was gone, scuttling out the open infirmary doors, the three prisoners paying him no mind.

"Hi, nurse Rachel," the man with the shank said. His face and the front of his sweatshirt were spattered in Spentz's gore. He was a powerfully built white man with a shaved head and a neck tattoo that said *Fuck Da Law*. His two companions were smaller. One had a mohawk, and the other was squinting badly from some of Spentz's blood that had gotten in his eye.

"How did you get in here?" the nurse managed. She was moving away as she talked and knocked over a tray of medical supplies with a clatter. She kept moving until she came up against her desk and then there was nowhere else to go.

"Door to our floor just opened for us," Shank said. "Like it was meant to be."

"It's okay," Mohawk said as he pulled his shirt off. "We just want a taste." He jerked a thumb at Squint. "Make sure we got some privacy."

Squint took up a position in front of a red button on the wall that said *Emergency* and blocked it with his body.

"Get the fuck out," Shank told Argento.

Argento didn't move. He felt the spigot of adrenaline turn on, but right now he needed to control it. He was taking in the scene. Calculating odds and angles, scenarios and possibilities.

Mohawk puffed his chest out. "You want some, new fish?"

"No," Argento said. "Even if I did, I'm in sandals. Be embarrassing for everybody."

"So step aside," Mohawk said, "so we can do what we came here to do."

Argento nodded. "All good. Rapists gotta rape."

"Don't leave me," the nurse pleaded with Argento, her voice climbing the ladder. "Don't you dare leave me."

"Lady," Argento said, "I don't even know your name." He moved past the three cons into the hallway, his shoes crunching on the shards of Spentz's broken radio. Spentz himself was slumped and very dead, his shirt soaked in blood. A crimson bubble popped on his lips. He looked like he'd been set upon by wolves. But, there was no point in dwelling on Spentz's demise. He couldn't resurrect him. Argento turned his attention to Spentz's belt. Pepper spray, which Argento didn't take much stock in. A flashlight too small to be an effective impact weapon, a glove pouch. A small cylinder of something called T46 Malodorant, which Argento wasn't familiar with, but which he assumed was some kind of chemical used for prisoner control. No Taser. The only thing of use was a twenty-one-inch collapsible baton. Argento took it out of the holder and his fingers closed around the metal handle. Not quite the heft he was used to, but it would do. He tucked it in his pants at the small of his back. Then he stood utterly still for eight seconds. Four seconds to inhale, four seconds to exhale. Combat breathing, to steady him for what was to come.

When he returned to the infirmary, the nurse was on her stomach on top of the desk, her eyes squeezed tight. Shank had his pants down and was yanking on hers. Mohawk leaned in close to the woman, and inhaled deeply by her neck.

"Don't worry," Shank said. "We won't tell him. Be our secret."

At the sound of the door chime, Squint took a step away from the alarm button to square up to Argento. "Fuck you back for?"

Argento raised his hands in a gesture of appeasement. "Forgot my smokes," he said, pointing with his chin at a spot just past Squint. Squint instinctively turned that way and Argento pulled the baton out, extended it with a flip of the wrist, and speared Squint in the windpipe as hard as he could.

Which was very hard.

Squint went down, eyes wide, gasping for air. The back of his head made a dull *thonk* on the tile floor. He jerked and was still.

Argento kicked off his sandals. No traction with those things.

"Next man up," he said.

Mohawk charged, sloppy and rushed. Argento went low and took him out at the knees with a baton strike and hit him on the back of the head with the return swing. Mohawk banged into the wall face-first but stayed on his feet. Argento's next strike was a golf swing that exploded up into Mohawk's groin, crushing his testicles. Mohawk screamed. Argento smacked Mohawk across the face with the baton. Bones audibly broke. Mohawk's eyes frosted over and he went quiet.

Time for the third one. The hat trick. Shank was slowed by the fact that his pants had just been around his ankles, but he had buttoned them during the fray.

"Fucking kill you," he shouted, eyes huge. "I'll fucking—" He held out the metal shiv, close to his body, parallel to the floor. But it was a small weapon and he was panicked, and Argento liked his chances with the length of the baton. He swung at Shank overhead like he was using an axe to make kindling. Shank was fast enough to throw his hand up to block the blow. The baton strike shattered his left forearm. Argento swung again, Shank blocked again, this time with his right. Another shattered forearm. Shank howled and the shiv clattered to the floor. Argento stepped in and clotheslined Shank with the crook of his arm, sending the man's legs skyward and his body crashing to the ground neck first. Shank tried to get up and Argento scooped up the shiv, leaned down, and punched it through Shank's neck, again and again, about as many times as Shank himself had stabbed Spentz.

When someone was trying to murder him, Argento wasn't big on second chances.

When he was done, he straightened and looked down at Shank. If he wasn't dead yet, he was knocking on the door. As a cop, he'd be obligated to try and save the man's life, even if it looked hopeless, even if the man had just tried to cut him in half. Breaths. Chest compressions. Applying direct pressure to major bleeding. But he wasn't a cop anymore, and the only physician in the house, the esteemed Dr. Lau, had tucked his tail and run. So instead he watched Shank's breathing fade from ragged gasps to quiet huffs to nothing. Argento looked down on him, his *Fuck Da Law* tattoo, his loose, rapist's pants, his jail shirt covered in the blood of a murdered guard. Argento wondered what the point of his life was anyway.

Argento heard a *thwack*ing sound. He looked up. The nurse had just slapped the red emergency button. Then she stayed very still.

"Your name is Rachel?"

The nurse nodded. Face taut, trying to control her breathing.

"Rachel, you have nothing to fear from me," Argento said. "Do you want me to stay until more guards come or you want me to leave?"

"Stay," she said. "Please stay... I... can't breathe... That was... I need to..."

Argento put his hands out in a steadying gesture. "Take your time."

She sucked in a deep breath. Pinched her eyes shut and then opened them. "Okay," she said. "Okay." She had pulled her necklace out from under her shirt and was running her thumbs over the beads as if to ground herself. The bottom of the necklace ended in a small round medallion that looked like half of the steering wheel for an old ship.

"You're having a normal reaction to an abnormal situation."

"Thank you for helping me."

"You're welcome," Argento said. "I'm new here and not up on protocol. How is it three prisoners are loose in this hallway?"

"I don't know. I don't... it never should have happened. Inmates come here one at a time and they're always escorted by a guard." She slipped her necklace back under her shirt and shook her head as if coming to. "Oh my God, Spentz."

"Dead."

"Are you sure?"

"I'm no doctor," Argento said, "but he has injuries incompatible with life. The guy at my feet is dead too. The other two probably need some serious nursing, but under the circumstances, I'd understand if you took a pass."

What he had done to Shank broke new ground. He had never stabbed anyone before. He was getting into just as many fights off the job as on and he had stopped two sexual assaults in two days. Maybe that could be his new purpose in life. A depressed widower walking the lands beating up sex offenders.

The doors to the infirmary opened, and Aguilar and another guard burst through, eyes wide, both out of breath.

"We're okay," Rachel said quickly. "They came after me." She pointed to Argento. "He stopped them." She looked around her, then found a pack of cigarettes on a tabletop. She lit one and inhaled deeply. It seemed to Argento a fair time to bypass indoor smoking regulations. He could have used one, too.

Aguilar did a quick scan of the three men on the floor. "Spentz is outside," he said. "He's gone." Aguilar took out his handheld radio and called it in. Argento heard a faint buzzing sound on the other end. He didn't hear any acknowledgment of Aguilar's transmission, but Aguilar didn't seem to notice. He was trying to take it all in: dead coworker outside, three mangled cons on the floor, a felony assault on a nurse, a new prisoner he had just fingerprinted standing next to her.

"What the hell happened?" the other guard asked. He had sergeant's chevrons on his uniform sleeves and his name tag said *LeMaines*. He looked Native American, a husky guy in his midfifties with shock-black hair streaked with white and professorial glasses.

Rachel told them. Her voice was quick and strained. She finished the cigarette and started on another.

"How'd they get buzzed through?" Aguilar asked.

"I don't know," she said. "It's never happened like that before."

"They're in red," LeMaines said. "That's second floor. How'd they get from there to here without an escort?"

"I...I don't know," Rachel said again. "One of them said something about his cell door just opening."

LeMaines turned to Argento. "You took out these three guys by yourself?"

"Used a club," Argento said. He found his sandals and stepped back into them. He didn't know what was going on with the three prisoners freely entering medical, but if there was going to be more fighting in here, he'd need to get new shoes.

Aguilar was pacing back and forth. Then he leaned down and handcuffed the two men on the floor who were still alive. Squint's leg twitched.

"I got a question," Argento said, looking at Aguilar.

"What?"

"Why isn't your radio working?"

CHAPTER 8

Julie

The man leading the tour had introduced himself as Assistant Warden Pillaire. He was well over six feet tall and gangly with dishwater-gray hair. He wore an off-brand brown suit that made Julie think of a budget undertaker; it was offset by a thick, jeweled college or fraternity ring that struck her as ostentatious given the surroundings. He seemed in a hurry. Maybe his haste was due to trying to get out early for the holiday weekend. Or maybe it was because there were things in the prison he didn't want Julie to see. Or some combination of both. Julie didn't much care. She had a passing curiosity about the inner workings of a large state pen, but corrections was her least favorite grad class, and mostly she wanted to get this over with, too. She thought back to her father's offer to get her out of this tour. She loathed the special treatment that came with being the governor's daughter, but every now and again she unloathed it. Wanted to claim it, to use it as a fast pass.

"Our ask was that nobody knows about this," Coates said. "I take it that's been honored?"

"We've kept Julie's visit under wraps," Pillaire said. "No need to get our inmates riled up."

"Is that what you think would happen if they knew?" Jamerson asked. "They'd get riled up?"

"There would be a number of appeals to ask her father for clemency," Pillaire said. "I fear they would be delivered in less than civil ways."

"Ever get any celebrities in here?" Coates asked. "Like Johnny Cash playing at Folsom?"

"We did have a comedian come once a few years ago. He had a ventriloquist act. It did not go particularly well."

"Shows your inmates have good taste," Julie said. She checked her phone. There was a message from Eric. It said State Prison-bring me back some mystery loaf and had a thumbs-up emoji next to it. She smiled. Eric was just on the right side of goofy. She had met him at a college friend's birthday party. Eric had brought his violin—he'd played since he was a child—and treated the group to a rousing version of "Happy Birthday." He'd also been kind and attentive to her friend's small children, remembering their names and showing them a magic trick with a quarter. He seemed genuinely uninterested in her father being governor, but definitely interested in her. She'd asked him out that day and never looked back.

"I'll need you to check that with staff," Pillaire said. "No civilian cell phones allowed inside the facility."

Julie was about to hand it over when she remembered what her father had said in his office about keeping it on her, prison regs be damned. Did she really want to play the My Dad the Governor Said I Could card?

Coates intervened. "The governor wants her to hang on to it during the tour."

"She won't get service in here," Pillaire said. "We have a cell net up. Prevents the prisoners from making calls even if they manage to smuggle a phone in."

"That's okay. She's getting married in a few weeks, lot of last-minute emails to look at. We can vouch for Julie."

Pillaire gave this some thought. "All right. It's not protocol, but I'll make an exception. Just keep it out of sight as much as you can."

Julie mouthed *Thank you* to Coates, and he saluted her in

return. She wasn't surprised her father had reached out to Coates to ensure she kept her phone. He was shepherdly like that. Sometimes it annoyed her. Most of the time it reminded her how much she loved him.

Pillaire led them to a security checkpoint manned by two correctional officers. Coates and Jamerson went behind the officers' desk and put their sidearms in lockboxes inside a closet-size room with a metal door so thick it looked like it would hold up to anything short of a howitzer. Wallets, keys, phones, Julie's school notebook, and the troopers' neck lanyards holding their badges went into small plastic bowls run into an X-ray conveyer.

"And the chew," one of the officers said to Jamerson. "No tobacco allowed inside."

"That's disappointing," Jamerson replied. He spat his plug in a nearby trash can and tossed his dip cup in after it. The three of them went through a metal detector. Jamerson was last, and it buzzed when he passed. "Knee surgery," he explained. "Got some pins and rods in there."

Pillaire nodded. One of the correctional officers came over and did a cursory pat-down on Jamerson and then stepped away.

"No offense," Pillaire said. "I know you're cops. But we've had issues in the past even with law enforcement."

"None taken," Jamerson said.

They started on the ground floor past the visiting area, which was conspicuously empty. Along one wall was a line of small, scuffed booths with a phone and a clear glass separator between visitor and inmate for noncontact visits. For everyone else, there were a handful of wooden tables dotted with playing cards and newspapers. The cuisine was supplied by a row of vending machines that sold chips, drinks, and premade sandwiches. Julie always felt that machines that sold sandwiches looked mournful.

"Nobody's here," Jamerson said. "Where's the holiday love? Private prisons have different rules for visitors than county?"

"No," Pillaire said. "As a private correctional facility, we have to follow all the same laws and codes as the county ones. But a good percentage of our inmates are from out of state, which cuts down on visitors."

"Do you think you'll run into any people you've arrested in here?" Julie asked the troopers.

"Possibly," Coates said. "But I've been out of field ops for a while. Some folks in the geriatric wing might remember me."

Jamerson shook his head. "Most of my narcotics cases go federal. They're doing ten to twenty years in Marion or Terra Haute, ruing the day they ran into one Maxwell Jamerson."

"Ruing the day," Julie said.

"I try to get him to talk less," Coates said. "It's difficult."

The next stop was the mess hall and kitchen. The hall was empty of inmates. The room was filled with square tables bolted to the floor, the tabletops stamped with the words *Remain Seated*. Each table had four spokes jutting out that each ended in a fastened-down chair, presumably so inmates had sufficient spacing between them and couldn't pick up the chairs and throw them at one another or staff. Two glum-looking inmate cooks clad in white manned the kitchen underneath signs that read *Keep Lines Moving* and *Diet Syrup Is Available Upon Request*. The first inmate was tall and lanky. The second was short and wide with a pinched face. Both had a prison pallor. Their height and weight disparity reminded Julie of the children's books she read to her niece about the adventures of Fred and Ted, two dogs that got into misadventures. Both men openly stared at Julie. The tall man's mouth hung open slightly. A generic meat smell wafted out from the food prep island behind them.

"What's on the menu for today, gents?" Pillaire asked.

"Ass of mouse," the tall man replied.

"With gravy," the short one said.

Pillaire forced a chuckle.

The tall man stayed fixed on Julie. "Can that wobbler help us in the kitchen? I got a job for her." He jabbed both hands toward his crotch and thrust it forward.

Coates automatically stepped between the men and Julie, and there in his posture was something she'd seen from Coates only a handful of times over the years he'd protected her—his genial serenity replaced by something coiled and hostile. "Ease down," he said, "before something bad happens to you."

Pillaire put a hand on Coates's back. The assistant warden smiled at the two men. "That's uncalled-for," he said without looking directly at them, and kept the group moving.

"My apologies," Pillaire said after they returned to the hallway.

Julie said, "Don't worry about it," but the experience left her feeling both guarded and greasy.

"You should know that I didn't smile at them because I approved of what they said. I smiled because I believe smiles are contagious, and that's part of our effort to normalize these inmates so they don't act out."

"Okay," Julie said, instead of what she really wanted to say, which was that Pillaire's contagious-smile comment was among the stupidest things she'd ever heard. "Why were they in white when everyone else is in orange?"

"A white uniform means they're prison trustees. It's a paid position they earn through good behavior. They have a lot more freedom of movement than the other inmates."

"Those two are trustees?" Jamerson snorted. "They look like they've been eating lead paint."

"What responsibilities do you give trustees in here?" Julie asked.

"They cook and clean, deliver mail, take out trash," Pillaire said. "But we hold them accountable. I'll write up the inappropriate interaction they had with you. It will go in their file."

"A note in the file. That'll show 'em," Jamerson said.

"What's a wobbler?" Julie asked.

"It's jail slang for 'a weak person,'" Pillaire said. "A person you can control."

Coates looked at Julie and chuckled. "Don't think he got that one quite right."

"Thanks, Derrick," Julie said to Coates. He held out his fist and she bumped it. She wrote the word *wobbler* in her notebook. Fodder for the paper she'd have to write on this visit.

The group stepped into the activities room, which was one of the most depressing things Julie had ever seen. A small space with bare walls painted lime green. A ping-pong table with a ripped net and no paddles in sight. A table of children's board games, no doubt donated—Connect 4, Sorry, Chutes and Ladders—like it was a prison for eight-year-olds from 1986; most of the boxes were torn open, with mixed pieces scattered about. She saw a crossword puzzle on the floor that someone had scrawled a large, erect penis on. The room felt confined and stagnant. As a private prison, Julie figured, the less money Whitehall spent on educational programs, the more money they had for their shareholders. The low overhead showed.

"We had a foosball table for a while," Pillaire said, "but the inmates kept ripping out the metal rods and using them as weapons against each other and the staff."

"Should have rewarded their initiative," Jamerson said. "Made them trustees."

On the way out, Jamerson held the door for them.

"Thanks," Coates said.

"No one takes care of you like me," Jamerson said with a wide grin.

The rest of the tour was unremarkable. They were taken to the laundry room, which reeked so strongly of body odor that Julie walked in and walked right out, the metal shop where a handful of prisoners were loafing with an equally disinterested guard keeping watch, and a modest-size chapel. The library, if you could call it that, was mostly old magazines and piles of dusty Westerns and science fiction novels with a few law books sprinkled in, all in paperback because hardcovers could be used as weapons, Pillaire explained. He showed them a small room filled with ten individual cells that were used for group therapy, but Julie didn't get the sense that anything constructive had happened there for some time. Everything looked dingy and poorly kept. It was supposed to be a new prison, built within the last five years, but it looked like the kind of place the health department might condemn.

"Why wasn't anyone working in the metal shop?" Julie asked. "I just saw lots of standing around."

"The class was about over," Pillaire said. "We're just able to run the one course a day at the moment. It's a matter of staffing."

When Pillaire led them into a room marked *Office/Clerical*, Julie was taken aback to see rows of old brick-style typewriters chained to desks with no computers in sight.

"I haven't seen an actual typewriter since high school," Coates said. "Didn't know they still made them."

"There's an aftermarket for them," Pillaire said. "We find the inmates like the sounds they make. They've done studies."

Julie said, "But when they're released and get into the workforce, isn't that a barrier to employment, only knowing how to use an obsolete typewriter instead of a computer?"

"Our computer instructor left and we haven't found a replacement," Pillaire said pleasantly. "If you know anyone..."

"She needs a job after grad school," Jamerson said of Julie. "I'm sure she'll keep you on the short list."

Touché, Julie thought. She'd give Jamerson that one.

Pillaire stopped and gestured toward the double doors. "We can't walk any of the wings themselves, for obvious reasons, but I can give you the breakdown. There's one central control bubble that has wall-to-wall video surveillance, plus each floor has a guard's station and a shower room. Every cell is the same—seven by twelve, immovable bed and desk with a toilet-and-sink combo. The first floor is general population, mostly run-of-the-mill property crimes and the white-collar inmates. The second floor is made up of violent felons. Third floor is sex offenders. Fourth floor houses those with intensive psychological disorders. Fifth floor is our Gang Pop. And last but not least, floor six, our Secure Housing Unit, which includes solitary and death row. That's the most restrictive floor. Prisoners go everywhere in restraints and their food is brought to them."

"Didn't think private prisons were allowed to have death row," Julie said.

"They are in Missouri," Pillaire said.

"What are those obvious reasons we can't walk the wings?"

"Some of these inmates see a woman walk by, they're gonna get stirred up. They're going to say and do things I'd rather you not be exposed to."

"I've heard bad words before," Julie said. "Sometimes I use them myself."

"Let me be more specific," Pillaire said. "There are a few inmates who will masturbate and throw their semen at you from in between the bars."

"Okay," Julie said. "That I could do without."

"Sensible," Coates said.

"I'm pretty good-looking," Jamerson said. "Would they throw any semen at me?"

Coates shook his head.

"I'm sure you'd get plenty," Julie said. "Maybe most of it."

Jamerson grinned. "Sweet."

Coates snorted. "It's these kinds of conversations that make it a real pleasure to come to work."

They moved on through a series of gunmetal gray doors back the way they'd come, and stopped at an alcove that led out to the prison yard. Pillaire held up a plastic card from a lanyard to a circular sensor on the wall. The sensor turned green, and he pushed the doors open. The prison yard was a large oval surrounded by a walking track. Two manned guard towers complete with large spotlights provided overwatch. Alongside one of the towers was a tall flagpole with the American flag, the Missouri state flag, and the black POW-MIA banner. The middle of the yard had a basketball court with netless rims and a couple of scuffed heavy bags. Julie didn't see any weights, but a dozen or so inmates were exercising—

pullups on a metal bar, jumping jacks, and push-ups. The four of them watched from the doorway.

"Every floor except for secure housing gets an hour out here. They use it well. Some of these men can easily do a thousand push-ups in a day," Pillaire said.

"I haven't done one push-up since the academy," Jamerson said. He tapped his chest. "You can't even tell."

"You can tell," Coates said.

Julie didn't even try to suppress her smile. She wrote this exchange in her notebook. It wasn't going to go in her paper. She just wanted to remember it. She could listen to Coates cap on Jamerson all day. But she did need to stay on task if she wanted to turn in an adequate summary of this visit.

She turned to Pillaire. "What are some of your main issues here with prisoners?"

"Inmate control," he said. "Our prisoners tend to practice antisocial norms, which means when they get bored, they break something or try to hurt somebody. Also, contraband cell phones. Prisoners use them to continue their criminal enterprises on the outside. They used to be smuggled in from visitors, even by a guard or two. Once we had a drone drop one off in the yard. But now we have the electronic hardware to jam their signals."

"Antisocial norms," Jamerson said. "I practice some of those myself."

Julie ignored him. "What's the inmate to guard ratio?"

"Fifteen to one. Our prison design and electronic surveillance lets us operate with a smaller staff than comparable facilities."

"What about programming other than foosball?"

"We have a cognitive intervention class that emphasizes nonconfrontation and affords the inmates a chance to talk about their feelings and how their belief systems affect their decisions. They keep a journal. It's therapeutic."

"How's that going?"

"There are challenges. Many of our inmates have what they

call oppositional defiance disorder, which is a pattern of hostile behavior toward anyone they perceive as an authority figure. Our last instructor resigned. We're in the market for a new one if you know of anyone."

Jamerson nudged Coates. "Coates maybe. Coates likes to talk about his feelings," he offered.

Julie ignored the trooper again. "What kinds of weapons are in the prison?"

"Melted-down plastic sharpened to a point is popular. We've seen papier-mâché spears fashioned out of newspaper. One of our inmates on death row took the elastic out of his boxer shorts to make a crossbow string."

Julie made notes. Flung fluids. Oppositional defiance disorder. Papier-mâché spears. This class paper was looking to be grim.

"Put up some signs that clearly state *No Weapons*," Jamerson said. "It would help with that." He looked at Coates and Julie for a response to his perceived wit.

"Can we return him to the reserve pool?" Julie asked. "Or maybe give him a dollar for every word he doesn't say?"

"Part of the path to wisdom," Coates told Jamerson, "is realizing how many things do not require your comment."

"I second that," Julie said.

"I like saying things," Jamerson protested. He was running one hand through the other like he'd just downed a pot of coffee. He seemed to be struggling without his dip cup.

Julie turned back to Pillaire. "Is there a prison code the inmates follow?"

"Don't snoop, don't snitch. That's the main one."

"How do the people of Rocker County feel about you?"

"They want us here. We're one of their larger employers."

"One last question. To make assistant warden, did you come up through the ranks as a corrections officer or were you hired from the outside?"

"From outside."

"What was your job before this?"

"I was in finance," Pillaire said. He turned from the alcove. "We can finish up in my office."

The four of them made their way back down the corridor and had just rounded the corner toward the entryway when Julie thought she heard something, a cross between a wail and a scream, maybe a floor or two above them. It stopped as quickly as it started. Pillaire didn't react to it and neither did Jamerson, but Coates looked up toward the origin of the noise. Julie caught his eye and made a palms-up gesture. After a moment of studying the ceiling, he returned it. Maybe that was just Whitehall's natural backdrop.

"Who are the absolute worst guys you have in here?" Jamerson asked Pillaire.

"How much time do you have?"

"Give me the top three."

"Okay," Pillaire said. "We have a man on the second floor named Howard Brogan, who made kids drink bleach. There's Raymond Janz. You probably saw him on the news. Murdered fourteen prostitutes before he was caught. All teenagers. Rearranged their faces with surgical tools and industrial glue. He put their lips on their foreheads, their tongues on their chins, switched their eyes out with their ears. He called them his queens."

"I read about him," Julie said. "*People* magazine or somewhere. He killed his neighbor's dog and then graduated to killing his neighbor."

"Yes," Pillaire said. "But if you can believe it, we have someone worse. That would be Dimitri Medov. He's an Armenian on death row in secure housing, and that's where he'll stay until he's executed, because any time we let him out of his cell, he tries to kill everyone he sees."

"You got someone worse than the face-rearranging guy?" Jamerson asked.

"That's correct."

"What did Dimitri do to get there?" Julie questioned.

Pillaire began to speak and then stopped. "Things you wouldn't believe." He didn't elaborate.

Julie didn't ask him to. She had about enough of Whitehall. It was Fourth of July weekend, and her friends were about to throw steaks on the grill and crack open some craft beers, which sounded like a whole lot better time than one more second in this place.

They were back near where they'd started the tour. There was a cork board posted that said *Staff Only* above it. On it was a placard advertising a 5K charity fund-raiser to battle MS. Julie noted that the date of the race was last summer. Nothing in Whitehall was up to date. Pillaire stopped at a door marked CP7.

"I'll show you our main control room last," he said. "It houses the main electronic guts of the place and has cameras that cover the prison and grounds." He pushed a silver button on the wall and looked up at a small orb in the corner surrounded by a protective metal shell. Julie assumed it was a security camera.

There was a distinctive metallic click. Pillaire pulled on the door but it was still locked.

"I'm getting old. I pulled a piece of wax the size of a raisin out of my right ear this morning," Jamerson said to no one in particular.

"It was probably your brain," Coates said and Julie chuckled.

"Nuh-uh," Jamerson said. "It was, ah, your brain."

Pillaire hit the button again. "Open on Seven."

Again the metallic click. Pillaire pulled on the door. It didn't budge.

A tinny voice came from the intercom—presumably from a corrections officer, Julie thought. "Seems to be sticking," the officer said.

"Your key card doesn't work?" Jamerson asked, gesturing to Pillaire's neck lanyard.

"Not on this door," Pillaire said. "If a prisoner got a hold of it, it'd be too easy for them to escape." He hit the intercom. "Unstick it," he said.

"I am, sir." A pause. "It's not opening."

"Who is this?" Pillaire demanded.

"Correctional Officer McVay, sir."

"McVay, run a diagnostic and then get the on-call tech." Pillaire turned to the other three again. "I think he's new." They waited. Nothing happened with the door. "I'll call them myself," Pillaire said. He picked a phone marked Comm Seven off the opposite wall, held it to his ear, and looked quizzical. He returned it to the cradle and then picked it up again. He shook his head. He took out his cell phone and checked it. "Our cell net that jams signals shouldn't reach this close to the control booth. I should have service here."

Everyone checked their own phones.

"Anyone?" Pillaire asked. There was a collective shaking of heads.

"Fucking Verizon," Jamerson said.

Pillaire hit the intercom button again. "McVay, get me the on-duty watch commander."

"Copy that," McVay said. "Acting watch commander is Sgt. LeMaines."

"A sergeant is our watch commander?"

"Lieutenant called in sick."

"Call the warden."

"I just did. He's not picking up."

Pillaire took his radio out and turned the volume up. It buzzed with static.

"This ever happened before?" Coates asked

Pillaire shook his head. A bead of sweat had formed on his temple.

"Could someone have knocked out the radio repeater?"

"I don't think so," Pillaire said.

"What are we talking about?" Julie asked. "What's a repeater?"

"The gizmo that lets radios talk to each other over a distance," Coates said. "It's usually high up, on a building or a hill." He turned back to Pillaire. "Where's yours?"

"I'm not sure... Our tech guy handles all that. He doesn't work weekends. But the radios are on a digital system like the doors, so if the doors are down, maybe that's affecting our communications."

Jamerson checked his phone again. Gave up. "I'm gonna get bored waiting."

"I'll find you a word search," Coates said.

Julie heard the sound again, from above. The cross between a shout and a shriek, clearer this time and lasting longer before tapering off.

This time Jamerson looked up. "Fuck is that?"

McVay's voice crackled back on the intercom. "Sir, we're getting an alarm from the infirmary. I'm sending Aguilar and LeMaines."

"What do you show up on the infirmary monitor?"

"It's blank. It's... something is going on with our video feed."

"I don't mean to be rude," Jamerson interjected, "but do either of you guys know how to do your jobs?"

Pillaire made a point to look at Jamerson, but there was no challenge in it. Another bead of sweat was making its way down his temple.

"Because it's gonna be inconvenient if you both decide to suck at once."

Pillaire didn't respond. Julie turned to Coates. "Are we worried?"

"I'd say we're at least confused," Coates said.

Pillaire hit the button again. "Anything?"

"I can't get anything on coms."

The four of them lapsed into silence.

Julie had no idea what to make of this situation. But Coates seemed calm, so she'd be calm. But then again, Coates was always calm.

"Hit the button again," Jamerson said to Pillaire. "Get a fucking update."

But Assistant Warden Pillaire didn't have to press anything to get an update. Ahead of them, just down the hallway, a door opened. Four people emerged, one right after the other. The first two were correctional officers, one a Hispanic man in his early twenties and the other a heavyset guard about fifty with glasses. Both looked highly stressed. The third was a female nurse, breathing heavily, who moved in an ungainly lumber. And the last was a hard-looking man of about forty with hair cut to the scalp. He didn't look stressed at all. Or out of breath. He was wearing orange prison garb, the front of which was spattered with blood.

CHAPTER 9

Argento took in the group in front of him. Two men in suits who looked like cops: one Black and middle-aged, with a solid frame; the other younger, white, and lean, with a ratty mustache. Next to them was a skinny guy with graying hair in a cheap brown suit. He looked skittish. Rounding them out was a woman, midtwenties with long brown hair tied back. She came in at about five-seven with a triathlete build and wore a plain gray sweatshirt and running shoes. Not staff, Argento reasoned, because she wasn't wearing any kind of uniform. Then he saw she was holding a notebook. Some kind of tourist. On a tour that had just gone very much awry.

Everyone but Argento started talking at once, Argento's group trying to explain what they had just witnessed and the men in the other camp demanding answers.

"We have a homicide scene we need to lock down in medical," LeMaines said. "Check that, two homicide scenes."

"What? So why isn't... why aren't you there instead of here?" Brown Suit demanded.

"Because we can't get radio reception and we can't get a fucking call through," Aguilar interjected.

"Did Dr. Lau come this way?" Rachel asked.

Brown Suit shook his head. He jammed his thumb on the intercom button. "McVay, what the hell is going on?" he shouted. "Call the warden, call MDC, give me status on comms and medical, and how about opening this damn door."

The Black man in the suit had stepped protectively in front of the woman in the running shoes. He was watching Argento intently. He pulled a lanyard out of his front shirt pocket that held a gold badge that said State Highway Patrol with an eagle on top and underneath read State of Missouri.

"Drop the stick," he said. "Right now."

Argento was still holding Spentz's collapsible baton. He would have preferred to hang on to it, but all things considered, it seemed best to comply. He let it fall to the floor and, as a courtesy, kicked it over to the trooper, who picked it up and shoved it in the back of his beltline.

The trooper gestured at Argento. "What's his deal?" he said to Aguilar and LeMaines.

"He saved me," Rachel offered. "Three prisoners killed one of our officers and came after me, and he stopped them."

The trooper gave the two correctional officers a questioning look.

"Seems that way," Aguilar nodded. "We lost one of our guys, and there's one dead prisoner and two mangled ones."

"What are you in for?" the white man with the mustache demanded. Argento figured he was Trooper Number Two and had already taken an instant dislike to him. Argento said nothing.

"Does it speak?" the white trooper said, taking a step closer to Argento.

"Assault," Aguilar said. "He beat up some deputies."

"Thanks for helping the nurse," the Black trooper said, locking eyes with Argento, "but you can go back to your cell."

Argento knew how he looked to outsiders. It wasn't just the prison orange he found himself in, or the blood decorating the front of his sweatshirt. His hair was cropped short, his eyes expressionless, his build that of someone who could hurt people. One of Emily's friends had once confided to her that he had a cruel set to his face. Pedestrians would occasionally cross the street to avoid him, especially late at night. Or lock their car doors. A female jogger had taken out her pepper spray once when he had walked in her direction. He resembled a short-tempered cattle rustler.

"He should stay," Rachel said. "He helped me. He can help you."

"He gets points for all that. But he's a convict we don't know," the Black trooper said.

The white trooper said, "So go screw."

"All right," Argento said. "They haven't assigned me a cell yet. Anywhere in particular you'd like me to go?"

"Yeah," the white trooper said, pointing in a random direction. "Fucking... away."

"Wait," Rachel said. "Just wait."

Argento didn't wait. He turned to walk. He didn't know why the prison technology had taken a dive at the Whitehall Correctional Institute, but it didn't have much to do with him. He figured he'd go find an empty cell or room and ride this one out, and if any more prisoners got in his way, he'd give them all they could handle. He had nowhere to be until Monday when court was in session. The troopers, the guards, and Brown Suit were no doubt big boys and could take care of themselves—and if they couldn't, that was on them.

But then there was the nurse. And the girl with the notebook. Neither were cops or correctional staff, and the prisoner assault in the infirmary showed the nurse already had a sizable target on her back. In this place, so would the girl with the notebook. There was something else about her. She was on a tour, not with a student group, but all by herself. And on a holiday, no less. That seemed strange to Argento. He wouldn't think the jail would have the time or inclination to take students on a tour one at a time. It meant something that they had catered just to her. And, not for nothing, she had a two-trooper escort. He wanted to know more, and the residual cop in him made him stop.

"Who's she?" he asked, pointing to the girl with the notebook.

"You don't even need to look at her," the Black trooper said to Argento. He took two steps toward him and then stopped short.

Because the white trooper had a gun in his hand.

It was a silver subcompact with a two-and-a-half-inch barrel designed to fit easily in a pocket. An NAA Guardian, Argento thought, with a short magazine that probably held no more than six rounds. The trooper pointed it at Argento's midsection, his arm fully extended. The adrenaline dump from the infirmary fight had faded, but seeing the gun leveled sent the chemical wash right back through him.

"We told you to piss off," the white trooper said. "So do it."

"How'd you get that in here?" Brown Suit asked.

"Crotched it," the white trooper said, his eyes flicking away from Argento toward Brown Suit.

"They patted you down." Brown Suit's voice trailed off.

"Guys don't like touching other guys' junk, even in here."

"You can't have–" Brown Suit began, his voice an ineffectual whine, and the white trooper cut him off.

"Don't care about your rules. I work narcotics undercover. I take a gun everywhere."

Brown Suit turned to the Black trooper. "Did you know about this?"

The Black trooper shook his head. "But given the circumstances, it ain't gonna hurt us."

"You can relax, Samaritan," the white trooper told Argento. "You don't need to know who she is. She's got all the help she needs. Now for the last time, walk. Or your head is where I'm gonna keep my bullets."

Your head is where I'm gonna keep my bullets. It sounded like a line he'd stolen from some shitty gangster movie. The white trooper was close to Argento. Too close. And his arm was still fully extended instead of held snug to his body for proper tight quarters firearm retention. He was used to pointing guns at people and gaining compliance. Argento's experience had been different as an officer in inner-city Detroit. He had pointed guns at hardened parolees who had laughed at him. Who had refused to prone out on the ground when commanded to do so. *I ain't no dog*, they'd said.

Argento put his hands up in resignation, but it was all for show. What he was going to do next required a supreme belief in his own abilities and no small amount of doubt in the abilities of the white trooper. The former he had. The latter was an educated guess. The trooper was full of bravado, and Argento was betting big on it not being earned. He had momentarily taken his eyes off Argento when Brown Suit had asked him a question, which was a tactical blunder. Plus he had a stupid mustache.

Argento had three more things going for him. The first was fast hands. The second was that the trooper's finger was off the trigger of his firearm, as all police training dictated, because he hadn't yet committed to shoot. And the third was that action beats reaction, every time.

Argento started backpedaling. *Make 'em think you're doing one thing*. Then he moved forward. *Then do the other.* He stepped in close to the trooper, at a forty-five-degree angle. He took the Guardian out of his hand with a sharp twist of the trooper's wrist and moved away, flush against the wall, the gun down at his side. It had been a risky move. The white trooper could have exceeded Argento's expectations and lit him up when he tried for the gun. But Argento had never been risk averse. Especially not these days. In fact, at that moment, he didn't care if he took a bullet. Getting shot might be a step up for him.

"If she has all the help she needs," Argento said, "then why was that so easy?"

The Black trooper didn't hesitate. He stepped in front of the woman with the notebook and backed her against the wall so his bulk covered her. If there were bullets coming her way, he would absorb them.

Argento ejected the chambered round from the Guardian,

caught it midair, and stripped the mag from the well. He tossed the gun back to the white trooper, who grabbed it with his mouth hanging open.

"Don't like guns pointed at me. Who's she?"

The woman stepped out from behind the Black trooper. His hand instinctively went up to stop her, but she had already moved to the center of the room.

"You don't have to ask them," she said. "You can ask me. My name is Julie Wakefield." Argento took note of her voice, which was surprisingly steady given recent events. "And they're with me because I'm the governor's daughter."

"There's fifty states," Argento said. "Which governor?"

"Here in Missouri."

Now that she was closer, Argento could see Julie had a light spray of freckles across her nose and cheeks. She was an attractive woman, which likely wouldn't serve her well in Whitehall. But there was something else in her posture and the set of her face. Something unruly or contrarian. Like she wouldn't put up with a lot of shit.

"What are you doing in lockup?"

"I'm on a tour for a grad school paper. What's your name?"

Argento glanced down at his prison band, which said *Chris Spielman*, the name he'd given to the Rocker County deputies and during Whitehall intake. It'd be too confusing to try and keep that alias up. "I go by Kurt. Who are these guys?"

"Missouri State Troopers. My protective detail." She pointed to the Black trooper. "That's Derrick Coates." She motioned to the white one. "And Max Jamerson."

"Protective detail," Argento said. He looked at Jamerson. Looked at the loose round and gun mag in his own hand. "When does your shift start?"

Jamerson looked both queasy and resigned. As if he was still processing what had just happened to him. Then he came back to life. "That's a felony what you just did," he sputtered.

"We'll deal with that later," Coates cut in. He was looking at Argento with a mixture of apprehension and curiosity. He reached his hand out. "Now how about those bullets back, Kurt."

Argento had liked how Coates had protected Julie. He liked how he didn't seem overly rattled. He liked how he wasn't Jamerson. He tossed Coates the magazine. Coates caught it and notably didn't give it back to Jamerson. Instead he nodded at his partner, who wordlessly handed him the empty Guardian. Coates loaded it and racked in a round. He dropped the gun in his front right pants pocket.

"Talk," he said to Argento.

"All right," Argento said. "Here's what I know. You've got doors that aren't working and some violent prisoners wandering free floor to floor. You've got at least one dead guard. You've got civilians at risk: Julie, Rachel, and whoever this guy in the brown suit is. I don't know what all that adds up to, but whatever it is, I'm going to be good at it. You may want to keep me on board."

"My name is Daniel Pillaire," the man in the brown suit said. "I'm assistant warden," he added.

"What'd you do for a living before you got locked up?" Coates asked Argento.

"You wouldn't believe me if I told you."

"Try me," Coates said.

Argento suspected the whole truth could only hurt him now. Saying he was an ex-cop who ended up in this place for assaulting other cops and then claiming the whole thing was a setup wouldn't pass the credulity test with Coates. He might as well claim he was a tugboat captain. "Garbageman," he said, which wasn't really a lie.

"You took my partner's gun away like you'd done it before. Where'd you get your training? Military?"

"From books," Argento said. "I like to read."

"Look," LeMaines broke in. "We got a dead colleague down the hall. Do you understand? We gotta see to that. Warden, what's the status on this door?"

The warden looked at the silver button on the wall as if he were seeing it for the first time. Then he jammed it with his thumb so hard the skin flushed red under the nail. Nothing.

"Sir, nothing's changed," McVay said on the other side of the door without prompting. "It won't open."

Argento was watching Jamerson, who was quiet. He was attempting to reset. Argento had never been disarmed before, but he knew cops who had, and they said there was nothing worse. No matter how helpful Argento would be to this group going forward, he had just earned an enemy. He'd taken the gun because he'd let ego get in his way plus anger at being treated like a piece of shit by what until recently had been his fellow officers. It had been a tactical error. What remained to be seen was how it would play out with Jamerson.

"Just pull on it again," Jamerson told Pillaire.

"I know how doors work," Pillaire snapped.

Jamerson pushed past him and yanked on the handle. It didn't budge.

"Okay," Coates said. He stepped forward and hit the intercom button. "I get that this door won't open. That's abundantly clear to all of us. What about the other doors?"

Silence. McVay no doubt checking.

"They're... Jesus." More silence. McVay came back on. "Exterior doors are shut. Interior, some are open, some closed. Cell doors, some are, ah, open, some are closed, all floors. I don't... I haven't ever seen anything like this."

"So give us an alternate exit," Coates said. "Because we are out of here."

"I'm... there's nothing close. Everything's magnetically sealed. Nothing's opening. And I can't get an outside line. And cameras are down. Just blank screens."

"Do you have comms with the officers on the floors?"

"Nothing."

"Unfuck this," Jamerson said to Pillaire. "And do it right now."

"I don't know how," Pillaire said. His voice was quiet. No one said anything. Pillaire was clenching and unclenching a fist. Jamerson was blinking more than he should have been. Julie was looking from Jamerson to Coates, as if expecting some kind of solution. Rachel was shaking her head almost imperceptibly, her mind probably still spinning from the infirmary assault. LeMaines and Aguilar were sweating, the latter so heavily his collar was speckled with perspiration. LeMaines tried his radio again. Nothing but static. He swore under his breath. Only Coates seemed largely unruffled.

Argento broke the silence. "So what kind of asshole designed this system?"

CHAPTER 10

"Our controls are nearly all digital," Pillaire explained, his voice regaining some strength now that he was talking about something he was familiar with. "Installed three months ago. We still use manual lock and keys for redundancy on interior doors. But there's been a few bugs in the system. The company that installed it quit before all the work was complete. Contractual dispute."

"Sorry to interrupt," LeMaines said to Pillaire, mopping his brow with his elbow. "But you gotta...just give us an order, sir. You want us to go back and secure the infirmary?"

"No," Pillaire said. "Too many unknowns right now. I have to figure out what our baseline is."

"Who takes point on murders inside here?" Jamerson asked, motioning between himself and Coates. "Us?" The trooper was talking louder than he needed to, trying to reestablish himself after having his gun stripped.

"No, local PD," LeMaines said. "We secure the scene and help coordinate but it's their show."

Coates hit the intercom. He wasn't waiting for Pillaire anymore. "The doors that are open. Does it seem random? Or is there a pattern? Like every other door?"

"Random, I think," McVay said. "Can't say for sure. There's lots of doors to track. I tried to reboot the system. It's a no-go."

Jamerson turned to Argento. "You said you were going to be helpful. You know anything about computers?"

"I did a spreadsheet once," Argento said.

Jamerson half laughed and looked at Pillaire. "So how do we get out of here? Is there a drainpipe we can climb down?"

Pillaire shook his head. "What windows we have are secured and we can't—"

"It was a joke, Warden," Jamerson snapped. He stared at Pillaire. "How about a big smile? Heard they're contagious."

"Enough," Coates said. "Where's the warden's office from here? Can we access it?"

"He said some doors are open, some are closed, I . . . I don't know," Pillaire said.

Coates looked at Pillaire. Then cast his gaze on the rest of the group as if mentally calculating their abilities and weaknesses.

"Let's go see," he said. He turned to Argento. Looked at Julie and Rachel. Argento could almost see him doing the math in his head. Weighing the known and the unknown, the risk and the reward. "Okay, Kurt. We'll give you a tryout."

Jamerson took a step forward. "That's a bad fucking play, partner."

"I'll take full responsibility," Coates said. "I got a feeling about him."

Pillaire put a hand up. "Gentlemen, I don't mean to pull rank, but I am assistant warden of this facility and as such, I maintain command."

Coates stared at Pillaire. The assistant warden slowly lowered his hand until it hung limply at his side.

"I've got the governor's only child with me," Coates said. "And I intend to see her out of this. I need you because you know this place, but you're not in charge anymore. We are." Coates nodded toward Jamerson to indicate who *we* referred to. "If you don't like that, you can take it up with our boss. His name is Christopher

Wakefield. He's in charge of the whole state, and he lives in a big house on Madison Street."

Pillaire nodded. Almost too quickly, Argento thought, as if he were relieved to be off the hook for decision-making.

Coates's hand went down to his front pocket and patted it, as if assuring himself that the Guardian was still there. "Now take us to the warden."

CHAPTER 11

The hallway leading to the office of Warden Ian Stroster was passable by two security doors that opened with a mechanical whoosh when Pillaire used his lanyard key card. Coates took point with the handgun out at the low ready position. Jamerson brought up the rear. Everyone else filled in the middle.

"I guess that's a good sign, right?" Julie said. "That the card is working."

"Been the first good sign we've seen," Jamerson said.

There were no signs of prisoners in the hallway, but the acrid smell of urine filled the air. Argento saw a yellowish pool outside the door marked *Warden*. Not a good omen. Coates opened the door. Paused.

"Wait," he said to the group. Then he went in. He emerged a moment later and locked eyes with Jamerson. "Hold this hallway," he told his partner and handed him the Guardian. "Pillaire, come with me." The assistant warden dutifully followed him inside. He walked out seconds later, face ashen.

"Problem?" Jamerson asked.

Argento moved closer to the open office door. There was no receptionist's area. Only the main office itself. A man he took to be

Warden Ian Stroster, dressed in a navy-blue Whitehall polo shirt, ID lanyard around his neck, was leaned up against the back wall, legs splayed out. The warden had been largely eviscerated. Like a frog dissected in science class. The stench of blood and voided bowels filled the room. The warden's face was set in a kind of confused repose, as if he thought he could escape his imminent death by simply not believing it. Coates was standing over the body. His eyes were hooded and he was very still.

"Maybe it was quicker than it looks," Coates said softly.

"Oh my God," Pillaire said. "Oh my dear God."

Jamerson remained in the hallway as a sentry, head on a swivel checking both sides of the hall. He made a point of having the Guardian in close to his body with Argento near.

"Warden dead?" Jamerson asked.

"Yes," Coates said.

"Are we sure?"

"I can see his lungs from the outside."

"Probably why he wasn't answering the phone," Jamerson said.

"Who did this?" Pillaire mumbled, his head tilted toward the ground as if he didn't have the strength to fully straighten it. "And where did they go?"

Jamerson continued to scan the hall. "They can't be far."

LeMaines and Aguilar framed themselves in the doorway. Took one look at Stroster and stepped right back out, LeMaines making the sign of the cross, Aguilar going pale.

Argento looked at Stroster's corpse. He didn't know the man. But this was how life was. People break or are broken. You're surrounded by their pieces. There was something clutched in the warden's hand. Something to use as a weapon to stave off his attackers. Argento looked closer. No, it wasn't a weapon. It was a purple feather duster. Stroster must have known that the prison had just entered emergency mode and had elected to clean. As a member of SWAT, Argento had cotaught a class at the police academy on disaster preparedness. How people cycled through denial and groupthink. So the feather duster made sense to him. He knew this was something the uninitiated did in crisis—busied themselves with mundane tasks to unconsciously shield themselves from what was coming. People in the Towers on 9/11 had taken the time to gather keepsakes from their workspaces instead of evacuating.

Argento scanned the rest of the room. A few framed diplomas. A small outline of dust on the desk where a picture cube had recently been. Above the warden's door was a quilted sign that said, *Courage does not always roar. Sometimes courage is the quiet voice at the end of the day saying: "I will try again tomorrow."* Argento guessed it was written by someone who had never won a fight. The quilted letters made him think of the sign Emily had hung in the kitchen that said *Only Love Completes This House*. He thought it was corny at first before it gradually became one of his favorite things. His home had him, his wife, and Hudson. It had been complete. When Emily had died, one night he'd looked at the sign, as if seeing it for the first time. Then he had pulled it down and torn it to shreds.

"Shouldn't we…do something with his body?" Julie asked, and Argento's mind came back to the present. She was still in the hallway, her hand covering her mouth to ward off the smell of the warden's innards. She was pacing from side to side but, Argento noted, looked otherwise composed. She was no longer holding her notebook. Good. She was going to need to have her hands free for whatever came their way.

"Like bury him?" Jamerson said. "We got enough problems with living people here to worry about the dead ones."

Coates picked up the warden's phone and held it to his ear. Shook his head. Picked up the warden's radio, which was in a holder behind his desk. All static. He nestled it back in the holder. Now Coates sat in front of Stroster's computer, which had a request for a password.

"You know it?" he asked Pillaire. "We could try to get an email out or look for anything that could help us."

Pillaire didn't look at Coates. He wasn't looking anywhere. He was lost somewhere inside himself. If he hadn't officially become worthless yet, it wouldn't be long.

Coates motioned Kurt over. "You can't be worse at computers than me. Can you try to get into that?" Coates stood aside. Argento took a seat. It was a comfortable chair. The warden hadn't skimped on ergonomics. Argento wasn't holding out much hope he'd be able to get into the warden's desktop. He wasn't much with computers. He had only done the one spreadsheet and he would have still been handwriting police reports if they'd let him. He got on the main screen that asked for the password. He looked around to see if it was taped to the desk. No such luck. He typed in Whitehall, both upper- and lowercase, and got a message that his entry was incorrect. He met Coates's eyes and shook his head.

Coates nodded. He moved to the door and picked up a straight-backed wooden visitor chair. Argento realized what was next. He stood, but Coates had already shut the office door behind him and jammed the chair underneath the handle, locking Argento inside. There was a small square window panel set in the door. Argento looked through it at the trooper.

"Nothing personal," Coates said.

"Thought you had a feeling about me."

"Still do. My feeling is you're too much of a wild card to keep around."

Argento watched the group depart. He couldn't fault Coates. If the positions were reversed, he would have likely done the same thing. He should have seen this coming. But he was too used to viewing himself as a cop and not as others saw him right now: a violent felon in an orange jumpsuit locked up for assaulting deputies. A man who was likely part of the problem, not any kind of solution.

Argento watched Jamerson circle back and return to the door. The trooper pointed at Argento and turned up his middle finger.

"Have the best day ever," Jamerson said.

CHAPTER 12

Julie

Julie watched Jamerson take the time to leave the group, walk back to the warden's door, and flip off Kurt. He was a man-child, she thought. The warden was dead with his guts hanging out, there was a murdered correctional officer outside the infirmary, prison doors weren't working, and he was playing sixth-grade games. Stress, maybe. It did strange things to people. Or maybe that was just how Jamerson always was. But she didn't trust him, and she was going to watch him.

Julie turned her attention to her own stress level. She could feel it keenly. Like something was trying to crawl out of her stomach. But she believed she could keep it at bay. Panic never solved any problems, her father had told her once. It just caused them. She needed to transition from student mode to survival mode. To that end, she had abandoned her notebook. Just dropped it on the floor. It would be mental notes from here on out. She'd need to keep her hands free.

She thought about Kurt. How swiftly he'd disarmed Jamerson. How Rachel had reported that he'd taken out three convicts to save her. Julie didn't doubt the latter. Kurt resembled the guy on a hockey team whose only job was to start and finish fights. It wasn't his size so much, although he was by no means small. It was the way he moved: decisive and economical. The way he seemed to talk through you instead of to you. He looked both intense and serene. There was something else about him, too, but she couldn't put her finger on it. Just a general sense that he didn't belong in here, not as an inmate. That he belonged on their side.

"I'm not sure we should have done that," she told Coates.

"Okay, Jules." He was the only person besides her father who called her that. "I hear you. But there's no playbook for what's happening here. I gotta make some decisions on the fly."

"Who responds to this kind of thing?"

"I looked into that when I found out we were coming here," Coates said. "Every private prison has state prison personnel assigned to shadow it. It's gonna be a SWAT team from MDC. That right, guys?"

LeMaines and Aguilar nodded.

"And since you're here," Coates continued, "my guess is they'll add some tanks and cannons."

Julie always appreciated how Coates treated her, if not quite like a peer, then like someone whose opinion he valued. He was right—there was no playbook—but she trusted his judgment. He could get her out of this. He could get them all out of this. Her father had told her about Coates's reputation before assigning him to her protective detail. She knew he'd seen his fair share of critical incidents before, from gang shootings to all-out riots in Ferguson. He was skilled and he was steady.

Jamerson seemed to be another story. Macho bluster she'd yet to see backed up by competence. When Kurt had taken his gun away, the image of the trooper left in Julie's head had been that of a poorly constructed toy.

As if he sensed her thoughts, Coates tapped Jamerson on the back and held his hand out. Jamerson gave him back the Guardian, somewhat begrudgingly. Coates held it at his side.

"Where to?" Aguilar asked. Neither he nor LeMaines had

bothered to challenge Coates's authority to supplant Pillaire in the chain of command.

"Control room," Coates said. "See if anything's changed."

The group retraced their steps to the control room door. Pillaire didn't even bother to step forward to press the intercom button. Coates did it for him. The trooper was calling the plays now, and Julie was glad for it.

"Status."

McVay's voice came crackling over the speaker. "Same. Everything's the same. Did you find the warden?"

"Murdered."

Silence on the other end. Julie couldn't imagine McVay's day was going much better than their own, but he was in the control room protected by doors, brick, and metal. She'd swap places in a heartbeat.

"You need," Coates said, "to walk out of this facility until you can get a cell or radio signal and call this in. Tell the dispatcher to send local PD, the state SWAT team, the fire department, and every ambulance they have. Tell them the governor's daughter is in here. They can activate the damn National Guard if they have to."

"You don't understand," McVay said, rushing out the words. "Our doors are locked, too. Magnetically sealed. You're locked out there. We're locked in here."

Jamerson ran his fingers over his scalp, leaning back until he was staring straight up at the ceiling. "You have gotta be playing with me."

Coates put his hands on the door and ran them down the metal to the floor, like a captain assessing the hull of a ship. "Can we blow it?"

"No way," Aguilar said. "We don't have anything that high-grade in here."

Julie heard a noise behind her. It was Pillaire. He was crying. He wasn't even trying to hide it. "I can't do this," Pillaire said. "I'm just . . . I'm not brave."

"Better work on that," Coates said, his tone of voice suggesting that if Pillaire was looking for sympathy, he'd not find it here. "This is an all-hands-on-deck situation and we need you."

"Leave me alone," Pillaire managed between snuffles.

Jamerson's face screwed up in disgust. "You should be happy there, Sniffly Sue. You just got promoted. You're acting warden now."

"Take it easy, Max," Coates said, the exasperation clear in his voice. "Now, let's run through this. There's a cell net over the whole prison so we can't make calls. The landlines and radios are down. The doors are screwed—some are open, some are closed, but we're sealed in here. We have a murdered warden, a murdered officer, and some dead cons. Am I missing anything?"

"That's about the size of it," LeMaines said.

"And there's no plan in place for any of this? No contingency?"

"Not for this," LeMaines said. "Hell no." He reached into his pocket, removed a small pink pill from a ziplock bag, and dry-swallowed it.

"What's that?"

"For my blood pressure."

"Fuck," Jamerson said. "We should probably all take one of those."

"When does the next shift come on?"

"Six hours," LeMaines said. "I know, that's a haul. But they'll figure out right away something's up when they can't get through the front doors."

"Six hours," Coates repeated. "Okay. Let's talk about what we do have. One working firearm with seven rounds. LeMaines, you and Aguilar have batons and pepper spray. That's not great, but it's better than nothing. Any Tasers around here?"

"Used to," LeMaines said. "Lost them to budget cuts."

"That ain't much," Jamerson said. "Maybe if we spread it all out on a table, it'll look like more."

Coates asked, "What about your armory?"

"We got a full weapons locker. Nine-millimeters, .223 rifles with thirty-round magazines. The works."

"Sounds good. Where is it?"

"Other side of that door," LeMaines said, his voice faltering as he nodded toward the control room.

"When we passed the yard, I saw guard towers. They have long guns?"

LeMaines nodded. "But none of the tower guys are working. We've got a skeleton crew today because of the holiday."

"Keys?"

"All cells are keyed the same on each floor. But the guards on the floor don't have any of the exit keys because it prevents prisoners from taking them and getting into the exterior stairwells. Guards have to be buzzed off the floor by Control."

"Is there a master key?"

"Warden has it. He wears it around his neck."

"That information," Jamerson interjected, "would have been a lot more fucking useful when we were in the fucking warden's office looking at his fucking remains."

"I didn't think of it then," Aguilar said, his voice rising in protest. "He was all split open. Give me a break."

"It's okay," Coates said. "Did anyone even see a key around his neck? Whoever killed him may have taken it."

"Hell, I hardly even saw a neck," Jamerson said.

"I didn't look at him for but a second," LeMaines said. Aguilar nodded in agreement.

"You want me to go back?" Jamerson asked.

"Kurt's not going to be very happy with us after I locked him in there," Coates said.

"Give me the gun," Jamerson said casually. "Then it won't matter what his mood is."

Julie put her hands out, palms up.

Coates shook his head as if to tell Julie, *Don't worry. Not gonna happen.* "Would that master key even work on this door?" Coates asked, thumping on the metal separating them from the control room.

"No," LeMaines said. "It opens all interior and stairwell doors. That's it. Doors that lead to the outside still have to be operated by Control."

"So it isn't going to help us much," Coates said. "Leave it up there."

"Anything else we have going for us?" Jamerson asked.

"We're all adults in good health," Julie said, speaking for the first time since they had reconvened at the control door. It felt good to talk. It gave her some semblance of a handle on this situation. "Some of you have training that will help us. And there's a finite number of prisoners."

"'Finite,'" Jamerson echoed. "Someone's got some book learning."

"What was that last part?" Julie asked, irritation quickly morphing to anger.

Jamerson waved her off. Julie made the decision to hate him.

"So what's the plan?" Aguilar asked.

Coates said, "We hold here. This area is as defensible as any. We hunker down for six hours until the next watch realizes what's up and they call for the cavalry. Any threat comes through a door at us, I'll give them something to think about." Coates held up the Guardian.

The plan made sense to Julie, although that didn't mean she liked the thought of just sitting there. But something else was occurring to her. "Derrick," she said.

"Yes?"

"What do we think this is? The system failure. Hackers?"

"If it's a hacking, Pillaire or someone from Whitehall should have gotten some kind of demand email, right? You know, pay us if you want your system back."

"Maybe it's some anarchist group," Aguilar chimed in. "They just want to disrupt shit."

"I don't know," Coates said. "And right now, even if we did know, I'm not sure how it would help us." He turned to Pillaire and the two correctional officers. "Since we're gonna be sitting here for a while, I want to know what could come our way while we wait for the next shift to show up. So tell me about this place."

Pillaire looked wilted. When he opened his mouth to speak, Coates shook his head.

"No. Not you. I don't want to hear the company line. I want to hear from Sgt. LeMaines. And no bullshit. Give it to me straight."

LeMaines looked at Pillaire. The assistant warden was silent, his head in his hands. Julie watched him with a growing sense of dismay. The one person with the most institutional knowledge was down for the count. LeMaines let out a breath. Leaned against the wall, as if this was going to take a while. "Okay," he said. "I'll tell you. But it ain't good."

CHAPTER 13

Julie

I've worked in other prisons," LeMaines said. "Some ran pretty well. I saw more than a handful of convicts leave as different men, get real jobs, function in society, all the things that you want. This place," LeMaines said, pointing at the ground for emphasis, "isn't one of those kind of prisons. This place makes everyone who comes here worse. Some of them, a lot worse."

"I don't know if that's the case," Pillaire said without looking up, but his heart wasn't in it. No one reacted to his words. After his breakdown, Julie didn't think anything he said mattered.

"Our inmates are seventy-five percent minority. Our staff is twenty-five percent minority. Makes for some racial tensions in what already is one of the most violent pens in the country. The prisoners run this joint even when all is well, even when we have a full staff and working doors. Our jobs training program, when we even have it running, is a mess. It's basically just the metal shop and it pays inmates twelve cents an hour. Outside of that, we don't have shit for programming, so our inmates get bored and they fight all the time. They try to kill the guards. We had two guys maimed this year. One's still in physical therapy, can't see straight. The other lost a leg."

"What else?" Coates asked.

"We're the worst-paid department in Missouri," LeMaines continued. "Our staffing is fucking horrible. They say it's one guard for every fifteen inmates, which is the lowest we can get away with under state law, but it's more like one for twenty-five. That's because everyone hates working here so they call in sick all the time. We just had half a dozen officers quit and they haven't been replaced. We don't have the staff to regularly search inmates and cells for contraband, and even if we did, we've had guards sneaking the shit in for prisoners in exchange for cash. There's gonna be weapons out there. There's gonna be prisoners hopped up on dope who are feeling no pain."

"If they're having that many problems with the guards smuggling in contraband, how come they don't search the guards?" Jamerson asked.

LeMaines laughed without mirth. "Per our union contract, we are to be paid for the time it takes us to suit up and walk inside. If you're going to search the guards, you have to pay us for that search time. That's five, ten minutes a guard. Multiply that by a shitload of guards over the course of a year. You're talking money that's not in the budget. This is a for-profit prison, man. It's Skimp City. We got a state inspection coming up where they're gonna check this place up and down, and I don't see how we're going to come close to passing without someone bribing someone."

Coates asked, "How many inmates and how many guards?"

"About five hundred inmates being watched by thirty-three guards, on a good day. And today's not a good day. We're probably looking at more like twenty-three. And Pillaire told you there's been a few bugs with the rollout of our digital security system, but that's the understatement of the year. When you have an incomplete setup like ours where some doors open via key cards and some have backup locks with actual keys, it just creates more opportunities for inmates to get their hands on those keys and those cards and gain access wherever the hell they want."

Jamerson whistled. "Well, that's for shits. With some doors open upstairs, and not a lot of guards to wrangle them, what do you think your inmates are going to do?"

"Depends on the floor," LeMaines said. "This place gets crazier the higher up you go. But generally speaking, some of them will stay in their cells and wait for order to be restored. They'll be as scared as some of us are. There's a couple short-timers, a few trustees that probably won't give us too much trouble. Others will wander around and see how far they can get. We got guys who will probably go to the kitchen looking for food or try to break into the canteen for the candy and donuts. Then there'll be the hunters."

"Hunters?" Julie asked. The word hung in the air. She had asked the question but she felt she already knew the answer. And it scared her.

"The hard-core cons," LeMaines continued. "They'll be searching for prey. Like the ones who came after Rachel. Or they'll track down guards who pissed them off. Some will hunt other prisoners who they think are beneath them, like the pedos. Or they'll look for rival gang members."

"How many hunters we talking about?" Coates asked.

"Plenty," LeMaines said. "Enough to give us all we can handle."

"Any visitors in here besides Julie?"

"Not a one."

"Any other medical staff?"

Rachel spoke up, her voice cracking when she spoke. "There's another doctor and a nurse who are on break but they're past the control pod. So it's just Dr. Lau and me. Like the sergeant said, it's a skeleton crew."

"Any idea where Lau went?"

"I would have thought he'd come here," Rachel said. "I don't know."

Coates continued. "Cleaning crew, counselors, other administrators?"

"The trustees clean this place, so we don't have civilian

custodians," LeMaines said. "Not cost-effective. And no other administrators. There should be at least a few guards per floor upstairs. God knows what's happening up there."

"We gotta go up there," Aguilar said. He had been squatting on his thighs but now he rose. "We gotta help them."

"No," Coates said. "They know their floors and they're going to have to hold them. I need you here."

"I don't work for you," Aguilar said. "Those are my brothers. We've already lost Spentz." He began pacing and threading his fingers together. "I don't even know what I've been doing sitting here all this time listening to you people. I gotta go to them."

Coates put both his hands up in a gesture of appeasement. "I understand that, Aguilar. I'm right there with you. We're all shook here. But we gotta stay together."

"Fuck all that," Aguilar said. A patch of redness had appeared on his cheeks and was spreading to the base of his neck.

"Listen to him," Julie said to Coates. "He's right, we have to help them."

"Julie," Coates said. "Let me work this."

"Tony," LeMaines said, putting a hand on the younger guard's shoulder. Aguilar shook it off.

"Settle down, kid," Jamerson said, a hard note of disdain in his voice. "This shit is way above your pay grade."

Julie winced.

Aguilar stopped moving. Got quiet. "Tell me to settle down again, cop," he finally said. "See what happens."

Jamerson didn't pause a beat. He squared up to Aguilar. "Settle down."

"You fucking—" Aguilar went for him, hands raised. Both LeMaines and Coates moved at the same time, stepping in between them. LeMaines pulled back Aguilar, and Coates yanked back his partner.

And then McVay's voice came on over the intercom, stopping the row before it started.

"Warden, I have an update and I don't think it's good."

The sound of McVay's voice seemed to rouse Pillaire. He stood up and pressed the intercom. "What is it?"

"Sir, on my main system terminal under Pending Events, it says System Purge."

"What does that mean?"

"I think it means this system is going to reset itself. The, ah, doors are going to open and stay open. Hallway doors. Stairwell doors. The cell doors."

"So this door between us?" Pillaire said, his voice rising in excitement. "So we can get out?"

"No," McVay said. "Not this one. The other doors."

"How many other doors?"

"Once you pass the corridor you're in," McVay said, "all of them."

Pillaire began to speak but Coates talked over him. "After the purge, can we still key the doors closed?"

"I don't think so. Looks like it's gonna be an electronic seal. If there's a manual override, I don't know it. I'm not tech support, man, but I don't think keys will do a thing."

Jamerson pushed past Pillaire and hit the button. "How much time do we have?"

"Screen says two hours."

It settled in. In two hours, every single prisoner in Whitehall would be free instead of just a random assortment. *Bad guys are in there*, her father had said. *I know they'll be behind steel doors, but watch yourself.* Now no more locked doors. They'd be free to go where they wanted. Do what they wanted. Julie reflexively put her hand to her mouth, as if she could prevent this information from infiltrating her. Someone said, "Holy shit." Then it was quiet, save for the collective sound of uneven breathing in the gray hallway.

CHAPTER 14

Argento sat on the warden's desk and cracked his knuckles just to do something. He had been in the office long enough to have gotten used to the dead body smell. Gruesome, to be sure, but he was well acquainted with being among the dead, and it barely moved the needle. He'd averaged about a body every other week on the job, ranging from natural deaths to industrial accidents to gunshot victims. One unlucky soul had his face sheared off by a passing train.

Argento had already studied the exit door. He'd kicked down a good many in his day, but this one was more than sturdy and there was the chair on the other side to contend with. He wasn't going to be able to horse his way through. Advantage Trooper Coates.

If he worked in this place, he'd stow a weapon in the office, preferably a firearm for situations just like this. There was almost certainly a regulation against it, but the people who made such rules didn't understand how bad things could get and how quickly they could get that way. The people who made such rules worked in committees and put white paper into manila folders and drank hibiscus tea.

He began a systematic search, mentally dividing the office into sectors. Like most of his days since Emily left, he had his mind half on what was in front of him and half on memories of her, even being in a small room with a murdered man. Because everything reminded him of her. They had fallen hard for each other. Emily used to joke that they were dating exclusively within the first twenty minutes of meeting. Introductions to their respective circles were made, and while Emily's family didn't quite know what to do with Argento, Argento's cop friends took to Emily just fine. She was engaging and down-to-earth and could be as bawdy as the rest of them.

He fell in love with her. Loved her so fiercely it scared him.

They were wed within a year. On the surface, the two of them didn't have much in common. Argento used to claim that it was an arranged marriage. But they reveled in each other's company. Hiking, camping, shopping at the city's antiques mall on Fisher Freeway, finding hole-in-the-wall ethnic restaurants off the marked path. After a hard day on the job, she would put on soft music and work the kinks out of his neck and back. He would try to reciprocate, because she had her own hard days, but his hands were rough and unpracticed, and she would laugh and tell him not to give up his day job.

They had gotten Hudson together, a rescue from a state wildfire, and brought him home to their Polish A-frame in a working-class neighborhood they relished. There were posters of tropical locales papered on the den walls. Key West. The Cayman Islands. Fiji. After they married, every time they saved up enough money for a vacation, they went somewhere warm. The beach was where he'd proposed. They were taking a morning walk along the surf when he got down on one knee. The water was coming in around them, warm and clear, dampening the bottom of her white dress.

Argento blinked and pulled himself back to the room. He was an inmate alone with a split-open body in a state prison where everything had just broken down. He didn't know who would have the ability and funding to pull off an operation like this, to electronically bedevil an entire state prison. Maybe some Whitehall office schlub had just spilled coffee on the control panels.

He thought about what was happening on the floors above him with random doors open and a scarcity of guards given the holiday. He had never worked in a prison but he knew cons. He'd been around them for more than half his life. He knew that even under the best of circumstances, they'd fight each other over issues of power and race, revenge for an attack, a slight, a theft, over drugs, over smokes, being too assertive, not being assertive enough. He figured it was a safe bet that things were going poorly in Whitehall for everyone involved. People were going to get hurt. People were going to die.

The group with the assistant warden were facing lousy odds. Seven people, only four of whom had relevant training, versus an entire jail didn't seem fair.

He had offered to help.

They said no.

He was about halfway through his search, having turned up nothing more notable than a half-eaten bag of gummy worms and an open pack of cigarettes with a lighter taped to it, when he saw movement by the door.

Someone was looking at him through the glass square.

"How can I help you?" Argento said.

He could see a Black face at the glass. Neatly trimmed hair, salt-and-pepper beard. Deep creases in the forehead and eyes beginning to pouch underneath.

"What's going on in there?" a throaty voice asked.

"Got a dead warden and apparently some computer problems with the doors," Argento said. "But not my doing."

"Warden's dead?"

"Warden's murdered."

The man's head got higher, as if he were standing on his tiptoes, which gave him enough of a vantage point to see the warden's body. He was wearing a white prison uniform.

"Holy damn," he said.

"Yeah."

"Didn't much care for him."

"Job's open if you want it."

"I already got a job. I'm a trustee. See how I got the white uniform here?"

"What's your name?"

"Malcolm Simmons."

"Any idea what's happening in this place, Mr. Simmons? Why the doors aren't working and cons are running around?"

"Don't know," Simmons said.

"Can you let me out of here? I'm sitting on this desk trying not to step on small intestines."

"Let you out? Don't know you. Maybe you killed the warden. Maybe you'll kill me next."

"I killed him and then trapped myself inside the crime scene with a chair under the outside door handle?"

"Okay, so someone else did that chair part," Simmons conceded.

Argento held up the pack of cigarettes and candy. Hard currency in this place.

"Yours if you open the door."

Simmons chuckled, which had nearly as much throat to it as his speaking voice. "Son, you think I'm gonna open that door over a stale pack of smokes and some candy worms? Momma didn't raise no fools." And just like that he was gone.

Advantage inmate Simmons.

Argento waited for a tick but Simmons didn't return, so he completed his sweep of the office, including the warden's pockets. There was nothing there that would help him. He took another look at the walls. One of the framed diplomas was from Columbia. Argento had heard of that university, which probably meant it was pretty good. He looked farther down the certificate. Underneath the large ornate lettering that spelled *Columbia*, in smaller letters, it said *Tech* and underneath that, in even smaller script, were the words *Community College*. Argento didn't think there was anything wrong with community college. He'd talked to Emily about going himself to get an associate's in criminal justice. But the warden wanted people to assume he'd gone to the fancy four-year school. It was a résumé hustle. Even the head of Whitehall was running a game. Argento turned to his seat on the desk. He didn't have a whole lot of other options. There were sounds filtering into the office from what sounded like far away. Sounds of metal on metal. Shrill sounds of laughter alongside screaming. Like a haunted house in full swing.

Argento looked down at his feet and the flimsy orange sandals that covered them. They weren't good for much. He looked at the warden's feet. The departed was wearing Merrell hiking shoes along with his Whitehall polo and khakis. Casual Fridays in the pen. Argento had a pair of Merrells at home. It was a sturdy shoe. He slid off the desk, pulled the shoes off the warden, and checked the size. Elevens. Argento was a ten, but it would work. He put on the dead warden's shoes. If the situation was reversed, the warden would have been welcome to his own footwear. He wasn't up on Missouri penal code, but he was fairly certain he was committing a crime. Theft from a Corpse or something like it. It was also probably poor form. But he was a civilian now, not a police officer. He had no plans to get hung up on legalese or bad manners. Bodies were stacking up in this place. He needed to be practical and use what was in front of him. He walked around the office in the Merrells. They felt right. Decent traction and support. He took another look around the office. There was a mini fridge behind the warden's desk. Argento realized he was thirsty as hell. He opened the fridge. It contained a few bottles of sparkling water. Argento's first choice would have been Löwenbräu, but he'd take what he could get. He drained a bottle and started on another.

After a time, another face appeared at the door, this one white. A regular jamboree in the hallway. Argento got off the desk, watching where he stepped, and approached the door. The man on the other side was about thirty. Stocky but not fat. His hair was slicked back, his arms dark with tattoos, including one that said *Bitch Splitter*.

"Hey boss," Argento said.

The con blinked. He had flat cheeks and a thin upper lip underneath beady eyes. His skull was too small for his neck.

"Fuck you doing in there?"

"Trying to get out."

"You ain't no one to me, wobbler."

"What's a wobbler?"

"You don't know that, you gotta be new," the inmate snorted. "You can stay where you are."

"Give you a pack of smokes if you spring me."

The con produced a pack of cigarettes from his back pocket, shook one out in his hand and tucked it behind his ear. "Don't need your charity, bitch. I do fine by myself."

Argento pocketed the warden's cigarettes and lighter. "Tough talk with a door between us."

The con stepped farther back from the door so Argento could see him better, and grabbed his crotch in response.

When he was a cop, Argento had dealt with people who were stupid. People who were so bag-of-hammers dumb, he was surprised they could walk without falling down. Plus they had no impulse control. The stupidity combined with a lack of emotional discipline meant they could be played like puppets. This guy seemed a good bet to fall into that category. With his small, pinched features, he also looked like a classic case of Fetal Alcohol Syndrome, which brought with it impaired cognition. Argento had been to a lot of police trainings, some of which touched on substance abuse, and he'd paid attention. He figured this was a good time to test out his theory.

"Okay," he said with a dismissive wave. "Go back to your shift in the nail salon. Think I just heard them calling you on the intercom."

The con stared at Argento. Argento could see his jaw clench. He spat on the window square and started walking away.

"Excuse me, little girl," Argento said. "Little girl. I don't think you're listening to me."

The man stopped dead. He walked back to the door. Squinted his little eyes at Argento. "You know what I did on the outside?"

"Something soft," Argento said. "Like a party planner."

"Fuck you. I was the hammer they called in to fuck people up."

"Sure, I can tell you're important. Probably been that way since you were the pride of the group home."

"Wasn't in no—"

"The hell you weren't. Probably where you got molested, which is why you look and talk so screwy."

The con's face was reddening. He slapped the glass square with his palm. "You don't know nothing about me, you peckerwood fag."

Argento had worked with gay cops on the DPD. They held their own as well as the straight ones. There had been no issues. But this guy would have issues. He saw the opening and took it.

"Bet you liked it when it happened. Bet you got all cozy with the guy afterward and asked for more. Probably started braiding each other's hair."

A large vein pulsed in the con's forehead. His palm was still on the glass, thick with calluses.

"Probably started riding one of those tandem bikes so he could be right behind you all day."

"You're the fucking homo, you fucking—"

Argento cocked his head and looked at the man like he was taking him in for the first time. "When you get mad, your voice gets high. Like Minnie Mouse."

"Gonna fucking kill you," the con shouted, jabbing a finger toward Argento. He was pacing now, face crimson, his hands clenching and unclenching.

"Look, I've made you upset. You gonna have a good cry?"

The con snapped his cigarette in half and started toward the door.

"Big girls don't cry," Argento said.

The man picked up the wood chair and hurled it to the side with a clatter. Argento stepped back. As soon as the door opened, the con lunged for Argento. Argento met him head-on and shot his palm out to break the con's nose. The man was quick enough and shielded his face and Argento automatically worked his unguarded lower body, imagining his fists and elbows finding and exploding the man's liver, spleen, and pancreas with quick, punishing blows. An ER doctor once told him you couldn't transplant a pancreas. The con groaned, and his hands dropped to cradle his midsection. Argento didn't need to hit him in the face. This thing was already over; the man fighting above his weight class. Argento watched him sit down next to the dead warden and hunch forward, still groaning, his eyes fixed on the floor, as if he was looking around for an extra gear he didn't have. Argento had been in a lot of hospitals over his police career, with both victims and suspects. He had always paid close attention to how nurses and doctors treated patients. He asked a lot of questions. The human body, with its strengths, limits, and peculiarities, had always interested him.

It was an interest that informed any melee he was ever in.

Argento often felt calm both during and after a fight. There was a purity to it, to doing something he was good at. He walked into the hallway and retrieved the chair. The con was still sitting with a glazed expression, a thin trail of spittle dribbling from his chin. He gave up too easy. Normally, Argento might have felt a twinge of guilt about inciting a man to fight and then pummeling him. Normally, it would have violated his sense of fair play. But there was nothing normal about these circumstances. Argento placed the chair under the doorknob, securing the con inside. It was his turn to be in a tight space with the recently departed warden. He looked left, looked right. No sign of Simmons. No sign of anyone. He could hear shouting somewhere above him, but it was faint and maybe a floor or two away. So where to? He took inventory of his possessions. One prison-issue orange jumpsuit, somewhat soiled. One decent pair of hiking shoes. He had given up his only weapon, the baton, to Coates. He was an unknown in this place not aligned with any group. If prisoners were roaming free, he didn't think they'd give him a pass. He was as good as anyone with just his hands, but he already had microfractures in most of his knuckles from hitting people in the head on the job. Palm strikes and elbows were still on the table, but a weapon would be better. This was a state prison and there weren't going to be weapons just laying around waiting to be claimed. So he'd have to go old-school. If he wanted a decent means of defense, he was going to need to fashion one out of the materials at hand.

Argento went looking for the metal shop.

CHAPTER 15

Julie

Two hours. All the doors open. It seemed like both an eternity and no time at all. The feeling deep in Julie's stomach, that something was trying to crawl out, enlarged itself. But now it was combined with a sense of disbelief, almost dizziness. Like she had just stepped into a distortion field. Her father's advice—that panic never solved any problems—still held, but with the doors to a jail full of poorly treated angry felons about to be flung wide open, panic was an understandable option. She took in a deep breath. Blew it out. It was the same thing she did at the start of a road race. She took her phone out and started a countdown timer for two hours. She saw Coates and Jamerson doing the same on their watches.

"Well, that's a kick in the dick," Jamerson offered.

An ugly possibility dawned on Julie. "Is this because I'm here? Is this some kind of plot against my father?"

"No one knows you're here," Coates said. "And even if they did, they couldn't have had time to mount something like this."

"Okay," Jamerson interjected. "So how's this going to go down now with all the doors open?"

LeMaines squeezed his forehead with both hands like he was

trying to cut a headache off at the pass. He looked hot and weary, his uniform stretched tight around his neck and protruding belly. Julie doubted that high blood pressure was his sole health problem. "Every factor in our favor is gonna disappear. It's going to be... more hunters. More people looking to settle scores, going after snitches, coming after us. More of everything bad." He looked at Julie and Rachel. "And for the two of them, they're gonna, it's gonna be—"

"I know," Coates said. "So much for staying put. Find me a way out of here."

"I don't know," Aguilar said. "Man, I don't think there is one."

"What about fire escapes?" Julie asked. "Doesn't this building have to have them?"

LeMaines shook his head. "They aren't required. This building is structured to be fireproof. The inmates' bedding is flame-retardant, no matches or lighters are allowed inside, we got a sprinkler system, all that is supposed to take the place of fire escapes." He steepled his hands and brought them to his chin. Closed his eyes. Was still for a good minute.

"Fuck, dude," Jamerson said. "You consulting your decision tree? Any time you're ready."

LeMaines opened his eyes. "The roof," he said. "If we can get to the roof, our phones should work again. The cell net doesn't reach up there. We find something heavy to seal the door behind us, call for help, and wait for rescue."

"You speculating about this or you know? You've made a call from the roof before with the cell net up?"

"I've been there," LeMaines insisted. "Phones work."

"He's right," Aguilar said. "I was up there last month. I called my mom."

"Okay, we go to the roof," Coates said. "That's six floors up?"

LeMaines nodded.

"Point us to the elevator," Jamerson said. "Let's hit it. Sick of this place."

Coates asked, "Elevators tied into the computer?"

LeMaines nodded.

"Then no elevator. With this system gone screwy, we don't want to get stuck."

Jamerson said, "Okay, let's do the stairs. They're close."

"We can't take those stairs," LeMaines said. "This is the north side of the building. Roof access is only off the south exterior stairwell."

"Why?"

"I don't know. I didn't build the place. Follow me."

"No," Aguilar said.

Everyone stopped talking and looked at the younger of the two correctional officers.

Julie had been watching Aguilar since he and Jamerson had almost come to blows over Aguilar's insistence that they go help his fellow officers. He had backed off when he heard McVay's announcement about the System Purge, but there was nothing in his expression or body language that suggested he had relented.

"We go help our brothers," Aguilar said. His face was red, his voice compressed.

"We'll help them after we get to the roof," Coates said.

"Once you get to that roof, you ain't coming back down."

"No time for arguing."

Aguilar stared at LeMaines expectantly. LeMaines shook his head slowly. Almost sadly. "Roof is the best play. Once we get up there and make the call, I'll come down with you myself."

"It's gonna be bad. We're gonna need all of them," Aguilar said. "Gonna need that trooper's gun."

"We can do this without you," Coates said.

Aguilar held up a thick ring of jailer's keys and gave them a quick shake, as if to demonstrate their heft. "No you can't." Then he pivoted and sprinted down the far hallway, thumbing through the keys as he ran. He had gotten ten yards before anyone reacted. Coates was first, chasing after him, arms and legs surging. But Aguilar was younger and quicker. He reached the end of the hallway, keyed open the door, and slammed it behind him with a resounding metallic clank. Coates put his hands up to stop his momentum as he thudded against the now-sealed door. The rest of the group had come up hard behind him.

Coates spun around. Took Pillaire by the arm and pulled him to the door like a parent dragging a reluctant child from the park. "Open it."

Pillaire held his electronic key card up to the digital pad next to the door handle. The door didn't open. The light stayed red.

"This should work," Pillaire muttered. "I don't know why it isn't working."

"You got manual keys?" Coates asked LeMaines.

LeMaines shook his head, his lips tight. "Just him."

"So we're trapped," Jamerson said.

LeMaines looked at the door. Looked around. Even looked up, as if there was an answer in the ceiling. "I don't know how far he's going to get," he said. "He's just a kid."

Coates persisted. "What's another way through?"

"There isn't one."

"No problem," Jamerson said. "We'll just wait here, in this god-forsaken corridor."

Coates put a hand on Julie's shoulder. "Just a hiccup. We'll work the problem. You okay?"

"I think so."

"We're gonna get you out of here."

"You better, Derrick. If I get killed, Eric and I won't get the deposit back on the reception hall." The remark about the deposit had just come to her. She figured it was a good sign that she could still joke. Meant the dread hadn't taken over yet.

"Today has kind of sucked," Coates said, "but it will make one hell of a grad school paper when you get home."

With all that had happened, Coates's expression and tone of voice largely remained the same. It was as if he had just been told the restaurant he was dining in was out of the pie he liked. He took bad news well, Julie knew. She tried to make his calm her own. She wished Eric was with her, too. He was no cop or brawler, and tended toward absent-mindedness, but he was smart and practical and, in his own way, deeply protective of her. He'd figure out a way to help. But her initial yearning for her fiancé gave way to cold practicality. No, she was glad Eric wasn't with her. Glad he was safe in his normal world of science and grant writing. She had to put thoughts of him behind her and focus on survival.

A commotion on the other side of the door that Aguilar had fled through broke through her line of thought. A strangled shout. Sounds of running drawing closer.

"That's Aguilar," LeMaines exclaimed.

"Think our boy is coming back," Jamerson said. "Change of heart."

Coates raised the Guardian. "Back off that door and get ready," he said tersely. "He's not alone."

CHAPTER 16

Argento turned down a different hallway than the one that led to the main guard pod. He passed a row of rooms: some kind of cut-rate activities center with a rickety ping-pong table and dated board games, a laundry room that smelled, for lack of a better word, like ass, a library, and a chapel. The metal shop was toward the end of the hall. He listened first outside the door. No sounds.

The shop had about a dozen different workstations. It looked like a plus-size version of the one from his high school, where Argento had spent a fair amount of time making things while his more highbrow classmates pursued honors English and AP chemistry. He recognized most of the hardware. Machines for cutting, bending, and steel fabrication. Welders. A prep-and-finish area with water hoses to cool off the superheated metal. Signs that said, *Danger Keep Hands Away from Machine* and *Do Not Operate Without Permission*. A couple of forklifts, wooden pallets, and plastic wrap for shipping to whichever outfit bought the prison's wares. It was one of the few places in a prison that could actually teach inmates work skills they could use upon their release. The fact that it was completely empty seemed about right for Whitehall. Argento checked the loading dock doors. Sturdy. Digitally locked. A keypad on the wall next to the doors blinked red.

He'd been a gentleman earlier and returned the trooper's gun as a sign of good faith, along with the magazine, but he'd held on to the loose round he'd ejected from the chamber and put it in his sock because his prison jumpsuit didn't have any pockets. In the midst of the chaos, no one had noticed. Argento hadn't exactly been sure why he'd kept the round. He hadn't given it much thought. That was how it went for him sometimes. Like he was equipped with a secondary processing system running just underneath the first that made decisions for him mostly by instinct. Decisions that, more often than not, turned out to be right.

So he had a bullet.

Now he needed a gun.

Years back, Argento had arrested a con named Latavius Marks for several counts of bank robbery and transported him to the county jail. There was a backlog in the booking area before Marks could be processed, so the two men had fallen into conversation. Argento had always been interested in criminals: how they operated, where they frequented, what they were thinking. He asked them questions because he was curious and because it helped him be better at his job. Marks was a seasoned felon who had been in and out of correctional facilities the majority of his adult life. He was resigned to going back to jail. It seemed to be almost a relief after months on the run. So he had been in an affable, talkative mood. The conversation steered to prison life and to protecting yourself. Marks had made some enemies along the way, both in and out of prison. So he'd given Argento step-by-step instructions on how to make an improvised firearm, a zip gun, using only what could be found in a standard DIY workspace. When Argento had gone home that night after his shift, he'd constructed one in his garage, just for kicks. It was easily concealable and not much bigger than his palm. He'd later tested it at the SWAT range and put a hole through the head of a paper target at ten feet. Marks's blueprint had been right on the money.

Argento still remembered what Marks had told him. He was

experienced with tools and knew his way around firearms. He had the full run of the metal shop and no guards to intervene with his project. Time to go to work.

His first step was the barrel. He looked around for the right size metal pipe. It took him a while but he found one about the size of a small flashlight. Next up was the grip, which Argento fashioned using a wedge of plastic that would fit his hand. Then the internal spring, which he retrieved from a pull-out drawer of miscellaneous tools on a roll cart. He attached the spring to a small steel rod that would serve as the firing pin. To operate it, he'd need to pull the firing pin out, then release it, sending the pin forward. The pin would strike the primer of the loaded cartridge he'd taken off Jamerson, expelling the bullet. He assembled the pieces and lashed the whole thing together with electrical tape. He had only one round, so a test fire was out, but he was reasonably sure he now had a working gun. It wasn't pretty and wouldn't be much for range or accuracy, but up close it would make an impression.

It wasn't anything Argento heard that told him he was no longer alone. Nothing he saw or smelled. It was more of a reckoning. Of two decades of suspicious readiness. A disruption in the stasis. He remained still and watched the open doorway. After a time, a man appeared in it. He cocked his head at Argento. And smiled. It was the first smile Argento had seen in Whitehall, but that didn't mean it was welcoming.

The man in the doorway was about Argento's height and didn't quite have his heft, but still looked solidly put together. His hair was blond, almost white, his eyes unnaturally shiny. He closed the door behind him and stepped into the room. Lithe. Like a gymnast. He wore red prison garb, the same color as the men in the infirmary. Argento recalled LeMaines saying red meant a prisoner was from the second floor. Lot of cross-pollination between floors one and two, Argento thought.

"Hello," the man said. There was an artificial cheerfulness in his voice, as if he were addressing someone at a corporate meet and greet. He was still smiling, but the smile didn't go with the rest of his face.

Argento nodded.

"What brings you here?"

Argento didn't say anything for a moment. He watched the man, who was moving, almost imperceptibly, from one foot to the other, as if testing his own balance. His hands were clasped behind him, like a nobleman out for a stroll.

"Just looking for a place," Argento said, "to spit out my gum."

"You don't seem to be chewing gum."

"I like to plan ahead. Case I find some."

The man motioned with his chin to a space next to him. "There's a trash can right there. Come see."

That would mean walking toward you, Argento thought. And the man gave off all the signs of someone he didn't want to walk toward, not without being able to see what was in his hands. "So it is," Argento said, still watching the man. There was a tall stack of metal chairs between the two of them on a roll cart, and Argento wanted to keep it that way.

"What's your name, friend?"

"Didn't think I'd make friends this fast in prison," Argento said. "Must be doing something right."

"So that means you're new here. What's your name?" the blond man asked again. Some of the sheen had left the pleasant lilt to his voice. He took a few steps closer, and Argento saw that he wore a rope necklace. Probably the only kind approved in Whitehall, to cut down on inmates strangling each other with metal ligatures.

"Trying to get people to call me Ace."

"Ace," the blond man said, rolling the word around in his mouth. "My name is Micah. But I don't think you look like an Ace."

Argento nodded without meaning. There were some orange coveralls hanging up on the back wall of the metal shop next to a pile of welder's masks. The coveralls had pockets, which would be useful. He kept one eye on Micah as he moved toward the back wall.

"What brought you here?"

"A big green bus," Argento said.

"No, I mean what's your crime, Mr. Ace?"

"Long story."

"I have time. I bet you do, too."

"I killed a bald eagle," Argento said.

A spot of color was forming on Micah's cheekbones. "If I didn't know better," he said slowly, as if trying to contain something, "I'd think you were messing with me. But that's not what friends do, is it?"

"No. Friends are honest with each other."

"Where'd you get your fancy shoes?"

"Won a raffle."

"Now you've told your second lie."

"It's your second stupid question."

Micah hung one arm over the stack of chairs with an athletic casualness, causing the trapezius muscles to swell under his prison shirt. "Come on over. I have a plan for getting out of here. I'll explain it to you."

"Sure," Argento said. "What could go wrong in a prison metal shop."

Argento had always been adept at predicting violence. It wasn't quite a sixth sense, but he didn't know a better word for it. He sometimes felt it like a change in the wind pressure. A suspect would start talking too fast, or too slow. Would take glances around, to get his bearings. Breath quickening in the chest, hands wiped on pants and then curling toward fist. This man, Micah, was right on the cusp. He confirmed it when he began moving toward Argento, his hands still behind his back. The metal shop wasn't that large. He was fifty feet away and closing the distance quickly. Forty feet away. Thirty.

"What are you holding in your hands there?"

"Part of the plan," Micah said. One of his arms was coming out in front of him. Argento saw a flash of steel. Twenty feet.

Argento pointed the zip gun at Micah's chest. "I got my own plan."

Micah stopped short. His eyes narrowed and he moved fluidly sideways, using an industrial cutter as cover.

"I don't know what your deal is," Argento said, "but I can use this on you or some other son of a bitch. Doesn't matter to me. You decide."

Micah's artificial smile had returned. "You've got it wrong. I couldn't hear you from that far away. I was just trying to get closer. Be rude not to."

"Not as rude as me shooting you in the head."

"You should be careful how you talk to people. You need allies in this place. No one lasts without them."

Neither man said anything for a time. Micah stayed behind cover. Argento took a pair of coveralls off the far wall and put them on, all while locking eyes with Micah. From his time on SWAT, he was used to changing fast. The coveralls had two deep pockets and were thick enough to give him some nominal protection against an edged weapon.

"Look at us," Argento said. "Both figuring out if we're going to try and kill each other."

"Look at us," Micah echoed.

"Take a walk. I'll be in the hallway in a minute. If I see anything I don't like, I'll shoot it."

"You've got the gun," Micah said. "You make the rules." He walked backward, keeping machinery in Argento's field of fire. He seemed to know what was behind him without looking, and easily made his way back to the entry door. The artful dodger. When he turned, Argento saw the words *High Control* stamped on the back of his prison jumpsuit.

"But you won't always have the gun, Kurt," Micah said.

Then he was gone.

Argento waited a minute. Gave it another. Then he approached the exit door and metered it with the zip gun raised. No Micah. No one else. He remained in the hallway. Listened. No footsteps, no screaming. Just the sounds buildings made, mostly behind the walls: metallic ticking, a fan turning on, water going through pipes.

Then he gave some thought to how that asshole knew his real name.

Argento had passed a chapel on the way to the metal shop but hadn't stopped inside. He decided to revisit it. A chapel seemed as good a place as any to be right now. Argento had been telling the truth when he identified himself as Lutheran to Aguilar at central booking. He'd grown up relatively unchurched save for Christmas and Easter, but Emily was a lifelong member of Trinity Lutheran in downtown Detroit.

Early on in their courtship, she'd invited him to come with her. Argento had agreed—he would have gone to a toxic waste dump with Emily. The services had been alien to him at first. He didn't understand the biblical references and he didn't know the hymns. But he grew accustomed to the rhythm of the liturgy. He took to the sermons about passing by temptation and being a good neighbor and how God would forgive people even though they were broken, imperfect vessels. Like himself. And he appreciated that the church was made up of people coming together around something bigger than they were and they weren't just talk. Trinity sent their members into the city to tutor at-risk kids and help build affordable housing. Argento had become a member himself. Then he'd been baptized. When Emily had become ill, he'd prayed for her recovery. And in the end, he'd been reminded that not all prayers were answered. The pastor at Trinity, a canny, robust woman of fifty who had been with the church for a decade, had tried to help him. She talked to him about how one of the ways mourners are able to ease their own suffering is to walk with their fellow sufferers.

"What if other people mostly bug the shit out of me?" Argento had asked.

"Kurt," the pastor said matter-of-factly. "You may need to work on that."

Argento had looked for answers elsewhere and hadn't found them. At the department's repeated urging, he had seen a psychiatrist, a chatty, effete man who knew nothing of law enforcement and kept using the phrase *grief journey*. After the first session, when the psychiatrist had gravely informed him that broken crayons still colored, Argento hadn't returned. One night, aimless and despondent, he'd found himself at the walk-up business of a low-rent fortune-teller and medium with a neon sign that said, *No Appointment Necessary*. She'd claimed to be able to serve as a psychic bridge so he could talk to Emily. By the time she was halfway through her séance, she'd gotten enough details about Emily's life wrong to remind him that all such people were frauds. He had overturned her table in a fit of rage and stormed out, cursing himself as a fool.

The chapel was small but well-kept. An immaculate floor led past ten burnished rows of pews up to a wood pulpit, next to which was a picture of Christ suffering on the cross behind an altar with a green velvet covering lined with candles. A banner on the back wall said, *This Is the Day That the Lord Has Made. Let Us Rejoice and Be Glad in It*. There was no Bible verse listed underneath, but Argento knew the passage was from Psalms.

Two men sat in the front pew. One was Malcolm Simmons, the trustee who hadn't been impressed with Argento or his candy and cigarettes. The other was a white man in a black shirt with a white collar. Argento slipped the zip gun into a coverall pocket and approached.

"Gentlemen," Argento said.

Both men rose. The man in the collar looked startled. Simmons's eyebrows raised at the sight of Argento.

"How'd you get out?" Simmons asked.

"The guy after you wanted those smokes."

"You mad?"

"No. I wouldn't have let me out, either." Argento turned to the man in the white collar. He had a compact build and looked to be around forty, his hair cut short like a soldier's. He had facial stubble and a scar running down the left side of his face from cheekbone to jaw. Even the ministers looked like convicts in here.

"You the prison chaplain or an inmate who killed him and took his clothes?"

"He the chaplain," Simmons confirmed and busied himself by chewing on a fingernail.

"Mark Van Dyne," the chaplain said, although he did not offer his hand. He was staring at the blood on Argento's shirtfront near the neckline.

"Haven't been getting along with everyone," Argento explained.

Van Dyne took it in stride. Argento supposed he probably wasn't the first bloody visitor to the chapel. "Do you know what's happening? With the doors and inmates running around?"

"Glitch in the system, I'm told. You an ordained minister?"

Van Dyne nodded.

"What denomination?"

Van Dyne paused for a beat, as if it were a strange question to ask in the moment. "Episcopalian," he responded. "Are you a man of faith?"

"On my good days, I'm Lutheran. Don't know much about Episcopalians."

"We've been described as 'unhurried,'" Van Dyne said. "Have you seen any other staff or officers?"

"Turns out the governor's daughter picked today for a tour. Couple of troopers are guarding her. They're floating around somewhere. They have two guards with them plus a nurse."

"You were with them?"

"Until they locked me in an office with the dead warden."

Van Dyne looked grave when he said, "Malcolm told me about the warden. He said you were in there, but he didn't think you did it."

"Any ideas who might have?"

"Lot of people had problems with the warden," Simmons said. "But if he got killed crazy, it was a crazy who did it. Crazies all be up on the fourth floor."

"Someone was able to make it down from the fourth floor, kill the warden, and then scamper back up there?"

Simmons shrugged. "Got people here that do that kind of shit. And the doors be jacked up. I've been walking around wherever I want for better part of an hour. Locked doors just all of a sudden open. No reason to it."

"What is this? A computer virus?" Van Dyne asked.

"I don't know," Argento said. "Beyond my skill set."

Simmons chortled. "If the governor's daughter is here, maybe the man himself will come down here and fix this place."

"It needs fixing," Van Dyne said. "Been saying that since day one, and I've been here since the beginning."

"Malcolm, I was just in the metal shop and a rangy fellow with blond hair took an interest in me. Said his name was Micah. Know anything about him?"

"Oh ho ho," Simmons said and moved his finger like a metronome.

"That didn't sound good."

"Micah, he in and out of here all the time. He a bad man."

"Lots of bad men in here. Anything that makes him different?"

"For one, he a gymnast. Like legit. They say he made the Olympics. Good shape, that one. Wins all his prison fights. Can't nobody get a hand on him, way he moves."

"So what happened?"

"That crystal meth found him."

"What does he do now?"

"Mostly hurts people for money. Anyone on the outside want you fucked up?"

"Someone's coming to mind," Argento said.

"Why are you in here?" Van Dyne asked.

"Misunderstanding between me and some sheriff's deputies."

"Lot of misunderstandings bring folks to Whitehall," Simmons said.

"Sure," Argento said. "So what's the plan here with you two?"

Van Dyne said, "I want to be helpful, but I can't reach anyone by phone. I was going to stay here and pray with anyone who comes into the chapel. Beyond that, I don't know what the drill is for this."

"Episcopalians known for miracles?"

"No. But we're really polite. Where's your place in all this?"

"Might just hang out," Argento said. "Got nowhere else to be."

The three sat in silence. After a few minutes, Simmons broke it. "Nobody asked," he said, "but I be Baptist. And I've seen miracles."

On the second *t* of *Baptist*, a loud cursing rang out down the hall outside the chapel. Sounds of running. Then a gunshot.

CHAPTER 17

Argento opened the chapel door to the sights and sounds of a battle. There was no other word for it. The group who had left him: the troopers, Julie, and the prison staffers, were locked in combat with a half-dozen convicts in orange. Aguilar was slashing his baton at anyone within range, LeMaines was wrestling with two inmates at once, and Jamerson was getting the worst of it from a con with a shaved head and pink scalp, the back of which was adorned with a tattoo of a hand grenade. Rachel and Pillaire had their backs flattened to the wall. Julie wasn't so docile; one of the cons struggling with LeMaines wasn't looking her way, and she kicked him in the groin like she was trying to put his testicles through the uprights fifty yards downfield. It was a crushing shot and took the prisoner to his knees. A gurgling sound escaped his lips that sounded like a man drowning on dry land.

Argento was used to sizing up chaos quickly. The flurry of activity in front of him was a lot to look at, but when he heard a gunshot, it made sense to first find the gun. His mind rolled back to the events of the last hour: He had taken the Guardian off Jamerson, then tossed it back to Coates. Coates had given it to Jamerson to hold the hallway while they were in the warden's office. But after that,

Coates had likely demanded its return. So Coates. Coates would have the gun. He scanned for the trooper.

He saw him near the end of the hallway.

A convict nearly twice his size was on the trooper's back.

The two men were struggling for control over the Guardian. It was in Coates's right fist, but the fat con had both his meaty hands on it and was rapidly gaining leverage. Coates tried to push off the ground to free himself, but the con was too massive. Two hundred seventy-five pounds, Argento thought. Maybe three hundred.

The fat con leaned in and chomped Coates's hand. Coates grunted, and the con spat out a chunk of flesh the size of a walnut. Coates hung on. His thumb was the break point. If he lost control of the thumb, he lost the weapon. The con leaned in again, closed his mouth over Coates's hand, and bit the trooper's right thumb nearly clean off, leaving the digit hanging by strands of tendon and flesh. The sound was loud and sharp, like he had just crunched down on a corn chip.

To his credit, Coates didn't scream.

But he had only four working fingers left to try to retain the weapon, so the con was able to wrest it out of the trooper's hands. He howled in triumph and pointed it at the back of Coates's skull. He didn't quite get to the trigger.

Because Argento was faster.

He reached over the convict's head, twisted the gun a hundred and eighty degrees, and slipped his own finger in the trigger guard.

Shots to the head didn't always kill. Bullets could loop and spin and sometimes carom off bone. But Detroit SWAT had taught Argento to imagine a T drawn on the target's face with the horizontal top of the T crossing both eye sockets and the base of the T running vertically down the nose to the upper mouth. Shooting someone in this zone meant the bullet would likely strike the working center of the brain and shut the body down. So Argento brought his own head hard up against the convict's to anchor it and avoid friendly fire. Then he shot the Guardian through the fat man's left eye. The inmate had a few seconds to look genuinely puzzled at this sudden reversal of fortune before he died.

Argento didn't linger. There was still work to do. He kept the Guardian out at low ready and moved back down the hall. The bald con was now in the process of strangling Jamerson, the effort reddening the convict's already pink scalp and infusing the grenade tattoo on the back of his head with a crimson hue. Jamerson was gripping the convict's wrists and trying frantically to shed him, the corded muscles on the trooper's slim forearms popping out with the strain. Argento shot the bald con through the nose from five feet away—any closer and he'd blow out Jamerson's eardrums—and the con sagged off the trooper and went still. Farther down the hallway, a wild-eyed convict had peeled Pillaire off the wall and was holding a razor blade affixed to the melted end of a toothbrush up to the assistant warden's neck as he shouted commands that bordered on unintelligible. Argento didn't give him time to further formulate a hostage plan. He had gone to the shooting range once a week for the last twenty years; he double-tapped Razor Blade between the eyes at fifteen feet. He didn't rush the shot. He didn't need to. He had been trained that slow was smooth and smooth was fast. The razor blade fell to the floor followed by the man holding it.

Two of the three remaining cons bugged out at the sound of gunfire and sprinted wildly in the direction of the metal shop. The third was the one Julie had kicked in the testicles. He couldn't sprint, so he flop-staggered after the first two, his hands beating the air like he thought he had wings. Argento let them go. He checked the magazine of the Guardian. After the round he'd heard in the chapel and the four he'd fired, there was one left along with the chambered cartridge. Plus he still had the zip gun with its single round. The double tap to Razor Blade might have been excessive, but other than that, he had done well with ammo conservation. He was now aware of his ears buzzing from the thunderclap of the bullets fired indoors, but he'd barely noticed when the shots went off, a physiological oddity called auditory exclusion that he'd experienced before during high-stress incidents on the job.

Coates was back on his feet, cradling his mangled thumb. Jamerson was still on the ground coughing. Pillaire was touching his own neck, checking for injuries and hyperventilating.

"Heard a round go off when I was in the chapel. Anyone hit?" Argento asked.

Coates didn't answer him. He was still breathing hard, his face furrowed in pain. He went to check on Julie, Rachel, and Pillaire. Then he helped his partner to his feet with his uninjured hand.

"You good?"

Jamerson gave him a thumbs-up. He was making a point not to look at Argento.

Coates turned back and answered Argento's question. "I shot the big one when he came after my gun. Hit him center mass. Didn't even slow him."

Argento hadn't seen the bullet hole in the fleshy con before Argento had descended on him. But someone of that heft with the right amount of will could fight a long time even with a round lodged in his upper chest. He handed the Guardian back to Coates for the second time. Coates took it with his one good hand and checked the magazine and chamber. Then he knelt next to Razor Blade and used the blade to cut a strip off the dead man's shirt and bind his thumb.

"How'd you get out?"

"Someone came along." Argento noticed how hard Coates was breathing. "Pace yourself," he said to the trooper. "It's going to be a long day."

"Haven't scuffled this much since I don't know when." Coates scanned the hallway where the three messy bodies lined the floor. "I like your way with people."

Argento didn't reply. After victory, that's when you're vulnerable. The last two minutes had infused him with adrenaline, and now that the massive chemical dump was over, the body just wanted to relax. You couldn't let it. He watched the hallway for any latecomers.

"What you just did," Coates said, "never seen anything like that."

"How's the thumb?"

"Once you get used to the excruciating pain, it's not so bad," he said between clenched teeth.

"That man tried to kill me," Pillaire said. He stared at the floor, arms wrapped around his chest.

"Yeah, but he didn't," Jamerson said. "So sack up and deal."

The convict that had been trying to throttle Jamerson had a scorpion tattoo on his neck, which Argento knew meant either he was from Durango, Mexico, or he was a drug dealer, as the scorpion was a good-luck charm for those in the narcotics trade. Or he was just a guy who thought scorpions were neat. Jamerson swore and kicked the body in the head. There was a wet sound and vomit spewed from the corpse's mouth.

"He's still alive!" Julie exclaimed.

"He's not," Argento said. "Dead bodies do that. It's just a reflex."

Julie looked to Rachel, as if seeking a medical second on this assessment, and the nurse nodded. She hadn't said a word since the hallway fight, which could be concerning, but Argento didn't think she was going to go the way of Pillaire and shut down. She seemed to have more grit than that.

"You know a lot for a garbageman," Jamerson said, talking to Argento but still not looking at him.

"I worked in Detroit," Argento said.

He had an idea why Jamerson and Coates had been on the losing end of their respective fights. Most of the brawls cops had on the job were with suspects who were trying to get away. The fighting was a means to an end—escape. Once the suspect broke free, the fighting stopped because they were running in the opposite direction. Suspects who went toe-to-toe with their arresting officers, who weren't trying to get away but were looking to hurt or kill them, were a rarer breed. The fighting was the end in itself and was sometimes part of their street cred; if they were going to jail, they wanted to go bloody with a story to tell. Whitehall was likely full of inmates like that, and Coates and Jamerson would have to adjust accordingly or Julie was going to be down two protectors and going it alone.

Van Dyne had emerged from the chapel. When Rachel saw him, she went straight to him.

"Oh my God, Mark," she said. The pastor hugged her fiercely and she returned it.

"I thought you said there was no more staff in here," Coates said.

"I'm so sorry," Rachel said. "Mark's the chaplain. I didn't know he was in this weekend."

"It's okay," Van Dyne said. "It was last-minute." But he wasn't looking at Rachel. He was looking at the three bodies on the floor. Then he looked at Argento. He was trying to think of what to say. Maybe something pastoral. A proverb or brief eulogy fitting for the occasion. But all he managed was "Are you're sure you're Lutheran?"

Argento nodded. "In good standing."

"Welcome to our get-together, Reverend," Jamerson said. He nodded to Argento and eyed Coates. "So, what are we doing with him?"

"How is that even a question?" Julie broke in. "We're in a building with the most dangerous people in the state running free and no one on the outside even knows it. We're going to need all the help we can get. He stays."

"He stopped those three men from killing me in the infirmary," Rachel said. "I believe God sent him here to deliver us."

"It wasn't God," Argento said. "It was the Rocker County Sheriff's Department."

"Doesn't matter who he helped," Jamerson countered. "Nothing's changed. He's still a con and I don't want him watching my back."

"Horseshit," Julie said. "Three men in the infirmary, plus three more just now. He's taken out six more bad guys than you, Jamerson, and we're letting *you* stay."

Jamerson wheeled, face twisted, and stuck a finger in her face. "No one talks to me that way you fucking cun—"

—and Coates stepped in and put his good hand on Jamerson's chest. "Cycle down, partner. Right now."

"You're the governor's daughter," Jamerson continued, spittle flecking his mouth. "A rich man's kid. You grew up in a mansion with a fucking pony. You don't know anything."

"Take a breath, Max," Coates said. He still hadn't moved his hand from Jamerson's chest.

"Yeah," Jamerson said. "I'm breathing."

"She's got a voice here, Max. Just like you. Now I need you straight and clear. You good?"

"I'm good," Jamerson said, his words at odds with the strained energy still coming off of him. "I'm fucking golden. You want to trust this guy, go ahead. Never mind that this whole thing started when he got here."

"You think he crashed the system?" LeMaines asked.

Argento gestured toward the bodies on the floor. "I give off a hacker vibe to you?"

"He stays," Coates said. He got closer to Argento. His voice didn't change but his eyes did. Something in them went flat and hard. "You saved our ass when you didn't have to. We owe you for that. I believe you can help us get through this. But that doesn't make us friends. You do anything sideways, compromise her safety, get in my way, and I'll end you out here. I promise."

"Fair enough," Argento said. "But while we're talking, how about you don't trap me in any other small rooms with dead guys."

Coates was quiet for a moment. Taking that in. Then he said, "Fair enough."

Jamerson got closer to Argento, like a poor man's pantomime of Coates. "Listen up, shit-stick. Make a wrong move, twitch, fucking do anything I don't like, and it's all over for you."

"Glad we're saying everything twice," Argento said. "So what'd I miss while I was gone?"

Coates brought him up to speed. "Aguilar took off with the keys. Then he came running right back with six inmates hot on his heels. We were scrapping with them when you showed."

LeMaines raised the key ring, as if to say, *They're safe with me now*.

"I'm not going to apologize for wanting to help my brothers," Aguilar replied, but there was more numbness in his tone than defiance. At the moment, he looked shell-shocked, Argento thought, and grossly out of place, like he was just a kid playing dress-up in a prison guard uniform.

"Hang on," Jamerson said to Aguilar. "I thought everyone had to be buzzed off the floor by Control. How'd you key that door when they were chasing you back to us?"

"He had the duty ring," LeMaines broke in. "It's got a key to get off the first-floor cellblock so we can let the vendors in and out."

"Aguilar," Coates said.

The guard just met the trooper's gaze.

"You can't help them alone. I can offer you the same deal as before. You come with us to the roof, we put through the call for help, then this place will be crawling with cops who will rescue whoever needs rescuing."

"I don't know," Aguilar said. "I just don't know."

"Kurt," Julie said. "In less than two hours, there's going to be something called a System Purge. All the interior doors are going to open. All the prisoners are going to be let out. That's why we have to get to the roof. It's the only place that will get phone reception."

"How much time do we have left?"

Julie checked her phone. "Hundred and eleven minutes."

Jamerson looked around at the assembled group and spat on the floor. It seemed to be his go-to move. LeMaines still looked out of breath. Pillaire had resumed his place with his back to the wall and was muttering something. Aguilar looked both tense and adrift at the same time.

"Gunshots are loud," Van Dyne said.

"Thank you for your insight," Jamerson said. He took another look at the group. "Quite the fucking squadron we got assembled here."

"Let's fall back to the chapel," Coates said. "Cement a plan."

"Is there time for that?" LeMaines asked.

"If we're going to be together in the middle of hell for the next hundred and eleven minutes," Coates said, "we can at least introduce ourselves."

CHAPTER 18

Malcolm Simmons was sitting in the front pew when the group came into the chapel. He rose at the sight of the two women, nodded, and sat back down.

"Who is this guy?" Jamerson demanded.

"His name is Malcolm Simmons," Van Dyne said. "He's our oldest trustee. You have nothing to fear from him, and I hope he has nothing to fear from you."

Simmons waved a hand without looking back.

Coates went right to the aging convict. "Sorry, man, I don't know you," he said and patted him down for weapons without finding any.

Simmons shrugged. "You just doing your job."

"We talking freely in front of this gentleman?" Coates asked LeMaines.

LeMaines nodded. "Mr. Simmons knows more than us about this place."

Coates said to the group, "Could an inmate have dreamt this thing up? Screwed with the the mainframe?"

"I don't think so. Not a lot of evil geniuses in here. Just evil dumb people. IQs below eighty. Guys reading at a third-grade level if they can read at all."

"They ain't all dumb," Aguilar said. "One of them told me he could always tell which guard was working just by listening to how he dangles the keys."

Coates spread his hands. "Does that leave any likely candidates who could be behind this?"

"Guy in general population named Sarrazin is in for computer fraud. I think he has a doctorate or something. But he's a head case. He's usually on suicide watch."

"All right. Head case or not, we may have to pay him a visit. Now, we already went over our equipment inventory. In terms of personnel, besides Max and myself, we have three officers who know the floors and a nurse who can patch up the wounded."

"That I can," Rachel said as she lit up another cigarette. She didn't bother to ask if anyone minded. Argento was pretty sure no one did.

"Reverend, you coming with us?"

Argento watched the chaplain, who had taken a seat next to Simmons, almost protectively, as if providing a buffer against the troopers. He was still trying to get a read on Van Dyne. He looked anchored enough, but it was too early to tell if he was going to be a net gain or loss.

Van Dyne nodded. "I'll do whatever I'm able to."

"Plus a minister. And then there's you," Coates said, eyeing Argento. "Whatever we're calling you."

"Just Kurt."

"And me," Julie said. "Trying not to be the fifth wheel."

"Saw you kick that con in the nuts in the hallway," LeMaines said. "Before you did that, he was all over me. You took him right out of the fight, saved my ass. You're no fifth wheel."

"Okay, so Julie is our designated nut kicker," Coates said, pointing two appreciative fingers at her. "Anything I'm missing? Anyone with other skills that will help us? Ex-military, a medic, good with locks, speak a second language?"

Argento wondered how the older trooper would answer that

question about himself. He figured that the governor's protective detail got some training beyond the standard state requirements. Courses in dignitary protection, evasive driving, evacuation procedures, maybe some extra range time. But academic learning without application in the field didn't mean much, and Argento didn't know how many hard skills the troopers had that would help much in here. Coates had given a valiant effort against the convict trying to take his gun, but the trooper was at least five years out of his fighting prime. He seemed to make up for it with a seasoned calm and his proficiency to run point. During a crisis, people automatically follow leaders, and Coates fit the bill. But he'd need plenty of help.

On the other hand, there was Jamerson, who had boasted about working undercover vice, which would make him a subject matter expert in narcotics. In the limited action in which Argento had seen him, though, he had seemed fairly useless. But there was something else Argento was picking up on with Jamerson. Something off, something jittery. Like he was missing a needed boost. Argento didn't know the trooper's baseline, so he didn't know if this was his normal. Plus the shit that had been happening at Whitehall would put anyone on edge. But it was enough for Argento to wonder if Jamerson was an addict. Cops who spent too long in narcotics sometimes found themselves walking down the same path as those they hunted.

"I'm a floater," LeMaines said. "I work all the floors. So I know almost every prisoner in here. The groups, the leaders, the followers. That could help."

"I'm from North Jersey," Aguilar said blankly. "It's the embroidery capital of the world."

"Sweet," Jamerson said.

"Look, does it even matter?" Aguilar protested. "When I keyed through that doorway and down the hall, you know what I saw? Cons. No guards, no allies. Just cons. They came after me in a second. And that's just Gen Pop I'm talking about, that's the most mellow floor we have. And we're going through six *more* floors, each one worse than the last? I'll do it. Don't doubt that for a second. Because any officers still alive up there are gonna need us and we're gonna need them. But do you understand that we're likely good and screwed?"

His words hung in the air. Nobody spoke for a time. Argento heard a sniffing sound. He turned in the direction of the noise. It was Pillaire. The assistant warden was sitting on the floor in the corner, his legs drawn in to his chest. Like he'd gone dormant.

Then LeMaines said, "Maybe not. Once we get through Gen Pop, we can take the south stairwell all the way to the roof. That's a single floor we gotta pass."

"Way our day is going," Aguilar said, "bet we ain't that lucky."

Julie broke the silence. "Do we really need to worry about every single prisoner? I mean, statistically speaking, aren't there some inmates in here that are innocent?"

"Maybe like two guys," Aguilar said. "Out of five hundred."

"Tops," LeMaines added. "And if they were good when they came in here, this place turned them the other way."

"Then this is gonna be nothing like easy," Coates said. "We're not invincible. But neither are they." He turned his level gaze to Argento. "I know you can handle yourself, Kurt. What else you good at?"

"Etiquette," Argento said.

"Would someone shut this guy up?" Jamerson half shouted.

"Why don't you?"

"Don't tempt me, man,"

"Or you could just stay there, keep making that stupid face."

"This is my show," Jamerson said. His nostrils were flared and he was jutting his chest out. Probably didn't even know he was doing it.

"Just because you're the loudest," Argento said, "doesn't mean you're in charge."

"I talk loud and slow to you because you're a garbageman, which means you're too stupid to find a better job. Want to make sure you hear me."

"I had a boss once," Argento said. "He was scared on the street. Scared off of it. You could almost see his knees knocking. But you wouldn't know it from listening to him. According to him, he was the best one out there. He could part the sea."

"So."

"You said, 'This is my show.' That's exactly what he used to say, from the safety of the office. You remind me of him."

Jamerson took a step closer. Showed his teeth. "Dude, you're nothing. You're just a cronk. I'll beat you down if I have to."

"Set more realistic goals," Argento said.

Jamerson charged. It didn't surprise Argento. He moved in toward the trooper instead of away, gripped his shoulder, and threw his elbow up at the trooper's face, making Jamerson recoil, lose his footing, and land on his back. It was an old aikido move that a fellow SWAT officer had once taught Argento, a way to stop someone's forward momentum without seriously hurting them. Jamerson bounced right back up ready to resume hostilities, and Coates stepped between the men once again. When he spoke, it looked like it required every ounce of his self-control not to scream. "We don't need this," he said slowly. "Kurt, you've proven you're a badass. We get it. Max, you don't like Kurt. Get that, too. But we are in a crisis situation where I need you both to be fucking adults. Truce this shit."

"You just assaulted a cop," Jamerson said, but it came out in a monotone, like he knew he had to say something and couldn't think of anything better.

"I'm already in jail for that," Argento said.

"Shut up," Julie said sharply to Argento. She turned to Jamerson and repeated the same words. The ferocity with which she spoke took Argento aback. "Quit provoking each other over nothing. Don't you see where we are and where we still need to go? Get the hell along. What's wrong with you two?"

Her words found him and cut through. Argento had trouble letting insults go, but it had been schoolyard bullshit with Jamerson.

She was a civilian he was supposed to protect, and instead he was wasting time they couldn't afford to waste.

"You're right," Argento said. "I'm sorry." He reached a hand out to Jamerson and the trooper reluctantly took it. Emily would have been ashamed of him for how he'd acted. But he knew it wasn't over with Jamerson. He was willing to let things be, but the trooper wouldn't forget Argento taking his gun away, having to save him from strangulation in the hallway, and then knocking him on his ass in front of witnesses. Not by a long shot. If Argento thought Jamerson was an enemy before, he'd just doubled down on it.

Coates turned his attention to Van Dyne. "Reverend, things are liable to get messy here. Can you fight?"

"No," the chaplain said. "Not even a little." There was no resignation or shame in his voice. Just a man reporting facts.

"If I give you a weapon, will you use it?"

"I think it would be wasted on me."

"Well, then how'd you get that scar?" Jamerson asked.

"An inmate here," Van Dyne said. "Didn't care for my preaching, I guess."

He got cut in the face and stayed on, Argento thought. That said something about the man's tenacity. Or maybe it said something about how no one else would hire him.

"We could use a preacher for what we're about to do," LeMaines mused.

Jamerson snorted. He had regained some of his cocksure strut. "For what? In case we want to bust out some hymns? God even in here?"

"Especially here," Van Dyne said.

LeMaines said, "We've lost two guys. Spentz, the warden, almost the rest of us if Kurt hadn't come along. And we haven't even gotten off the first floor."

"That's *why* we need to get off the first floor," Coates countered.

"Might as well make it three guys out of service," Jamerson said, turning up his mouth at the sight of Pillaire, who was somnolent on the floor. A few minutes earlier, when Van Dyne had shut the chapel doors behind them, Pillaire had given an exaggerated start: the startle response under stress. He had lapsed into silence since. "Wake the fuck up," Jamerson said in disgust. Pillaire made no indication he heard him.

"Easy," Van Dyne said.

"Don't tell me easy," Jamerson said. "You don't know what we've been through."

"Look," LeMaines broke in. "We don't know what's up there. We're going in blind. You saw what happened with Aguilar. After two minutes, half the floor was chasing him."

"May I say a word?" Simmons said. He had walked over without anyone noticing and stood patiently with his hands folded in front of him.

The group turned to look at him.

"Nobody cares—" Jamerson began, and Van Dyne cut him off.

"Go ahead, Malcolm."

"This place like a small town," Simmons said. "Word travels fast. By now, everyone knows the doors ain't working right and the guards is scattered and that two suits are down here with a good-looking white girl and pretty Nurse Rachel. Bad folks in this house. There's an Armenian fellow named Dimitri on the sixth floor, they say he pulls people apart like they're made of bread. I heard you talking about all these doors opening in two hours. When that go down and you stay in one spot, he'll come for you. They'll all come for you. Ain't no barricade you can make that will hold."

"Movement is life," Julie said.

"Come again?" Jamerson said.

"I heard someone say that in a movie once. I can't remember which one, but it was someone who was in a lot of danger."

"It was the zombie one with Brad Pitt," Aguilar said.

LeMaines frowned. "We're gonna let Hollywood make our decisions for us?"

"We have two options," Julie said. "Go or stay. They're both bad.

But I don't want to sit and wait to be a victim. I want to keep moving." Her voice was strong and clear. A voice worth listening to, Argento thought.

"I'm with her," Rachel said. "Three men attacked me in the infirmary. But only three. In two hours, with no locks on doors, it'll be the whole jail after us."

"They're right," Coates said. "So is Mr. Simmons. We don't want to be a stationary target." He walked up to the front of the church, in front of the pulpit. As if about to deliver a benediction. "We're going to have to push through this place. If we can hit the south stairwell that leads to the roof straightaway, then we're in solid shape. If not, then it'll be floor by floor until we reach the top. Between the keys that LeMaines has and the access card from Pillaire, we should be able to go where we need to go."

"I might have missed something in transit," Argento said, "but why the south stairwell? Why not take this one?"

"No roof access here," LeMaines said. "I know it's screwed up. But this place was built by the lowest bidder. Surprised they even knew buildings have roofs."

"Then any reason we don't take this stairwell up to six and cross over?"

"Because then we have to pass through death row. And you absolutely don't want to do that. The guy Simmons was talking about, Dimitri? If he's out of his cell..." LeMaines didn't seem to have the energy to finish his sentence.

"This place gets worse as you get higher," Aguilar said. "So any officers on this floor or above us, we're gonna need bad. We can add them to our group. Like a caravan."

"We'll take whoever we can get," Coates said. "But for now, here's how it will be. We're a line. I'm on point with the pistol. Behind me is LeMaines with the keys, then Julie, Aguilar, Rachel, Pillaire, Kurt, and Van Dyne. Jamerson takes rear guard. We're going to stay on the edge of the hallway but away from the cell doors. Move when I move, stop when I stop. Something happens, do not separate from the pack. Do not take individual action. We keep it tight. The only way we're going to make it through here is if we stay together. But if we move with enough purpose, there's enough of us that when we go down the hall, folks are gonna think twice before taking us on."

"Can you shoot with your left?" Argento asked. "With that thumb, your right ain't gonna do much."

"If I gotta use this thing, I'll be so close up I could fire it with my toes."

"And what of the warden?" Argento asked.

"I'm not going," Pillaire said. His voice warbled. "I'm staying here. Something will come up."

"The 'something will come up' plan," Jamerson said. "Sure. Wish we'd thought of that."

"You have to come with us," Julie said. "You'll die here."

Pillaire responded by closing his eyes. Profiles in courage, Argento thought. He figured the warden was maybe half a tick away from all-out catatonia.

"He's an adult," Coates said. "He can make his own decisions."

"No problem," Jamerson said. "He's a bureaucrat, not a fighter. He'll just be in the way." Jamerson leaned in and snatched Pillaire's key card off his neck. "You got anything else useful on you? Fucking... snacks?"

Pillaire didn't respond.

Coates motioned to the two correctional officers. "Either of you want to weigh in on your boss?"

LeMaines eyed the warden. Made a chopping motion with his hand. "He's supposed to be the leader here. When we were at the guard pod and he cried and said 'Leave me alone,' that's where he lost me. I don't care what he does."

"Aguilar?"

Aguilar's lip curled in what Argento took for contempt. "What Sarge said."

Julie shot Coates a look. "We can't leave him."

"Not gonna throw him over my shoulder and carry him like a sack of grain," Coates said.

"We can't, Derrick."

"We can, Julie." There was steel in Coates's voice. "And we will."

"Malcolm?" Van Dyne asked. "What will you do?"

"I'm too old for people to fuck with," Simmons said. "I'll be fine here. Be fine anywhere. I'll keep an eye on your warden best I can. No guarantees, though. Not in this place."

"Warden, you okay with a convict being the only one watching out for you?"

Pillaire said nothing but Simmons chuckled. "You look at me and I know what you see, but I own my crime and I know it's right I do penance for it. I killed a man in a tavern twenty years ago. His name was Rodney Musgrave. I have to honor him in everything I do."

"This guy for real?" Coates asked.

LeMaines nodded. "Victim's mother ended up forgiving him. Now she comes to see him every month. Damnedest thing I've ever seen."

Coates was watching Pillaire. The trooper opened his mouth as if to say something to him. Like *Good luck*, Argento assumed. Or *Be careful*. But then he didn't, as if deciding the warden wasn't worth the effort. At this point, Pillaire was just a bag of protein and water. He could compost in place.

The trooper turned to address the group. "One more thing. This is a maximum security prison for some of the worst offenders in the state, which means we're going to be passing by some folk who aren't too civilized. We've already seen some of that. You are objects to them, so it will be easy for them to kill you. So don't hesitate to kill them first. Use whatever you have. A knife, a club, your hands. If you can't do that, then become the person who can. Right here and now. Because that's who you need to be to survive this."

"Damn right," Jamerson said. He gave Coates an approving nod.

Coates shrugged. "Every once in a while I give a speech." He reached behind his back and took out Spentz's baton, the one

Argento had turned over to him. Coates handed it back. Argento took it. Felt the reassuring metal in his palm. Jamerson started to say something and then stopped.

Argento didn't need a speech. He was ready. He was used to thinking through emergencies. And here was a genuine crisis, rapidly evolving on uncertain terrain with extreme danger and imminent violence. It felt like home. He was getting down in the mud. Part of him was looking forward to it.

"Reverend," Coates said, "you want to take us out with a blessing?"

Van Dyne nodded. He bowed his head. "Lord God, though we walk through the valley of the shadow of death, we shall fear no evil, for thou art with us. Your rod and your staff comfort us. Lord, we ask that you heal the broken in this place, and if it is your will, reveal to us the safe path. In your name we pray, Amen."

"And Lord, may we smite the living fuck out of our enemies," Jamerson added.

"Amen," Coates said.

"Amen," Julie added. She checked her watch. "We have a hundred minutes even."

"No more talking," Coates said. "Let's do this."

CHAPTER 19

The first stop was the infirmary, which meant stepping over Spentz's bloodied corpse in the hallway. LeMaines made the sign of the cross. Van Dyne said something softly that Argento took to be an Episcopal valediction. Aguilar stopped short in front of the infirmary doors. Then he pushed them open without having to key in.

"These should be locked," LeMaines said. "When we came in here earlier today, I had to use my key card to buzz in."

"That's what Simmons said in the chapel," Argento said. "That some locked doors would just open. No pattern to it."

"Doesn't change a thing," Coates said. "Plan is the same."

Rachel put her cigarette out and splinted and rewrapped Coates's battered thumb while Jamerson kept watch at the entrance. Shank's corpse remained inside along with the still-unconscious handcuffed Mohawk. In his mind's eye, Argento went back over the strike sequence with Mohawk: knee, head, groin, face. Even if Mohawk woke, he wouldn't be in any shape to retaliate.

Squint was nowhere to be found.

Julie had come into the infirmary with the others. She flinched at the sight of the bodies, but stood her ground.

"There was a third guy," Argento said. "He's gone."

"Do we have to worry about him?" Coates asked.

Argento thought back to Squint hitting his head hard on the tile floor and imagined the convict's brain slapping against his skull like a wave on a water piling. Plus Aguilar had handcuffed him. Even if he got his hands on a cuff key, he'd be a hot mess.

"Wherever he is," Argento said, "he isn't breathing right."

Coates was surveying the room. His eyes came to rest on Argento's footwear. "Where did you get those shoes?"

"From the warden. I'll fight better in these than slippers."

"That is some cold-ass shit," Jamerson said.

"Says the guy wearing shoes with traction."

"You took shoes off a dead man," Julie said, then lapsed back into silence. She hadn't necessarily said it in an accusatory tone. More like a fact-gathering one. As if she wanted to better understand the strange and violent microworld she now found herself in. Argento had made peace with it. He was the doer of unpleasant tasks. The warden's estate could bill him.

He watched Rachel tend to Coates. She moved with seasoned practice, but he could see her hands weren't steady. She was back in the place where the assault had happened. Revisiting a nightmare.

As if sensing Argento's thoughts, Coates eased to his feet. "We can finish this outside if you want," he said to the nurse.

"I'm fine," she said, too quickly. "I'm almost done."

Argento had Spentz's reclaimed baton in his front coverall pocket. He had the zip gun in his coveralls as well but didn't feel the need to announce it to the group. It would make Jamerson too nervous. Probably the rest of them, too.

"Can you pack a go bag," Coates told LeMaines as Rachel finished with his wound. "Bandages, antiseptic, N95 masks, QuikClot."

"There's a backpack in the corner," Rachel said. LeMaines found it and started stuffing it with supplies.

Jamerson took another look around. "Any food in here? I missed lunch."

"No time for that, but water would be good. Everyone needs to hydrate."

"And some pain meds," Jamerson said. "For Derrick and the rest of us if we get banged up."

There it is, Argento thought. The addict coming out. Argento had a dim view of drug addicts. He had once administered Narcan to revive a dying junkie, who woke up furious that his high had been interrupted and stabbed Argento in the knee with a corkscrew.

Rachel went to a digitally locked medicine cabinet and punched in a code. The door to the cabinet clicked open. She took out two bottles and ran a UPC-type scanner over them. "With this system gone haywire, I wasn't even sure if that would work. But here's Percocet and Vicodin. It's as heavy as we go in here without knocking you out. Normally, I have to log it but..." She looked around as if seeking guidance.

"It's fine, Rachel," LeMaines said. "When I write my report on all this, I'll explain the circumstances. The bosses will understand. They'll have to."

"The report," Aguilar repeated, putting his hands behind his neck and letting out a puff of air. "Holy shit, it's gonna be like a hundred pages. You want me to write it?"

"Tony," LeMaines said, "when this is all over, there's going to be an investigation to end all investigations. Local cops, DOJ, probably the inspector general. And if by some miracle we make it out of here, they're going to hold us accountable for everything we did. For everything we didn't to do. Senior guy should write this report."

"Damn," Aguilar said. "When you put it that way."

"Besides," LeMaines said, laughing without mirth, "I could use the overtime."

Rachel held out a pill bottle toward Coates. He waved her off. "Gotta stay sharp," he explained. She tossed LeMaines both bottles and he dropped them in the backpack.

Jamerson was standing next to Van Dyne. He scrutinized the preacher, like a curiosity at a museum. "I'm not much for church," Jamerson drawled, "but I was in a fraternity in college. Delta Chi."

"That counts," Julie said. "That's the same."

Jamerson gave Julie a fuck-you smile and turned back to Van Dyne. "In a situation like this, even you gotta be thinking all your hippie religious shit is a joke."

Van Dyne looked unfazed by Jamerson, as if he was used to this line of questioning. "You know what the most common command in Scripture is?"

"Something about oxen. Or fucking... myrrh."

"It's 'Do not be afraid,'" Van Dyne replied patiently. "To me that means scary circumstances are when faith is most relevant."

Jamerson sneezed and then ran the back of his hand across his nose. "I ain't afraid," he said blankly.

"Good guess about the oxen and the myrrh, though," Julie said.

As Rachel was rummaging through a pull-out drawer near one of the infirmary beds for more supplies, Julie's gaze fell on Argento. "What's your take on this?"

"Don't fraternize with the inmates," Jamerson said.

"Go forth and shut up," Julie told him. She looked at Van Dyne. "Was that biblical?"

Van Dyne half smiled. "Leviticus, I think."

"My take is it's good to have a man of God on our side," Argento said. "But good to have some weapons, too."

"You think we're going to make it?"

She wanted assurance from him. The whole group did. In a different life, the life he had with Emily before she died, he might have offered some. But now, in this place, with the hand he'd been dealt, he had little to give.

"I probably will," Argento said.

"Comforting," Julie replied. "You sure you're not the pastor instead of Van Dyne?"

Argento didn't respond. He wasn't for everybody. A police psychologist had once told him, during mandatory counseling after an officer-involved shooting, that he was emotionally detached. And Emily had warned him he was too blunt with people. He told her he liked to be honest. Plus, in this case, he wasn't going to give anyone a false sense of security. He was a good pickup for this group, but they had some tough sledding ahead of them. They couldn't overly rely on him. Everyone was going to have to pull their own weight.

"If you help us get out of here," Julie said with something approaching earnestness, "it could work in your favor. My father might be in a position to see about your sentence."

"I don't have a sentence yet," Argento said. "Haven't even seen a judge."

"Well, what could my father do for you?"

"Maybe some different jail activities. Like a handbell choir."

Julie winced. "Is this really the time for jokes?"

It was. Argento knew that if you could joke when things were going to shit, it helped unfreeze you and get you back toward equilibrium. He had mastered this approach as a patrol cop, a survival tool when you had a job where the deadly and ridiculous happened to you on a weekly basis. Officers who couldn't do it tended to flame out.

Above them, near the ceiling, a mechanical whirring noise kicked into high gear and just as suddenly, stopped.

"What was that?" Julie asked.

Aguilar got down on his knees and put his hand near an air vent at ankle level.

"I think that was the air-conditioning shutting off."

"It's July," Jamerson protested.

"If the AC is tied into the digital core of this place, why wouldn't it shut off?" Coates said.

Jamerson scowled. "Whitehall sucks ass. All the ass."

They left on that thoughtful note, silently filing out of the infirmary in the tactical conga line that Coates had designated. The trooper led the way with the Guardian in hand, the rest in the middle, and Jamerson taking up the rear with the go bag on his back. As they approached the entry door to General Population that Aguilar had initially entered before fleeing back toward the group,

Rachel halted in her tracks, her shoes making an audible squeak on the tile floor.

"I don't know if I can do this."

Coates looked back at her. "You're tough," he said. "You can."

"Lady, someday we'll all look back at it and laugh," Jamerson added.

Argento watched Julie put a consoling hand on the nurse's broad shoulders. "We've got this," she said softly.

Rachel looked back at Argento. "Stay close to me," she said. "Okay?"

Argento gave her the thumbs-up. He could hear labored breathing behind him. LeMaines. With his blood pressure and excess weight combined with extreme outside stress, he was probably the only one in their group who might drop of natural causes.

"How you doing?"

"I'll make it," LeMaines said. "Can anyone see anything through the windows?"

"Looks quiet," Coates said. "So here we go." He held Pillaire's ID up to the keypad. It hadn't worked before when they were chasing after Aguilar, but this time the door clicked green.

"Random-ass joint," Jamerson said.

Coates opened the door and the group filed in, tense, watchful, prepared for anything.

A rush of stagnant air greeted them. The block was divided into an upper and a lower floor of numbered cells with short interior staircases connecting them. Sixteen tables took up the middle of the room with four circular stools around them, all bolted to the floor. To the right was a correctional officer kiosk surrounded by Plexiglas. Computers, log book, office supplies. There was no one manning the station, but a cup of coffee on the counter still had steam rising from it.

Ten or so convicts were out on the floor. Several more were secured in their cells. Some cell doors were open, McVay had said. Some were closed.

Coates led the group down the kiosk side of the block, gun in hand. The inmates watched them silently.

"Just passing through," Coates said. "But I'll shoot anyone I have to."

None of the inmates blocked their passage. Maybe they'd heard the gunshots on the other side of the door earlier. Some felons still respected the gun, even here.

They made their way to the other side without incident. LeMaines keyed the door, and just like that they were in the south exterior stairwell that led to the roof. The stairwell housed a service elevator, the doors of which were stuck open.

"That went better than it should have," Coates said.

"We want to try this elevator?" Jamerson asked.

"Elevators are digital. And if the doors close on us, we won't be able to open them from the inside. So no elevators." No sooner had Coates spoke then the doors to the elevator closed and the lights above it showed it rising.

"Jesus," Jamerson said. "We coulda taken that one. We'd be where we need to be."

"Or it could just get stuck open," Aguilar said, "and inmates would pull us out piece by piece."

"Stairs it is," Coates said. He started up the steps and stopped. He held his hand up. Put his back to the far wall and metered up the staircase. Ascended a few more steps. And backed down slowly, keeping his gun and attention forward.

"No good," he said, keeping his voice low. "Got a party brigade up there waiting for us. Maybe seven guys. They've got weapons."

A voice sounded down the stairwell. Weak at first and then gaining more strength.

"It hurts," the voice said. "Help me."

A second voice, deeper and raspier, said, "Hey there's a guard with us and he's hurt. You gotta get up here."

Coates shook his head. "Trap. One hundred percent."

Aguilar moved to the front of the line. "What's his name?" he demanded. "The officer."

"He can't talk," the raspy voice said. "He's knocked out."

"What's it say on his name tag?"

"It says... Johnson," the raspy voice responded.

"We don't have a fucking Johnson," LeMaines muttered. "Guy's too stupid to even make up a real name."

"On me," Coates said, and reversed the line as they headed back toward the entrance to General Population.

"But we just got past them," Rachel protested. "Why are we—"

"No other choice," Coates said. "Those guys in that stairwell were in red. That's second floor, all violent cons. Better if we take our chances back in General Pop and cross over on another floor."

"Do you think they know we're trying for the roof?" Julie asked. "And they're trying to intercept us?"

"Could be," LeMaines said. "I wouldn't put it past them."

"Fuck," Aguilar said, speaking for all of them. "But that same group is still going to be in the same stairwell we need to get to the roof even if we cross over a floor above."

Argento said, "When you're in a stairwell, positioning is everything. Hard to fight uphill with someone who knows what they're doing. If you're above your target, he's screwed."

"Garbageman knows his tactics," Coates said.

If he had felt like expounding, Argento would have told Coates about some of the fights he'd had in the stairwells of high-rise housing projects. Some quick, some drawn out, most of them brutal. He'd had to throw one gang member down the stairs after the banger tried to take his gun and had been thrown down a stairwell himself when he was outnumbered, snapping his arm. Afterward, he'd tried to avoid battling in such a venue. Experience was a hard teacher.

When they opened the doors back to General Population, one man had separated himself from the others. He was an older con with reddish hair parted down the middle and he wore a plastic crucifix around his neck on a string. He approached the group.

"Hold up," LeMaines said. "This guy we can talk to." He nodded at the red-haired man. "Inmate Scroggins."

Scroggins nodded back. "Hell's going on in here?" he asked. "Doors are all screwy. What caused this?"

"Liberals," Jamerson said.

"So six guys from the floor ran down there after your man," Scroggins said, jutting his chin at Aguilar. "Don't know if they were trying to fuck with him or just trying to make it to the canteen for free chips. I tried to stop them, but you know how people are. The three that came back didn't look so good."

"Where are the officers that are supposed to be on this floor?" LeMaines asked.

"Screws cut and ran. Don't know where."

"How'd they get out?"

Scroggins shrugged. "Like I said, doors are messed up. There's one on the second tier that just keeps opening and closing all by itself."

Argento had moved toward the cells so he could have his back against something. There was a prisoner inside one of them watching the De Niro–Pacino movie *Heat* on a mini-TV. It was on the part where the hold-up crew, led by De Niro, were shooting it out with the cops outside the bank.

"Seen this like nine times. This movie good," the con said gleefully. He was a scrawny guy with pockmarked skin and a partially burned face. Meth lab accident, Argento guessed. The crystal industry didn't always follow OSHA guidelines.

"Ending's bullshit," Argento said. "Pacino would never hold hands with a bank robber who tried to kill him and other cops."

The prisoner nodded slowly, as if chewing this over. Then he shrugged. "Naw, it still good."

"What's the name of the computer fraud guy you got in here?" Coates asked LeMaines.

"Sarrazin. He's probably the smartest inmate we have."

"Take me to him."

"We got time for this?" Jamerson asked.

Coates checked his watch. Tapped it. "We've got eighty-two

minutes. We're already here. Maybe he's involved with the system going down or maybe he knows how to fix it. If he's the smartest one in Whitehall."

LeMaines led the group up the interior stairs to the second level. They found Sarrazin easily enough. He was in his open cell, hanging from a section of what looked like shower curtain that was lashed around a ceiling pipe. He was a portly, soft-looking man in plaid boxers with a postdeath, grayish cast to his face. Suicide, or someone had done him the honors, although Argento knew it was damn hard to string someone up who didn't want to be hung.

"Lord Almighty," Julie said in disbelief.

"Told you he was on suicide watch," LeMaines said.

Julie took a step back from Sarrazin's body. "What does that even mean in here? Guy commits suicide and afterward you watch him?"

"There's supposed to be guards checking in with him every fifteen minutes."

"Should we cut him down?" Van Dyne asked.

"Not unless you want his fluids in your hair," Jamerson said. "Dude's gonna leak."

"Wait, you said a lot of the inmates have cell phones, right?" Coates asked the two troopers.

LeMaines nodded. "Enough that it made us put up the cell net."

"Any chance the smartest guy in here has a tricked-out phone that might work even when ours don't?"

"Maybe," LeMaines said. "Worth a shot."

"Where do they keep them?" Jamerson asked.

"We find some in cell tosses, but they're small. About the size of a deck of cards. They usually keep them in the vault."

"The vault?" Julie asked.

"Up their ass," Aguilar explained. "Put that in your paper."

Jamerson was already tearing the cell apart. Aguilar and LeMaines joined him. Mattress, books, clothing, toiletries, all shaken or torn apart and then dumped on the floor without ceremony. The three men occasionally bumped into Sarrazin's feet, causing the hanging man with the gray face to sway gently above them. They came up empty-handed.

"Kurt," Jamerson said to Argento. "If you want to be useful, check that guy's buttocks for a working phone."

Coates stepped toward them, anticipating another dustup.

Argento waved him off. "No problem." He held his hand out to Aguilar. "Could use some gloves."

Aguilar wordlessly went into one of his belt pouches and handed Argento a pair of blue latex gloves. And without hesitation, Argento checked the anal cavity of the smartest man in Whitehall for any mobile device that could put out a call for help. A pungent odor filled the cell. Everyone hastened out. Argento remained until he was sure there was nothing to find, stripped off the gloves, and washed his hands in the cell's sink for good measure.

"Thanks for trying," Julie said, because she probably thought someone should say something.

"You told me to get along with him," Argento told Julie evenly. "So I did what he said."

Jamerson seemed momentarily baffled by Argento's cooperation. He opened his mouth as if he were about to acknowledge him, but thought better of it. "Okay," he said to no one in particular, "so who's second smartest?"

CHAPTER 20

Julie

The group trekked back through the rest of General Population without confrontation. Scroggins presented as the informal leader of the first floor, and it seemed that if he was willing to let them pass, then the rest of the inmates would, too.

They had now reassembled in the north stairwell.

"We should go up to the second floor and cross there," Aguilar said.

Julie watched him. Beads of sweat had formed on the young correctional officer's temple, making his already gelled hair glisten. Her own hair was damp at the roots. The AC hadn't kicked back on, and the swelter was beginning to take hold. She took a deep breath in, letting the warm air fill her lungs. She slowly exhaled. She was scared, as scared as she'd ever been, but she would let the fear come. She would use it to keep her senses sharp. If she was going to survive this, she needed to see everything. Hear everything. She checked her phone again, out of habit. No signal. She clutched the phone in her hand until her palm was red, as if it were a talisman meant to ward off an approaching storm.

"Second floor? Through a block of violent felons? Why don't we cross on the third floor with the sex offenders? Sex offenders are pussies," Jamerson said.

Aguilar shook his head. "Because there are guards that are going to need our help, and the second floor is better staffed than the third. When they join us, there should be enough of us to take those seven guys in the south stairwell."

"Trooper?" LeMaines asked of Coates, looking for guidance.

"Let's all just take a breath," Coates said.

The sight of the hanging man had unnerved Julie. His paunchy body suspended off the floor, discolored and still. It seemed worse somehow than the other deaths she had already seen in this place. Maybe, she thought, it was because Sarrazin's decision to kill himself almost seemed like a reasonable response to the situation they found themselves in. He had anticipated a worse fate to come, she presumed, so he took action now.

She had taken note of Kurt's reaction to Sarrazin, or lack thereof. There was no sign of shock or surprise on his face. He seemed unmoved. Almost like he had expected it, like people hung themselves all the time in his day-to-day life. Julie realized that she both wanted Kurt close by and at the same time was considerably wary of him.

The man in question was leaning against the wall, arms crossed, a placid expression on his face. As relaxed as he seemed, Julie thought, he might as well be a damn farmer chewing on a stalk of wheat.

Rachel had walked up to him, almost tentatively, and Kurt gave her the slightest of head nods. Not warmth, necessarily, but not hostility.

"When do I stop being scared?" Rachel asked him, running her fingers over the beads of her necklace.

"Be crazy not to be scared in a place like this."

"You don't seem scared."

Kurt looked down at his orange Dreamsicle jumpsuit and coveralls, now blood-stained and torn. "Scared of dying in these pants."

Van Dyne put a reassuring hand on Rachel's back. He turned his attention to Kurt. "Why are you helping us?"

Kurt didn't say anything for a moment. Julie thought he was going to ignore the preacher's question.

Then he spoke. "When I see trouble, I do something about it."

"Why?"

"Seems wrong not to."

"It's the garbageman's code," Jamerson interjected.

Van Dyne let the trooper's comment pass. "In church," the chaplain said, "we might call that a kind of covenant."

Kurt shrugged. "Sounds better than what I said."

Coates had been looking through the door's window onto the second-floor cellblock. "I see two guys close by that might be trouble. LeMaines, you want to take a peek?"

LeMaines came up to the window, adjusted his glasses, and peered through. "Those are the Canche brothers. They only speak Mayan."

"How do you communicate?"

"When our phones are up and working, we got a language line."

"What'd they do?"

"Kidnapped the man who they thought raped their sister and burned him alive."

"That shouldn't even be a crime," Jamerson said.

"Yeah, but turns out it was the wrong person. Cops arrested the right guy a week later."

"Okay," Jamerson said, "now it's probably back to being a crime again."

"They're actually some of our best-behaved inmates. I don't see them bothering us."

Coates said, "Other than the Mayan boys, there's a handful milling around, but all in all, looks pretty clear. We cross here. We'll go straight to the south stairwell, pick up any loose guards on the way, and then up the stairs to the roof. If those seven are still waiting for us, there's a good shot we'll have the high ground on them."

"You see any officers on the floor?" Aguilar asked, hope in his voice.

"Not yet."

LeMaines's face tightened. "Where the hell are our guys?"

"Let's go see," Coates said. "Everyone on me. We're moving." He clicked the door open with Pillaire's ID and strode onto the floor with the group following behind. Rachel was so close to Kurt she stepped on his heel.

The Canche brothers moved aside at the sound of their arrival. They were short and stocky and essentially looked interchangeable. Both brothers gave off the impression they'd just woken up. Coates communicated to them with a thumb jerk. They got out of the way, but when Julie passed, one stepped toward her. Kurt shook his head and drew his finger across his throat. The man stopped. Kurt gave him an approving nod. Both brothers gave him toothy grins in return.

Who needed a language line? Julie thought.

There were several red-clad prisoners on the block, but Coates's raised firearm provided enough incentive for them to stay put. The group passed an empty guard station and then three occupied cells in a row. One inmate was Asian, the second was Black, the third Hispanic.

"Let me out," the first inmate said. "I'll be good." He took a deep pull off a meth pipe and blew out, Julie picking up on traces of what smelled like glass cleaner.

"They be putting fake cases on a brother," the second inmate said. "I'm a political prisoner."

"I'll look into it," Coates said as he kept moving.

"If you ain't gonna let us out then let the bitches in," the third inmate said, rubbing his groin with both hands.

Under different circumstances, Julie would have stayed and tried to think of an insulting retort, but the group had already passed the cells and were approaching the south exterior stairwell door. In less than two hours, the three inmates they'd just passed would be free to roam. Rivulets of sweat ran down her back. It seemed to get hotter inside the prison walls with every step she took.

"I like the people here," Jamerson said. "They're diverse."

Just before they reached the end of the block, a room opened up on their left. A sign above the doorway said *Group Therapy*. The room contained a desk with an obsolete brand laptop on it. At the head of the room was a whiteboard that someone had written a quote from Margaret Thatcher on: *You May Have to Fight a Battle More Than Once*. The bulk of the room was taken up by a series of gray metal cells, spaced a foot apart, that ran along all four walls, each about the size of a shower stall with a stool inside to sit on. It seemed an odd setup to Julie. Therapy in cages? Was it to keep the inmates from attacking each other and staff? But the thought was fleeting, because her attention was drawn to the insides of the cells themselves.

Every single one was filled.

With a uniformed correctional officer.

At the sight of the staff, Jamerson's face contorted in disbelief. "Hey, I found the guards."

Coates waved the group into the therapy room. Jamerson kept watch on the outside hallway. LeMaines and Aguilar stared at the assembled men.

"What—" LeMaines began and seemed unable to finish his sentence.

One of the officers, a man of about fifty with graying hair and a nervous bob to his head spoke. There was a squeak to his voice. "What were we supposed to do? The doors aren't working, we can't get anyone on the phones, the radio. And they said if we stayed in here, they wouldn't kill us."

"Who's they?"

"The whole block," the first officer said. "Whole block is rising up against us. 'Cept for those Mayan brothers. They seem to think this is some kind of vacation."

Coates looked around the room, and then back at the first officer. "These cells aren't anything. They only lock from the outside. You're not protected in here. You're sitting ducks."

"You don't work here, man," a second officer said. "I ain't gonna listen to shit you got to say."

"Well, *I* work here," LeMaines said. "And I'm the acting watch commander. We have a mission. It's to get these two ladies and the rest of this group to the roof where we can make a call for help. So come on out of there and join us. We're gonna need every single one of you."

"Sarge," the first officer said plaintively. Bob bob went his head.

"Heard the warden's dead," a third officer offered.

"He is," LeMaines said.

"Heard Spentz is, too," the third officer continued. "Maybe some other guys. So fuck ending up like them."

LeMaines didn't reply.

"You know why this place is going haywire?"

"No," LeMaines said. He lowered his voice so only those in the room could hear him. "But I know that in about seventy-five minutes, every door on every floor is going to open up and inmates are going to have full run of it. You think it's bad now? Bad is still coming."

The first officer put his hands up in a sign of surrender. "Gonna stay put, Sergeant. No disrespect. But we ain't equipped to handle this."

"Kilpatrick?" Aguilar asked, training his gaze on a young officer with a flat top. "We're in the same softball league. Our kids go to school together. Get the hell out of there and help us."

"This isn't for me," Kilpatrick said, a note of remorse in his voice. "No offense to you or the sarge, but I get paid fourteen bucks an hour. I'm out."

"You're safer with us," Coates said.

"Says you. I don't know what's out there." Kilpatrick gestured beyond the room. "But I know what's in here. What's in here we can handle."

"This is the governor's daughter," Jamerson said from the doorway. He gripped Julie by the shoulder and pushed her forward so the whole ring of cells could see her, like she was on auction. "So maybe at least a few of you could postpone your nervous breakdowns and pitch in."

"Who cares?" the second officer said. "I didn't vote for the guy."

Julie twisted out of Jamerson's grasp, irritated that he had singled her out. She looked around the room. Most of the officers were looking away. Some were looking at the floor. No help to be found there. She asked, "Is this the best use of our time?"

Kurt had been quiet since they entered the room, but now he spoke. His expression remained neutral, that of a spectator, not a participant, but Julie thought she detected something more behind his eyes, a flash of animation, even anger. "Always remember," he said to the room of guards, "that when your coworkers and these women were in danger, you chose to hide in here."

"I'll help," one of the officers said. He pushed his door open and stepped out, almost dramatically, Julie thought, like he was posing for a picture. He was a fun-size twenty-year-old with a plump, pimpled face shiny with sweat. His belly pushed several inches out over his uniform belt. "What should I do?"

"Get back in here, Radke," Kilpatrick said. "You ain't gonna do shit."

Radke looked at Kilpatrick and cast a quick glance at Julie and her group. Then he did as Kilpatrick said without a word of protest, stepping back into his cage and closing the door without meeting anyone's eyes.

"Just as well," Jamerson said in disgust. "You're too fat to be useful."

It was the first time Julie had agreed with the trooper. The kid was supposed to be a Whitehall first responder, which meant he'd lost the right to be out of shape, but he looked like a sack of jelly.

"We're done here," Coates said. "Moving. South stairwell."

The group stepped back into the hallway. Rachel looked back at the room with the do-nothing officers and gave them a departing middle finger. "Those guys. Fuck. I mean, just...fuck."

"Yep," Julie seconded. It seemed a more than adequate summary.

Coates approached the door and tried to peer through, but the window was covered from the outside by a black piece of clothing. The trooper stopped short. He didn't like that he couldn't see through to the other side. But there was nowhere to go but forward. "Be ready for anything," he said and clicked open the door.

Then it all went to hell.

CHAPTER 21

As soon as the door was open, the seven inmates in the stairwell poured out, like the gate to a cattle pen had been lifted, a rush of prisoners in red, all sinew and clatter. Coates shot the first man point-blank through the throat and the second in the upper chest. Both went down. The slide to the now-empty Guardian locked open. The shots stopped the prisoner surge, but Argento knew it wouldn't last.

"Stairs," Coates shouted, and the group sprinted up the interior stairs two at a time to the second level of the cellblock. Argento wasn't sure if Coates was reacting blindly to the threat or if he was thinking tactically, but the narrow stairwell and subsequent thin walkway that ran the length of the second floor would both blunt the capacity of the five remaining inmates to attack at once and also protect the middle of the group, which included Julie and Rachel. It also meant the two ends of the line, Coates and Jamerson, would have to hold their own.

The five cons had resumed their pursuit, trampling over the two fallen inmates and giving chase up the south end of the stairs.

But they weren't alone.

On the north end of the stairwell, two inmates detached

themselves from the wall and moved to the base of the stairs. The first was a Hispanic man of about thirty with long hair and forearm tattoos of writhing snakes. The second was an older Asian man with loose skin around his neck and a permanent up-twist to one side of his lip.

Which meant the group was trapped on the second-floor walkway.

When Argento was on field training as an officer in Detroit, his field training officer had passed on one of his favorite expressions to him. He said, "The plane is crashing. Do something." In other words, if presented with an awful set of circumstances, don't be a passive witness to your own demise. Make a decision.

Take action.

Do something.

In this case, the math was easy. Two men on one side, unknown if armed. Five men on the other, likely with edged weapons.

Argento watched Snake Tattoo and Twist Lip approach. You could tell a lot in the first ten seconds. How they carried themselves. How they set their feet. What they did with their hands. The unknowns were pain tolerance and will. So far neither man was giving off signals that they were going to distinguish themselves in unarmed combat. Even if they had a trained fighting skill, it was likely one that Argento was familiar with and knew how to counter. Wrestlers sometimes gave him problems, but he had learned plenty of ground defenses over the years. Neither of these men had a wrestler's build.

Snake Tattoo stepped ahead of Twist Lip and eyed Jamerson, who readied his baton but had his hands spaced too far apart from the grommet, which made Argento wonder when he'd last used it. Narcotics cops were almost exclusively plainclothes. Plainclothes cops didn't carry batons.

"Bienvenidos, puta," Snake Tattoo said. Argento knew enough Spanish to know the man wasn't paying the trooper tribute. As Snake Tattoo slipped metal knuckles on his right fist, Argento shouldered past Jamerson and expanded his collapsible baton. Snake Tattoo's hands automatically went up to cover his face and Argento hit him in the gut. The con covered his stomach, and Argento hit him in the face with a second baton strike. Hands to face, another gut shot. Hands to gut, another face shot. Snake Tattoo went down.

A lesson is repeated until learned.

Argento had hoped Snake Tattoo's quick disposal would have given Twist Lip a moment of pause, but the inmate lashed out with a hard right that connected flush with Argento's cheek and rocked him back on his heels. Argento fought to keep his balance and then someone shot past him and wrapped his arms around the inmate like an orderly in a psych hospital trying to keep a patient from hurting himself. It was Van Dyne. Twist Lip rewarded the chaplain with a savage headbutt, which dropped him straightaway. But it gave Argento the time and space to bounce back. He took rough hold of the con under the arms, hoisted him over the second-floor railing, and dropped him. The convict landed on his back on the cement floor fifteen feet down, his body making the same sound a steak makes when you slap it on a cutting board.

There was no time to waste. The five inmates coming up the south stairs had halted when Twist Lip took his fall, but that only bought Argento a second or two. He moved past Coates and blocked their path.

The five of them were straight prison issue. Tattoos of guns and dollar signs and their street names on their forearms, faces, and necks. The lead guy had a throat tat that read *Fuck You Pay Me* and a swollen physique. He gripped a homemade knife with a four-inch blade.

Argento raised the baton parallel to the floor. He swung, hard and fast, targeting the side of the neck at the base. The technical term for it was a diffused strike. DPD had banned it years ago because of injuries and lawsuits, but Argento was no longer beholden to their rules. Do the diffused strike right and according to the Detroit Police Department manual, it was an incapacitating technique that "resulted in the instant but temporary cessation of the subject's aggression." In other words, it knocked the target out cold. Do it wrong and it could kill. Throat Tat had a knife, so Argento elected to do it wrong. He swung for the fences.

Throat Tat said something that sounded like "Blergh" as the scything power of the weighted baton blew up his neck. Argento followed up by crouching low and gripping the large con around the waist. Throat Tat was considerably heavier than Twist Lip, so it took more horsepower, but Argento hauled the con's limp body over the railing and let him drop. Throat Tat landed next to Twist Lip with the same smacking noise. Maybe it was his imagination, but Argento thought he could hear Throat Tat's veterbrae crack.

"You see how this is gonna go," Argento said to the four inmates who remained. His breath came high and hard from the intense physical exertion of the previous twenty-five seconds. The cons instinctively backed up.

"We're gonna walk back the way we came," Argento continued. "Follow us and more of you will end up down there." He jutted his chin in the direction of the lower level. "Floor's made out of cement, but you're not." He spoke slowly and forcefully, as if he found himself in this position all the time, as if he tossed convicts over railings on a routine basis. He had to sell it, unblinkingly. It was like being at the casino table and betting too safe. Scared money doesn't win.

"Man with a plan," one of the four said with a curiously soft voice. He sported a lone puff of hair on the center of his head and a long, sullen face. "But what if we don't like your plan?"

"Like it, don't like it," Argento said. "It's happening either way."

The convict didn't reply. Argento tapped Coates, who was behind him. "We're moving," he said.

"Okay," Coates said, but he said it a tick slow, as if his brain was still trying to process everything that had just happened.

The band moved down the north stairs, Jamerson leading the group and Argento walking backward to keep a visual. The four remaining cons from the stairwell stayed put. The remaining inmates on the floor cut them a wide berth. One of the Canche brothers returned Argento's approving nod from before and gave him a wide grin, as if to say, *Nice work up there*. It was so surreal it made Argento want to laugh.

But when they reached the northern exterior stairwell door, Argento spotted two more inmates, neither of whom was a welcome sight. The first was Squint, one of Rachel's attackers in the infirmary. Although Aguilar had handcuffed him, his hands were now free. All the guards carried handcuff keys on their belts, so it wouldn't have been hard for Squint to procure them, especially given how the guards in the Group Therapy room had lain down and given up. He still looked dazed and disheveled from Argento's earlier barrage. He was pointing at Argento, but it didn't seem like a challenge. The gesture seemed more like childlike recognition.

The second person rated far higher on the alarm scale.

The second person was Micah.

CHAPTER 22

"Back up," Argento told Jamerson.

Jamerson did as instructed. The group moved halfway up the north interior stairs. Argento moved quickly to the front of the line.

"You again," Argento said.

"Me," Micah said.

The blond-haired con stood on the balls of his feet, relaxed, almost tranquil. His arms were once again behind him, like a leisurely gentleman. Although it was baking on the cell floor, Micah didn't look to be perspiring at all. The Canche brothers moved away from him, yielding the floor. Rachel was next to Argento and he felt her tense up. Like she knew Micah and what he was capable of.

"What are you doing with her?" Micah asked. Behind him, Argento heard what he thought was Julie's breath escaping as she no doubt saw Micah's target gaze. It was a fair question. Argento didn't seem the type to be getting face time with the governor's daughter.

"Call it, Kurt," Coates said.

"Stand fast." Argento stole a look around. The four inmates were still on the upper stairwell. The remaining inmates on the floor were a distance away. Only Micah blocked their egress. But he was enough.

As if to illustrate the point, Micah strode toward Squint and delivered the best snap kick Argento had ever seen. It struck the con straight in the abdomen and drove him into the closest wall, his breath exploding out of him. And then Micah was behind him, pulling his head back and cutting his throat with a wicked-looking knife, through the windpipe, the vagus nerve, the jugular, all with one savage, practiced stroke. Squint thrashed and spewed blood. His last few words on earth were a gurgle. Micah let go and Squint fell face-first to the floor. If the severed vagus nerve hadn't already stopped his heart, he would have drowned in his own blood.

Micah knelt down and used Squint's shirt to wipe a long line of the dead convict's blood off his forehead. The rope necklace he wore slipped out of his shirt, revealing a quarter-sized medallion on the end that looked like a half moon. He tucked the necklace back in, stood, and extended a hand toward the corpse.

"What'd you think of that?" he asked Argento.

Argento didn't answer. He had never seen anyone's throat cut in front of him before, but he had seen equally awful things on the job. It had blunted his capacity to be shocked or surprised. Add in the numbness he had felt since Emily died, and Micah might as well have playfully tweaked Squint's nose for all the effect it had on him.

"Oh my Jesus," someone said from behind Argento. It sounded like Julie but the voice was so distorted it could have been Van Dyne.

"Someone's paying you to kill me," Argento said. "Probably the Rocker County sheriff."

"How you figure?" Micah asked. The knife had gone behind his back again. Argento wondered why he did that. Wasn't as if he would forget the inmate had it.

"Haven't been in Missouri long, so it's a short list. Plus, you called me Kurt. Only the sheriff would know that name. No one else could have told you."

"You have quite the imagination."

"I'm not blaming you. It's probably good money the sheriff promised. Sitting there, waiting for you, all stacked up and green."

Although he stood in more or less the same position, Micah hadn't stopped moving. Nothing dramatic. Just small steps from side to side, minor adjustments of his hands, eyes scanning his surroundings.

"Maybe I just don't like you."

"Everybody likes me," Argento said. "Now I'm going to give you a choice. You won't like it. Either way, you don't get paid."

"I'm listening."

Argento took another look around. The four inmates still on the upper stairwell. The remaining inmates on the floor a distance away. If they all converged, it would likely be over for Argento and his group. But he didn't think they would. With Snake Tattoo and Twist Lip out of the fight, they didn't have a leader at the moment to organize them.

"Lot of shit going on," Argento continued. "I got no time for you. So either you back off, or I'm going to hurt you. I know you're some kind of Mary Lou Retton. But I'm good at hurting people. Dance around all you want, won't make a difference to me."

Rachel had visibly started when Argento had talked about hurting Micah. She had seen enough carnage in one day, Argento guessed, and didn't want to see any more.

"Look at you with the tough talk," Micah said with something feigning appreciation. "You should be in a movie about cowboys."

Sensing some ambivalence on Micah's part, Argento took out the zip gun and pointed it at the inmate to help him decide. He hadn't wanted Coates or Jamerson to know he had the weapon because they'd want to take it from him, but the clock was ticking and they were on a floor of violent criminals who were trying to figure out if they were still worth attacking.

"Your little friend," Micah said. "Thought you'd have used it by now."

"Step aside."

Micah hesitated.

"Not big on saying shit twice."

Micah moved. Even Olympians couldn't dodge bullets.

"Farther away," Argento ordered, to factor for a gymnast's speed.

Micah complied, moving a good thirty feet from the door.

Argento led the group down the remaining interior stairs and covered Micah with the zip gun while Coates used the ID card to open the north door to exit the block. Rachel turned to face Micah. Argento couldn't see her face from his vantage point, but she was squared up to the inmate and it almost seemed some kind of moment had passed between the two of them. Rachel standing her ground, showing that she wasn't scared of Micah? Asking for mercy? Argento wasn't sure. Julie seemed to notice it, as did LeMaines, who ushered Rachel toward the door. When the lock clicked open, the group rushed out into the safety of the exterior stairwell, jumbled, shaken. Argento remained until the last of them had passed by.

"You won't always have the gun," Micah said for the second time as Argento closed the door between them.

CHAPTER 23

When they were on the other side of the closed door, Rachel slid to the floor, eyes shut, hands to her face. Then she fumbled for another cigarette and lit it. Julie sat close enough to the nurse to inhale the plume of nicotine. Both looked utterly spent. Van Dyne threw up, most of it going on his shoes. Jamerson was pacing. LeMaines seemed rattled and Aguilar didn't look much better. Only Coates remained stoic, even after having to shoot two men. Argento kept the zip gun out in case Micah reversed course and came through the door into the stairwell. The door was locked and there wasn't supposed to be a key on any of the guards' rings to get off the second floor and above. But the doors weren't reliable in this place, and even if they were, he wouldn't put it past the gymnast to figure out a way to walk through walls. He'd already figured out a way to get from the first floor to the second.

"Any more like him in here?" Argento asked LeMaines.

"No," LeMaines said.

Coates began to speak. Probably a call to action. Urging them to keep moving. But he looked at the assembled group and stopped. Sensing they needed to downshift after what they'd just seen.

"Those were clean shoots, brother," Jamerson said to his partner, taking Coates by the arms and searching his face. "I'll take the stand and say the same. Everyone here will."

Coates didn't reply.

"Are you okay?" Julie asked Coates from her position on the floor.

"First-rate," Coates said, although his thoughts seemed elsewhere. Argento had been where the trooper had been. Typically after a police shooting, the officer involved got medical attention if he needed it, then was hustled away from the scene by a supervisor to whom he'd give a brief statement and then be taken to a down room where he could decompress, eat if he was hungry, and call his family and tell them he was okay. None of that was going to happen here, which meant Coates would have to stay in the field and function even after doing one of the most stressful things a cop could do. Argento figured he was up for it. Coates had some time on the job and came off as composed and resilient. But he was going to have to watch him.

The heat was stifling in the stairwell. Coates wiped his brow. "Pass some water around," he told Jamerson. It was a good sign. It showed that Coates was already able to step out of himself and think of the needs of the group. Jamerson fished into the go bag and distributed some bottles. Everyone drank greedily. Aguilar poured a bottle over his head and shook off the excess water.

Argento turned to Van Dyne, who was finished puking. "Thanks for the help back there. Although you might be the worst fighter I've ever seen."

"You're welcome," the chaplain said, wiping a string of vomit from his mouth with his shirtsleeve. The inmate's head butt had left a large red blotch on his forehead.

"I hate this place," Julie said after she drained her bottle and flipped the empty plastic down the stairs. "I hate it so much."

"Who the hell was that blond wing nut?" Jamerson demanded.

"His name is Micah," Argento said.

"The man you were talking to Simmons about in the chapel," Van Dyne said.

"You ran into him before?" Coates asked.

Argento nodded. "In the metal shop."

"You said the sheriff of Rocker County had hired him to off you. Why would he do that?"

"Long story," Argento said. "No time for it."

Van Dyne had recovered enough to ask, "If the sheriff is after you, do you think he could have engineered this power outage?"

Argento didn't have to give that much thought. The sheriff could barely engineer his roadside assault. "No. I don't see it."

"Better question," Jamerson said, his voice louder than it needed to be. "How the hell is that fucker Micah getting through all these doors and following us?"

"He's got the warden's master key," LeMaines said. "There's no other way. Which means he's probably the one who killed him."

"Why'd he carve up the rando by the door? They have a prior beef?"

"I think he was trying to show what happens to people who cross him," LeMaines said. He was speaking to the group but Argento noticed LeMaines was watching Rachel. Probably trying to see if she was holding up. If she would break. Julie didn't know Whitehall, but she had grit and would fight. This put the nurse as potentially the weak link among them, especially considering she'd already suffered enough trauma in the infirmary to last a lifetime.

Argento observed Jamerson, who was still pacing and whose lips were moving ever so slightly, as if muttering to himself. While Coates was getting calmer as things got worse, Jamerson was getting progressively more unglued. Hell, *he* could be the weak link. It wasn't a good look for a state trooper guarding the governor's daughter. Jamerson didn't have the right to panic. But this was a different kind of pressure. Some people fold.

Given that Squint was one of the three who assaulted Rachel, Argento was of the opinion that Micah killed the right guy. No need for a candlelight vigil. But the fact that he had done the killing in front of multiple witnesses meant something. Micah was locked up, but he was no lifer. He was going to be released from custody eventually, and he'd want to spend whatever money the sheriff had pledged to him for killing Argento. Which meant he was confident none of Argento's group was going to make it to the stand to testify against him. Highly confident. Eerily confident.

"Hey," Jamerson said to Argento. "When you were dealing with those four cons, why didn't you have them clear out so we could hit the south stairwell?"

"They would have had to retreat back the way they came. They wouldn't like that because they'd look weak. Would have made them more inclined to fight."

"Shit," Jamerson said, just to be saying something.

"Maybe you could have negotiated something better."

Jamerson let the comment pass. His lips moved again but no sound came out. Then he said, "How you know all this stuff?"

"I've spent some time around dangerous people."

"Garbageman psychologist. Okay, I get it. But why not take Micah out right then and there so we don't have to worry about him on our back?"

"Not a fight we needed."

"He's one guy. You've been dropping them left and right."

"He's different," Argento said. Over the years as a street fighter, he had learned to read people. The average joe with no weapons and little training would come along and beat a guy like Argento maybe once every hundred years. Like a true solar eclipse. But Micah was not average. Argento wasn't confident enough that the fight would go his way.

"So we keep him in our rearview," Coates said.

"That's why we have a rear guard," Argento said.

"Awesome," Jamerson the rear guard said. "Anyone want to switch with me?"

Aguilar finished his water bottle and rolled the plastic in his hands. "I'm ashamed of our officers," he said without prompting. "Hiding the way they were. I'm sorry."

"Not your fault," Argento said. "You did what you could to rally them." A knocked-out tooth was pinched between his cheek and gums. He spat the bloody tooth on the floor and briefly examined the corresponding hole in his gumline with a thumb. Twist Lip had landed a solid punch.

"Are you okay?" Rachel asked.

Argento nodded. Nobody had ever died from a missing tooth. It was a vanity injury. He looked at his hands. They had put in some work over the last few hours. He was missing a nail and the middle finger on his left hand was canted in an unnatural crook that he couldn't straighten or bend. It was either broken or a tendon was torn from jamming it during a punch. He'd seen it happen to basketball players before when a hard pass hit their fingers.

Argento had confidence in his physical abilities. He saw the world differently than most. He was always thinking of ways to defend himself and others. A two-by-four on the ground wasn't just for building, it was a cudgel. The corner of a car door could be an offensive weapon when smashed into someone's eye. He was used to hitting and being hit. He could endure physical punishment as well as anyone. But to survive this, he—all of them—would need to be smart and they'd need to be lucky. He couldn't fight every inmate. The law of averages said he'd eventually meet someone nastier than him or get ganged up on. If he was in the wrong spot at the wrong time, he'd lose. And with each clash, with each injury he sustained, the odds against him spiked. No one went undefeated.

"You're a fucking warrior, dude," Aguilar said, meeting Argento's gaze and raising the crushed plastic bottle in the air in salutation. "I don't know what your story is but I'm glad you're with us."

A warrior. Argento had once had a conversation with Emily about whether cops should have a warrior mindset, or if that was too destructive for what was supposed to be a peacekeeping job. Argento opted for the former. He figured if people shot at you with rifles, it was a war.

"What if instead of a warrior, you were more like a knight?" she asked once when they were sitting on the porch. "Knights are good to people. But they're no pushovers. They'll draw a sword on that dragon."

"They don't give us swords."

"If you were a knight, you'd have one. You'd impale that dragon's brain with your sword. Then you'd say something tough like, I don't know, like 'Something on your mind?'" She'd laughed, her full, tapering laugh, the most pleasant and familiar sound he'd ever known. A few months later, after complaining of a persistent cough and trouble swallowing, she had gone in for tests and gotten the diagnosis.

Coates gestured toward the zip gun in Argento's hand. "How'd you come by that?"

"Made it in metal shop during a break."

"Hand it—" Jamerson said, but then stopped himself before he said *over* as he realized he'd be issuing a directive he couldn't enforce.

"Keep it," LeMaines said. "Maybe it's strange, me telling a prisoner to hang on to an illegal weapon, but he's the only reason any of us are alive right now. I'll even put it right in my report. I don't give a shit."

"I second that," Aguilar said, pointing approvingly at Argento.

Coates didn't argue.

"You gonna keep that Guardian in play?" Argento asked Coates.

Coates closed the slide with a metallic *snick*. "Yeah. Crooks won't know it's empty."

Jamerson leaned back against the wall. "You still hanging on to your faith there, Van Dyne?"

"I am," Van Dyne said. He was clasping his hands together and looking off at some spot in the distance. As if gathering himself.

"Because Jesus loves everyone? Thinks we're all special?"

"Pretty sure Jesus thinks you're an asshole," Julie said. She wasn't looking at Jamerson but was fiddling with a ragged hole in her sweatshirt sleeve she'd picked up somewhere on the last two floors.

"Julie, I will..." Jamerson started angrily.

"Finish the sentence," Julie demanded, now giving Jamerson her full attention. "You will what?"

Argento broke in. "I stopped riding him when you told me to. It was good advice. How about you do the same?"

Julie stayed quiet. Then she said, "Giving advice is more fun than taking it."

"So now what?" Rachel asked. She was on maybe her seventh cigarette—Argento had lost count.

"We cross on three," Coates said. "Maybe there'll be some guards there that are actually worth a damn. Plus, and anyone correct me if I'm wrong, those inmates roaming the south stairwell that just came after us on the second floor are trapped on the block now, right? Because you said no one, not even the guards, have the keys to exit the second floor and above."

"That's right about the keys," LeMaines said. "But how did they get in that stairwell in the first place? That shows us that some doors that were closed are now open and the other way around. We can't count on anything right now."

"Plus you have Micah with the master key," Argento said. "He could decide to spring them."

"Why would he do that?"

"Maybe he wants to throw enough inmates my way to where I have to use this." Argento held up the zip gun. "Then he'll come for me. More of an even fight."

"You should have used the zip on him straightaway," Jamerson said. "If not him, then who you saving it for?"

Argento didn't answer. He wasn't quite sure himself. So far, it had just felt right to keep the zip gun in reserve.

"All right," Julie said grimly. "Third floor it is. This weekend is already shot—might as well go mingle with the pervs and pedophiles." She stood, drained the rest of her second water bottle and cast it aside. Plucky, Argento thought. She'd need that spirit and then some to make it through.

Coates did his routine of scanning the floor before opening the door. For all the good it had done them up to this point. But Argento was slightly distracted. Something was ticking in the back of his head. Like a nagging reminder of something he should be seeing that he wasn't. He couldn't put words to it, so he let it be. Maybe this place was just playing tricks on him. He was used to stress but he wasn't immune to it. The heat wasn't helping. Whitehall had turned into a violent sauna.

Coates said, "I can see one inmate. Looks like he has one of the guards' key rings for the cells but I don't see any guards."

"That's not a good sign," Rachel said.

"How many good signs have there been since we got here?" Julie asked.

"That's a point," Coates said. "Everybody ready?"

Van Dyne threw up again. This time he was able to aim in the corner. "I'm sorry," he said when he had finished retching. "I think it's the heat and—"

Rachel handed him some water and he took it.

"—and all the murdering," he added.

Coates used Pillaire's ID card to open the door, the Guardian out and ready. The gun was empty, so it amounted to no more than a bluff, but it was a solid one.

"Step lively," he said.

CHAPTER 24

Julie

The inmate swinging the guard's key ring around was doing so jauntily. He was a shirtless, reed-thin guy clad in purple pants. When he heard the door open and saw Coates pointing a handgun at him, he dropped the keys like his hand was on fire. He sprinted into the closest open cell and dipped behind the bed.

"I think I scared him," Julie said. It was false bravado, but it seemed to help control the balloon of panic in her chest that had been there since everything had touched off. Fake it until you make it. Sweat trickled down her back, which was already damp. The heat made everything worse. She was so hot, she felt feverish. She had noticed something on the floor below them that was bothering her, not the bloody confrontation, something far more subtle. But she couldn't name it. She was too hot to even think.

"This is more like it," Jamerson scoffed. "Told you sex offenders were soft."

LeMaines scooped the keys off the floor and took a hard look around.

Some cell doors were open and some were closed, but every prisoner was in his cell. Not a soul was on the floor. The cell block felt airless and smelled of metal and unwashed bodies. The guard station was abandoned, just like the first two floors.

"What's happening in here?" a voice from one of the cells called out.

"Shut up," Jamerson said.

"We're having some technical difficulties," LeMaines said. "Stay put and wait for further instruction."

They moved straight through the cell block to the south stairwell door, encountering no resistance. The remaining prisoners they passed stared at them from their enclosures. A human zoo.

"Should be at least two officers on this floor," Aguilar said. "Where the hell are they?"

Coates had already reached the south door. "Worry about that after we get to the top," he said. He held up the ID to the keypad.

Nothing happened.

Coates wiped the ID on his pants and held it up again.

The key pad remained red.

"Little help here," he said.

LeMaines took the ID. Held it up just as Coates had. But the pad didn't turn green and the door didn't open.

"Fuck the reader. Key that bitch," Jamerson said impatiently.

LeMaines ignored him. He held the card up again to the reader. Still red.

"I said key it," Jamerson growled.

"I told you, I don't have keys to get off the floor," LeMaines shot back. "Just for the cells."

"You've got to be fucking kidding me." Jamerson snatched the key ring off LeMaines's belt and started trying each one of them on the lock.

"It's not going to open," Julie said, trying to keep her voice even. "Just like the keypad downstairs that led to the control room."

"We're not doing something right," Jamerson said. His voice was high in his throat. He jammed another key in the lock to no avail.

"Hey man," Aguilar said, taking a step toward Jamerson. "It's not gonna work."

Jamerson ignored him. He was halfway through the ring, sweat dripping from his forehead onto the floor.

"Hey," Aguilar said again, getting closer.

"Let him finish," Kurt said. "He needs to see for himself."

Jamerson jabbed the final key into the lock. It didn't turn. He swore, and started in with the first key again.

"Max," Coates said. His voice was patient, almost melodic. "We're burning time."

Jamerson hurled the key ring against the wall. "It would be nice. If we could get to *the fucking south stairwell.*" He bellowed the last few words, his face mottled. LeMaines picked up the keys and put them back on his belt. He began to say something to Jamerson.

"Quiet," Julie said. She had heard something. It was close. A scratching sound, like fingers on wood. She oriented herself toward the origin of the noise. A janitorial closet on the far wall.

"That closet big enough to hold folks?" Coates whispered to LeMaines, who nodded. Coates readied his Guardian and made a hand motion for Kurt and Jamerson to join him. The rest of the group backed up. The scrabbling sound stopped.

Coates flung the door open.

It was a cramped room. Slop sink, mop bucket, industrial cleaners. But there was just enough space for the two uniformed correctional officers inside. Both flung their hands up in front of their faces.

"It's us," LeMaines said. "The good guys."

The guards lowered their hands. From the heavy lines on his forehead, the first looked to be around fifty. The second was in his twenties, with a shiny moon face. His uniform shirt was untucked and one of the breast pockets had been ripped halfway off.

"Either of you injured?" Coates asked.

Both men shook their heads.

"Then come with us. We're going to the roof to call this in."

Neither man moved. Julie smelled the sharp tang of urine. She eyed the moon-faced kid. He had wet himself. He saw her looking at his stained pants and his face flushed.

Jamerson wrinkled his nose at the smell. "First time away from Mom?"

"Fall in, fellas," LeMaines said. "We're getting out of here."

The older man looked tired and uncertain. The younger's red face had become a mask of panic.

Jamerson was done waiting. "Just like those weak-ass guards downstairs. I ain't having it anymore. Do your job," he growled, reaching into the closet and pulling the first guy out by the shirt collar. He pushed him against the far wall and went for the second one, who recoiled and tucked himself deeper in the closet, halfway under the sink.

"I'm going to die in here," the moon-faced kid said from his hunched position. "I'm going to die in here and I have a baby boy at home."

"Shannon," Aguilar said. "Come out. Best chance you and your kiddo have is to link up with us."

"Right now," LeMaines said, "every one of the inmates on this floor is in a cell. But our system's crashed so in less than two hours, all the doors are gonna open. These guys are gonna be sitting in your laps. Same with the cons on the floors above you and below you. And no one is gonna be with you to help. And the phones are down, so there ain't no calling for backup."

"C'mon, kid," the older guard said. "It'll be okay."

From his cell across the block, a man in his sixties was lying on his back on the floor, using his folded hands as a pillow, and watching this drama unfold. He had cracked skin, sunspots near his temples, and his hair was dusted with white. Kurt seemed disengaged with the two correctional officers from the janitor's closet, but he was watching the inmate watching them with quiet interest.

"What do you think of all this, OG?" Kurt asked the old convict.

"Troubled times," the man said.

"What do they call you in here?"

"Nintendo."

"Seems like a young man's nickname."

"I think they was making fun when they gave it to me."

"What'd you do?"

"Robbed some pharmacies. Just with notes, though. No gun."

"Why are you in with the rapists then?"

"No room in General Pop. There was space up here."

"Why are you down on the floor?"

"Makes the room look bigger."

"These two fellas from the janitor's closet worth keeping?"

"Nope," Nintendo said. "Older one is too old and the younger one's too scared. Neither can fight for shit. They just gonna slow you down."

Julie noticed a harmonica on the stand near Nintendo's bed. Kurt saw it, too.

"That's bad news. You want to play me a sad song?"

"Why not?" Nintendo said. "I ain't doing nothing." He picked up the harmonica, played a few practice bars, and started in on a bluesy number that rose and fell skillfully.

At the sound of the harmonica, the inmate in the adjacent cell roused himself from his bunk. His cell door was open and he leaned against it, as if taking in the day for the first time.

"Is my penis talking too loudly?" he asked the group. He was parchment pale with sunken eyes and bowed legs. Like he originated from a crematorium.

"It's fine," Coates said, without taking his eyes off the moon-faced kid in the closet. "It's at just the right volume. But stay in your cell, keep it that way."

"What's his story?" Kurt asked LeMaines.

"Benjamin Queenan. He sodomized seven people. He promised not to hurt them and then told them it was Opposite Day."

"Kick-ass," Julie said. "Think I prefer Nintendo on harmonica."

"He's got AIDS, herpes, and syphilis," LeMaines continued. "He's basically a diseased dick with feet."

Jamerson cut in. "We done with our jam session?" He stepped into the closet and closed his hands on Shannon's hair, who yelped in response and tried to crawl farther under the sink. The other tail to his uniform shirt had come undone and gotten hiked up, freeing his chalk-white belly to spill out over his belt.

"Max, slow it down," Coates said.

Jamerson gave Shannon's hair a sharp tug and then released his grip. "Fucking hell."

Coates said, "You gotta come out of there, Shannon. Because otherwise you'll be the worst thing a person can be."

Shannon didn't meet the trooper's gaze. He was studying the floor in front of him.

"You know what that is?"

"No," Shannon said, still looking down.

"A coward. You won't ever shake it. It'll stain you. And when your son grows up, it'll stain him, too."

Now Shannon looked up.

"It'll be okay," the older guard said.

Coates's words took hold. Shannon stood and tentatively made his way out of the janitor's closet like he was discovering his legs for the first time. He retucked his shirt.

"Strike force just got stronger," Jamerson said.

"We'll take who we can get," Coates said. He introduced himself to the two correctional officers. The older one's name was Bryant.

"To answer the questions you're about to ask, no, I don't know what's going on with the doors or the comms, this woman is the governor's daughter, this inmate's name is Kurt and he's been helping us immensely, and our plan is to get to the roof and make a few phone calls to clean this place up." Coates paused and held up the Guardian. "And this gun is out of bullets, but don't tell the bad guys."

"Okay," Bryant said. "That's a lot, but okay."

Shannon looked at Bryant as if for confirmation. "Okay," the younger guard echoed.

"Back to the north side, up to four?" LeMaines asked Coates, who nodded.

"Lots of step retracing up in here," Jamerson said. "Feels like one long retreat."

"Just playing the cards we're dealt," Coates said. There was a decided note of weariness in his voice that worried Julie. Coates was her rock.

The group filed back toward the north door, but Queenan wasn't quite done. He put his hands to his cheeks and waggled his tongue. "Come over here and give me some of that sweet meat," he told Kurt.

Kurt paused, as if considering this offer. Then he said, "It wouldn't work out between us. You are from the country and I am from the city."

Julie burst out laughing. It was an odd reaction, all things considered.

"What do you...how do you?" Julie didn't even know what she was asking Kurt.

Nintendo gave one last toot on his harmonica as the group departed. Kurt pointed at him approvingly.

"Is this really happening?" Van Dyne mused. "It's like some kind of street theater."

"Add the harmonica part to your grad paper," Kurt told Julie. "Have some music in there."

I will, Julie thought. And she'd add the hanging man. And Micah cutting a convict's throat. And Queenan. And the kid who hid in the closet and peed himself. She'd put it all in. Her professor was a tough grader, but she'd probably at least get a B+ on the strength of the source material alone.

Back in the north stairwell, deep breaths, more water, resetting.

"How we doing?" Coates asked the group. A collection of nods. Coates checked his damaged hand. Noticed Julie looking at it. "Good enough for government work," he said with a faint smile. Kurt flexed his fingers. He seemed to be having hand trouble of his own. Jamerson turned his back to the group and fished a bottle of water out of the go bag. Julie noted he seemed to be busying himself with the bag longer than it took to just hydrate. She checked her phone. Fifty-four minutes left.

The group was cutting Shannon as wide a berth as they could in the confines of the stairwell, in part because of the odor of urine emanating from him and in part, Julie thought, on the chance his case of nerves might be contagious; the group was rattled enough as it was. The younger officer had recovered enough to take a photo out of his lone undamaged shirt pocket. Kurt was closest to him.

"So a little about me," Shannon said, forcing a smile. "I grew up in Branson and had my own small business before I joined the Whitehall staff. I'm married. I was talking about my son before. He's three months old. Want to see a picture?"

"No," Kurt said.

CHAPTER 25

Julie

Van Dyne said, "This system failure seems random to me. Like a glitch or a virus. I don't think there's some evil mastermind watching us on a monitor. If someone had really wanted to do us harm, they'd open up all the doors from the start except for the south ones, so there'd be no chance of escape at all."

Jamerson was drumming his fingers on the stairwell wall. He stopped when Van Dyne finished talking. "Doesn't matter how it started. We just need to ship outta here."

"Maybe you're both right," LeMaines said. "Now let's hit the fourth floor."

"Remind me who's on four?" Julie asked.

"It's the Psych block," LeMaines said. "In the academy, they tell us that sociopaths are about two percent of the adult male population in general. I'd say at least a third of this floor is. Maybe half."

"Four is complete crazies, man," Aguilar added. "They're probably playing soccer with a human head right about now."

"Do we want to try crossing on a higher floor?" Julie asked.

"One level above us is gangs," LeMaines said. "No good. Above that is death row. That's even worse. The folks on Psych are bad news, but a lot of them are heavily medicated. Makes them docile, on a good day."

"Medicated with what?" Coates asked.

"Depakote. Seroquel. Thorazine. Some other ones I can't pronounce."

"There's a guy who thinks this whole jail is a spaceship that's going to Reno," Aguilar said. "And another one who put a skillet on his head and robbed a Carl's Jr. with a drywall hammer. Then he ordered a milkshake, paid for it with his own money, not even the money he just got from the register, and when the police came, he was asleep in a booth."

"He comes to chapel sometimes," Van Dyne said. "He falls asleep there, too."

The group filed out onto the fourth floor. Shannon and Bryant took up position in back with Jamerson still on rear guard. No one was playing soccer with a human head. It was quiet. Even quieter than the sex offender floor had been. Which was somehow worse. They walked past yet another damningly vacant guard station. Two inmates were playing chess on one of the cellblock tables. They didn't look up at the sound of new arrivals.

Then Julie realized it wasn't completely quiet. She did hear something. Soothing music was playing at a barely audible volume. It was classical compositions interspersed with the sound of waves and rain. She looked at LeMaines and pointed to the ceiling.

"The Muzak is supposed to settle them down," LeMaines explained.

"Does it work?" Julie asked.

An inmate was running at them. Not quite on an intercept course, but close enough. He was completely naked except for a filthy pink head band. His entire body shone with sweat. Coates leveled the Guardian at him, but the inmate didn't even blink. He sprinted past them down the cell block to the far wall, touched it with his palm, and sprinted back. Then he did it again, running with high knees, making good time. He paid them no mind.

"Not really," LeMaines said.

"That guy's medication might be off," Kurt said.

"Some of them you could dope up all you want, they'll still show you the crazy."

Most of the inmates looked to be in their cells, but a few were shuffling along one wall, their padded slippers making rustling sounds on the floor. They wore tan jumpsuits that said *Psych* on the back and bulky sleeveless tops with Velcro strips on them. They looked vacantly at the newcomers. One of them waved. Without thinking, Julie waved back.

"Why are they wearing a different kind of shirt?" she asked.

"They're safety garments," Aguilar said. "Standard on this floor. The fabric they're made of is too tough to rip so it can't be made into a rope or a noose. And they've got no buckles and zippers they can cut themselves with."

The ten of them moved cautiously through the floor toward the south exterior stairwell, as if any kind of rapid movement would agitate the sluggish inmates. They approached the two chess players.

"Are those...?" Julie began, looking at the brown lumps the men were using for game pieces.

"Human turds? Yeah," Aguilar said. "We had to take the chess pieces away. They kept swallowing them."

Jamerson stopped and stood over the two players. He made a show of stroking his chin.

"Pawn to rook four," he suggested.

One of the two inmates looked at him. He had a half-shaved head. There was a glimmer of something in his eye, Julie thought, maybe comprehension. She wiped the sweat from her face. It was so damn hot, she could easily be seeing things.

"Who are you?" the man asked.

"Captain America," Jamerson said.

"Where are the rest of the Avengers?"

"They're coming. Hawkhead and Mothman."

The inmate nodded, as if this meant something. His opponent wasn't moving, but his hair was. A fat cockroach glided over his curly scalp.

Jamerson took a quick step back. "You fellas got any big holiday plans?"

"What are you doing?" Van Dyne asked. "This isn't getting us anywhere."

"Relax," Jamerson said. "Just trying to make peace with the locals."

"Enough," Coates said, casting a glance backward. "Check around. Look for more guards. Aguilar, go with him."

Jamerson walked away from the chess table with a bit more strut in his step. Julie figured that after Kurt made the trooper look like a fool at least twice, Jamerson needed that interaction, needed to come across as clever and cool, to exert his superiority over someone, even if it was just two sad-sack mental patients playing a board game with feces.

Aguilar and Jamerson swept the cell blocks. No guards. One prisoner on the lower level was rhythmically banging his head on his cell door, eyes closed, his forehead streaked with blood.

"Stop that," Aguilar said.

"Biscuits," the man replied without opening his eyes. He kept up the steady banging. Aguilar looked at LeMaines.

"I don't know," LeMaines said.

Julie couldn't blame him. She didn't know, either.

Jamerson stopped at a closed cell that bore a placard that said *Attention Staff: A.P. Inside*. "What's A.P.?"

"Assisted Person," Aguilar said. "Means they need a two-person escort getting out of their cell, for health or security reasons."

Julie walked toward the cell. She wasn't sure why. Coates followed her. "Stay close," he said.

The man inside the A.P. cell was small and bony, with thin lips. His face was angular and touched off by dark, almost black eyes. His features combined to make him look like a demented ferret.

"What's his malfunction?" Jamerson asked

"That's Raymond Janz," Aguilar said.

"Why does that name sound familiar?"

"The warden was talking about him," Julie said. "He killed prostitutes and scrambled their faces."

Janz was rocking back and forth and putting his longish hair in his mouth.

"Why does he do that?" she whispered.

"Probably because other people won't let him put their hair in his mouth," Jamerson said.

"Dude was just born bad," Aguilar said. "When that nurse handed him to his mother, a bunch of hookers were gonna die and there wasn't shit anyone could do about it. Be glad his cell door is shut."

"What's his diagnosis?" Julie asked.

"It's a lot of shit. He's bananas. When they arrested him, he was in the food court of a mall with no pants and wearing a dress shirt tucked into his underwear. And guess what was in the front pocket of that dress shirt?"

"Don't answer that," Rachel said. "It doesn't matter. Can we go?" The nurse looked openly irritated by this sidebar. Julie figured that was progress, Rachel showing anger. Better than being walled off by fear.

"Sorry," Aguilar said.

The group moved away from Janz's cell. "It's not a bunch of shit," LeMaines said. "He's been diagnosed with paraphilia sado-masochism, which is a disorder where sexual excitement is derived from pain and humiliation."

Jamerson looked quizzical.

"Been taking some online psychology courses," LeMaines explained.

"I have a secret," Janz called after them. His voice was high, but otherwise entirely without affect, as if he wasn't from anywhere. "Come closer."

"No thanks," Julie said without turning back. She liked her face where it was. Janz was enough to make her miss the inmates on the third floor.

"I don't do bad things anymore," Janz said. "I'm all better. Fixed, fixed."

Van Dyne was trailing a few steps behind the rest of them.

"Pastor?" Janz asked hopefully. "A quick prayer for a man who needs one?"

Van Dyne took a few steps to the cell. Julie thought nothing of it at first. It was his job, Julie figured. He was going to go do his job. She checked her phone. Forty-five minutes left before all the doors in Whitehall opened. She'd give the chaplain about thirty seconds before she gave him a time check.

Coates didn't want to even wait that long. "Don't," he told the chaplain. "Stay together."

Van Dyne turned in the direction of the trooper. Which meant he took his eyes off Janz.

Julie noticed motion behind her. Rachel had stepped forward and was pointing at Janz's cell. "His door!" the nurse called out. "It's not closed all the way!"

She was immediately proved right when Janz's cell door opened.

The inmate came out on all fours, scurrying. Like a crab. The movement looked natural, as if it were his preferred mode of travel. He had a small knife in one hand and he used it to make a long, hard cut on the back of Van Dyne's left ankle. The motion was so quick Julie had trouble tracking it.

Van Dyne let out a shout of surprise and pain and dropped to his knees.

Janz put the knife to Van Dyne's neck and pulled him back into his cell, showing surprising strength given his small frame. He shut the door behind him and dragged the chaplain to the back. He sat behind him cross-legged, the knife now a few inches away from Van Dyne's neck, but moving in small circles in the air.

"That was my secret," Janz proclaimed proudly. "Secret, secret. My door wasn't shut."

"Motherfucker," Jamerson shouted.

Coates moved quickly to the door. "Turn him loose," he said, pointing the Guardian through the bars at the con. Julie felt a stab of hope that the gun would spur Janz to let Van Dyne go.

"Stop talking to me," Janz said to Coates. "I don't like darkies."

"You got a key for that cell door?" Coates asked LeMaines without looking away from Janz.

LeMaines scanned the ring and thumbed up a key. "Yeah."

At the sight of the key, Janz put the knife back up to Van Dyne. A dribble of blood moved down the chaplain's neck to his shirt collar. He was breathing heavily and his eyes were darting left and right.

"I'm sorry," Van Dyne said, locking eyes with Coates. "I was stupid. Just, just go."

Jamerson grimaced, looked at Coates, and pointed to his wrist as if to say, *We're on the clock.*

"No," Julie said. "No, we aren't leaving him." *We're on the clock.* Julie thought of Jamerson's pointless, time-wasting conversation with the two men playing chess and wanted to stuff him in Janz's cell in exchange for Van Dyne. She took Coates's arm. "Derrick. Making it out of here isn't going to mean anything if we let him die."

Coates swore under his breath. He rarely swore. It took Julie aback. She could almost see him deciding what to do about the chaplain. Stay or go. Stay or go. He had the Guardian, but even if there was a shot to take that wouldn't unduly risk hitting Van Dyne, he didn't have any bullets.

"We can't," Julie repeated. She checked her phone. "We still have time."

"We have to—" Coates began and Kurt walked past him.

"I'll take that cell key," he told LeMaines, pulling him aside.

LeMaines looked at Coates for guidance. Coates did nothing for a few long seconds. Then he put his good hand over his bad one, as if this would help him make the decision. He nodded. LeMaines unfastened the key from the ring and put it in Kurt's palm. Julie knew that under normal circumstances, it would be absurd for a correctional supervisor to voluntarily hand over one prisoner's cell key to another prisoner. But she hadn't seen normal circumstances since this tour began.

"Tell me about him," Kurt told LeMaines.

"Huh?"

"Tell me about Mr. Janz."

"Ah, okay. His full name is Raymond Janz. He's a paranoid schizophrenic. He started off having sex with dogs in his neighborhood and killing them. Graduated to killing fourteen prostitutes. Cut up their faces and put them back in a different order with tools and glue."

"What do you call him?" Kurt asked.

"He likes being called Ray and hates being called Raymond. I think the regular guards on this floor make a point to call him Raymond because, well, fuck him."

"You have any kind of connection with him?"

"No," LeMaines said. "Hell no. I'm not up on this block enough."

Kurt turned to Aguilar, who shook his head. Kurt looked like he was going to ask Shannon and Bryant if they had an in with Janz but seemed to think better of it. Julie figured the two guards were of limited use to him. Kurt walked up to the front of Janz's cell.

"What you're saying isn't going to mean anything to him," Aguilar said. "He's insane."

Kurt ignored him. He sat outside the bars, cross-legged just like Janz was. Like he was about to catch up with an old friend.

What is he doing? Julie thought.

"Hello, Ray," Kurt said.

CHAPTER 26

One of Argento's former police supervisors, a lightweight sergeant transferred in from Written Directives, had once noted on Argento's annual performance evaluation that he had problems with interpersonal communication. *Too blunt*, the sergeant had written. *Not considerate enough.* He wasn't wrong. Argento knew he was not a social creature. Even when Emily was with him, he was content to go all day without speaking with anyone else. But when he did decide to talk, Argento thought he communicated just fine. So when he joined Detroit's SWAT team, he had taken an interest in hostage negotiation. His teammates used to joke that for someone who hated everybody, Argento was surprisingly good at it. He was able to connect with certain people. Calm them. Assure them. He had talked a battered wife out of shooting her husband and convinced an unhinged transient not to throw acid on a four-year-old boy.

But he had never had to work under the kind of time constraints he was facing in Whitehall with Raymond Janz. Even the most artful negotiations could take hours. Sometimes the better part of a day and into the next. But every minute he spent with the inmate was another minute closer to all the cell doors opening and their threat matrix expanding exponentially. And there was the failed air-conditioning to contend with; it had been Argento's experience that extreme heat never made anyone more reasonable. The totality of the situation he was faced with reminded him of something his father used to say: Things are never so bad that they can't get worse.

"You called me Ray," Janz said. "Everyone in here calls me Raymond."

"Which do you prefer?"

"I want to be Ray," Janz said in his toneless voice. "My mother called me Raymond. She bites. When I was seven, no one came to my birthday party."

"What are you in here for, Ray?"

"I changed people," Janz said. "They didn't like that. They didn't understand."

"I'd like to understand," Argento said. "But it's hard for me to concentrate when you have my friend in there, especially because he's hurt. Could you let him go?"

"I miss them," he said and gazed at the ceiling. The knife wasn't touching Van Dyne's neck anymore, but he still held it close.

"You miss the people you changed?"

Janz didn't answer the question. He looked at Argento, as if for the first time.

"Who are you?"

"My name's Kurt. I'm just a traveler."

"You have cameras in your eyes."

"I'll turn them off," Argento said. He put his hands to his eyes and made a twisting gesture with his palms.

"We're on deadline here," Jamerson began and Argento cut him off, addressing him without looking at him.

"Quiet," he said. "Until I say otherwise." He pointed at Jamerson apologetically. "I'm sorry. He's not with us. He's with them."

"Them," Janz agreed.

Jamerson began to speak again and Coates cut him off with a hand on his shoulder.

"Let him work," Coates said.

"The universe is a friendly place," Janz said. "We see ourselves in poison sprays. Rabbits have their eyes cut out."

"That sounds sad, Ray. About the rabbits," Argento said. Relaxed. Conversational. Just a casual chat with a madman who had just hamstrung the jail chaplain and now had him at knifepoint.

"Are you from the Agency?" Janz was holding the knife back up to Van Dyne's throat. Van Dyne shuddered and then stayed completely still. Argento's instincts told him it was better not to be from the Agency, because he couldn't imagine a man like Janz finding anyone from a business or organization taking his side. His instincts also told him that if Janz didn't like his answer, Van Dyne would be geysering blood. "No. I can't be. I'm part German. The Agency won't hire anyone from Germany." He watched Janz's reaction.

The inmate grinned. Accepting this response. He lowered the knife. "The Agency bites," he said.

Argento looked around Janz's cell. It was the standard size. Bed, stool, and desk, all bolted to the floor along with a toilet-sink unit. There was no television. There were no books or pictures. No art. No indication of any hobbies or interests. Nothing to stimulate the mind. It looked like a place specifically constructed for people to go to be insane.

Janz spoke again. "A spider was in my hair. It's retired now. End worms on hooks."

"This isn't working," Van Dyne said. Sweat was pouring down his face and he was holding his lacerated leg with both hands. "You can leave, Kurt. Everyone can. It's okay. I'm giving you permission to go."

"Reverend," Argento said. "With all due respect, zip it."

Janz said, "I have forty-eight and I'm trying to get to zero."

"Count backward by twos," Argento suggested.

"It's not working."

"Then stop," Argento said. "Tell me something you see."

"I see bars."

"Tell me something you hear, Ray."

"I hear your voice. You look rough but your words float."

"Tell me something you feel."

"I feel," Janz said. "I feel hot. The turbines are off."

The inmate was spot-on about that. The sweat had soaked through Argento's shirt to his coveralls, and perspiration was popping out on his brow.

"Ray, are you taking your medicine?"

Janz smiled widely. He had no teeth to speak of. Argento wondered if other prisoners had knocked them out, or if they had been like that.

"They make me take them," he said.

"Does it help?"

Janz answered, "The bees light on your fingers and show their engineering. I have achieved larva stage. They walk on my face and whistle."

"Do you like when that happens? Or does it bother you?"

"It reminds me I'm wicked. Wicked, wicked."

"Don't be so hard on yourself," Argento said. "It's the sin we worry about. Not the sinner. The sinner is doing the best he can."

Janz nodded, two quick nods and one long one. He liked that. "I am doing my best," he agreed.

"This man's name is Mark." Argento gestured toward Van Dyne. "Ray, why did you take Mark into your cell?"

"He's my treat."

"What if I gave you a different treat? Would you let Mark go?"

"I want friends." Janz scratched his lips with a dirty thumbnail and then narrowed his eyes. "Can I smell your tongue?"

"Ray," Argento said. "What if I gave you a different treat?"

"I want an airplane."

"Nobody's flying anymore. Gas is too expensive."

"I want ice cream."

"Okay. Let Mark go and I'll get you some ice cream. The guards have some in their refrigerator. I've seen it."

"Ice cream first," Janz said.

One of the cardinal rules of hostage negotiation was never give in to a demand, especially one for food or a beverage, until you get some semblance of cooperation. Otherwise you were just feeding and hydrating your target and giving them the fuel to extend the standoff. "Can't," Argento said. He jerked a thumb back toward LeMaines and Aguilar. "They won't let me. It's one of their silly rules."

Janz put the knife back up to Van Dyne's neck. The tip penetrated flesh and another trickle of blood ran down the chaplain's collar, turning the white crimson. The chaplain let out a soft grunt but remained still.

"Ice cream first," Janz said again. It was as coherent as he'd sounded.

Argento had to change tactics. Time to be more direct. It was risky, because he knew Janz was ultimately going to make decisions based on his own internal logic, however twisted, no matter how reasonable Argento or anyone else tried to be. But it was a risk he'd have to take.

"I need you to let Mark go," Argento said. "Even if you don't want to. Then I'll get you ice cream."

"Ice cream," Janz said. "What time is it? It's ice cream o'clock. Home van flies away because the formula is missing. They brought me a little bride." The tip of the knife went in a fraction deeper. Van Dyne twitched.

"Ray, I can be the good guy here or I can be the bad guy. I got both guys in me."

Janz withdrew the tip of the knife from Van Dyne's skin. "I want you to be the good guy."

Progress. "So do I," Argento said. "Will you let me be him?"

"Okay."

"Do you like jokes?"

"I like animal jokes."

"You're going to get two before ice cream. I'm going to give you one animal joke now and another when you let Mark go."

"What do you think?" Janz asked. He wasn't looking at Argento. He was staring in the direction of his bed. He moved the knife an inch farther away from Van Dyne's neck.

Van Dyne said, "I don't—"

"Not talking to you," Janz said. "Talking to her." He nodded at his pillow. He said something barely audible to it and then appeared to be listening.

"She says yes. She says we are goldfish in a bowl."

"I think she's right," Argento said. "So here goes. You ready?"

Janz blinked repeatedly and said nothing. Argento hoped he'd finessed a clear signal through the noise in Janz's head and the blinking meant yes. One of Argento's SWAT partners had children, so Argento always had a few kid's jokes at the ready. Most of them had to do with animals. "What do you call a camel with no hump?"

"When I was a boy, I had a dog," Janz said apropos of nothing. "Her name was Petunia Picklebottom."

"Humphrey," Argento said.

Janz remained utterly still for a good five seconds. Argento waited. Then Janz laughed without moving his head. The laughter didn't go with the rest of him. Like the sound had been piped in.

"Another," he said.

"Let him go, Ray."

"Another," Janz said, "but from him." He slapped the flat part of the knife on Van Dyne's neck and looked at the chaplain expectantly.

This was not part of the plan. That happened a lot with negotiations and you had to be nimble. To be prepared to launch Plan B when Plan A showed every sign of not working out. But Argento found himself at a temporary loss for words. He rushed through the metrics of putting the key in the lock, entering the cell, and trying to disarm Janz before the convict cut Van Dyne's neck open in a way that couldn't be repaired. Low probability of success.

"Another," Janz said in that affectless voice, flipping the knife around and introducing the tip back into the meat of Van Dyne's neck.

Low probability was better than none. Argento steeled himself for what he was about to do. No time to fumble with the zip gun. It would be a straight rush into the cell. Van Dyne would get cut. So would he. It was just a question of how badly. He was a half second from moving when Van Dyne spoke.

"Why do they call them chicken fingers? Birds don't have fingers."

"Ha!" Janz chortled. "Humphrey. Chicken fingers." He dropped his knife hand. Van Dyne didn't wait for any official declaration of release. He crawled toward the cell door. Argento sprang up, keyed the lock, and pulled the chaplain out with one hand. LeMaines slammed the cell door behind him.

"Ice cream, ice cream. I'm eating ice cream in heaven," Janz said in singsong.

Argento breathed deeply and handed the cell key back to LeMaines. He looked at the small convict, who had put his hair back in his mouth. Maybe he had grown up hard. Maybe he had parents that hurt him. But he had never learned how to be a person and it was too late to teach him now. "There's no ice cream for you. No heaven, either. Too many dead girls."

"Will you come to my birthday party?"

"Nobody's coming, bugnut," Jamerson said. "No one is glad you were born."

Rachel was attending to Van Dyne's cut ankle and lacerated neck. He was sitting down, a look of both pain and relief creasing his face. She dressed both wounds and wrapped them with gauze from the go bag.

"I can't put weight on it," he said.

"You're not going to be able to," Rachel responded. "I think your Achilles tendon is severed."

"You shouldn't have messed with our chaplain, Raymond," Aguilar shouted at Janz. "You *need* a minister. You need a team of them working around the clock."

Janz sat down on his bed with his shoulders slumped and pulled his pillow close. He said something to it. Then he went still. Almost catatonic. Argento didn't know what it would take to restart his brain but there was no need to stick around and find out.

Coates turned to Argento. "How did you do that? Where'd you learn it?"

"He's crazy. I speak crazy. I bet you do, too, but he said from the jump he didn't like Blacks, so he wasn't going to hear you. Not your fault he's racist."

"Trashman, right?"

"Had some interesting folks on my route."

"All right," Coates said, back to business and addressing the group. "Shannon, Bryant, can you help Mark get mobile? We need to roll out. I'm hoping we're about to hit our last stairwell."

The two guards came forward, seemingly glad to be needed. They hoisted Van Dyne to his feet with a grunt and he put one arm around each of their shoulders.

"Your joke was better," he said to Argento as he tested the weight on his remaining good leg.

"My Achilles wasn't cut," Argento said. "I could concentrate more."

"Didn't see you praying in there, Reverend," Jamerson said.

"I was praying. I was just keeping my eyes open. So I could see what was coming at me."

"Raymond Janz!" Jamerson exclaimed. "Man, some people have real problems."

"I forgive him for hurting me. He may not even know why he did it. Men like Janz, I don't know their inner life."

"Don't know if he has an inner life," Argento said. "Cut that guy's brain open and there'd be a couple of squirrels playing with twine."

"Maybe if the world had been kinder to him."

"How about if he'd been kinder to his victims?"

"I do not condone his crimes. But God will judge him, not me."

"All right, enough," Jamerson said. "This is why I quit Sunday school."

Van Dyne didn't reply. The chaplain likely didn't see the point. He knew he wasn't going to change Jamerson and Jamerson wasn't going to change him. Van Dyne hopped forward with the support of the two guards, and the group reassembled and moved forward through the rest of the cellblock. And stopped.

At the end of the fourth floor, just in front of the south stairwell, someone had strung up several grimy bedsheets as a long makeshift curtain. There were wide swaths of blood on the sheets, like a Civil War field hospital. The sheets were high enough and long enough that Argento could see nothing behind them. He felt an immediate and tangible sense of foreboding in an already foreboding place. This was the Psych floor, populated by violent, damaged inmates, some of whom had undoubtedly gotten their hands on cutting tools. The sheets might have resembled a makeshift field hospital, but behind the sheets, Argento knew, nobody was getting healed.

Jamerson spoke for the collective group. "What the Sam Fuck is that?"

CHAPTER 27

Julie

"What the Sam Fuck is that?" Jamerson repeated, as if someone had come up with the answer in the last two seconds.

"I don't know," Coates said. "But I don't think I like it."

A man emerged from behind the curtain, pushing it aside with a flourish, and walked briskly toward them. He was wearing the fourth-floor tan prison jumpsuit but he'd adorned it with a clip-on plastic flower. He was holding something in one hand. Julie couldn't tell exactly what it was, but she had the sense it wasn't a weapon. Coates pointed the Guardian at him. It might as well have been a water pistol for all the attention the man paid to it.

He stopped twenty feet away. "Hi hello," he said loudly. Like he was the official greeter of the cellblock. He was tall and broad, with thick arms and a woodsman's beard.

"Give him some space," LeMaines whispered. "That's Peter Vorbach. He's in here because he ate most of a guy."

"If he's got to eat one of us, I nominate Shannon," Jamerson said.

"Wait," Shannon protested.

Julie watched Vorbach keenly. He opened his hand, revealing what he held. It was a small plastic picture cube with family photos.

The kind you keep on a desk. She looked at the photos with a sinking realization. "Is that . . . the warden and his family?"

"Hi hello," Vorbach said.

"Whaddya got there, Peter?" Coates asked carefully.

Vorbach proudly held up the cube for the group to see. "It's my family. But they never visit."

"Okay. What's behind the sheets?"

"We made a fort."

"Where are the guards who were on this floor?" LeMaines asked.

"Some ran away. We kept one. I can show you. But don't get mad, okay? We'll clean it all up when we're done. Hi hello."

"Oh fuck me," Aguilar said quietly.

"Why would we get mad, Peter?" Coates asked.

"Jail is broken. Everything is canceled. So we made our own fun."

A chill shot up Julie's body. Like an auger boring into her chest. This bizarrely friendly inmate wearing a plastic flower holding the warden's picture cube. The bloody sheets. The absent guards except for one they kept. Something that needed cleaning up. And what was that smell? Curdled yogurt?

"I bet their idea of fun," Jamerson whispered, "is not our idea of fun."

"What do you want us to do here?" Bryant asked.

"Stand by," Coates said without looking at him. "Peter," he addressed the inmate. "Can you walk back over to the sheets and pull them aside? We'd like to see what's in there before we go any farther."

Peter turned and trotted back to the sheets. Eager to comply. The floor yes-man.

"Close your eyes, Julie," Coates said.

She couldn't. Wouldn't.

"Hi hello," Peter said. He pulled the sheets away, clamped his hands over his ears and began to hum.

Julie saw it in flashes then, not as a whole. There was no way to process the whole. Her brain struggled to make sense of even the few images her eyes were taking in.

There was a dead prison guard on the floor just past the curtain line. He was on his back, still in uniform. A canoe had been made of his body. There was no other word for it. His upper torso had been cut open, the rib cage cracked clear, the innards removed. An inmate in a tan jumpsuit was sitting inside him, his rear end plopped down in the hollowed-out stomach and his legs on top of the corpse's legs. Upon the curtain being opened, the inmate pantomimed rowing with an oar, as if part of some macabre performance art he and Peter had put together to entertain the floor.

Julie opened her mouth to speak but no words came out.

A second body was propped up against the wall near the south stairwell door. It was the corpse of an inmate, this one dressed in the purple of the third floor. His arms had been hacked off at the shoulders. An inmate in tan was sitting in the body's lap, drenched in blood. He had a meat clever in one hand and was reading a comic book. He looked up. Used the cleaver to point at the comic book.

"No," Julie said. Her voice came out as a croak.

Behind both men, the south stairwell door was blocked with mattresses and metal bunk beds. There was a third body on one of the mattresses. Medium size. White medical jacket. Probably male. But Julie couldn't be sure because something had been done to the body. Something... Julie turned away. LeMaines was still but Aguilar did a bunny hop backward, as if he had just touched something hot, and the motion caused Van Dyne to sag to the ground on his good leg. Julie looked at Kurt, who was normally expressionless. Even his face was drawn. She started to move. Coates put a hand on her shoulder and she shrugged it off and began walking briskly back toward the north doors, stifling the overwhelming urge to scream. She wasn't going to stay one more second there. She wasn't going to spend any time looking for logic where there wasn't any. This wasn't just the worst place she'd been. It wasn't just the worst place there was. It was maybe the worst place there could be. And she knew that even if the fourth-floor south stairwell doors opened automatically for them and there was a team of Army Rangers and armored Humvees on the other side waiting to spirit the group away, she would not pass by those bodies and the inmates using them as furniture in order to try and reach safety. It was a bridge she would not cross.

She looked back once before she reached the north door. LeMaines and Aguilar had picked Van Dyne back up and were moving as fast as they could with the injured chaplain, which wasn't very fast at all. The rest of the group was following. There was nothing else for them to do. But she saw Kurt separate himself from the pack. He approached the fringe of the open curtain and picked something up off the floor. Then he jogged back to join the others.

The naked man was still doing his wall-to-wall sprints. Slower now, but remaining on the go. He approached the caravan, cutting them a wide berth. Jamerson stepped off line and gave the inmate a violent shove, knocking him backward to the floor like a human pinwheel, sending up a spray of sweat from both men. It was a vicious and pointless act by the trooper, but after what she had just seen behind the curtain, it struck Julie as grotesquely amusing. Why not. She knew she had just passed over a sort of mental threshold. No, not just passed over. Bounded over, to meet whatever darkness waited on the other side.

Coates used Pillaire's ID on the north stairwell door. It opened and he ushered everyone through before slamming it behind him. "You okay?" Coates asked Julie, although he hardly looked okay himself.

"Yes," she said, the clearest lie she'd ever told.

CHAPTER 28

The only sound in the north stairwell was the group's ragged breathing. Julie broke the silence. "Some people are let into this world by mistake."

"Could you tell who that guard was?" Aguilar asked LeMaines, his voice breaking.

LeMaines shook his head. "Carrasco and Smitty are supposed to be working up here but there wasn't... enough to... I couldn't tell."

"Maybe it was an inmate we saw? They just put a guard uniform on him? I mean, they're already doing fucked-up shit."

"Maybe," LeMaines said, a note of hope in his voice.

Argento didn't buy it for a minute. Another one of their coworkers was dead and they didn't want to face it. He couldn't blame them. But it was magical thinking.

"I don't think God likes us very much," Aguilar said. He had untucked his uniform shirt and used it to wipe the sweat off his face.

"Maybe he just thinks highly of our abilities," LeMaines said gruffly.

"Fuuuck," Jamerson said. "Not sure about all that. But what I do know is that I'm gonna start saying 'Hi hello' to people. It's like twice as friendly."

"Was that Dr. Lau?" Aguilar asked. "On the floor? In the white jacket?"

"Don't know," LeMaines said. "The clothing fits, but... no face."

"Jesus, the guy with the comic book and the cleaver," Julie said. "Who was that? What was he locked up for?"

"I can't remember," LeMaines said. "But I'm pretty sure it's bad."

Aguilar rubbed his face with his hands, as if willing himself back to a reality that made sense. "Should we have tried to push through anyway? I mean, the dead people were already dead."

"Don't know if you saw but the stairwell door was blocked off with beds," Coates said. "Would take a minute to clear it. I don't imagine those boys with the cleavers would just stand by and watch us work."

"Rachel?" Aguilar asked.

The nurse was on the floor, hugging herself, both hands wrapped around the beads of her necklace. Shut down inwardly.

"Rachel," Argento said. "Can you check Mark's ankle?" It would give her something concrete to focus on besides what they'd all just seen.

Rachel nodded wordlessly. She rose and examined Van Dyne's ankle. The minister was seated on the stairs. Despite being the most injured of them all, and what he'd just witnessed, the chaplain seemed strangely at peace.

"How about that floor?" Jamerson said with an odd casualness. "Those dudes need to slow down so they'll have something to do tomorrow."

"You talk too much," Argento said. He was close enough to the trooper to smell his odor. The heat and exertion had them all dripping. Jamerson's pupils looked bigger than they should have. He was also measurably more relaxed than he'd been on the floors below. Oxy. From the go bag. Argento figured he must have snuck some on the fly. "You leave enough for the rest of us?"

"Enough what?"

"Painkillers. Your pupils are blown up."

"Nah," Jamerson said, looking at a space between Argento and the wall. "You're confused."

"I don't get confused. Being on pain meds when you're just chasing the high is gonna slow you down. Dull your reflexes. Means you're a liability. Means you're not qualified for the job you're holding."

"I'm sick of you," Jamerson countered. "When you get killed in here, and it's gonna be soon"—the trooper pointed to Argento for emphasis—"I'm just gonna fucking laugh and laugh."

"Max," Coates said.

"What?"

"You straight? You clear?"

"You really asking me that? Based on what an inmate says?"

"I can see your eyes, too," Coates said. "How many did you take?"

"Don't you check me in front of these civies," Jamerson replied. "Don't you dare."

"Uh, Kurt?"

Everyone looked toward the sound of the voice. The tension was momentarily broken. It was Julie and she was staring so hard at Argento her eyes were nearly shut.

"Why do you have that?" She was fixated on what Argento was holding, the item he'd picked up from near the bedsheet curtain. It was a severed arm from the inmate's body that the man with the meat cleaver had been sitting in. It still had part of a purple sleeve attached.

"I want to know, too," Coates said. "And I kind of don't."

"We might need a prop," Argento said. "Owner of the arm won't care."

"A prop for freakin' what?" LeMaines asked.

"I'm thinking ahead. To the fifth floor. Where we're going to need to get their attention."

"Is this something that people do?" Julie said, looking at the arm and then looking at Coates for confirmation.

"I don't know," Coates said. "But I didn't know that people could do what was going on behind those bedsheets, either, so it's a day of firsts." He turned to Jamerson. "That conversation we just started, we're gonna finish it when we get out of here. And you're not going to like how it goes."

"Yeah" was all Jamerson could manage in reply. He did a slow roll of his neck and eyed Shannon and Bryant. Both men had looked dumbfounded since setting foot on the floor. "You clowns have anything to add to any of this?"

Both men shook their heads.

"Super glad we picked you up for the team."

Van Dyne rose to his feet and hobbled to the stair's handrail. "I have some things to say."

"Chaplain," Coates said. "You have the floor."

"First, thank you. Kurt, for getting me out of that cell."

"That situation was avoidable. You can make it up to me by keeping your distance from the rest of the maniacs."

"That won't be an issue. I'm leaving."

"Leaving?" Julie was visibly taken aback.

"You got a secret exit we don't know about?" Jamerson asked.

"I'll go back down these stairs to the chapel. That's where I should be. I can't walk anymore. It takes two men to move me and even then, it's slow. My presence will just put you all in more danger."

"Mark, you don't have to," Julie said. "We have enough people here to get you to the roof."

"All I've managed to be since I joined you is a liability. It's not fair."

"Like she said," Coates said. "We'll carry you on our shoulders."

"My decision is made."

"Shannon, Bryant," Argento said.

The two guards looked his way.

"Why don't you escort the good chaplain back. Stay with him, make sure he's safe."

"Yes," Shannon said. "I'm . . . I'll do that."

Bryant nodded in assent.

"Will that suffice?" Coates asked Van Dyne.

"More than I deserve. I appreciate these men coming with me. But God is my fortress."

"Some fortress," Jamerson said. "Remember when you got cut and captured by a freak with a knife."

"Whitehall is dangerous. I knew that when I accepted the call to serve. My goal is to bring God's word here. But under these circumstances, I am dead weight to you."

"So we're just supposed to abandon you to whatever hell is downstairs?" Julie asked.

Van Dyne shook his head. Sweat dewed his scalp. He looked exhausted but resolute. "To continue with you like this would be to turn my back on my calling. And I'm not abandoned. I have these two men, I have God, and I have whoever is waiting for me in the chapel."

"You trust in God even through all this?" Julie asked.

Van Dyne nodded. "Who else is there?" He turned to Argento. "I'm a minister, so I hope you'll allow me this, Kurt. I see suffering in you and doubt. I don't have all the answers. My faith doesn't tell me what God is up to in all this. It just tells me I'm called to be in Whitehall. You have to figure out the same thing. Where you're being called." He extended his hand and Argento shook it. Still a working chaplain even with a debilitating stab wound. It was a plus in the Episcopalian column. LeMaines flipped through the duty ring until he found the key that would get the men through the first-floor stairwell and handed it to Bryant. Van Dyne hobbled down the stairs, Shannon in front of him and Bryant to the rear. Shannon's shirt had come untucked again and he was now missing a shoe.

"Are you guys good or—" Shannon began just as they rounded the corner.

"We're good," Coates said, cutting him off.

"I'll never forget you," Jamerson said. He turned to LeMaines. "Impressed with your quality personnel."

"That's what a starting wage of fourteen dollars an hour and crap training gets you."

"Let's move," Coates said.

"Up to five?" Julie asked.

"Up to five." Coates reached his hand out toward Jamerson. Something unspoken passed between them. Jamerson handed Coates the go bag, his face utterly expressionless. His narcotics supply had just been cut off.

Julie moved in close to Argento. "Can we trust him?" she asked quietly, a clear reference to Jamerson. It surprised Argento, because it sounded like a question she'd ask Coates instead. But maybe she wasn't sure if Coates could be objective.

"Not a lot of other options."

The seven of them trudged up the steps to the fifth floor. Gang Population. Coates looked through the window. Then he stepped aside. "Everyone take a look. I need some feedback on what I'm seeing."

They all took turns. Argento smelled a whiff of something burning. Saw a host of inmates in black prison togs with equally dark skin. Congregating like it was a picnic. A few were practicing knife takeaways. One was doing handstand push-ups against a wall. A trio of inmates were lounging in chairs in the guard station, one of them flipping through the log book. The source of the burning smell was a smoking mattress near the back of the block. The good news was Micah wouldn't show up here, at least not anywhere near this crew. Given the racial animus in most state pens, it was no place for a white man, not even a fast one with a knife.

Rachel followed after Argento. He could hear her breath accelerate upon seeing the cellblock full of threats.

"That's a lot of inmates and a lot of open cells," Rachel ventured. "The most we've seen so far."

"Too many," LeMaines said. "And these guys don't play. They got all damn day to sit around and think of creative ways to hurt people. Most of them will kill you for a blunt."

"We'd need a magician to get through there," Aguilar said. "The Vegas kind."

"Let's hold off on making plans until we know what the problem is. Break down the demographics for me," Coates said, turning to LeMaines and Aguilar.

LeMaines took the question. "We've got two main prison gangs on this floor plus a few stragglers. First is Westmob, a Black gang, and second is the Kindred, our Aryans. The cellblock is divided by a security gate because they can't play nice. Westmob is on the north side, the side we're seeing. The Kindred are on the south side."

"So we're just seeing half the floor right now?" Jamerson asked. "The Westmob half?"

"Right."

"So if we can get past Westmob, we still have to deal with the Aryans on the other side of the security gate."

"Who's worse?" Julie asked.

"Kindred are more volatile, but they're both organized and disciplined. All these cons have is time. Time to train, to practice fighting. You should see them in the yard. They do group exercises. This whole floor is a fucking death squad. And I know they have weapons. There's probably a knife for every man on the floor and then some."

Julie put her hands up, fingers spread apart, as if she could physically measure the metrics of their choice. "What if we dropped back down to three? See if that door is opening by now?"

"Way things have been going," Coates said, "I don't like the odds."

"Then up to six?"

"No," LeMaines said. "That floor, it's all monsters. Every last one. There's a lifer up there, Dimitri Medov, he...I don't even know where to start. The police had to shoot him in the head to stop him. Didn't even kill him—it just gives him migraines when it's too loud."

Aguilar asked, "So we gonna plow through a floor full of angry Westmobs? With an empty gun and your bad hand and two women they're gonna want to take from us? And then go through a door and do the same with our Nazi fucks, who are even worse?"

"Maybe they'll fight us one at a time," Jamerson said. "Like in the old karate movies."

"We're on the fifth floor but it's like we haven't made any progress," Rachel said. "We're still trapped." Her hair had come partially undone from the band, and she retied it. Julie watched her and did the same. It was a good play, keeping your vision unobstructed when inmates with meat cleavers were close by.

"Like Janz's pillow told him," Aguilar muttered. "We are all goldfish in a bowl."

"Okay, let's put our heads together," Coates said. "Best plan wins."

An idea meritocracy, Argento thought. The smartest ideas would rise to the top. His wife had taught him the word *meritocracy*. She'd been a reader.

After a moment, Coates asked, "Anything?"

Everyone was looking at Argento. The curse of the competent.

"Do we have the key to the door that separates the two sides?"

"Right here," LeMaines said, patting his key ring. "Even if the key card doesn't work, we can pop it manually."

"You said the gangs don't play nice. So what if we opened that middle door? Let the Westmob have at the Kindred and vice versa?"

LeMaines nodded slowly and then with increasing head speed, until he looked like a Bobblehead. "It'd be a bloodbath. They're spoiling for a fight. That's why they're divided in the first place."

"So they tussle. We wait a tick until the dust settles and hope they cancel each other out enough that we can cross."

Coates said, "Thin the herd."

"Is that... right?" Julie asked.

"Right as in correct or right as in ethical?" Argento asked.

"Ethical."

"Look around," Jamerson said. "This the best time for ethics?"

Argento would have to agree with Jamerson. It was true a lot of the bangers on the floor probably didn't have a hell of a lot of choice in what became of them. When you were a drug lookout at age nine and carrying dope and guns for the older set at twelve, you were on a doomed trajectory. You expected to be here, in state prison. This was where your friends went. Where your parents went. You were in the place where generations of poverty and awful role models, drug abuse, and shitty choices invariably brought you. But Argento wasn't going to get too sentimental about it.

He told Julie, "The people on this floor probably aren't going to be rehabilitated. It's okay not to feel bad if they decide to hurt each other. And we'll be giving them a chance to fight for a cause they believe in, even if it's wrong."

Julie didn't respond.

"Hell, we're not telling anyone to fight," Jamerson said. "If they do, it's on them."

"Our plan depends on them fighting," Julie said.

"Don't penalize us for knowing human nature."

"I know everything has gone to shit," Julie said forcefully. "But we are going to be judged for our decisions here."

"I think," Argento said, "that a judge is going to cut us some slack."

"Julie, I respect where your head's at, but I agree with Kurt," Coates said. "You want tidy answers, but I don't have any. We gotta give ourselves a little room to operate on this one. Now, I can go in there and open the connecting door. I'm the only one here who's the same color as Westmob. It ain't much, but it's going to have to do."

"No," Argento said. "I'll go."

"Why? You tired of living?"

Argento thought about that. This life might not have much more to offer him, but he was too stubborn to leave it. He had the Pacific waiting for him. Emily in his head telling him to do his best, her voice clear even in this hellhole. And now he had the added motivation of returning to the Rocker County Sheriff's Department and giving them some much-needed attention. "I try to do one nice thing per day."

"How do you plan on accomplishing that without getting shanked the minute you step on the floor?"

"That depends," Argento said, "on whether the good Sgt. LeMaines is willing to loan me something on his belt."

CHAPTER 29

LeMaines looked down at his waistline and looked up without comprehension. "What do you want to borrow?"

"Tell me about that can of T46 spray," Argento said. He had first noticed the cylinder on Spentz's belt, the guard who had been killed outside the infirmary. It was labeled *T46 Malodorant*.

"It's—" LeMaines began and then raised his eyebrows. "Hell, I can't tell you much. I've never even used it. It's military surplus. The bosses got it for cheap a couple of years ago in case of prison riots, but they were supposed to be used along with gas masks so the guards didn't breathe in the fumes. But when we got our shipment of masks, some of them didn't fit right and some of them were broken. So most of the cans have just been collecting dust. The only reason a few of us old-timers still carry it is because we already put the holder for it on our belt and it's a pain to strip all the shit off the belt and then rearrange it the way it was before."

Argento glanced at Aguilar's belt. The younger guard didn't have the T46. He was probably too new to have been issued one. Argento was familiar with military surplus. There was a time when the U.S. Armed Forces were selling gear on the cheap to police departments across the country. DPD had gotten in on the action. Argento had been on SWAT at the time, and his unit had received an armored vehicle, a truckload of smoke and gas grenades, and some rifles with bayonets. There was nothing in the DPD's manual authorizing bayonet use, so Argento had hung one bayoneted rifle up in the SWAT armory for kicks and put the rest in deep storage. He didn't know the military fire sale had extended to private prisons.

"How bad does it smell?"

"The brochures we got said it's like diarrhea and spoiled eggs. I guess it was designed by Israeli Defense Forces as a crowd-control measure against Palestinians. They sprayed it with a hose."

"Sounds promising. I'll put some of that on, Westmob will steer clear of me, I'll unlock the door, and come on back."

"We don't have a decent mask for you," Aguilar pointed out.

"I'll hold my breath."

"Okay, but then we'll all be retching from your smell when you return," Julie said.

"We'll need something to neutralize it. What did the brochure say about that?"

"There's some kind of special soap that clears it out," LeMaines said, "but I don't know if we have it. They said a fire extinguisher would more or less do the trick, too. Absorb the odor."

Argento nodded at the fire extinguisher in a case across from the stairwell door. "Done."

Coates asked, "How'd you think up a thing like this?"

"When I was on the first floor fishing around in Sarrazin's ass for a pirate cell phone, it smelled bad. Everyone stepped away from me. I'm banking the T46 will be like that, except worse."

"Couldn't you just use pepper spray to clear the floor?" Julie asked.

LeMaines shook his head. "It's most effective against people with lighter skin, which Westmob does not have. Plus, some of them seem inoculated against it. Last time I sprayed a guy on this wing, he opened his mouth and asked for more. Like it was flavoring he'd put on his meat."

"T46," Coates said. "If it's good enough for the Israeli Defense Forces. How much are you going to use?"

"All of it," Argento said.

"That," Coates said, "is going to be as unpleasant as hell. Let's go back to Plan A. I'll do this. We've already asked a lot out of you, Kurt. Plus I'm actually getting paid right now. You're not. Doesn't seem right to ask you to work for free."

"How many kids you got, Derrick?"

Coates paused. Giving personal information out to convicts would go against his better judgment. But Argento must have built up enough credit in the bank because he said, "Three."

"How old are they?"

"Eight, eleven, and fourteen. All boys."

"So why don't you sit this one out? It's gonna take two good arms anyway, and you only have one."

Coates looked down at his bandaged hand. He looked back up at Argento. Something different in his eyes. A reassessment, or realization.

"Garbageman," he said, almost to himself. "Right. Westmob isn't going to much like seeing a white face on the floor."

"I have broad appeal," Argento said.

"No doubt. But you've been pushing hard. How much you got left in the tank?"

"About two-thirds. More than enough to get us home."

Jamerson said to LeMaines, "Lemme see that shit." The guard handed the trooper the canister. Jamerson squinted while he read the instructions. "Says here not to get it in your eyes. Also says it won't stain garments." He handed it to Argento.

Aguilar asked, "Is this going to work?"

"Trust the process," Argento said.

"What process? There's a process here?"

"I think he's being sarcastic," Julie said. "He does that a lot."

It was a familiar refrain to Argento. Emily used to say the same thing. She had chided him about it: *You make jokes but you don't care if anyone gets them. Plus you're so deadpan, it's confusing. It makes it hard for people to relate to you because they don't know when you're joking.*

Long as you know, Argento had said.

He had worked on that. For her. But now she was gone and it didn't matter. "It might work," Argento said to Aguilar. "They can't stop me if they won't get near me."

Aguilar said, "It just sounds like you're guessing."

"Well hell, kid," Argento said, turning to the guard. "I don't think I've done this before."

Jamerson chimed in. "What if, when the door opens, the two sides form society's first harmonious interracial gang?"

"Then it'll be another chapter for Julie's grad paper."

Coates checked his watch. "We've got thirty minutes left. Anything else you need?"

"I'll take an N95. It's not much but it might take the edge off. Safety glasses if you have them."

Coates rifled through the go bag with his still-working hand. He gave Argento a paper N95 mask with a rubber band strap and took one for himself. "No glasses. I wasn't planning for whatever we're calling this. Anything else?"

"Some intel," Argento said. "Who are the two worst guys on this wing from Westmob?"

"Take your pick," Aguilar said. "They're all awful."

"Uncle," LeMaines interjected. "He's the worst. Runs the whole block. Like a cult leader. Big slug-looking guy. Why do you ask?"

"I'm guessing the door separating the two wings isn't going to stay open by itself. I'm going to need to wedge it."

Aguilar looked confused. "You're gonna use an inmate to do that? How? You're just going to ask nicely?"

"No, I'm gonna make them do what I want. I shouldn't have to explain this to you."

"Sorry," Aguilar said. "I've never met anyone like you before. I'm just trying to keep up."

"Uncle is a big boy," LeMaines said. "Runs over three hundred. It'll be hard to move him. Besides, he mostly just stays in his cell. People come to him, bring him what he wants. But there's plenty more to choose from. We got a guy they call Gizmo. He robbed a church for the collection plates and shot an usher who wasn't moving fast enough."

"He robbed a church," Argento said.

"Yep."

"How will I know him?"

"He's about six-four and has a big tattoo of a centipede on his right cheek."

"Okay, how about a backup in case Gizmo is locked in his cell?"

"Dude named Chewy did a drive-by of a rival but accidentally shot his own passenger and paralyzed a bystander. Little girl, six years old. Fucking tragic."

"What's Chewy look like?"

"He's about five feet tall, bad acne. Real bad. Like he's got gulches in his face."

"Gizmo and Chewy."

"You shouldn't go in there alone," Julie said. There was a look on her face that Argento took to be genuine concern.

"It was his idea," Jamerson said.

"They're my fellow inmates. I'm sure we'll get along fine."

"I'd never forgive myself if something happened to you," Jamerson said.

"Ignore him," Coates said. "He's not good with people. I want to thank you. For everything you've done and what you're about to do."

"It's the Lutheran way," Argento replied. "Now I'd suggest everyone give me some room. I'm about to dump this stuff on me here and hit the door. Have some water and that extinguisher ready for when I come back."

The group didn't hesitate to oblige and moved down the stairs, giving Argento the fifth-floor landing to himself. He donned the N95 mask. LeMaines went through the key ring, removed the key to the door dividing Westmob from Kindred, and handed it to him. Argento held his breath and popped the top off the canister of stink spray. Then he used the key card to open the door. It would be one combined movement, stepping through the doorway while dumping the contents of the vial over his coveralls and letting it trickle down to his shoes, sparing his eyes and mouth. It would be bad. But Argento already knew what bad looked like.

Time to tilt the odds in his favor.

Time to wake the fifth floor up.

CHAPTER 30

Argento vomited as soon as the stink spray made contact with his shirt, which meant he was no longer holding his breath. He was just fast enough to raise the bottom of his mask so the vomit didn't cake the insides. The odor was as advertised. It was diarrhea, old eggs, and rotting flowers. It was ripe offal mingled with curdled cheese. A dead whale festering in a gassy sewer. All of it augmented by the heat. The smell burrowed itself in the scent receptors in his nose, and added a foul layer to his skin. His eyes watered and he coughed up more vomit. This time he wasn't fast enough and the regurgitation spattered the inside of his mask.

It occurred to him he might not have fully thought this plan through.

The overwhelming smell had consumed all of his senses, temporarily shutting off the outside world, but he found his footing. Audio began seeping in. Shouts. Curses.

"Wood on the floor," someone yelled. *Wood*. Prison slang for a white man. Or maybe it was the specific word for a puking white man.

His throat tightened. He was built to withstand this. To focus on the mission. To suck it up and deal.

"Motherfucker stank!" someone howled.

An inmate with wild hair ran at him. Stopped within ten feet. Threw up. A second inmate approached, but from farther away. He threw up, too. Either the odor reached that far or he was just a sympathetic vomiter.

"Get the fuck out, wood," someone behind him growled.

Argento didn't reply. It was all he could do not to heave again. He moved briskly toward his goal, the door separating Westmob from the Kindred. He could see it in the distance, a haze filtered through watering eyes. He passed two guards, prone, bodies twisted beyond repair, both with shirts stuffed in their mouths. One had a knife sticking out of his chest. Maybe they at least went down swinging. Sometimes that's all you can do in this life. The odor propelled him forward. He dry-heaved. His stomach had nothing more in it. He had already thrown up everything he'd ever eaten and everything he ever would. Moving fast now, sweat rolling off his hair, down his forehead, into his eyes. The door was dead ahead. It was a shit assignment he'd chosen. It should have been someone else's job.

Except he was the someone else.

He always had been.

CHAPTER 31

Julie

The conga line had spread down the stairwell when Kurt had said he needed room. Coates was the closest to the stairwell door, with the extinguisher at his side, a silent watchman. Behind him was LeMaines, then Julie, Aguilar, and Rachel, with Jamerson taking rear guard. It was the same configuration they had started their Whitehall ascent with, except Kurt was on the floor on his mad mission and Van Dyne was no longer with them.

Julie ran her tongue over dry lips. There were salt stains on her shirt from sweat. The stairwell felt like a hundred degrees. She knew she had to be focused. But her thoughts drifted to her fiancé, Eric, who was quick to laugh, slow to anger, and would always wake before her and have coffee ready. To her best friends who would be there on her wedding day wearing the ruffly pink bridesmaid dresses her mother had picked out that they would all laugh at but wear without complaint. To her father, who would move heaven and earth to take her away if he knew what was going on in this place. To her mother, who would drop whatever she was doing and join him.

Whitehall Correctional Institute was an example of entropy, which meant complex systems tend to split apart and get chaotic. One of her grad school profs liked to refer to it when discussing high-crime neighborhoods. But an advanced degree wasn't required to call what was behind her and what was still in front of her chaotic.

Julie wasn't blind to how the world worked, especially for those people who grew up hard. She had volunteered at a low-income health clinic using her college Spanish to translate for indigent clients. Her Teach for America experience in Philly trying to manage a raucous high school classroom featuring angry, damaged kids, some of whom towered over her, had at times been harrowing. But other than kicking the inmate in the groin on the first floor, the only physical altercation she'd been in recently was shoving a handsy drunk in a college bar. The imminent prospect of danger had been a largely abstract concept to her. What she understood now was that in a place like this, the difference between life and death was paper-thin.

She noticed one of her hands was trembling. What she felt wasn't just fear. It was terror. No, that wasn't it. More than terror. It was horror. Horror that wanted to take root in her and spread its gnarled branches.

"You okay?" Coates asked her again. The avuncular kindness in his words and face made her want to give him a ferocious hug. He had his own problems. His injured hand. His flighty partner. Getting back home to his wife and boys. But all she could see him worrying about was her.

"Just trying to keep my head above water."

"Me too." He looked through the window. Checking Kurt's progress.

"That canoe that one man made out of another man. You're not going to top that." She wasn't trying to sound flip, she couldn't if she wanted to, it just came out that way. But Julie figured that if she could name it, this unimaginable thing, then she could face it, and if she could face it, she could overcome it.

"Jules," Coates said, still looking out the window.

"Yes?"

"We got this. We're gonna get you home. I don't care if these prisoners eat each other or burn this place to the ground. I care about getting you out of here safe and sound. That's the mission."

"How's he doing? Kurt?"

"Lost sight of him a minute ago. But looks like everyone on the floor is giving him all the space he needs."

Could Kurt pull this off? It seemed like a fool's errand. But she had seen him already dispatch half a dozen men who were trying to kill them. When he took action, when he fought, he made it seem natural, practiced, like something he had done thousands of times before.

She looked for Jamerson. He was standing alone, tapping his baton against his thigh, far enough away to be out of earshot.

"What about Max?"

Coates drew in a breath. "Gonna watch him. Gonna keep him on a leash." Then he met her gaze. There was pain and regret there. "Julie, I messed up. I know I vouched for him, but I vouched for the guy I went to the academy and worked the streets with. That's not him anymore. He didn't used to be like this. Antagonizing everyone, making bad calls in the field. He's trying to hide it, but I think the dope's got him bad."

"You didn't know. It's okay."

"It's not," Coates said.

"I have to go to the bathroom," Rachel said. Her voice was unnaturally loud in the close confines of the stairwell.

Julie looked behind her at the nurse. Rachel hadn't spoken for so long that she wasn't sure she had heard her right.

"What's that?"

"I have to go to the bathroom," Rachel repeated.

Rachel's statement was the first time Julie remembered the nurse saying she needed something, and it was just out of place enough to make something flicker in the recesses of Julie's mind. Something else out of place that she'd seen on the second floor. The thought was still only half-formed.

"Can you, ah, hold it?" Coates asked, still training his gaze on the window.

"No. I can just walk down the stairs and go in the stairwell. I don't need a bathroom. It's gross, but I'll make do."

"I'll go down there with her," LeMaines said. "Keep an eye out."

Julie could see Coates working this through. "I don't know how long Kurt is going to be on the floor, but when he's done, we'll still need to wait a while for it to clear. So we have a minute. But make it fast, please."

Rachel turned without another word and descended the stairs. LeMaines followed.

"I need to talk to you," Julie heard LeMaines tell Rachel. Something in his voice. Not quite urgent, but close to it.

Then the sound of their footsteps faded and they were gone.

CHAPTER 32

As Argento pushed ahead, he was aware of motion around him. Something small and metal whizzed past his head. Was it a paperweight? No, you wouldn't be allowed paperweights in state prison. It would have to be some kind of hand-crafted missile weapon. He was hoping no one had gone further and jerry-rigged a crossbow. Or a zip gun like his.

He took glances left and right as he moved. Looking for Chewy and Gizmo. He passed two men having sex in a cell. It looked consensual. Good for them. Anywhere you can find love in this world. But they weren't Chewy or Gizmo. He might have to grab a ringer. The heat and smell were creating a visual haze that made him want to squeeze his eyes shut. Steady. Steady now.

A man well over six feet tall loomed in Argento's vision. He turned to get out of the way of the toxic plume approaching and Argento saw the long centipede tattoo on his cheek. Gizmo. The gangster who robbed a church and shot an usher. Argento headed right for him.

"What you doing, fool?"

Acquiring a door stop, Argento thought. He took hold of the inmate and dug his fingers into the nerve underneath his ears, the mandibular angle pressure points that, when he'd been a street cop, had made suspects rise on their toes and pledge allegiance to Argento's cause. Gizmo gagged and flailed weakly. A shooter, not a fighter. Argento frog-marched him to the door separating the two gang sides. He opened it with the key card. Gizmo's eyes widened. He didn't have any friends on that side of the block. Argento bent, twisted at the waist, and unloaded a diffused strike at the base of Gizmo's neck that rocked the man into the wall.

"Don't rob churches," Argento managed to say without vomiting.

Gizmo improbably stayed on his feet. He wasn't out yet. Argento hit him with another blow to the same spot, faster and more vicious. Sometimes he got better results the second time. Gizmo's eyes went dark and Argento caught him before he fell and laid him down in the door opening to prop it.

"Don't shoot ushers," he coughed out. Opening his mouth let in more of the stink, but it needed to be said. He allowed himself a quick look up to the Kindred side. A dozen white faces with bald heads and swastika tattoos. The usual bullshit. More pointing. Shouting. Men approaching. Argento didn't think they'd charge through the door. It would take a minute for both sides to get oriented to what was happening. But it was time for him to make a dignified exit.

The path back to the north stairwell door looked clear. He moved toward it, the image in his mind that of a diver straining back up to the water's surface. Argento wasn't getting used to the smell, but he could breathe a shade better. No one was throwing things at him anymore. Westmob's attention had been drawn away from him to the open door and the imminent Kindred threat. He saw Westmob forming up ranks. Argento looked back and watched a few Kindred step through the now open door over Gizmo's still form.

Argento was twenty feet from the exit when the inmate blocked his path. He was about thirty with a powerlifter's build, African-dark skin, and a long, braided goatee. But that wasn't what struck Argento about the man. What drew Argento's eye was that something was protruding from both the man's nostrils. A thin, fleshy growth. Argento knew just enough biology to identify it as nasal polyps or something in the same family. Whatever the case, it was a natural barrier that would drastically reduce the inmate's sense of smell. Which meant that to this inmate, Argento's T46 odor weapon wasn't a weapon at all.

Argento's first thought was *You gotta be kidding me*.

His second thought was to duck. Because the man was swinging a standard issue prison sock at him. Argento moved in time and the sock missed his head and tagged him high on the left shoulder. He heard a clicking sound. The pain was immediate. The sock was weighted, likely with a padlock, and was the equivalent of getting smacked with a pair of nunchakus.

Fucking kidding me, Argento thought.

Argento expanded his baton and smashed it down at the closest striking surface available to him, which was the inmate's right arm, aiming for the dense nerve cluster in the forearm that would cause him to drop the padlock and renounce fighting for the rest of his natural life. He hit pay dirt and the inmate cried out, a howl that died as soon as it left his lips. The body's instinctive reaction to pain was avoidance, and the inmate staggered back a few steps. Argento went with the momentum and rushed the man, pushing him down on his back. Argento stood over him, raised the warden's borrowed size eleven Merrell hiking boot above the man's head, and stomped down once. An unearthly sound escaped the inmate's lips. Argento stepped over him on the way to the door. No time to admire his handiwork. The din behind him had intensified. Westmob and Kindred. Introductions were being made. Weaknesses were being assessed. Knives were coming out.

He banged on the door once to announce his return. He heard the door lock click from the other side. Other than his blurred vision, throbbing shoulder, and general unsteadiness on his feet, everything was going his way. This penitentiary was a cinch. He threw the door open for the big finish, barreled through, and held his mask to his face to avoid inhaling as he was greeted with a shower of white foam.

CHAPTER 33

Rachel

While Argento was still working the floor trying to open the door between Westmob and Kindred, Rachel was taking the stairs two at a time, putting much needed distance between herself and the group. She stopped when she reached the first-floor landing. LeMaines had matched her pace and was right behind her. Rachel looked up. No cameras in the stairwells. The company that had tried to take Whitehall fully digital was supposed to install them, but had never finished the job. It was typical for Whitehall. The place was a bad joke. The last, desperate stop for someone seeking employment. But Rachel was a nurse with two drunk-driving convictions and her job opportunities were few and far between. She couldn't afford to be choosy. And even her tenure at Whitehall was far from secure. There had been complaints. She heard through back channels that Dr. Lau had filed one himself, accusing her of negligence. Of insufficiently securing medications. Of failing to maintain proper boundaries with patients. His death would slow the investigation but wouldn't stop it. If her license was revoked, not even Whitehall would keep her.

LeMaines stayed midstairwell while Rachel pulled her pants down, squatted, and relieved herself in the corner. Like an animal.

But it wouldn't be that way for her, not for long. She had plans. She had a partner. And they shared the same vision. They would start over, leave Whitehall far behind them, like it never was. When she had finished, she started back up the stairs.

"Rachel," LeMaines said. He came down to the first-floor stairwell. Partially blocking her path. She looked up at him. LeMaines had taken his professor glasses off. He wiped them on his shirt pocket, as if girding himself for a difficult conversation. A blotch of sweat ran from his shirt collar to his belt line. He looked exhausted. He was an out-of-shape man not used to maintaining this kind of pace. None of them were. "This place," he said softly.

"This place," Rachel echoed.

"I know about you and Micah," LeMaines said. "There's been rumors floating around for a while, but today sealed it." He searched her face for a reaction, but Rachel didn't give him one. He pressed on. "When I saw Micah kill that inmate, I knew. There was no reason for it unless it was personal. Micah killed him because these walls talk and he must have found out the man attacked you in medical. Then I saw you mouth a word to him on our way off the second floor. I'm no lip reader, but it looked like you were saying 'roof.' Telling him where we're going."

Rachel nodded. Denying would only make it worse. It would make LeMaines more on guard. He was no moron, not like the rest of his colleagues. She wasn't surprised he'd figured it out. She was only surprised she had kept it a secret as long as she did. She knew it was risky whispering to Micah, but it was a risk she had to take.

"How long has it been?"

"Not long," Rachel said.

"How'd it start?"

"He came in for treatment. Dr. Lau left us alone for a minute. We got to talking. It just happened."

"You really think there's any future in it?"

"No," Rachel said. Painting on her most disappointed-in-herself face. "There's no future. It was foolish. You know how Whitehall is.

How it can make us. I was weak. Lonely. I'm trying to break it off. He won't listen."

LeMaines looked up at the ceiling, as if for guidance. Then his gaze fell back on Rachel. "The others have to know. They have a right. This changes things. It puts us all at risk. He's still after us."

Rachel nodded some more. Going along to get along. Trying to buy some more time to think. "I understand. I'm sorry." Humble. Contrite. What he wanted. What he expected.

"Rachel, it's against the law to have relations with prisoners. I can't let this go. Even with all of this going on around us, I can't. I'm a sergeant."

Rachel was nodding so much she thought she'd get a neck cramp. "I know, Ronald," she said. Using his first name. The personal touch. Putting him at ease. "I appreciate you not bringing it up in front of the group. It would be embarrassing."

"We've known each other a while. Figured I owed you that much. Better if it comes from you first. But you have to go upstairs now and tell them. No need to get into all the details. Just keep it simple. And when this thing is over and DOJ sweeps in here with their fifty investigators, you can get out in front of the story. I'm sure he pressured you. Maybe he threatened you. Maybe he's done it before. There's gonna be mitigating factors. You can explain. And I'll do what I can to help."

Mitigating factors. Pressure. Threats. LeMaines with his cheap online psych courses, talking above his station. Micah had never threatened her. He hadn't needed to. Rachel wanted to be with him just as much as he wanted to be with her. She wasn't lying when she said she appreciated LeMaines not bringing her and Micah up in front of the others. But not because it would embarrass her. Because it made what she was contemplating doing just that much easier.

"We need to go back upstairs," LeMaines said.

"I know," Rachel said. She'd been a trauma nurse for fifteen years. She had treated serious stab wounds before. She knew how they were inflicted, so she knew how to inflict them herself. Micah had showed her. Her hands closed on the scalpel she had taken from the infirmary and kept in a plastic holder in the pocket of her scrubs. A shiver ran through her body. Was she going to do this? Did she even have a choice?

"Rachel are you okay?" LeMaines had put his glasses back on and was now looking at her attentively.

No. She wasn't. She was about to do something she couldn't take back. She felt like she was being controlled by some force outside of her. Like Micah was standing next to her whispering guidance in her ear. Earlier, he had proven his love for her when he'd taken the life of the inmate who'd assaulted her in the infirmary. Now she would demonstrate her love by taking a life for him. She hated Micah for making her do this. And she loved him for making her do this. Because it meant they could still be together, not in the pit that was Whitehall, but out in the real world.

"Ronald," she said.

"Yes?"

"What's up there?" She pointed to the ceiling. He looked. Human nature when you weren't as suspicious as you should be. His chin tilted up, exposing his wide, sweaty neck. She swung the scalpel. Aimed for the artery. He never saw it coming. The bright red blood spat out and hit the wall eight feet away, like a high-pressure hose, and kept spraying, painting the wall crimson. LeMaines sank to the floor, both hands reaching up to his throat, trying vainly to stop the torrent of blood. Rachel got out of the way. LeMaines looked up at her, shocked, pleading. Rachel knew that the arterial bleed meant he had about another thirty seconds to live.

"I'm sorry," she whispered. "I am. But I lied. We do have a future." She shut her eyes and pushed LeMaines's body down the stairs with her foot. His body flopped over itself and was still. And then, just like that, it was over. She had done it. It was already behind her. She took no pleasure in the act. She liked LeMaines. He had always been civil to her. But he was in the way. They were all in the way. But Micah would show them. They had a plan, the two of them. She would help him get out of Whitehall in the medical supply truck that came by once a week. She knew the driver, knew the schedule, knew the truck itself and all its hiding spots. Once he was sprung, she would quietly tender her resignation, citing stress. They would reunite. They had a place all picked out. Winnipeg, Manitoba. One of her distant relatives had a cabin on an inland lake that was all but abandoned. It was rugged. Quiet. Neither of them minded the cold. No one would come looking for them there. They could fix the cabin up. Find jobs using the forged documents Rachel had bought on the street, using a contact from one of the inmates in General Population in exchange for narcotics from the infirmary. They could begin their life together.

Rachel was still trying to fully process how today's events would affect their blueprint. Perhaps it would accelerate things. Micah had the master key. Could they leave earlier? Could they leave today? Micah would know what to do. She just needed to talk to him.

She took hold of the beads of her necklace. Ran them through her fingers. The medallion at the end of the necklace that she kept hidden under her shirt looked like the steering wheel of an old-fashioned sailing ship, but it was actually half of the Buddhist Dharma Wheel. Micah wore a necklace with the other half. Neither of them were remotely Buddhist, but Rachel had chosen the Wheel because it symbolized serenity and represented what her life with Micah would be like on the lake in Winnipeg. They had worn the necklaces covertly for months, and it gave her a secret thrill to walk the halls of Whitehall with it on.

When Rachel had composed herself, she went back up the stairs. The group was still spread out from the fourth floor to the fifth waiting for Kurt to save them all. They were stressed, banged up, and on an infernal ticking clock. And they trusted her. Which meant even if they thought of the right questions to ask about LeMaines, no one would go looking for him, not even Aguilar.

"All good?" Jamerson asked.

She nodded. Transformed back into the scared, docile nurse they were used to.

"Where's LeMaines?"

"He took off. He said Van Dyne would need more help in the chapel."

Jamerson shot her a quizzical look. So did Julie. Julie's gaze lasted longer than it should have. Did she...? No, Rachel thought. She didn't know anything. She was a pampered political heiress out of her depth in here.

"I think that might have been an excuse," Rachel said. "I think he was just scared to go farther. With his weight, his blood pressure, everything that's happened."

"Are you serious?" Aguilar asked, his face bunched in confusion. But he would believe her. They would all believe her. She was a reliable senior member of the Whitehall staff. A medical professional. And they were fools.

Trooper Coates was the only one she wasn't so confident she could sell. He seemed to know people. But he was distracted. He hadn't taken his eyes off the window since Rachel had returned. Too busy tracking Kurt on the floor. She saw him stiffen and put on his N95 mask. "Everybody stand back," Coates shouted. "He's coming in hot."

A bang on the door. Coates opened it with the key ring. Even though she was a flight and a half of stairs away, Rachel caught a huge whiff of the worst odor of her life. Then she heard Coates let fly with the extinguisher. Kurt was back. The target. The man that Rocker County Sheriff Rokus had called her about. Booked under the name Chris Spielman, but actual name Kurt Argento. Looked like a guy from action movies. It wasn't the first call she had taken from Sheriff Rokus. She was the conduit for all of Micah's messages and delivered them during his frequent visits to the infirmary. She knew exactly how much Rokus would route to Micah's account if he completed the assignment. It was the seed money they would need for their new life on the lake in the ice and quiet.

Kurt had saved her in the infirmary, there was no doubt. That meant something. She would tell Micah this so he would kill Kurt quickly. No need for him to suffer. But if Micah couldn't get to Kurt somehow, then she would. His money was her money now. They were bound together and they were no longer meant for Whitehall.

They were meant for the cabin in Winnipeg.

And Rachel was going to ensure that they got there.

No matter where it led.

No matter how it ended.

CHAPTER 34

Argento was so disoriented from the pain to his left shoulder and the redolent odor of the T46 that when he came through the stairwell door, he collapsed on the floor, making sure to go down on his right side to shield his collarbone. He had the presence of mind to hold his N95 mask to his face and squeeze his mouth shut when Coates doused him with the white dust of the fire extinguisher. He didn't want to inhale any more chemicals. He could hear Coates gag.

"Get another one," the trooper coughed. A ten-second delay, and then Argento was hit with another blast from a second extinguisher. And just like that, the odor of the T46 dissipated, absorbed by chemical foam.

Argento ripped off his mask. The desire to rub his face was intense, but he used a water bottle to rinse off so he didn't get fire retardant in his eyes. He used another to run over his torso.

"Talk to me when you can," Coates said.

Argento gave him a thumbs-up.

Aguilar was bouncing on the balls of his feet, like he was watching his team retake a fourth-quarter lead. "He did it. Told you it would take a magician to get through."

Presto, Argento thought. His vision looked like it was being filtered through oatmeal. He shook his head to clear it. He had to figure out whether he should tell LeMaines and Aguilar about the two dead correctional officers on the Westmob side of the floor. If he broke it to them now, it could shut them down. If he said nothing and they saw the bodies for themselves, it'd be the kind of horrific surprise that would compromise them on the floor. He opted to stay silent. No clear reason why. Just a gut feeling. He rose and tried to move his left shoulder. A piercing pain ran through his collarbone from the inmate's padlock. He winced as he handed the key back to Aguilar.

"What is it?" Coates asked.

"My collarbone's broken."

"What does that mean for us?" Julie asked.

"Nothing for you. Means I need to drink more milk."

"Rachel, can you—" Coates began.

Argento cut him off. "Don't put a sling on me."

Coates nodded. He knew. It would make Argento look vulnerable, chum in the water for the predators of this floor. "That couldn't have been fun."

"My sinuses are clear." Argento took a look at the group. "Where's LeMaines?"

"Cut and ran," Jamerson said. "Showed his true colors."

"Doesn't sound like him." It seemed, in fact, like the exact opposite of the veteran officer. Seemed a lot more like Jamerson.

"Enough about that coward," Jamerson said. "How does Westmob look?"

"A little rowdy," Argento said.

"What's next?" Julie asked.

"I think some bad things are gonna happen to some bad people."

Coates went back to the window, leaving footprints in the white powder that coated the floor. He used his shirtsleeve to wipe the flame retardant off the glass.

"They're having at it," he said. "Full tilt."

There was a colossal smack on the stairwell door. Coates instinctively took a step back. The smack was followed by continuous banging.

"That door gonna hold?" Jamerson asked.

"Not an expert on doors, man," Coates said.

"It'll hold," Aguilar said. He caught Rachel's eye. "Tell me about LeMaines again?"

"He left. Said his key card would get him through. He just didn't seem himself. But he wanted to see about Van Dyne in the chapel. He told me he was sure we'd be okay."

"I can't believe it." Aguilar put his hand against the wall and leaned into it. "Guy was steady."

Argento noticed blood spatter on Rachel's shirt that he hadn't seen before. He tried to recall which floor of Whitehall it might have come from. It was hard to pin down. There had been a lot of bleeding on a lot of floors.

On the other side of the door, the banging had subsided. Faint shouting could be heard. The occasional sound of metal on metal. Then relative silence. Coates used his other shirtsleeve to clear the rest of the window.

"I see something," Coates said.

"What is it?" Julie asked.

Coates strained forward. "Bodies."

CHAPTER 35

From what Argento could tell through the window, there were a few downed members of Westmob but the Aryans had suffered the worst of it. Several of them were scattered across the floor, bloody and motionless. Westmob must have MacGyvered a crossbow because one of the Aryans had what looked like an arrow stuck through his head. Not an undesirable outcome. No one would be playing the harp for dead white supremacists.

"We're walking this floor," Coates announced. "And we're going past the south door and up to the roof. I don't care if there's another flesh canoe at the end. I don't care if there's a butcher army with knives. This is the last stop and we're going to push through. Whatever it takes." His voice was clear and unruffled. A proclamation. It was what the group needed to hear.

"If the door to the south stairwell works," Aguilar said.

No one answered. If that door malfunctioned like the one two floors below...Argento could see the group collectively trying to process it. What that would mean. How it would feel. But Argento figured the universe needed to give them a break. They were long overdue.

"It'll work," Coates finally said.

Aguilar went to the window and peered out. "Kurt made some inroads, no doubt, but there's still Westmob on the floor and probably some Kindred that retreated back to their side. Looks like the rest are locked in their cells."

"Hardest part isn't going to be the fighting," Argento said. "Hardest part is going to be talking our way out of fighting." He picked up the inmate's severed arm he'd collected and brushed the white from the extinguisher off it.

Aguilar looked incredulous. "You're gonna use that as what, a club?"

"If you want to be taken seriously, sometimes you have to show you're a little crazier than the other guy." Argento motioned to Coates. "Hand me that go bag." The trooper complied, and Argento tossed the arm on top of the rest of the gear.

Jamerson said, "You need to be released back into the wild, dude. You should not, like, be among people."

Before he met Emily, they used to joke that DPD's Internal Affairs had a dedicated Kurt Argento wing. But she'd changed him. Not overnight, but eventually. She had told him to be good to people whenever he could. To not forget that everyone came from a mother and a father. To try and put himself in other people's shoes. When the Detroit Police Department had assembled a task force to review their policies and procedures spurred on in part by protests for racial justice, she said he should be on it. He didn't think it was a good fit, in part because he hated meetings, but she told him DPD needed some work and they could use people who were fair and honest. He'd listened to her. He'd agreed that DPD needed work, although probably not more or less than any other city agency in Detroit. But he tried to picture himself in that meeting room biting his tongue the first time some fired-up activist claimed the police were clearly the single biggest problem in the inner city. Sometimes he had a glimpse of that room. But when she got sick, he stopped trying to picture it. He couldn't sit in a room. He needed action, movement. Violence. And with her death, that was all over. He was back to his old self. His true self. Jamerson was right. He did belong in the wild. He was a savage.

"You want to go over your general game plan here?" Coates asked.

"Gonna make it up as I go. But if we're going to pull this off, I'm the only one who talks. The only one who says anything at all. You copy?"

There were murmurs of assent, save for Jamerson.

Coates held a hand up. "Hang on. What are you gonna say?"

"I'm gonna say what I'd listen to if I were a gangbanger and some con I didn't know came on my floor and flexed on me."

"You are one interesting son of a bitch," Coates said. He was looking at Argento with respect. Not the kind of grudging respect he'd shown earlier, but with the kind he might show a colleague.

"It's gotten me this far."

"Okay." Coates wiped his hands on his pants. "Kurt's on point. Everyone else fall in. We ready?"

"Ready," Rachel said with the most resolve that Argento had heard from her.

"Ready," Julie said.

"Ready," Aguilar echoed.

Jamerson was silent. Almost expectant. As if he was waiting for someone to tell him he didn't have to go. He didn't like Argento being on point, but maybe he was too doped up to care.

"Max?" Coates asked.

"Sure," Jamerson said finally. "Why not."

Argento put his hand on the door. He had been telling Coates the truth when he said he was making things up as he went. He didn't know exactly what he was going to say to any Westmob or Kindred who blocked their path. But he knew it would have to be stark. Uncompromising. He'd have to sell it in word, deed, and posture. Inmates could sense false bravado. Saying all the right things wouldn't mean jack without the body language and intent to do grievous harm that went along with it. And saying the wrong words at the wrong time? Like a spark in a mine full of coal dust.

Argento held up Pillaire's ID card. The door went green. He opened it and stepped back through the looking glass.

A foul odor washed over them. The T46 still hung in the air, fading but still pungent. It wasn't enough to make Argento throw up again, but it did start his eyes watering. He walked over Nose Polyp, who was laid out flat on his back, sock padlock still in hand, intermittent shallow breaths the only sign he was still in the land of the living. The five remaining members of the group filed in behind him. It would have been nice to have LeMaines. Argento already missed his steady presence and knowledge of the floors and their occupants.

Argento counted eleven Westmobbers in front of them, spread out on the floor. From their ranks, a group of three came to meet them. Like a scouting party. A big man with a thick neck, beard, and prominent pop eye took the lead. His tattoos were all black and blue. It would take ten minutes to read them all. Argento assumed the base colors were because they were done in jail. Hard to get colored ink in the joint. All three men's faces were devoid of expression in standard jailhouse fashion.

"Ain't you the stinky fucker that was just here?" the bearded man asked. "Let those peckerwoods in from next door?"

"Yeah. Liked it so much, thought I'd come through twice."

"We cleaned them up good," the bearded man said. "Some of them is still crying. Don't think they was ready for us."

"You be in the wrong place, wood," the second of the group of three said. He was about half the size of the bearded man but louder.

"No, I'm in the right place. I just walked onto your fucking ship. But I don't want it. Got my own ship I'm captain of. Just passing through."

"We already got a captain," the bearded man said. "His name Uncle. He in there." He motioned behind him to a cell that Argento couldn't see into.

"I'm sure he's running things the way they're supposed to be run."

"I don't know you," the second man said. "And if I don't know you, you ain't shit."

"I'm new," Argento said. "And you don't want to know me."

The bearded man looked at the five in the group behind Argento, who were silent. "This all you got for backup, whitebelly? Thinking of partying with your ladies."

"Maybe later."

"Fuck later," the second man said. "Talking 'bout now."

Argento assumed some, if not most, of the Westmob members he was looking at were armed. He didn't see any weapons, but that didn't mean anything. When he taught officer survival at the academy, he showed a training video where a skinny, unassuming teenager wearing a windbreaker started taking out concealed firearms and placing them on the table in front of him. He took them from his windbreaker, from his pants pockets, front waistband, rear waistband—a total of eight handguns, including an Uzi. For the coup de grace, he removed a pump-action shotgun from his pants leg.

"Let me tell you how this is gonna go," Argento said. "I'm walking these folks to the south stairwell door. Tell your people to stand down."

"What you got planned for us, wood?" the third con asked. He had a hoarse voice and a lined face.

It was time to show them. Argento set the go bag down and pulled the severed arm out. He tossed it at the bearded con, who flinched when it landed at his feet. The fine art of persuasion.

"Look to your right," Argento said.

The bearded man stared down Argento defiantly. Then his eyes flicked right to the second man.

"See him?"

"I see him."

"Now look left."

His eyes flicked left to the third man.

"You see?"

"You know I do, wood."

"You jump bad with me, say your goodbyes. Both dead. Then we'll do you and work on the rest. We might not get you all, but we'll get most. And that's on top of anyone you've already lost today."

No one said anything. The bearded man raised a hand in a slow-down gesture. Took a step back and craned his neck toward the cell he'd indicated was Uncle's.

"What's Uncle say?" he hollered.

A pause. Then someone from inside the cell shouted back, "He say it up to you."

The bearded man turned back to Argento. "You got sack, talking to us like that."

"That's why I'm the captain."

"I ain't got nothing to fear from you. My guardian angel won't let me be harmed, blood."

"Sorry to be the one to tell you this," Argento said, "but she took the day off."

"We got us one problem," the second man said.

"What's that?" said Argento.

"We seen how you done Gizmo and Lester."

"Don't get all broken up over Gizmo. He robbed a church. Lester the one with the unusual nose?"

"That him."

"Gizmo'll live. He'll just wake up with a headache. And Lester didn't give me much choice swinging at me the way he did. He might talk funny for a while but he'll be all right."

"You got all the answers, boy," the bearded man said.

"I got some. Now back up and let us through."

The bearded man hesitated. He didn't seem used to hesitating.

Argento decided to fill the silence. "You don't have to think on it. I already did your thinking for you. Besides, it's too damn hot in here to be fighting."

"Give up the shorty," the bearded man said, pointing his chin at Julie. "Rest of you can pass."

Argento wasn't going to give them Julie. Rachel. Or Aguilar, or either of the troopers. He wouldn't have given them a bottle of water or a crust of bread. He knew who he was dealing with. Wolves. If he gave them anything, they'd keep coming back until they'd taken it all.

Argento took out the zip gun. It was time for it. He pointed it at the bearded man.

"Fuck, son," the bearded man said. "That little toy ain't nothing."

"Put a hole in your face you didn't have before."

You don't know how absolute someone's position is until you've tested it. Argento was testing the bearded man. Banking on the zip gun, their numbers, the shock value of the severed arm to put them over the top. It all came down to this. Whether this man would fight or whether he would stand down so he didn't risk losing anyone else.

The bearded man made his decision. He stepped aside, his paunch jiggling with the motion. Made a gesture to the open space behind him.

Argento signaled the group forward with bladed fingers like refs did to show a first down. They moved ahead in their makeshift conga line. The bearded man and his two companions let them by but followed because that's what wolves did. They were passing the guard station where the two murdered correctional officers lay and Argento glanced at Aguilar, but he was so focused on the three men from Westmob that he walked by without noticing his fallen colleagues. A rare victory on a day of losses. The group approached the separation door that Gizmo's body was still propping open. Apparently the rest of Westmob hadn't thought highly enough of Gizmo to reposition him. Maybe they didn't like people who robbed churches, either. Just because they were in the same gang didn't mean they were all fast friends.

Argento let the group file out in front of him through the door and covered their exit with the zip gun as he walked backward. There were few Kindred to speak of. Several were in their cells watching the group. When they saw Aguilar, they shouted to be let out. The ones free of their cells on the floor looked to be in rough shape from the Westmob brawl. One was in the corner screaming, a jagged piece of bone sticking out through his upper thigh. Not one of them appeared ready to mount an attack at the moment, but Argento stayed close to the back of the line in case that changed.

Argento tossed Coates Pillaire's ID card and then stepped back so he could watch the three followers from Westmob and the trooper at the same time. Coates held the card to the reader. The light turned green. He heard Julie gasp. Heard someone else hiss "Yes." Good, Argento thought. Time to evacuate. Jamerson was standing near him. A few feet to his left. A few feet behind him. The trooper turned. Squared up to the three bangers.

"That's right, bitch," he said reflexively and then stiffened as he realized what he'd done.

A ripple went through Westmob.

The wrong words said at the wrong time.

Like a spark in a mine full of coal dust.

CHAPTER 36

The bearded man moved first, much faster than his heavy frame would suggest. He got in front of the door to the south stairwell just as Coates was opening it and slammed it shut. The second man shouted "West side!" The third stabbed Jamerson in the arm with a screwdriver, and the trooper howled in pain.

The conga line collapsed.

There were times when the best tactical decision was to hang back and take in the scene, then plot the safest and most effective course of action. And then there were times when you simply accelerated. Argento went with the latter. There was no clear field of fire, so he pocketed the zip gun and lashed out with the baton. He battered the bearded man in the head and hit the second man with the back swing. But he wasn't fast enough to get to the third man, the one who had just stuck Jamerson. Jamerson was furiously sidestepping, but the third man was still coming hard at the trooper. Until Jamerson took hold of Aguilar and pushed him in front. Using him as a human shield. The third man stabbed Aguilar in the upper chest, once, twice. Aguilar stayed on his feet and struck out weakly with his baton. Jamerson seemed momentarily paralyzed by what he'd just done. Then Coates bashed the third man in the head with his own baton, straight down, like he was driving in a tent stake. The third man's skull audibly cracked and he was out of the fight.

More bangers from Westmob were coming through the middle door fast, like a dam had been unblocked. At least seven, drawn by the second man's howl. The hue and the cry. Two Kindred Argento hadn't noticed before must have been waiting in the wings for them because they rushed to intercept and then backed off when they realized that Westmob had arrived and they didn't have the numbers. Coates tried to open the door again. A Kindred materialized and tackled him to the floor. Argento kicked the convict in the head, making his body flip from his knees to his back.

"What do we do?" Rachel shrieked.

"Stay behind me," Argento rasped. His left shoulder was on fire from swinging the baton. The oncoming Westmob had been only momentarily slowed by the two Kindred. They were upon them. Argento went to work. He was quick. Ruthless. He was what the situation required. He dropped the lead man with a blow to the knees. Someone got behind him and wrenched his baton from his grasp. He wrenched it back. Smashed a Westmob face into the concrete floor. Elbowed a Kindred in the throat. A burly Westmobber caught Argento around the neck and squeezed. Argento went to one knee and flipped the man over his shoulder. The gang member landed with an audible "Ooomph." Argento strangled him with both hands until the capillaries in his eyes broke.

He looked up. Exhausted. He could see Coates out of his peripheral vision using the Guardian to pistol-whip the man who had tackled him. He searched for Jamerson. Saw him hunched over Aguilar's still form, mumbling something, an apology, an excuse, but it didn't matter because then the trooper was on the run, pursued by several members of Westmob. It looked hopeful for him for a moment. He was fast enough and was using all the space available to him, like a defensive back going sideline to sideline. At one point, he tried to scale the sides of the bars to reach the second level. But there was nowhere to go. Jamerson was pulled to the floor, kicking and twisting, a fish trying to avoid the net. He took a savage blow to the head from what looked like a lead pipe. He stopped struggling. And just like that, he was pulled through the doorway to the Westmob side of the divide.

There were only two more members of Westmob to contend with and no Kindred in sight. The first looked young and uncertain. The second was older, short, with a heavily pimpled face. Chewy. The one LeMaines had told him about who'd paralyzed a six-year-old in a drive-by. They were looking at one of their fallen, the man that Argento had just strangled on the jail floor.

"Get up, blood," Chewy said.

"He's not getting up," Argento said.

"I'll kill you," Chewy proclaimed, although his breath was labored and there wasn't much steam to it. Like Gizmo, he was a shooter, not a brawler. A five-foot nothing trying to save face in front of his fellow gangster.

There was some type of verbal judo that was called for in response but Argento couldn't think of it so he said, "You can't. Fuck off."

Chewy stayed put for just long enough to say he had, and then took two stumbling steps back and left with the first man, disappearing through the divider.

The floor was now as clear as it was going to get, so Argento assessed the damage. He started with himself. He had taken some hits, but all his major systems seemed good to go. There was a white finger on the ground nearby. Argento checked his. He had all ten so it came from some other bastard. He looked for the rest of the group. Jamerson was gone. Coates was standing in front of Julie, his suit torn at the elbows and knees, a stream of blood running down his temple. Julie and Rachel both looked shaken but uninjured. Aguilar...

The correctional officer was motionless on the floor on his side. Argento hadn't been able to track what had happened to him in all the chaos, but his injuries were far beyond the two stab wounds Argento had witnessed. Blood had seeped out of his ears and a clear liquid dripped from his nose that Argento knew was spinal fluid. Julie sat down next to the guard and held his hand.

"It's okay," she said. "It's okay. You're not going to die."

"He is," Argento said.

"We can save him."

"We can't. He's got head and spine trauma. His fingertips, they're blue. He's not breathing."

Julie looked at Argento. Looked at Rachel for a second opinion. The nurse nodded, holding her fist to her mouth, on the verge of tears.

Argento unhooked the jailor's key ring from Aguilar's belt and put it in his coverall pocket. He'd never learned Aguilar's first name. It bothered him.

Coates shuffled over. Breathing hard, moving slow.

"Derrick, where are you hurt?" Julie asked.

Coates waved off the question and asked his own. "Where's my partner? Where's Max?"

CHAPTER 37

Jamerson

Maxwell Jamerson's arm stung from getting cut with the screwdriver. But not as much as it would have if he hadn't taken the pain pills from the go bag. He'd started with four of them. Julie had been watching, but his back was to her and he didn't think she'd seen. Then he'd taken two more afterward when he was sure no one was looking. That made a total of six Oxys in his system, and the familiar, welcome warmth that sluiced over him had taken the edge off all that was Whitehall Correctional Institute. Jamerson wasn't kidding himself. He knew, at some level, that he was on the verge of being an addict. But he could still control it. He was still calling the play. And with the narcotics rushing through his system, it was the first time he'd felt up to scratch in this godforsaken place.

He was standing outside a prison cell. He felt shaky on his feet and flushed from the heat. When the men had pulled him from the bars he'd been climbing, something had happened to his head. He touched his fingers to the top of his skull. They came away sticky. He couldn't quite reconcile why he'd been trying to climb the bars. Who was he trying to get away from?

"You bring me a wobbler?" he heard someone say. The voice was deep and muffled. Like it started somewhere low and had a distance to travel before it came out of a mouth.

"Yeah, Uncle. How's this one?" someone else said. Jamerson felt himself shoved forward.

"He'll do," the deep voice said.

He had heard the word earlier today. *Wobbler*. He couldn't remember what a wobbler was. He couldn't remember if it was good or bad. He felt wobbly standing, though. Maybe that was what they meant.

He knew he was supposed to be doing something right now. What was it? His head ached. It was hard to think clearly. There was something wrong with his head. What was his job? It was watching someone. That much he knew. Then a moment of clarity. The girl. He was supposed to be watching a girl. The governor's daughter. That mouthy bitch. He was blanking on her name. He'd just had it and it slipped away. The one who was trying to spy on him when he took the pills. It didn't matter. Screw her. She was on her own. And screw that bald-headed con who was trying to be so tough, trying to do his job for him, looking to show him up. He was on his own, too. Everyone was on their own in this place. Except his partner. His partner had stood by him. Jamerson blinked. His partner. He couldn't come up with his name, either. It didn't feel right, forgetting his partner's name. And then there was the prison guard who had stepped in front of him and took a knife to the chest. Took a knife for him. It seemed odd that someone would do that for Jamerson. Was that how it'd gone? The pills, Jamerson thought. He might have taken too many.

He was vaguely aware of others close by. An enormous man sat in front of him in the back of the cell on a bed. He wore no shirt and had rolls of glistening fat on his belly. That was good, Jamerson figured. Fat people were jolly. Jamerson wasn't sure what to do. He decided he should say something. "What's next?" he asked.

A voice next to him said, "Uncle will decide."

"Who's Uncle?"

"I am," said the large man with the belly rolls. The source of the deep, muffled voice Jamerson had heard. "I decide."

The large man was wearing black pants. People in black—what had the prison guards said about that color? They were trustees? Yes, that was it. Prisoners in black were trustees. They could be trusted, the trustees. Jamerson smiled at the wordplay. And there was something...protective in Uncle's voice. It was nice to hear that tone after being in this stressful, violent place. Where people judged him and tried to make him look stupid.

"You decide," Jamerson said gratefully. He liked that a trustee like Uncle was in charge here. Uncle could give him needed direction. Jamerson was not himself. It was his head. It hurt. It was foggy. But Uncle would take care of him. Jamerson could confide in him. Which was good, because there was something inside of him that needed to come out. Something he needed to say.

"I am," Jamerson began.

Uncle made a vague motion with his hands. Jamerson took it to be a sign of encouragement, a sign to go on. The fog in his head parted slightly.

"I don't think I'm a good person," Jamerson managed.

Uncle said nothing, but Jamerson thought he understood.

"I was scared and I ran away."

"You got scared," Uncle said. Uncle did understand. And probably even forgave him for running. Why stay on a sinking ship with the bald con and the woman? Wasn't that just dumb movie hero shit?

"But I don't want to be," Jamerson said. He struggled to complete his thought. It escaped him. He pressed his fingers to his temple until it returned. "I don't want to be remembered for that."

Uncle curled a finger toward him. Jamerson dutifully moved closer. He couldn't walk in a straight line. He had to sit down. He crossed his legs. Uncle loomed over him. Like a teacher gazing down on a pupil.

"Pimp rules, you mine," Uncle said.

Jamerson didn't quite get what Uncle meant by this. But he knew Uncle was his friend. Uncle's thick fingers worked their way into his sweat-soaked hair. It felt good at first. Then Uncle's fingers began to yank. It hurt. Jamerson tried to pull away.

"Be nice," Uncle said. "If you aren't nice, we can't play."

Jamerson stopped. He nodded. Uncle was right. He needed to be nice. Uncle knew things. He would help Jamerson. Help him clear the fog in his head. Guide him to wherever he needed to go next.

Uncle withdrew his fingers and patted Jamerson on the top of his head. It reminded Jamerson of how he petted his collie back home.

"One of us is the slave," Uncle said. "One of us is the master."

"Yes," Jamerson said.

"Guess which one you is."

"I'm the slaster." No, that didn't sound right. He had gotten the words mixed up. "I'm the malave," he tried.

Uncle chuckled. "Close your eyes now."

"Close my..."

"Ssshhh. No more talking. You're going to get me in trouble."

Jamerson wasn't sure about this part. But he did not want to get Uncle in trouble.

"Do as you're told, or you're gonna bring out the devil in me."

Jamerson did as he was told. He closed his eyes. His head swam. He thought he heard something rustling nearby. There were other people in the cell. They were getting closer to him. He felt a rough hand on his cheek. He kept his eyes closed.

"Your skin is soft," Uncle said.

Jamerson smiled. It was a kind thing to say. No one else had shown him kindness today.

"You the police?" Uncle asked. His voice sounded a little harder now and Jamerson wasn't sure why. But he nodded and kept his eyes shut tight, as Uncle had ordered. There was more rustling around him. More people getting near. Jamerson felt a dawning sense of unease. He felt like he needed to stand. He kept his eyes shut but started to rise.

"I didn't tell you to get up."

"I'm not trying to get up. I swear."

"He swears," someone behind Jamerson said. "So it must be true."

"Open your eyes," Uncle said. Jamerson did. There were other men in the cell now and Uncle was naked. A great mound of wet, sagging flesh. This was not right, Jamerson knew. He had said or done something wrong. He started to rise again so he could apologize. Someone hit him in the kidneys from behind and he gasped in pain.

"I brought my friends," Uncle said. He put his fingers back into Jamerson's hair and pulled. His breath, Jamerson noticed for the first time, smelled like rancid meat. "You gonna be our pet."

The fog lifted then, momentarily cleared by some deep-rooted sense of danger housed in the lizard brain, and Jamerson realized what was going to happen to him. And then it did. He bit. He spat. He fought. It didn't make a difference.

"I'm a cop," Jamerson howled.

"Up in here," Uncle whispered, "that don't mean nothing."

"Stop," Jamerson insisted. "It hurts." Then he shouted it. Then he screamed it.

Uncle and his friends didn't stop.

CHAPTER 38

Stay here with them," Argento told Coates. Before the trooper could protest, he made his way back through the dividing door, zip gun in hand. With each step, his left collarbone reminded him it was fractured. It hurt, but he knew pain.

He heard Jamerson before he saw him. The sound was coming from a cell toward the back of the block. It was like nothing Argento had ever heard before. Unearthly. Shattering. Helpless. Argento slowed. Walked to the far wall to get just enough of a vantage point to look in the cell without being too close to it.

And saw Jamerson.

The trooper's pants were off and he looked limp and ragged, like a broken doll. He wasn't dead. Not yet. But a half-clothed inmate was having his way with him and three more were waiting in line for their turn. In the back of the cell was a completely nude blob of a man sitting on a bed whose face and body looked they were made of soft cheese. Argento got the sense that the fat man wasn't just watching the spectacle but was presiding in some way.

It wasn't the worst thing Argento had seen that day, not with the human canoe a floor below. But he looked away.

Two members of Westmob stood on the outside of the cell

keeping watch. They both locked eyes with Argento but neither made a move. Devoted sentries.

Argento's innate drive to help a cop was as powerful as it could be. But he was also able to recognize a lost cause when he saw one. Even if Jamerson was still alive in two minutes, he wouldn't be able to walk—and regardless, Argento was both spent and battered. He wasn't going to be able to get Jamerson out of there. Not with six able-bodied Westmob standing in the way. Not even with Coates, not even with the zip gun.

He walked back to the other side of the floor. Coates was leaning against the far door, Rachel and Julie at his side. Rachel was scanning the trooper for wounds to patch but Coates moved away from her upon seeing Argento.

"Where's Max?" Coates said, his voice weighed down with pain and fatigue.

Argento wondered, for a split second, if it would be better to lie and tell Coates that Jamerson was dead. But it wouldn't matter. The trooper would insist on seeing the body. So Argento told the truth. "In a cell. Hurt. Heavily guarded. We're not getting in."

"Got to," Coates said. There was a faraway quality to his voice. He pushed off the wall. The bandage on his hand had come undone and was dripping blood. He shrugged off his suit jacket. There was another laceration stretching across his chest that looked like it had bit deep. He handed Pillaire's ID to Argento. Argento held it to the door. It went green again. Freedom on the other side. Coates stared at the green. As if momentarily transfixed by how close he'd come to getting out. Rachel hurriedly propped the door open with the go bag. In case it changed its mind.

Argento tried once more. "There's four, five men inside with him. Two more on the cell door. If he isn't dead already, he's on his way. You can't save him."

"He's my partner."

"He spent the last two hours popping pills and picking the wrong fights. All he's done is put you and Julie in danger."

Coates picked a baton off the floor. Held it in his left hand. His right kept dripping blood.

"You save that guy, you're just giving him another chance to fuck us."

"He's still a cop." Coates walked slowly toward the dividing door, his voice fainter now, his eyes unfocused. Argento kept stride.

"You've only got one good hand. You've lost a lot of blood. You won't make it. And you wouldn't leave Julie."

Coates blinked sweat out of his eyes. He kept shuffling forward but trained his gaze on Argento. "You were a cop before."

Argento could let the garbageman cover go. Coates knew. They were approaching the door. Gizmo's prone body was still holding it open. Between the Kindred and Westmob, there had been enough hard foot traffic over the downed convict that his face looked nearly inverted.

"Twenty-one years on the Detroit PD."

"What happened?"

"I didn't fit into their plans anymore."

Coates nodded. As if this new information made his final decision easier. He turned to Julie.

"It'll be a hell of a paper."

"Derrick," she said, her face ashen.

"Tell my boys and Vanessa I love them. Tell them I wasn't afraid."

"Derrick." There was a tremor in Julie's voice. "My God, don't do this." She took hold of his left arm. Coates gently pushed her away.

Argento handed him the zip gun.

"No," he said. "That's for protecting her. Get her out." Sweat salted the corners of his mouth. His voice was steady now save for a faint tremolo.

"I will."

"Swear it. Cop to cop."

"I swear," Argento said.

Coates stared at him for a moment. As if taking one last measure of Argento's worth. Then his mouth became a hard line and he walked through the doorway toward the cell that he would die in.

CHAPTER 39

There was nothing to do but walk away. Leave Coates, leave Aguilar's body behind. Both deserved far better. Argento, Rachel, and Julie went through the south stairwell door to the fifth-floor landing. The stairwell was quiet. Still. As close to an oasis as they'd seen since everything began. Roof access was just a floor above them. The promised land.

Julie was crying. Quietly at first and then openly. Argento had retrieved Aguilar's baton from the jailhouse floor. He handed it to Julie.

Julie took in one long shuddering breath and wiped her face. "What do I do with this?"

"The fighting might not be over. Go for the head first. Then the groin and spine. Then knees and elbows."

Argento studied Rachel. Her face looked raw, her scrubs stained. Blood on her collar. She'd been through the wringer. Then he noticed that Julie was studying her, too.

"Are we ready to get out of here?" Rachel asked.

"Damn right," Argento said.

Rachel started to move and Julie held out her hand to block her. "I have one question first," Julie said, her voice still thick with emotion from Coates's likely fate.

"What's that?"

"How long has Micah been your boyfriend?"

Rachel blinked. Reset her feet. Then cast her eyes down, looking toward the go bag. Argento was still processing what Julie had just said but he'd reclaimed the bag from the fifth floor where Rachel had used it to prop the door and instinctively pushed it behind him with his foot. The bag had trauma shears in it that he didn't want in Rachel's hands until Julie said more.

"I don't—" Rachel began.

Julie turned to Argento and her words came out in a tumble. "Something Micah said on the second floor. He looked at us and asked, 'What are you doing with her?' We thought he was talking about me, because I was the odd one out, the one who didn't belong. But he didn't care about me. He was talking about Rachel. He was wondering where we were taking his girlfriend."

"That doesn't even make sense," Rachel said, an edge to her voice Argento hadn't heard before.

"Then when you walked down those cellblock stairs, you turned so you were face-to-face with him. I saw the way you looked at him. You weren't afraid, even though you'd just watched him nearly cut a guy's head off. There was something else in your face."

"This is all because of a look?" Rachel demanded.

"I'm a woman, too, the only other woman in this fucking place," Julie said. She was speaking slowly now and with purpose. Argento took in every word. "I see things the men don't. And I know what new love looks like. I'm getting married next month."

"As the only other woman in this place," Rachel snapped, "I thought you'd have my back."

"I'm not finished," Julie said, edging closer to Rachel and punctuating her words with a pointed finger. "You and LeMaines went down the stairs together but you're the only one that came back. You said he ditched us? Bullshit. That wasn't him. I heard him say he needed to talk to you just before you left. I bet he guessed your relationship with Micah way before me. That inmate from the chapel, Simmons, he said Whitehall was like a small town. People talk. Rumors spread. I'd say he confronted you about Micah and you didn't like it. And I'm not positive about this last part, because a lot of people have been hurt and killed around us the last two hours, but I'm pretty sure you have more blood on your clothes now than when you went down those stairs with LeMaines. So what'd you do to him?"

Rachel pointed to Argento, as if summoning an ally. "I don't... I'm not even mad at her right now. It's this place. It's making her crazy."

Argento had to disagree. Julie wasn't crazy. In fact, what she was saying had unlocked the thing that had been bothering him about Rachel since leaving Micah on the second floor. He couldn't articulate it then, but he could now. Because more had happened since. Much more. And the cumulative effect had made him see the earlier events in a different light. The first warning bell should have gone off when the three men had burst into the infirmary to assault Rachel. Shank had said something to the nurse that didn't strike him as odd at the time, something like *Don't worry. We won't tell him.* Argento hadn't thought to ask who the "him" was that Shank wouldn't tell. Now he suspected it was Micah.

The second warning bell was a reevaluation of Rachel's visceral reaction to seeing Micah on the second floor. She had been standing next to him and he recalled her visibly tensing. Argento thought it was because she was scared of him. But it wasn't that. She was scared *for* him. Scared that Argento or one of the troopers would hurt her man on the way off the block.

And the third was right in front of him, but he'd needed Julie's help to see it. The blood on Rachel's shirt collar that had been there right after she'd claimed LeMaines had left the group to join Van Dyne in the chapel. Argento had initially chalked it up to spillover from one of the group's violent encounters on a lower floor, but when he went over it again in his head, it didn't seem to fit. It was blood spatter on Rachel's clothing, not blood smear, which meant it originated from an actively pumping wound, not transfer blood from someone who was already down and out.

Had Argento seen Rachel near anyone spurting blood like that? Would it have to have come from LeMaines?

Argento had never been a detective. He didn't have the patience for it. He hadn't wanted to wear a suit and get soft and move case files around. Plus he had seen the obscene amount of overtime committed detectives had to work if they wanted to stay on top of their caseloads, the time they spent in court and in district attorney conferences. It was not for him. He wanted to spend his life with Emily, not with the job.

But while he'd never formally been an investigator, he had been to an untold number of crime scenes. He knew how bloodstains worked. And he knew that charismatic prisoners were sometimes able to form sexual relationships with otherwise conscientious and committed staff members. And if someone like Sheriff Rokus wanted to get a message to a prisoner, he couldn't very well just dial that prisoner up directly. He'd need a go-between on the staff. Someone very much like Rachel. There was a lot stacking up against the nurse. But suspicions, as strong as they were, weren't enough. He'd have to be sure before he moved on this.

"Tell me about Micah," Argento said. "And tell me about LeMaines."

"There's nothing to tell," Rachel said. The entire countenance of her face had hardened. Her skin looked like it was on too tight. She pulled on her beaded necklace as if it would hold her up. The necklace. The one that ended in a small medallion that looked like the steering wheel of a boat. But not the whole wheel. Just half.

Argento reached for Rachel and pulled the medallion up from under her shirt. "I've seen the other half of this design. Micah wears it around his neck. It fell out of his shirt after he killed the man who tried to assault you."

Rachel snatched the medallion back and held on to it with both hands. "No. That's not true."

"Remember who you're talking to," Argento said. "I was a cop. I've heard all the lies before."

"I can explain when we get out of here," Rachel said. Talking too quickly.

"You can explain now."

"We have to go!" Rachel blurted. "We're on a two-hour clock."

"Not yet," Argento said. "Can't have you behind us. We'll get a knife in the back. My guess is that's what became of LeMaines."

Rachel was about to make her play and show them both her true nature. She was already showing all the signs. Head unconsciously tilted down to protect the neck, feet repositioned for better balance. Everyone had a giveaway. Argento had read an article not long ago about how poker players were getting Botox to immobilize their faces so they wouldn't have tells at the table. Rachel reached down. But not to the go bag. To her pocket. Her weapon was in her scrubs. Argento decided not to wait to get cut. He pivoted to her side, and trapped her right hand while it was still deep in the pocket. She strained against him and he used his bulk to pin her against the wall. Then he drew her hand out while it was holding the scalpel. She hadn't bothered to clean it. It still shone with LeMaines's blood.

"Let go," Argento snapped, "or I'll break your fingers."

Rachel dropped the scalpel. Argento picked it up and dropped it in a pocket of his coveralls. Then he checked the rest of her pockets for anything else that would hurt him. Clear.

"He's not my boyfriend," Rachel said. "He's my fiancé."

Julie stared at Rachel in open disgust.

Rachel's voice picked up strength. "You saw what he did to the man who attacked me. And now he's not just fighting for himself but for me, too. You can't beat him."

"Stop," Julie snapped. "What was your plan here with him? Slip out together in the confusion?"

"He's got the master key," Rachel said.

"LeMaines was a decent man," Argento said. "Whatever you did to him, he didn't deserve it."

At the mention of the dead guard's name, the cadence of Rachel's voice changed. It was smoother now. Consoling. "If we stick together, I can still help you. I'm the only one left who knows this place. We can all get out. We don't have to be enemies."

"No," Argento said. "Let's be enemies." He took firm hold of Rachel in a twist lock grip, bending her arm behind her back. She tried to jerk away, and he applied enough pressure to her wrist to make her curse out loud.

She craned her neck to look back at him. "What are you going to do to me?"

"Kurt," Julie said, alarm rising in her words. "You can't just let her go. She killed LeMaines. She was just about to kill you."

"Tell me," Rachel demanded. "What are you gonna do?" There was something in her eyes that seemed lost. Like she was unable to keep up with the speed of the world rushing at her. But just because she was adrift didn't mean she wasn't a lethal threat to him and to Julie. Argento made a decision. He had to take the nurse somewhere away from them. He wasn't going to open the fifth-floor door again to face off with the Kindred and Westmob. But he knew where to go.

He marched Rachel briskly forward in the bent-arm hold. Julie followed wordlessly. They went down two flights of stairs. They encountered no inmates. Given the effort they had undergone to get to this stairwell, it was almost perversely quiet. But it seemed everyone who wanted to kill them was now on the other side of the south stairwell doors. They arrived at the third floor. The sex offender floor. Argento used the access card on the door. It flashed green.

"Julie and I are getting out of here, Rachel. And after what you did, you can't come with us. So I'll give you a choice. I can either kneecap you with the baton and leave you in the hallway with no weapons. Or you can take your chances on this floor. When we walked through the first time, most everyone was locked in their cell. Don't know if that's still the case. So I'll give you your scalpel back to even the odds."

Rachel screamed. She tried to make her body dead weight. Argento cranked on her wrist and she gasped in pain.

"No," Argento said. "Don't play the victim. You're no victim. You're a volunteer. So decide."

Rachel strained to see through the small window of the door that led to the third floor. It looked clear. She stared at the baton tucked underneath Argento's arm. Drew in a shaky breath as if calculating how much damage he could do to her with it.

"I'll go on the floor," she said. "Give me the scalpel."

Argento opened the door. Rachel walked through it. He took the scalpel out of his pocket and tossed it in after her just before closing the door. The sporting chance. She was a monster, but he was trying damn hard not to be one, too.

CHAPTER 40

With Rachel gone, they double-timed back up the stairs. Argento got a clock check from Julie. Five minutes until all the doors in Whitehall opened. So far the prison had a monochromatic color scheme of gray from wall to floor, but the door they passed on the sixth floor was forest-green and marked *SHU*. Secure Housing Unit. The condemned. Where the inmate named Dimitri Medov, the one that LeMaines had talked about in hushed terms, called home. Argento was all for a worthy challenge, but he was fine with passing up this floor. He didn't need to run into Dimitri. He had met enough memorable people for a day.

"Good catch on Rachel. I should have seen it sooner."

Julie didn't seem to hear him. She looked like she was somewhere else entirely. Then she stopped short and gripped Argento tightly by his shirtsleeves and looked at him intently. "With Rachel. With just... everything. I feel sick."

"That's because you're a good person. We'll debrief the rest later. We gotta move."

Julie let go of Argento's sleeves, first one then another. She gave a quick head nod, refocusing. They set off again and she scanned the ceiling as they moved. "There." She pointed to a ladder adjacent to the sixth-floor elevator. "It has to go to the roof."

Argento nodded. The trapdoor that the ladder fed to was secured with a lock the size of a soda can. He had LeMaines's keys, which were marked with colored rubber heads. Black, white, purple, orange, tan, and yellow. They'd have to correspond to the color of the prisoners' uniforms.

"Yellow," Julie said. "Sixth floor has to be yellow. It's the only color we haven't seen yet."

Argento rifled through the ring to get to the yellow section, which had a glob of keys all its own. They weren't labeled beyond the color codes, the two cents it would have cost for a sticker that said "Roof" not included in the Whitehall budget. Argento put his foot on the first rung of the ladder. And stopped. He heard something. Faint. Below them. They weren't alone in the stairwell.

"What?" Julie asked.

"Company." Argento pointed down.

Julie stood utterly still. "Are you sure?"

Argento held a finger to his lips. He eyed the elevator directly across from him. The elevators were tied into the mainframe. So maybe it would go up to roof level. Or maybe it would trap them inside. *Screw it*, he thought, and pressed the up button. It didn't light. The elevator doors didn't open. No sounds of cables or wires. It didn't surprise him. It had been that kind of day.

"Your shoulder's hurt," she whispered. "There's only two of us. We have to hide."

"Not big on hiding," Argento said. "And there's nowhere to go."

Footsteps. Growing closer. Heavy. Maybe two men.

"Hurry up with the keys," she hissed.

Argento reached into his pocket and showed Julie the zip gun. "This works by the pullback spring. Aim for the upper chest. It's got one bullet, so make it count. Small round but they'll feel it." He handed her the keys. "If I'm down, don't stop. Keep going to the roof. Make the call for help."

Julie took the keys but not the gun. "You need this for whoever is coming up those stairs."

Argento pressed it into her palm. "Climb that ladder and look for the right key. I'll hold the fort down here."

Julie didn't argue further. She surged up the ladder and began trying the keys as fast as she could. Argento could see her hands shaking. Fine motor skills went to shit under stress.

The threat materialized before Julie had gotten halfway through the ring. Two men. One was tall and the other was short. The short guy's face was misshapen, like it had been squeezed in a can compressor. They both wore white prison jumpsuits and they both had knives, big carving blades that looked like they belonged in an industrial kitchen. Six inches long at least and several inches wide, probably manufactured in Germany somewhere with a solid brand name like Wüsthof or Henckels.

"Cooks," Julie said. "From the first floor."

Both men stopped midstairwell and looked at Julie with the predatory gaze Argento had seen so many times before. The one that said *two dogs, one bone*.

"We saws you before," the tall one said. "With two guys in suits. One of them was a smoke."

"I got this," Argento said. He took two steps back. Controlling the distance between them. Julie kept cycling through the keys.

"What happened to the smoke? He smell watermelon, go try and find it."

The short one chuckled. "Try to find chicken," he added.

"Fuck you," Julie's clipped voice came from the ladder.

"Oh you right about that," the tall one chortled. "There's gonna be fucking." He eyed Argento. "We just want the girl."

"Can't have her." Argento tapped the baton against the wall. Once. Twice. "You'll have to stick to each other."

The tall man hadn't gotten the reaction he wanted, and now he wasn't sure what to do. Argento calculated that the two men had maybe three brain cells between them. Rattling around like BBs in a bucket.

"Then we'll take you first. Then her."

"She won't let you have me, either. We come as a set."

Argento saw a vein pulse in the tall man's neck. He blinked. He began to speak again but the short man cut him off.

"We're gonna take that bitch, go on a date," the short man said. "Might let you walk if you're with the movement."

"Which movement?"

"Aryan Power."

"Listen," Argento said.

Both men looked at him.

"You listening?"

Both men nodded slightly.

"You can't have her and I don't give a fuck about your knives or your white brotherhood. Get closer and I'll kill you both with this baton. It'll take me about twenty seconds."

He watched them, to see if they'd make their move now or mouse down. He was playing the odds. If they just used the knives for the kitchen, then their blades would be shiny but of limited use. Like a party favor. But if they were the kind who practiced knife fighting—feints, parries, kill strokes—odds were he was going to be murdered in this hallway and then Julie next after they'd finished their date.

Something unspoken passed between the two men. Argento knew they'd made their decision and he knew what it was. There was a woman right there front and center and no rules, and only one obstacle to stop them. They liked those odds. He was about to be in a knife fight and he didn't have a knife. But he knew that when there was a blade involved, the key was to protect the upper body and the neck. He'd get cut, but he could still function. Still stay on his feet.

The short man smiled. He was confident about what was going to happen. Both of them moved in, but their approach was too slow, their spacing wrong, the set of their feet off; they were already making mistakes they didn't even know about. It told Argento he was dealing with amateurs. He met them, the cool metal of the baton in his palm. There was a cavern inside him that needed to be filled. He would fill it with this fight, a fight he would not allow himself to lose. He figured he'd be wiping that cocky smile right off the short man's face.

But he was wrong about the twenty seconds.

It took him three minutes and cost him a pint of blood.

CHAPTER 41

Julie

It took everything that Julie had to concentrate on finding the right key while the fight between Kurt and the two cooks raged six feet beneath her. At one point, she almost dropped the ring from her sweaty palm and a cold jolt ran up her body. The second-to-last key did the trick. The lock clicked open and Julie let out an involuntary cry of triumph. She pushed on the trap door. It rose a fraction of an inch before falling down.

Something was blocking it.

No.

They wouldn't.

Let her.

Leave.

This.

Place.

Julie Wakefield had been battling panic since Whitehall had gone haywire some two hours ago. But this new obstacle didn't make the fear worse. It did something different. It made her angry. Blow-the-roof-off angry. At Whitehall, Pillaire, the inmates, Jamerson, the Westmob gang members whom Coates would have to somehow bypass to try and save him. She looked down. Kurt was bleeding heavily. Favoring his left arm. The short man was down, wet globs of what Julie believed were bone and brain all around him. At any other time, in any other place, this image would have stopped her cold. But here, after what she'd been through, it was just part of the scenery. The air smelled of the iron tang of blood. The tall man was circling with the big knife. The one who'd called her a wobbler in the kitchen while pointing to his crotch.

She had to do something. The zip gun Kurt had given her? No, she'd need both hands for that and she didn't want to fall off the ladder. But something. Something right now. Because Kurt was going to die.

Julie hefted the lock in her hand. She reared back.

And threw it at the tall man's head.

It wasn't a direct hit. She had never practiced throwing locks at people. But when it glanced off the man's arm, he looked skyward in surprise. Took his eyes off Kurt. And that was all the time Kurt needed. He moved in and laid a walloping blow with the baton across the tall man's cheekbones. The cracking sound resounded off the stairwell walls. The tall man's face went slack. Kurt followed up with a violent shove and the tall man went airborne, landing directly on his neck midstairs with an awful crunch.

"Are you okay?" Julie called out. She needed him to be okay like she needed air.

"Tip-top," Kurt said. His face was pale, his voice subdued. He was bleeding from the arms and torso. The cooks' knives had found their mark.

"You're cut."

"Door first."

"It's stuck."

Kurt slung the go bag over his shoulder, climbed the ladder to the trap door, put both arms up, and pushed. Julie saw him wince as he moved his left arm above his damaged collarbone. The door moved a few inches. His face turned red with the strain. Julie climbed the ladder right alongside him and pushed with both hands, straining with all her might. The door moved a few inches more. Then half a foot. And then it flipped up and Kurt nearly fell off the ladder, Julie grabbing him by the front of his coveralls. They clambered through the opening, Kurt first with Julie right after him.

The top floor of Whitehall was essentially a large storage room, filled with rusty file cabinets, rolls of carpet, bins of tools, and random debris. The item that had been blocking the trapdoor was a heavy cardboard box. The air was noticeably cooler, as if the AC had just cycled back on. The favorable dip in temperature was exceedingly welcome, but Julie didn't want it to distract her. No time for a victory lap. She listened intently. Listened so hard she thought blood would burst from her ears. She didn't hear a thing. If an inmate had somehow made it all the way up here…She didn't need to see any more of the residents of Whitehall. Didn't need to see any more of Whitehall itself. The tour was fucking over.

She helped Kurt move the cardboard box back over the trapdoor, plus another box nearby to augment it, sealing them in. She checked her phone. They had gotten to a spot with roof access, and the two-hour clock for the doors in Whitehall had just expired. Timing was everything. She felt a twitch of something akin to security. Almost hope. She didn't know if they were actually safe now. But they were safer. And she'd take what she could get. She turned her attention back to Kurt. He had sat down and was searching through the go bag. He'd lost an alarming amount of blood. Julie took out several small green envelopes marked *QuikClot Combat Gauze*.

"These?" she asked.

"Yep." His face drawn. Voice hushed.

They were simple dressings. She had basic first aid and CPR during summer lifeguarding. She began applying the gauze to cover lacerations on his arm, rib cage, and thigh, wrapping it an inch above and an inch below the wounds. Kurt applied direct pressure himself with his palms on the cuts she hadn't gotten to.

"How's that so far? I know it's not perfect."

"Perfectionists never get anything done." His voice was still so quiet. Like by keeping it low, he was conserving the rest of his strength.

"Have you been stabbed before?"

"First time being stabbed in Missouri."

"Derrick," she said. "He gave you the ID and keys but with all the doors open, he doesn't need them anymore. He can still get to us." She searched Kurt's face for confirmation if that was even possible, but found none. She continued. "I'll listen for him. He could come to the same door we used."

"I'll listen, too," Kurt said.

"I think I understand why he did what he did."

"It was his partner. I would have done the same."

I would have done the same. Kurt had told Derrick that he'd been a Detroit cop. Julie knew inmates lied as easily as they breathed. But this wasn't a lie. Kurt was one of the good guys. Maybe the scariest good guy she'd ever met, but good nonetheless.

"Why didn't you tell us you were a cop?"

"I didn't look the part. Didn't think you'd believe me. Thought people would think I was crazy."

"I would have believed you."

"Thanks for chucking the lock at that guy's head. Timely."

"Thanks for the homemade gun. It's my first."

"Early wedding present."

"We registered for one, but I didn't think anyone would actually get it." She smiled thinly. If she could make a joke, then maybe she was somewhere in the vicinity of normalcy. It made sense to talk about normal things now. Keep her mind elsewhere. If she was half-way near normal, then maybe that meant they were actually getting out of Whitehall. But she knew she still had to compartmentalize. Put thoughts of Derrick and seeing Eric and her parents to the side. If she thought about them, she would cry. And if she started to cry, she might not be able to stop. Fatigue ran in a tight cord in the back of her eyes. She realized she'd been holding her breath. She let it out in one strong exhale.

"Smart," Kurt said.

"What?"

"Working on your breathing."

"I," Julie said, parsing out the words, "have been so damn scared."

"You're allowed to be."

"I feel like it's taking over. The fear. Like it wants me to stop moving."

Kurt checked one of Julie's dressings. He seemed satisfied with it. He looked at her and she felt the full weight of his attention. "Feel your feet on the ground," he said.

Julie looked at him without understanding.

"It's what an old SWAT instructor used to tell me when we were under high stress. Feel your feet on the ground. For one, it tells you your feet are still attached to your body and you can move. Second, it takes you outside of yourself, just for a minute. It reorients you."

"Feel my feet on the ground," Julie echoed.

"Then you look ahead. That's what you can control."

She finished with the last of his dressings.

"Thanks," he said. "I might still need a hand up."

She extended both her hands and helped hoist him to his feet, using all her weight as leverage because he wasn't light.

"Roof," he said.

The roof. There was so much junk piled up in the storage room that she couldn't see where the roof access even was. Julie hadn't bothered to ask LeMaines and Aguilar. She'd assumed they would have been around to show her.

Her phone buzzed. One of her apps giving her an update on her step count for the day. Step count. Who gave a squirt of cold piss about such things after all they'd been through?

Her phone. If it was making noise, she had service. The cell net didn't extend beyond the sixth floor. She looked at the screen. One bar. Then she saw texts popping up from her father and Eric, asking if the tour was over and telling her to call.

"Kurt!"

"Call the cavalry," he said wearily. "Tell them we already did most of their work for them."

Her father's number, the one solely for emergencies, on the phone he swore always to have on him, always charged, the phone he would always answer no matter what the hour, no matter who he was meeting with, no matter what he was doing. She had only used it once, in college when she'd had too much to drink, got separated from her girlfriends, and wandered into an unfamiliar neighborhood in St. Louis. He was in town giving a speech and had come with Derrick in a town car in twenty minutes. She'd blearily apologized and he said he didn't care and thanked her for calling and hugged her so tight her mascara made an imprint on his cheek.

She made the call.

CHAPTER 42

Argento heard Julie on the phone with her father. She communicated their situation clearly. Succinctly. Without being overwrought. It would have been understandable, especially for a civilian, to get lost in the violent drama and sputter on the who/what/when/where details that her father would need to help them, but she stayed in business mode. It reminded him of a good dispatcher giving a patrol cop enough information to respond to a call without cluttering things up with unnecessary crap. He was impressed. The kid had grit. Then she said "Hello? Dad?" She held the phone away from her.

"Call just dropped. But I got through. Holy shit, Kurt, I got through."

"Who's he sending?"

"Everybody. Starting with a SWAT helicopter straight to the roof."

"Any ETA?"

"I didn't get one before I lost the call. But he's the governor. People move fast for him." Julie was talking quickly. Buoyed by hope.

Argento nodded. His head was swimming. He had bled a lot. It wasn't catastrophic bleeding; his wounds weren't quite at tourniquet level. But probably in the neighborhood of a pint and change. He could stand to lose a pint without much fuss. That's how much they took at the blood bank. But there was something else wrong with him. His left leg throbbed at the hamstring, and it felt like injury, not just discomfort. Something was torn in there. It was already slowing him. His legs didn't have the same spring. He clenched his fists. One of his knuckles was dislodged. He could move it from side to side under the skin like a marble. His body was breaking down. But that was okay. The mind always gave up before the body. The body would go as far as the mind would let it.

"You want something for pain? Max didn't take all the pills."

Argento echoed what Coates had said earlier about taking the Oxys for his hand. "Don't want to get cloudy. We're close but we ain't out yet."

Julie checked her phone again. Even with all the doors in Whitehall now open, the only way to get to them now was the trapdoor they had just barricaded and the elevator across from them, which Argento had tried a level below and wasn't working.

"I'm going to find the way to the roof," Julie said. "See if I can pick my phone signal back up. Just stay here. You look like you might need a breather."

He didn't argue. She disappeared behind a stack of storage bins and returned a few minutes later. He could see in her face she was about to deliver welcome news.

"Got it! It's another ladder, about the length of the one below us. I already checked. The way to the roof is easy. No lock. And there's plenty of room to land a helicopter."

"Not sure I can climb that at the moment. Gonna open up some wounds. Plus my left leg seems to be malfunctioning."

Julie absorbed this information without missing a beat. "Okay. We'll hole up here until we hear the helicopter. Then I'll climb the stairs and wave them down to get you."

"Should stop here anyway. I'm an inmate. If I try for the roof, they'll probably charge me with escaping."

She sat cross-legged across from him. He took the pack of cigarettes out of his coverall pockets that had a lighter attached to the box. He lit one. He didn't smoke much, but it seemed right, given their current situation.

"Where'd you get those?"

"Off the dead warden."

Julie didn't bother with a follow-up question. She held her hand out and Argento gave her the pack and lighter. When someone was stressed, having something in the hands to manipulate could divert their thinking and steer them away from shock. Julie took out a cigarette and lit it. She inhaled deeply.

"Haven't smoked since my sophomore year of high school."

"Been a while for me, too. But I'm thinking about starting again."

They smoked and were quiet for a time.

"So," she said.

"So."

"I don't know anything about you. After all of this...I feel like I should."

There was a bag of gravel within reach that had partially spilled out onto the floor. Argento picked up a pebble and tossed it at the wall. It made a metallic plinking sound. "I like food trucks," he said. "That's something about me."

"Is that it?"

"I like football."

"Anything else?"

"Not much."

"What don't you like?"

"Food trucks that are out of food. Guys with ponytails."

"My fiancé, Eric, has a ponytail."

"Ditch him," Argento said. "There's still time."

"You used that arm," she said. "That man's cutoff arm. I don't think I'll ever forget that."

"I know what I did," Argento said. "Just not sure what it makes me."

"How did you even think of something like that?"

"Standard operating procedure in Detroit, Michigan."

Julie ashed her cigarette on the floor and pushed some sweaty strands of hair off her forehead. "What was it like being a cop there? What kind of neighborhood did you work in?"

"Some good people. Some evil. Spent more time with the evil ones."

"How did you get here? To Missouri?"

"My wife died. Work wasn't going well. They said quit or get fired, so I walked. Drove west. I stopped a man from hurting a girl. Man's brother was the sheriff. Sheriff found me and put me in here."

"Your wife?"

Argento nodded. "She got sick. Started as a sore throat. Turned out to be esophageal cancer."

"I'm sorry," Julie said. "I am so sorry."

"Even if they can get some of the cancer, the esophagus doesn't heal. It leaks. They just kept pulling fluid out of her lungs."

"How long was she sick?"

"Forever," he said. He threw another pebble at the wall.

"I'm sorry," she said again.

Argento didn't reply.

"Does it get any better?"

"Still waiting for that part."

He could see his wife's face. She used to make him hot tea when he was angry or frustrated with something at work. He didn't particularly care for tea, but he liked that she brought it to him. When her doctor had told him it was time to talk about end-of-life care, Argento had cornered him and asked every question he could think of, and the doctor had said "We've discussed that already" without looking up from his chart. Argento had slapped the clipboard out of his hands, papers scattering over the corridor floor. The doctor had seen the murder in his eyes and backed down the hallway.

But the doctor wasn't wrong. Emily was close to the end and they couldn't fix her. When he visited her, one thin, veined hand clung to the edge of the bed, her other hand clutching the top of her head, as if to ward off something trying to writhe into her skull. He brushed her teeth and held the small sponge soaked with water up to her mouth, but she wouldn't take it. It was three days before her death when he broke. He entered his church after it had let out for the evening service, sat in a back pew, and squeezed his eyes shut.

"Help her," he prayed to anyone who was listening. "Help her." And he kept saying it over and over until the words were just guttural noises combined with his sobbing, the sound of misery released into the void.

He picked up another pebble. Plinked it off the wall. Got his mind right. Focused on the now.

"Tomorrow around this time, you'll be with Eric eating pancakes on some terrace and looking back at this and having a good chuckle."

"All you just did was remind me how hungry I am."

"Where you from, Julie?"

"Kirkwood, Missouri."

"They raise 'em strong in Kirkwood."

"My dad didn't do much coddling."

Argento cast a sidelong glance at Julie. She had slowed her breathing from ragged to steady. She had scratches on her face and a bruise under her eye. She was lean, muscular, and alert in maybe, at this moment, the most foreboding place on earth.

"No, he did not."

They were quiet again. Then Julie said, "I don't like pancakes."

"Good to know."

"No, a second ago, you said I'd be eating pancakes on a terrace. I don't like pancakes."

"So what's your favorite breakfast?"

"I don't know. Waffles."

"And to drink?"

"Coffee with whole milk."

"Tomorrow at around this time, you're gonna be eating those waffles and drinking that milk coffee on the terrace and looking back at this and having a good chuckle."

"Before I eat that, I'm going to wash my hands for so long the skin's gonna chap. Then I'll split a plate with you."

"Deal."

They were silent again. Julie massaged her temple.

"Favorite athlete?" she asked.

"Joe Dumars is up there. Detroit Pistons."

"Why?"

"Gentleman assassin. Only guy that could ever guard Jordan. You?"

"Easy. Kurt Warner. From shelf stocker to Super Bowl MVP. How about favorite podcast?"

"Podcast," Argento said. The word didn't sound right on his tongue. He wasn't sure he'd ever actually uttered it.

"Ah, never mind," Julie said. "Favorite beer?"

"Löwenbräu."

"Do they still even make that?"

"It's hard to find. Makes me appreciate it more."

"Heineken for me. Bet Eric and my friends are drinking it right now."

"Favorite band?"

"Knit by Wolves."

"Favorite band I've heard of?"

"U2 by a hair over the Stones. You?"

"Metallica," Argento said. "All day."

"Yes," she said. "That fits." She looked down, and her attention turned to her arm. There were deep teeth marks on her right bicep. She waved it off. "Man, I don't even remember being bit."

"What are you studying in grad school?"

"Public admin and criminology."

"What's next after that?"

"I don't know. Maybe law school. Or I'll just show up in DC, tell people my dad's a big deal, and expect to be handed a sweet job. But that's just what my people do when they don't know what to do."

"You could write your application essay about Whitehall. Set you apart from the other candidates."

"I bet these surviving-a-prison-riot stories are a dime a dozen."

Argento laughed. He couldn't help himself. He couldn't remember the last time he'd laughed. "How about being a cop?"

"Don't you think I might be a little over—" She didn't finish the sentence.

"Overeducated? Not all cops are stupid. Some of us can read and write."

"No offense. But be a cop where?"

"Whatever city you care about the most."

"I wouldn't want to be in some suburb writing parking tickets on the night shift."

"Wrote maybe one parker my whole career," Argento said. "Plenty of other stuff to do out there. Front row seat to the greatest show on earth. Right now you're in school for criminology. Nothing wrong with that. But it can help to have a job where you deal up close with the criminals first. So you know if your professors are full of shit."

"Got any other advice?"

Argento took a long pull of his cigarette. He missed smoking. He'd been a fool to quit. "Be who you're supposed to be. Sometimes that means trying something new. You could be the best fighter of all time, but until you throw a punch, you don't know."

"This is the weirdest career counseling session I've ever had." Julie took the last bottle of water from the go bag and offered it to Argento. He declined. She drained it.

"Best part of this whole place," she said, "was the guys playing chess with turds."

"I liked the assistant warden," Argento said. "He was hardy."

"My Lord," Julie exhaled. "That guy? It was good he didn't come with us. At the next sign of trouble, he would have put his hand to his forehead and swooned."

"Like ladies do in the black-and-white movies."

"Exactly like that."

Another silence. Neither felt the need to fill it until Julie asked, "That man, Janz, you didn't hurt or kill him."

“After we got the chaplain back and shut him in his cell, he wasn’t a threat to us anymore.”

“I thought you were going to.”

“Would it have bothered you if I had?”

“No,” Julie said. “I don’t think so.”

“There are rules even in here. But they’re my rules, not yours. You can go back down there and knock him around if you want.”

“I’ll pass. But you aren’t what I thought you were.”

“Got layers to me,” Argento said. “Shitload of layers.”

“So what are you going to do when you get out of here?”

“Drink a beer in the shower.”

“You still act like a cop.”

Argento didn’t reply.

“My father says if you do something long enough, that’s what you are.”

“Sounds like a wise man. You should be listening to him instead of me.”

Julie stood. “I’m going to get on the roof and call him again. I’ll see if anything is flying our way, get a better ETA.”

“Go for it. You should call Eric, too.”

“I can’t,” Julie said. “I... I don’t want him to hear this place in my voice.”

Argento knew what she meant. He had been the same way with Emily, sparing her the gory details of his days in the field. He wanted there to be a wall between her and the city he policed.

Julie headed toward the direction of the roof ladder and then stopped. Turned to face Argento. “Are we actually getting out of here?”

“It’s looking damn good.”

“Do you really believe that?”

“I do.”

“Before you said it was probably just going to be you getting out.”

“I get more optimistic over time.”

Julie paused. Then blew out a breath. “I’m really glad we didn’t get raped.”

"Me too," Argento said.

She turned back and walked toward the stairs. Argento heard the creak of the rooftop door opening. A few minutes passed. He thought about how long it would take for the governor of a decent-size state to marshal up a helicopter full of cops and send it to the target location. He figured it would depend on a host of factors. Personnel working that day, what kind of assignment the chopper was currently on, where it was launching from, how much fuel it had on board, and probably a bunch of other crap that he wasn't thinking of. Detroit PD hadn't been equipped with a helicopter. When they'd needed eyes in the sky, they had to sweet-talk the Highway Patrol.

Argento looked around the room some more. There wasn't much to see. Haphazard equipment, poorly maintained and randomly organized. It seemed to be the Whitehall way. There wasn't much of use in view. No weapons that would trump his baton. He could use a beer. And some hand sanitizer. A lot of hand sanitizer. All the hand sanitizer. He just happened to be looking right at the elevator when the floor light above the doors lit up.

Then the doors opened.

And Micah stepped out.

He didn't have the knife behind his back anymore in his faux impression of a gentleman. It was out in front of him. He stared at Argento. The corner of his mouth twitched, the beginnings of a smile or a grimace.

The elevator door closed behind him.

Argento didn't have the zip gun. He had no backup. What he had was a splintered collarbone, a torn hamstring, multiple stab wounds, and a left hand that wouldn't fully close.

No shortcuts in Whitehall.

No shortcuts at all.

CHAPTER 43

Micah moved lithely to the side, employing a file cabinet as cover. But then he looked at Argento's empty hands and stepped out from behind it. "I said you wouldn't always have the gun."

When Argento started to get up from his seated position, his bad hamstring protested. He pushed through the pain and rose fully to his feet. He scooped the baton up from the floor. Wondered if it would be enough.

"This is a bad time," he said. "How about you come back later?"

"You don't stop trying to be clever, do you?"

"Don't know how."

Argento moved to the center of the room, putting a series of metal drums between himself and Micah. Using the terrain as obstacles to slow him. It was a reversal of their roles when they had first met on the ground floor.

"Where's Rachel?"

"I'll tell you if you tell me how much the sheriff paid you to off me." As far as he knew, no one had ever formally plotted Argento's murder before. Be good to know the going rate.

"When this knife goes in you," Micah said, gliding closer, "you're going to tell me everything. Where's Rachel?" He had the blade up parallel to the floor in a reverse grip. A professional's grip.

"You just missed her. She went down to the third floor to find a new boyfriend. Said you were annoying."

Micah blinked. Sniffed. If Argento could make him mad enough...It had worked with the con outside the warden's office. Micah might not be so easily manipulated. But Argento had more ammunition now. He had the fate of Micah's fiancée to play with.

"You shouldn't have said that. Now I'm gonna do you slow. Give you time to beg."

Micah advanced. Slowly. Precisely. Like the gymnast he was. Simmons had called him a bad man who won all his fights. Argento already knew his plan to goad him into a mistake wasn't going to work. Plans were like that. His leg banged against one of the drums he was using as an obstruction. The drum lifted off the floor. It was empty or close to it.

"Where's all your jokes now?"

"I just know the one," Argento said. He was looking straight ahead. Directly past Micah to the area behind him. It had his full attention.

Because the elevator doors had just opened again without a sound.

And there was no elevator there.

Micah was fast. Argento had to move. He pushed the oil drum onto its side. And began rolling it at the inmate. It looked ridiculous. No one had ever defeated their opponent with an empty oil drum. Micah wasn't going to stand still and let it pancake him like in a cartoon. But Argento just needed it to be enough of a distraction for Micah not to look back. And he needed momentum. Plenty of momentum.

When the drum got close enough to Micah, the inmate eyed Argento curiously and simply sidestepped, the blade up and ready. But Argento was already running at him, hands above his waist to protect his heart and neck. He absorbed the first slice on the meat of the forearm. You don't charge a knife fighter and expect to go unscathed. But taking this first hit allowed him to trap the knife against Micah's chest, wrap the inmate's upper body in a football tackle, and propel him backward toward the empty elevator shaft. Micah was agile and powerful, but he couldn't overcome simple physics. Argento kept him moving backward on his feet until he was within range. Then he gave him a simple two-handed push, like you'd see in the schoolyard between two kids who weren't sure if they really wanted to fight. But this one was strong, decisive, and backed by velocity. The blond man staggered, stopped himself, and then teetered on the precipice of the elevator shaft. There was no more fluidity. No grace. Just flailing arms trying to grasp something solid, an awkward half spin, like one of those inflatable tube men you see outside of car dealerships to announce a sale. Then he fell without a sound.

Argento looked down the shaft. He could see Micah facedown on the top of the elevator, which appeared to be on the ground floor. Which meant Micah had plummeted six floors onto a surface with no give, putting him well on his way to the big penitentiary in the sky. Argento had just made the state of Missouri a safer place.

Argento went to the go bag and retrieved another bandage for the blood already dripping from his lacerated forearm. The cut was deep, but Micah didn't seem to have sliced any nerves. He checked the rest of his dressings. Still in place. He sucked in cool air. That encounter had actually gone a lot better than he thought it would. The elevator had been a straight-up fluke. But Argento would take it. It'd been a rough afternoon. With someone like Micah, you had to be lucky and good. He had no idea why the doors had opened without the elevator present. It was another casualty of Whitehall's buggy digital system. But it would have been a damn shame not to take advantage of it.

He called for Julie. He wasn't confident the elevator was going to stay on the ground floor. It could easily return with more homicidal inmates in it. They both needed to get to the roof right now. And he would need her help to do so.

There was no response when he spoke her name. Then something caught his eye. The boxes they had put over the trap door. They'd been moved out of the way. The trap door was wide-open, like an open mouth, mocking him.

Julie was gone.

CHAPTER 44

Dimitri

The air-conditioning was out in Whitehall and his cell was an inferno, but Dimitri Medov still punched his wall. One hundred blows with his right fist, one hundred with his left. Then he sat on his bed and spread out his hands to examine them. The daily ritual of hitting concrete had flattened his knuckles to the point where it looked like nickels had been grafted to them. He was still regaining his breath when his cell door clicked open. This was unusual. He listened. Heard nothing. Stepped to the door, pushed it out all the way, and entered the hallway.

Every last door on the block was wide open. He saw more inmates begin to appear, looking around uncertainly, like gophers emerging from a hole. He despised raising his voice because it hurt his head, but he shouted, "Go back inside," because he didn't feel like company. A red bolt of pain shot through his temple as everyone complied. They knew his voice and they feared him. They were right to be scared. This was Dimitri's floor. He had proven that time and time again since he had arrived here four years ago.

His door opening was surprising, but not entirely unexpected. He'd heard from the guards' schoolgirl chatter in the hallway that the governor's daughter was at Whitehall on some kind of tour. Not long after, he'd heard a guard, a skinny man who somehow had a fat face, say some of the doors were broken because of a bug in the system. Then all the guards had left their posts. He didn't know if the first thing was related to the second and third things. What he did know was that it was typical behavior of Americans to flee. When the going got tough, they turned into vakhkots.

The governor's daughter, though, that meant something to Dimitri.

Dimitri had a bone to pick with the governor.

The man currently had him on death row and had denied him clemency.

Dimitri had come to the United States from Armenia. He'd had a good life there. He was a respected and decorated officer in the Armenian army, married with an infant son. But one night his son wouldn't stop crying. Crying turned to wailing. Dimitri didn't do well with noise. He took hold of the boy until he stopped crying. Then he stopped breathing. He thought nothing of it. If his son was that fragile, it couldn't be his own blood. His true son would never have been so weak. His wife had flown into a panic. The racket she'd made. He'd warned her to be quiet but she hadn't listened. When the three police officers came to his house to investigate the neighbors' reports of screaming, he was sitting in his living room eating a bowl of soup. The officers had looked at the bodies of his wife and child. Looked at Dimitri. Dimitri rose from his chair to his full six-foot-four height, showed them his three hundred pounds. The first officer reached for his nightstick. A second, who knew Dimitri and had once seen what he'd done to a man's skull in a tavern brawl, shook his head and the first officer let his hands fall to his sides. They let him pass, even stood by while he packed. Dimitri left the country that night. Changed his name. Eventually ended up in America to seek some version of fortune.

He hadn't been able to stay in one place long. He had hooked up with an Armenian crime family in Philadelphia as an enforcer, opting to work midnights when the city was quieter and wearing earplugs when the weekend revelry around him got to be too much. Then one day, he'd found a shop that sold the American Nike sneakers that were never available in his home country. A little man had walked too close to him and stepped on one of his new acquisitions, leaving a faint scuff mark on the toe of his right shoe. The man had not apologized. Dimitri had not bothered to tell him the error of his ways. He liked to show people. People remembered it more when you showed them.

He'd lifted the man up and slapped him down on the pavement like he was shaking out a rug. The man had died at the scene in front of a dozen witnesses, and the police were called. Dimitri had to leave once again. He had wandered for a time, ending up in some nothing town in Missouri. With no job and no prospects, he'd taken to stealing like the petty thieves he'd despised in the motherland. A security guard had tried to stop him when he was helping himself to lunch from the hot food aisle of a grocery store. He stabbed the guard through both lungs. The police had gotten there quickly and hadn't let him leave like their Armenian counterparts. Dimitri had made them pay. He'd killed two with his hands before they shot him in the head, and he was taken to the hospital handcuffed and in full restraints. The bullet made him prone to migraines when things got too loud, but other than that it had done no lasting damage. Dimitri had been a soldier, so he knew guns could be strange like that.

At the hospital, Dimitri had choked a cop to death who was guarding him bedside prior to booking. The officer's partner had gone to the bathroom, and when the remaining officer had taken one of his cuffs off so Dimitri could use the bedpan, the Armenian had grabbed him with his meaty hand, taken the hospital sandwich he'd been given for lunch and shoved it down the officer's throat. Kept pushing it farther and farther down as the officer bucked and thrashed until Dimitri's fist was in the man's mouth to the wrist. When the nurse rushed in, Dimitri had calmly requested a second sandwich, because, as he explained in his heavily accented English, the officer had eaten the first one.

His trial and sentencing on the three capital murders had been via a remote camera because he was considered too much of a security threat to be allowed inside a courtroom. He had laughed when the judge had sentenced him to death and said he was a cunt, which he'd learned was the worst thing you could call someone in America. Said he wished he could have killed more officers. Said he wished he could kill them all. He'd started at the Jefferson City Correctional Center where he'd had trouble coexisting with others. They were too loud. They gave him migraines. He had stomped one talkative guard's testicles into mush. Cornered a rowdy inmate in the laundry room, broken all his ribs, and shoved him between two dryers, watching him slowly suffocate as his chest vainly tried to expand for breath in the tight opening between the machines. Since Whitehall had accepted him, his home had been the sixth floor, where food was always brought to him through his feed slot so he wouldn't mix with the other inmates and he was shackled anytime he had to move.

There was no natural light on the sixth floor. Little to no human contact. No programming, nothing allowed in his cell, no visitors, no phone calls. Nothing to distinguish one day from the next. Gray walls. Gray floor. Gray ceiling. Gray food. After a time, Dimitri began to forget things. Talk to himself. See objects and people that weren't there. After several years of this, Dimitri came to the conclusion that this existence was driving him insane. But that wasn't a particularly troubling revelation for the Armenian. He didn't have anyone or anything to be sane for.

Dimitri went down the hallway to the exterior south stairwell. The door was open. On the other side were two dead inmates. One was short and one was tall. The short one was on the stairwell landing. He'd been beaten to death. The tall one was farther down the stairs, his neck cocked at an obscene angle.

He looked up. A ladder led to a trapdoor. There was no lock on the door. Dimitri had seen this door during one of the few times they'd let him off the floor and there had been a lock on it. He figured that whoever had killed the inmates might be up there. Maybe they would know where to find the governor's daughter. He put one foot on the short man's skull and pressed down with all his weight. The grinding sound it made pleased him. Then he climbed the ladder and pushed up on the door. It moved a foot but then came back down. Something was blocking it. But Dimitri would not be blocked. His strength was natural, not the artificial kind forged in a gym. Dimitri had gone to a gym only once. He'd done the bench press, starting at 315 pounds, then 495, then 675, oblivious to the gawkers who watched him, stopping not because he got tired but because he got bored. He pushed again on the trap door, using both hands, the muscles in his arms and shoulders expanding, working with singular purpose. It flew open. He climbed through.

There was a girl standing there. She wheeled at the noise and stared at him. Then froze. She was in her midtwenties, with brown hair tied back and a runner's frame. No uniform, which meant not staff. It was her. The daughter of the man who wished to take his life. There was no one else it could be. Four years of torment in Whitehall and now this, a gift, right in front of him, ready for the taking. Dimitri reached for her. She had unfrozen herself and tried to dodge him, but he'd always had fast hands. When he was a child, his father had taught him to fish in the river without a pole. Like a black bear. Just lean an arm in the bitterly cold water, still, patient, and when a fish got too curious and too close, snatch it right up. Dimitri's fingers found her ankle and he pulled her to him across the floor. The black bear had his catch. He would take this little fish apart. Piece by bloody piece. A visual lesson for her father. He liked to show people. People remembered it more when you showed them.

CHAPTER 45

Julie (Five Minutes Earlier)

Julie had just reached her father again on the cell when she heard voices downstairs. She hesitated and lowered the phone. The voices couldn't mean anything but serious trouble. She and Kurt were the last ones left in their party, which had started at nine strong. Whoever Kurt was talking to wasn't going to be an ally.

"Dad, I have to go." She tried to keep the edge out of her voice. "I have to... I'll call you right back." She pocketed the phone and started down the stairs to the storage room. To be going down again instead of up toward certain rescue made something come untethered in her chest. But she forced her arms and legs to do the required movements. Whatever was happening downstairs, she wasn't going to be a passive bystander. She was in good physical condition; she had a baton and she would crack someone's skull if it came to that. Whatever Kurt was up against, she could help. She *had* to help.

What she saw when she reached floor level made the untethered feeling in her chest expand. Kurt and the inmate named Micah were squared off on the other side of the room. Micah had a knife and was circling. Kurt was trying to keep both distance and objects between them. But Julie remembered how fast Micah moved on the lower level when he had cut the throat of the inmate. She felt an immediate wave of helplessness. She fought it off and began to run toward the two of them, with no earthly idea what she would do when she got there.

That was when Kurt began rolling what looked like an oil barrel toward the inmate. It was a maneuver that struck Julie as downright peculiar. But something told her to stop running and see this unfold. She watched Micah easily sidestep the barrel and slice open Kurt's forearm. But Kurt had built up enough speed that he plowed into Micah and drove the blond inmate backward, like a defensive lineman driving into a practice sled. The elevator, Julie realized. The doors were open but no elevator was waiting. That was where Kurt was going. He was going to drop that fucker down an elevator shaft.

And with a hard stop and then an even harder push, Kurt did just that. She saw Micah fight to keep his footing, teeter, and fall. Saw Kurt limp to the edge and peer over. That was awesome, she thought. She knew it was a bizarre word choice when referring to the loss of a human life, even someone like Micah's. Like she was commenting on a skateboarding trick. But so much had happened within these savage, loony walls, and the prospect of escape was so close at hand that she felt almost giddy. She had thought Micah would have gone down harder but Kurt had made short work of him. *Piece of cake*, she thought. *Whitehall is a piece of fucking cake.*

Noise behind her, rising. She turned. A man exploded up through the trap door, the boxes blocking it tumbling away. No, not a man. A giant, with long stringy hair. The giddy feeling evaporated, and for the first time since she'd set foot in Whitehall, she froze. It was system overload, seeing yet another threat when she thought the danger had passed, and her muscles seized, rooting her to the spot.

The giant's hand shot out and gripped her ankle so hard she gasped in pain. Then he descended the ladder, pulling her along the floor like she weighed nothing at all. When she hit the opening of the trap door, he gave a quick jerk and she fell past him. She landed on her hands, but the impact drove her stomach into the floor. She rolled to her side, the wind knocked out of her. The giant plucked her from the floor and dragged her by her wrists behind him back through the open door onto the sixth floor. Julie's feet bumped and dragged on the concrete walkway as she fought for breath, taking in gulps of overheated air; the cooler temperature of the warehouse above her was already far gone.

Even when her breathing returned to her, Julie felt the overwhelming sensation that she was drowning on dry land. Her mind screamed one thing: *Get Out*. But the giant had her in a vise grip. His hands were twice the size of hers, his knuckles as wide and flat as bottle caps.

A man on fire ran past her, emitting an otherworldly shriek. Then he was gone. Did that just happen? Did she dream that? No, she could smell the broiled flesh. If Whitehall had a sprinkler system, it wasn't working. People were burning on the sixth floor because there were no rules anymore. She had just been on the roof of Whitehall awaiting rescue. Now she was being dragged back into the abyss.

She was aware of others on the cellblock, shapes mostly, some voices, but they did not approach and they seemed to fade back at Dimitri's approach. She shouted at them for help. Not a scream. A demand. Help her. It was a call out to anyone on the floor, a guard, an inmate who was protective of women, a trustee, Kurt, in case he could hear through floors and walls, to her father, Eric, God above.

"No one come," the giant said. His voice was a heavily accented growl, his hair so long it was hard to see his face. He lumbered as he dragged her. Like some kind of damn forest ogre. Then he spoke again. "Dimitri's floor."

Dimitri Medov. The name sent a spasm through her core. She had asked Assistant Warden Pillaire what Dimitri had done. She remembered his response. "Things you wouldn't believe." Dimitri was right. No one was going to intervene. They were scared of him. And Kurt didn't know where she'd gone. She was on her own.

They stopped in front of a wide metal door. Julie tried to pivot out of Dimitri's grasp, her heels scraping the floor, but he hurled her against the wall without letting go of her wrists and she heard something crack in her side. A rib, it had to be a rib, and she cried out in pain. He opened the door, his mass filling the entire span of the doorway, and pushed her inside. Closed the door behind him.

The room she found herself in had a cement floor and bare white walls. There was a large floor-to-ceiling mirror on the far wall flanked by heavy curtains. Dominating the middle of the room was a strap-down hospital bed with extended brackets for arms and legs and a digital clock above it. It took a moment for her mind to get there. This was the sixth floor: Secure Housing and death row. They were in an execution chamber. It made a kind of grim sense.

Dimitri stood in front of the door looking at her. No, not looking at her. Inspecting her. He was well over six feet tall, maybe three hundred pounds. His tattoos began at his neck and ran down both arms to the knuckles. Images of barbed wire, foreign words that Julie guessed were Armenian, naked demonic creatures with huge breasts and knives where their hands should be. His eyebrows were thick and tangled, his wrists thick, his arms like a power lifter's. He looked like he could just pick her up, drop her into his mouth, and consume her whole.

Julie was in a kind of numb freefall. Her side where she'd slammed into the wall sent shivers of pain up her body. She had to break out of this inertia. She began by saying the first thing that came to mind, which was the opposite of how she felt. "You don't scare me."

"Yes I do," Dimitri said.

She had to reassemble herself and she had to do it now. She still had the baton. Dimitri saw it in her hand but hadn't bothered to take it from her. She'd make him fucking regret that. Kurt had told her where to aim. The head first. Then the groin, spine, knees, elbows. She decided not to go quietly.

She attacked.

Swung the baton at Dimitri's head, the movement setting her injured side afire. But he was too tall and the blow bounced off his massive neck. She tried for his elbow on the backswing and hit the wide wall of flesh that was his upper arm. Dimitri didn't budge. Didn't try to stop her.

"More," he said.

She swung again, without effect, and when she did, the tears came. Tears borne out of anger and pain, frustration, fear. She dropped the baton. It didn't work. She lashed out with her fists and feet. She clawed at his eyes but couldn't reach them. She kicked at his groin and he turned and her foot glanced harmlessly off his massive thigh.

"More," Dimitri said.

She knew she was in full panic mode. She needed to regroup. To find at least a thimble of calm. Wait. *The zip gun.* Kurt had given it to her. How had she blanked that out? And where had she put it? Had it fallen out while Dimitri had dragged her down the hallway? She took a step back from him and plunged her hands into both pockets at once. Her fingers closed around the cool metal tube. She drew it.

Julie saw Dimitri's huge open hand come at her, but she couldn't get out of the way in time. It struck her square in the cheek, and the room spun and darkness rolled in. She thought that only a few seconds had passed when she came to, feeling disoriented and queasy. But she was no longer on her feet. She was on the gurney and Dimitri was tying down her legs to the brackets with the thick leather straps. No. She could not let this man tie her up. Once she was tied...she tried to rise and he gave her a short, almost casual punch to her bad rib. The pain was exquisite and stopped all her movement. Dimitri finished securing her legs and began tying down her right hand to the extended arm bracket.

"Don't...don't do this," Julie gasped. She wasn't so terrified that she didn't realize how ridiculous it sounded. As if that was how it worked. A murderer is about to kill you but you just ask politely and he lets you go. What had Kurt said? Feel your feet on the ground? What if your feet weren't on the ground anymore? Her skull felt overstuffed. Terror took over.

Dimitri leaned toward her. She could feel his breath on her face. It carried with it a smell of wheat, as if he'd stopped for a dinner roll just before taking her. She tried to bite at his nose but he was just out of reach. A droplet of his sweat splashed on her forehead. "Your father wants me dead in this bed. So I beat you dead in same bed. Nothing left of you when Dimitri done. Like paste. Then Dimitri and your father even. You see? Even."

"I see," Julie said, her voice cracking, because she did. She understood. She understood that although she had seen awful things in Whitehall, this was what evil looked like. What it sounded like. What it smelled like. She understood now that she wasn't going to make it out of here. She wasn't going to get married or graduate. Wasn't going to see Eric again or her parents or her friends. She was going to die in this room and she was going to die horribly and alone at the hands of an insane death row inmate who hated her father. And she understood that however scared she was, it wasn't nearly enough.

Dimitri finished tying her right arm to the bracket. Then he chuckled, like he'd just thought of a joke. He was so close the ends of his long hair brushed her cheek.

He started in with her left.

CHAPTER 46

Argento moved to the trapdoor as fast as his damaged leg would allow. Forced himself to slow when he descended the ladder to the sixth floor. If he tumbled off the ladder, he'd be no good to anyone. He stopped at the landing. Listened. Listened as hard as he ever had. He didn't know who took Julie or where they'd gone, but he couldn't be far behind. Whoever had her would have to carry her; Julie wasn't going to go meekly along with their program, that was for certain. He heard nothing on the sixth floor. Felt the panic rise, mingled with the heat of the floor. It was the first time he'd felt anything like it since he'd arrived at Whitehall. Since Emily's passing, his life had become a void and his own death didn't scare him.

Hers did.

There was no question he'd go back for her. Going toward danger was what he knew. But it was more than that. What could happen to her was unthinkable. And he had made a promise to Coates that he would get her out. He intended to keep that promise.

Hearing nothing on the sixth floor, he was about to descend to five when a faint sound echoed from somewhere far down the cellblock. Then again, stronger. A voice. He couldn't make out the words, but it was unmistakably female. Julie. Sounding off and making her location known. *Attaway, kid. Attaway.* He opened the sixth-floor door. The only floor he hadn't yet been on. No key was needed now. The door creaked. An overpowering sense of resolve made him forget about the throb of his wounds.

The cellblock was strangely quiet. He smelled something burning, saw a faint layer of gray smoke curling up toward the ceiling but didn't see another soul. The burning smell wasn't wood, wasn't plastic. It was meat. No livestock up here. A person had been on fire. Julie? Had they burned her? A fierce prayer to his Maker to find this woman alive fumbled on Argento's lips. He listened so hard his head hurt. He had no margin for error. *Please say something, kid. Let me know where you are.* Then sounds ahead. Up and to his left. He moved down the hallway, quick, quiet, until he reached a wide steel door that said *Authorized Personnel Only* but was otherwise unmarked. He heard voices behind it. A male voice, low, guttural. And a female voice.

No time for tactical breathing. No time for anything. Argento opened the door.

A massive inmate was tying Julie to a strap-down hospital bed in the middle of the room. He wore yellow Whitehall prison garb, the back of which was stamped with *High Control.* A wide tattoo of brass knuckles ran the length of his formidable neck. Argento took in his surroundings. The bed. The curtains on either side of a large mirror. A large digital clock. This was the room where the state ended people's life with a syringe. Argento didn't know who this inmate was or why he had made the effort to take Julie here for some kind of fucked-up ceremony. But it didn't matter. He wasn't going to ask the man a lot of questions. He was just going to kill him. Argento tried to get a look at Julie, to gauge her condition, how injured she might be, but the inmate completely blocked his vantage point. Argento didn't see any blood on the floor. That was a good start.

The inmate turned to face him. Slowly. Untroubled by the presence of this stranger in their midst. He smoothed his hair back with both hands. There was color to both of his cheeks as if he had just come in from the cold. He was the size of an industrial refrigerator.

"Ask me name," the inmate said. His voice was a low rasp, his accent Eastern European.

Argento could see Julie now, at least enough of her to realize that both of her feet and one hand were secured to the gurney. As soon as the inmate's attention was drawn away from her, she started working to untie herself with her lone free hand. She was still in the game. *Attaway.* But he needed to draw this out to give her more time to undo the straps. He'd play along with the industrial refrigerator.

"Sure," Argento said. "What's your name?"

"Dimitri." The inmate smiled. It looked unnatural, like more of a facial tic. "You know Dimitri?"

"I don't know Dimitri," Argento said. "Not yet. Bus just dropped me off today."

"I kill this girl."

"Okay," Argento said. "All the same to me." He fought to keep his voice neutral. Dimitri was the inmate Simmons said pulled people apart like they were made of bread. But the convict didn't know him, either, and likely wouldn't assume he'd entered the room to attempt a rescue. "You want a smoke before?" He took out the dead warden's pack, shook one out, and lit it. Then he handed the pack toward Dimitri. Trying to burn seconds. To keep him engaged. Maybe he was lonely. There was no one to talk to in Secure Housing.

Dimitri eyed Argento and the cigarettes.

"After," he said. "Get out." There was nothing in his eyes but an animal glaze, as if his frontal cortex had slowed its development early on and then just stopped. He reminded Argento of an unsocialized dog.

Argento readied himself. Dimitri would be plenty strong. But strength only took you so far. It got you to the door, but you still had to walk through. Argento had fought big men before. They tended to be overconfident. They were used to getting their way. Introduce the hurt, some dysfunction, and it quickly cut them down to size. Argento was injured, but he could make one final push. One last good fight. Use his own pain as fuel to drive and feed him.

Argento took a step to the side. To check on Julie's progress. She had just unbuckled the strap on her right hand. She was breathing hard. Not looking at him. Not looking at Dimitri. Just locked in on the task of freeing herself.

Dimitri had told Argento to get out and he hadn't. This seemed to genuinely puzzle Dimitri. As if it had been a long time since someone hadn't done what he'd said.

"What I look like to you?" he demanded.

"Runt of the litter," Argento said, and leapt forward. The action took Dimitri by surprise, and he was too slow to stop Argento from putting the lit cigarette out in his right eye. He clamped both hands to his face and Argento punched him in the kidneys. Dimitri dipped forward but took the blows without a sound. Argento tore his right ear clean off his head, like he was ripping half a ream of paper in two. Now Dimitri howled, and the booming sound of his own voice seemed to agitate him further. Argento flipped him the ear like a lucky penny. Then he took his baton out and drove it into the convict's chest like he was spearing a fish. He reared back for a second blow, just as hard, center of mass, aiming to steal Dimitri's breath, to take him out of the fight. But Dimitri reached out and snatched the baton away from him. The movement was so fast, Argento was still processing it when Dimitri broke the baton over his quadriceps, something Argento had not seen a human being do before. Then he elbowed Argento in the face, his arm just a blur.

The blow knocked Argento down and away. Made his vision swim. He had never been hit that hard. He was sure of it. It was an explosive blow. Like a cannonball. He tasted blood in his mouth.

Across from him, behind Dimitri, Julie had just freed a leg. One more limb to go.

Argento rose. His hamstring twitched and burned. He moved

in on the Armenian, conscious that his hands were empty. He punched Dimitri in the gut. His broken collarbone screamed. It was like striking a redwood. He hit him in the side of the face with a hammer fist. It should have stunned him but there was no give. Dimitri grunted. Didn't move. If he was aware he was missing an ear and his right eye was burned, he didn't let on. Then he took hold of Argento by the leg and bent his right knee in a way a knee isn't supposed to bend. Argento heard a distinct popping sound. Felt a wash of pain. His right knee buckled and he went to the floor. The Armenian loomed over him and scratched his jaw, looking down at Argento like he was an experiment that at first had interested him, but now the novelty had worn off.

Argento rose a second time. Went at Dimitri, dragging his now useless right leg, clumsy and slow. Fighting was exhausting. Even the most fit brawler needed breaks. If a street fight lasted more than a few blows, the winner was usually the person who could delay fatigue the longest. Dimitri was fresh and Argento was already spent. He tried for the diffused strike but he didn't have a stable platform to generate enough force, and the blow glanced harmlessly off Dimitri's bolted-on neck. Argento lost his balance and stumbled into a small steel table near the room's entry door. On top of the table was a clipboard with a pen attached to a chain. He reached for it, but Dimitri was faster. He clamped a hand on Argento's chin to hold it in place, yanked the pen off the chain, and stabbed Argento in the face. The instrument went straight through Argento's left cheek and partway out his right. Argento went down again, a noise rising from his throat that sounded like a squelch.

Dimitri looked amused and pointed at Argento. "Pen face," he said.

Argento had once seen a traffic accident where a transient had wandered into the street and been hit by a delivery truck. The guy flipped over the hood and landed on the pavement. He promptly stood, said, "I'm okay, I'm okay," and walked casually to the curb, where he then collapsed. The doctor later told Argento he had two broken femurs. You could ride the crest of adrenaline for a short while before you crashed. But the crash always came. Argento was already there. The pen currently lodged in his mouth was the least of his problems. His broken collarbone was hampering his ability to hit. There was a ringing in his ears and his legs didn't work. That was when he understood something. That even if he wasn't injured, even if he had a weapon, even on his best day, he could not beat this man. Dimitri was too big, too strong, too impervious to pain. The only thing that would work would be to shut down the Armenian's brain. And Argento didn't have a way to do that.

He was going to lose this fight. It was the final test, and he was failing.

"You here to rescue girl, pen face?"

Argento tried to get up again, his chest heaving, the pain from his legs, shoulder, and face surging through him in electric loops, like a frayed power line. At least one of his QuikClot bandages had loosened, and he could see his blood dripping on the floor. He didn't think he had any broken bones other than the collarbone, not yet, but the cumulative effect of his injuries felt like he was nearing total skeletal collapse. His right leg spindled under him and he went down once more. He flipped to his side, keeping his less damaged left leg up and coiled. Ground defense for whatever Dimitri brought next. It wasn't much but it was all he had left.

"Bad rescue," Dimitri said.

Behind the hulking Armenian, Julie rose from the gurney.

CHAPTER 47

Julie

As soon as Julie had untied herself, she sat straight up on the gurney. She could see Dimitri had hurt Kurt badly. Julie wasn't sure what was even keeping Kurt going. He had taken Dimitri's eye, taken his ear, and the convict was only gaining strength. It was up to her now. She was going to finish this. She jammed her hand in her pocket to retrieve the zip gun.

It wasn't there.

The fear spread through her like tendrils. The force of Dimitri's blow must have knocked it out of her pocket.

Julie rolled off the gurney, away from the two men. She frantically scanned the floor. Was it there? Had she heard it fall?

Ten feet away from her, Dimitri's knee slammed into Kurt's lower back and the sound that Kurt made in response let Julie know he was close to the brink. So was she. But she wasn't going to die on some shitty penitentiary floor. Like Junger had said in his book on war, she wasn't quite at the bottom of the valley. She had more of herself to give. She had more in her than this psycho piece of shit. He was an obstacle to overcome. Like the Mammoth on the Centurion road race. Feel your feet on the ground, feel your feet…

"Go," Kurt gurgled, his eyes wide, searching hers. What she saw there she hadn't seen before from him. Desperation.

"Quiet, pen face," Dimitri said. Pleased with his nickname.

Dimitri's mention of quiet unstuck something in Julie's brain. Something LeMaines had said about the police shooting Dimitri and the resulting injury giving him headaches whenever it got too loud. And how Dimitri had reacted when Kurt mangled his ear, how the sound of his own howl seemed to hurt him more than the injury itself.

Dimitri put his bready forearms around Kurt's neck. Kurt was limp, his eyes dull. Dimitri was going to break him, she thought. Right in half. Then he was going to break her. No. That wasn't going to happen. She wouldn't let it. She came at Dimitri. Straight toward the danger, not away from it. Strode up to him. The air felt thick, as if she had to wade through it. But she felt her feet on the ground. Her rib burned, but the searing pain gave her clarity of motion.

She leaned in.

And screamed in his remaining ear.

The sound originated in some deep recess inside her. It was lung capacity fueled by ten years of road races and cross-training, augmented by the horrors of Whitehall, the pain from her cracked rib, her fervent desire to leave this place and see all the people she loved, her father, her mother, her Eric. It was the chemical dump of adrenaline, the blood flowing to her muscles, the heat rising off the floor, the fear in her gut. It was all the furies she could muster.

Dimitri stumbled back and clapped both hands to his good ear. His mouth contorted and he barked something in Armenian. Julie saw the metallic glint on the floor by his feet. The zip gun. The Armenian had been standing on it. She picked it up. Leveled it at him. She felt like she was moving underwater. Heavy. Slow. Dimitri looked confused. Almost offended. As if to say, *You draw a gun on me in my own house?* He reached out. Tried to grab hold of her arm. But her entire upper body was slick with sweat and his meaty fingers slipped off as she twisted away.

Julie pulled the spring back just like Kurt had taught her.

And, without pause, shot Dimitri in the face.

He was too large to miss. She thought she could see his skin flutter on the bridge of the nose where the bullet went in. He made a garbled sound. Bewildered. As if he couldn't imagine how it had come to this. Then he toppled face-forward onto the bed, his hands loose at his sides, and slid off it to the floor.

Julie put the gun back in her pocket. Then took it out and pointed it at Dimitri. Put it away. Then took it out again. She was dimly aware she was caught in some kind of stress-induced loop.

Across from her, Kurt was saying something. She moved closer. He was so still. His lips were barely moving. She got closer.

It sounded like *Attaway*.

CHAPTER 48

Julie leaned over him. "Where are you hurt?"

Argento didn't respond. The question had too many answers. The initial spasms of pain had grown to long, unyielding ropes. His back felt broken from where Dimitri had bludgeoned it with his knee. His body wasn't listening to his mind anymore. All his earlier bravado, about belonging here in Whitehall, about this being the right place for him, was gone. Belong here? He didn't belong anywhere. He was tired of fighting. Tired of getting hurt. Tired of the weight he was carrying with him—the job, Emily, this prison. It would feel good to set it down. He didn't need to go the last mile. He had done things in his life. Helped people. Taken felons off the streets. He had loved and been loved. And he had lived a violent life. It made sense it would end violently. He had nothing left to finish, nothing left to prove. No one that would miss him. It was zero hour.

"I'm gonna slow you down," Argento managed through gritted teeth. "Leave me here. Just let me die."

Julie didn't look at him. She was assessing her surroundings. As if making calculations. Then she did look at him. There was blood smeared on her face and her jaw was tight.

"Like hell," she said.

He couldn't put weight on either leg, so she took Argento out of the room in a fireman's carry, all 210 pounds of him, each step propelling the breath out of her lungs like a bellows. When she staggered down the hallway, no one tried to stop them. The sixth-floor lifers remained in their cells for reasons Argento's pain-clouded brain couldn't fathom.

"They're not coming out," Julie said with labored breaths, as if she sensed his question. "They're scared of him."

As soon as she made it past the exterior south stairwell door, she sagged to the floor and Argento went down on his hands and knees. The trapdoor ladder loomed above them.

"Can you?" she began, using her forearm to clear her face of sweat but didn't wait for a response. She knew he couldn't climb it. She jabbed the elevator button and looked up. "Lord, I'm asking for one fucking break here. Just one."

The elevator dinged.

An interminable pause.

The doors opened.

Julie push-pulled Argento into the elevator. Hit the *R* button. They might drop into the basement, but they were still doing this because there was no way she could get Argento up that ladder. The doors closed. Another pause. The seconds stretched out, distended. Argento watched Julie hit the button again. Jabbed it with her finger. Then squished it with both thumbs, taking in deep, steady breaths, as much air as she could manage, and letting them out. Then the elevator ascended.

"Okay," Julie said. "Okay."

When the doors opened to the roof, she dragged Argento out of the elevator and collapsed on her back beside him, too spent to celebrate. She stared at the blue sky laced with clouds, a snapshot of freedom, and for a moment Argento thought she was going to reach up and try to pull the blue closer.

Their respite lasted less than a minute. The elevator dinged and a man stepped out. He looked like one of the Kindred from the fifth floor. Bald. White. Tattooed. He held a clawhammer. *Some kind of apparition*, Argento thought. They had already beaten the fifth floor. He was in so much pain, he was seeing things. But when Julie cursed and stood in front of Argento, putting her hands above her waist in a boxer's stance to defend them both, he knew the inmate was real. There it was, the lethal absurdity of having yet another man to fight. They had made it this far, and now some random white-power grease spot would seal their fates.

"I got this," Julie said, her voice hoarse, but Argento knew she didn't have this, no more than he'd had when he'd squared off with Dimitri.

He watched her bite through her lower lip in fear and frustration. Gal had heart, Argento thought. Too bad she was wasting it on him. He couldn't get up in his condition, so he started to crawl toward the Kindred. The pitch of the roof was flat or he'd try to wrap the inmate up and roll off the edge with him. He'd die, but Julie could still make it. As it stood, the only thing he could think of was to yank the pen out of his own mouth and use it to try to slice one of the arteries on the convict's leg. He'd take a clawhammer to the dome, but at least he was going to die outside. He'd have a few more seconds to see the sky.

If Argento thought he had already reached the apex of agony, his efforts to move toward the inmate proved him wrong. It was all pain. It was only pain.

The inmate looked undecided. Go after Julie or for the man improbably crawling toward him. He had probably never been on top of a penitentiary roof faced with this type of choice before. *I'll help you decide*, Argento thought, and jerked the pen from his mouth to ready his futile attack. The action didn't move his pain meter, because it was already at saturation point. He was a few feet from the convict now and had the grim realization that he'd be lucky to generate enough pressure simply to write on the Kindred's leg.

The Kindred's mouth came together in an expression that was

part confusion, part disgust, as if wondering if he had to take Argento's advance seriously. He raised the clawhammer. *Fuck you,* Argento thought, and raised the pen. He heard a crack, which he assumed was the sound of the hammer burrowing into his skull.

But then the Kindred's scalp peeled back from his head.

Argento's full senses came roaring back to him. A helicopter hovering. Now landing on the roof. SWAT cops with helmets, heavy vests, and rifles, some of them wearing jeans and T-shirts, as if they'd gotten the call when they were in training or off duty and had suited up without wasting time on uniforms. Their voices came closer. Argento didn't move. To them, he was a con in an orange jumpsuit within arm's reach of their target package. If he even wriggled toward Julie, they'd light him up.

"Julie Wakefield," he heard a voice roar. A cop's voice, penetrating the din of the copter. He didn't have the strength to raise his head to look.

"Are you injured?"

"I'm good," Julie shouted.

"We gotta go. Right now."

"He's a cop. He's coming with us."

"No, he is not."

"He's coming with us," Julie bellowed, "or I'm not getting on."

"What the fuck we doing here, Sarge?"

"Do it," a different voice sounded. "Cuff him and stuff him."

"He's been stabbed and he's bleeding," Julie shouted. "His legs and his back are hurt, too. Watch his back. Watch everything."

Argento was handcuffed, frisked, rolled onto a gurney, and inserted in the helicopter, which thumped off without delay. The drone-like buzz filled his head. He felt someone checking his bandages. Felt pressure on his right hand. Julie was holding it. Someone had given her a headset to protect her ears from the copter's din. He tried to squeeze back but there wasn't much there. A SWAT cop sat across from him. The cop's tactical helmet had a sticker on it that said, *I Hunt the Evil You Pretend Does Not Exist.*

This made Argento want to laugh but he wasn't sure why. Then he thought back to how Dimitri had called him pen face, and that made him want to laugh, too. He looked around the copter without moving his head. Although he was handcuffed, one of the SWAT guys sitting across from him was training a handgun at his face. Nobody seemed to like him. He tried to say it, but it came out as more of a croak. He was too tired to talk. Too tired to move. Too tired to think. There was pain that accompanied his fatigue, pain from his back and leg and face, but now he was almost too tired to feel it.

A sound caught his attention, rising above the whir of the copter. It was Julie. She was screaming. He tried to move toward her, to help her, but then he realized she wasn't screaming in pain or in fear, but in elation. In release. Screaming because they were out, they were wheels up in the sky, leaving the underworld behind.

CHAPTER 49

When Argento woke from a drug-induced sleep, he was in a hospital bed, his wrist handcuffed to the rail. He was disoriented at first. Why was he in cuffs? He was a Detroit police officer—he put people in handcuffs, not the other way around. It came back to him, in pieces at first, and then as a whole. He was an ex-cop in custody for assaulting a sheriff and his deputy and he was in the hospital because he had been stabbed and then an Armenian had nearly beaten him to death. Nearly. But Julie Wakefield had shot the guy in the head with a zip gun, which had taken all the starch out of him. That's why you play until the final whistle.

He looked around the room. There were two cops in straight-backed chairs on sentry duty. Their uniforms were too crisp to be veterans. Both were on their phones. They looked bored but when they saw his eyes opening, one of them stood.

"I'll get the doc."

The doctor was a middle-aged man with a confident way about him and hair that looked longish for a physician.

"I'm Dr. Sinco," he said. "Nice to see you're alive."

Even with the drugs in his system, everything hurt. "If you say so."

"How are you feeling?"

"Like an angry Armenian tried to kill me with his hands."

"Armenians can run hot," Sinco said without missing a beat. He looked at Argento's chart. There must have been a lot to look at because he took his time before saying, "Well, this is a sad state of affairs. How many Armenians did you fight?"

"I just remember the one."

"Well, let's get to it. You have facial fractures around your eyes and cheekbones. Your left collarbone is fractured. That'll take four to six weeks to heal. Your stab wounds missed your vitals and won't do any permanent damage; you'll need to be on antibiotics and painkillers for a time, but the prognosis is decent there. You tore your left hamstring nearly off the bone. That may require surgery. Your right knee is a mess. That's a conversation I'll leave to our ortho department. As far as your back goes, you have two large left paracentral herniations to the lumbosacral disc. If you're experiencing sciatic pain, we can talk about some other options, including physical therapy and epidurals. And to round things out, your left middle finger has a torn tendon, which is why it's crooked. It's called mallet finger. We'll splint it. You'll be back to committing crimes in no time."

"Is that it? Thought I was actually injured."

"You don't seem too bothered."

"I'm used to things not going my way," Argento said.

In addition to Dr. Sinco's medical rundown, there was a ringing in his left ear and he couldn't lift his right arm above his shoulder. But the arm thing felt muscular, not as a result of any kind of tear, and the ringing he'd had off and on since he started with Detroit SWAT from firearms and flash bangs.

"Even with all that, you're stable, so you'll be discharged soon with a good pair of crutches. Anything else?"

Argento shook his head. When the doctor departed, the two cops guarding him went back to whatever app they had on their phones. Argento was left to muse. When he thought of Emily, he tried not to think of her last days, but how she was before. But he was in a hospital, and the last time he'd been in a hospital was with her. At the end, she had looked so tiny in bed. Tubes running into her. The machines and monitors with their blue lines and green lines rhythmically beeping.

"I love you," she said, her voice as small as she was.

He tried to give her an ice chip from a Styrofoam cup, but she pushed it away. He couldn't form any words, couldn't control the trembling of his hands. He touched his forehead to hers. He forced himself to speak.

"I want," he began. He stopped, his throat constricted. He spoke slowly, pushing each word out. "I want to take you out of here. I want to walk you home."

The machines hummed.

"I'm scared," she whispered. And died.

He touched her arms, her face, her lips. Then he lifted her off the bed, no more than an eighty-pound weight now, and held her to his chest. He opened his mouth to howl, but no sound came out. That made sense. There was nothing more to say.

Argento closed his eyes. When he opened them, Julie Wakefield stood in front of him. She wore a college T-shirt and blue jeans, and her hair was wet from a recent shower. Argento was a prisoner and hadn't been expecting visitors. He figured Julie was allowed in only because her father had made a call.

"Hi," she said. Almost cautiously.

"Hey, pal."

"'How are you' doesn't seem to cover it, but I don't know what else to ask."

He pointed to the holes in his cheeks. "When I chew tobacco, it's gonna spill out the sides."

She shook her head, the hint of a smile playing on her lips. "Okay."

"You?"

"Broken rib. Not much they can do for it. Guess they heal on their own."

"From Dimitri?"

She nodded.

"That guy was a real jerk."

Julie's smile broadened and turned into a laugh. She winced and cradled her side with the broken rib. "Total jerk."

"Got a little rough in there toward the end. I think we earned a break."

"You came back for me." Her voice was quiet in the still room.

"Rain or shine."

"What you did... I don't know what the right words are."

Argento didn't say anything. He didn't know the right words, either.

"The preacher?" he finally said.

"He made it." Julie's face lightened. "They found him in the chapel deep in a prayer circle."

"Pillaire?"

"They're still combing through that place. No sign of him. But there are bodies that haven't been identified. I don't think Rachel ever made it off the third floor, either. Maybe that should bother me, but it doesn't."

"Coates?"

She shook her head slowly. Then she put her hands to her face and cried. Silent at first and then barely muffled sobs, naked grief mixed with maybe some guilt.

"He took on a fight he knew he couldn't win," Argento said. "That's courage most people don't understand."

She nodded without speaking.

"It was a privilege to know him."

"Coates, LeMaines, Aguilar. All the others. I hope I was worth it."

"It's not on you. You didn't ask for this. Be proud of how you carried yourself in there."

"Well, I was glad to get out," she said, wiping her eyes. "I was getting pretty fed up with that place. Gonna let them have it on Tripadvisor."

It was Argento's turn to laugh now. It hurt, and he stopped as soon as he began.

"How do you put something like this behind you?"

"Everyone's different," Argento said. "Maybe you don't, not all the way. But time goes on and you do other things. Getting married and working, maybe having kids. Scrapbooking."

"Scrapbooking?"

"I hunt and fish, work with metal. I don't know what other people do."

"I have a question that might sound kind of strange, all things considered."

"Ask away."

"What are you doing three Saturdays from now?"

"I don't know. Why?"

"Will you come to my wedding?"

A wedding. That hadn't been in the plans when he started on his swing out west. But a lot had happened since.

"If I'm not still in the custody of the state," Argento said, "it would be my distinct pleasure."

"I'd like that very much."

They held each other's gaze for a time. The two cops in the room still had eyes on their phones, but Argento could tell they were listening. Probably wondering why a commoner like him was getting such fancy guests.

"My dad's here," she said. "He wants to see you."

Both cops looked up from their phones. *A visit from the governor? Who was this guy?*

"Send him in," Argento said. He turned to the two cops. "People know me."

"Hot shot," one of the cops replied with an upward head nod.

"Kurt," Julie said.

He looked at her.

"Thank you."

He looked away. Looked down. He needed time before he could speak, and when he did, there was a catch in his voice. "You're welcome," he said.

She rose and approached him. One of the cops stood.

"It's okay," she said. She put her hand on Argento's cheek, kissed him on the forehead, and walked out of the room. She smelled good, Argento thought. Like citrus and clean rain. Her scent was the opposite of Whitehall.

Even though he was handcuffed to a hospital bed and had already been searched several times, the two officers in the room patted him down before the governor entered. Argento didn't mind. He would have patted someone like him down, too.

Christopher Wakefield was tall and crisp looking, with gray hair and a politician's bearing. He came in with a trim, middle-aged Hispanic man who held a tablet. Together, their suits probably cost more than Argento's truck.

"We're good," Wakefield said to the two cops.

"Sir, we—"

"We're good," Wakefield said again.

The two officers looked at each other, and then stood. When they'd left, Wakefield said, "My name is Christopher Wakefield. This is my chief of staff, Alfredo Rosales. I wanted to meet the man who protected my daughter."

"Other way around. She dragged me to the roof when she had a broken rib."

"She's strong, my Julie. But I don't know how she survived in there."

"She never gave up," Argento said. "You can't beat someone who never gives up."

"If I had known—" Wakefield began and then stopped. Cleared his throat, struggled to keep the emotion out of his voice. "If I had really known what kind of place Whitehall was, I never would have let her go. I should have known. Should have looked into it more. I'm the damn governor, for God's sake."

The governor was right. He should have. Especially if there were warning signs. But Argento figured he had a lot of insitutions to keep track of. There had to be at least ten to twenty prisons in the state. You have to figure at least some of them were doing their jobs. And the governor had sent Coates. Without Coates, none of them would have made it. He thought these things but didn't say them. The governor would already know.

"How are you holding up?"

"Got some medical problems," Argento said, "but sounds like nothing they can't fix."

"Good. We're still in the early stages of figuring out what happened at Whitehall. I can't tell you everything. But I want to tell you what I can. We don't think the system shutdown was some outside hacker group or an inmate getting access to facilitate escape, and it had nothing to do with Julie's visit. At this point, we believe it was a disgruntled contractor who put the new system in but wasn't paid, so he inserted a virus through a back door as payback."

"If that's the case, what happens to that guy?"

"I'm not an attorney," Wakefield said, "but a lot of awful things happened in Whitehall stemming from what was essentially a business dispute. Whatever it is, it will be all bad for him."

"One dork good at computers can do a lot of damage."

"That he can. Mr. Argento, I did my homework. I know who you are and I know why you were arrested. You were the right person at the right time for my daughter. I owe you a debt I cannot repay. But the allegations against you are serious crimes against police officers. It would not be appropriate for me to intervene there. Your case is going to need to run its course."

"As long as you're here," Argento said, "it didn't go down the way the deputies wrote in their report."

"How so?"

Argento told him. All of it. From the start of his run-in with Donny Rokus at the carnival to Micah pursuing him for the sheriff's bounty. He kept expecting the governor or his aide to cut him off. To walk out. The governor was a busy man. He had places to be, hands to shake. But they let him talk. It took about ten minutes. Wakefield absorbed it. Rosales took notes on his tablet.

When Argento was done, Wakefield said, "I understand what you're saying. Be helpful if you had corroboration."

Argento mentally traced back to the roadside dustup. The sheriff shoving him at the deputy to manufacture an assault charge. Argento's hand landing on the deputy's chest camera. His hand had not been idle. "I hit the record button on the deputy's body camera at the traffic stop. Figured I'd need the footage to tell my side of the story. In the heat of the moment, I don't think he noticed, especially because the sheriff said they'd just gotten them. Don't think he even knows how all the controls work."

"How'd you know to do that?"

"We had the same cameras when I was on with Detroit. When you hit record, it picks up the previous thirty seconds of footage. After you dock them, the footage is automatically uploaded to a server. I think only DOJ can erase it. Some kind of state mandate."

"Which means the unprovoked assault on you was recorded."

"You bet," Argento said.

"If what you're telling me is true, I'll find that footage and we'll deal with everyone responsible."

There was a cardboard pint of milk on the tray next to Argento's bed. It was room temperature but he was parched from talking so much and drained it. When he set down the empty carton, he said, "It's the government. No one is ever responsible for anything."

"Give me a chance," Wakefield said, "to show you different."

CHAPTER 50

Wakefield was true to his word. He did show Argento different. He was released from the hospital and police custody after a few days of tests and observation, which meant he had missed the Fourth of July holiday and then some. Independence Day was one of the few holidays Argento enjoyed. He liked the steak and beer that accompanied it. He was also rather fond of his country and picked up the occasional history book, so he knew that in 1776 some American colonists had gone to a rally in New York City where the Declaration of Independence was read—Congress had just officially adopted it. They were so fired up, they marched to a local park, knocked the statue of George III off its pedestal, put the head on a spike, and melted the rest down to make musket balls for American soldiers.

That was the kind of nation Argento liked being a part of.

He was given a pair of crutches, a jumbo bottle of pain meds, and the governor's personal cell phone number before he left. His truck was waiting for him in the hospital lot. It looked none the worse for wear, and he didn't even see a bill for the tow fee under the windshield wiper. He limped over to it and opened the hidden compartment. His wallet was still there with all of its contents.

Apparently the Rocker County Sheriff's Department had never been to vehicle trap training.

He was a free man once again, and he used his new liberty to drive to a hotel he could afford outside of St Louis, order some decent takeout, and have a beer, which he mixed with the painkillers and muscle relaxers he'd been prescribed just like the doctors told him not to. Apparently, having a personal connection to the most powerful man in the state yielded results. The body cam footage had indeed been uploaded—the deputy completely unaware he'd been recording—and when a Rocker County assistant DA reviewed it, she declined to file any charges against Argento and instead had contacted her boss, who'd contacted his boss, who was already on the phone with the governor, who was sending a state DOJ team to launch an extensive investigation into Sheriff Rokus and the Rocker County Sheriff's Department.

Two grave DOJ agents had interviewed him at length in the hospital and he'd taken the bare-bones story he'd told Governor Wakefield and added the meat to it. Told them everything he knew and a few things he suspected. Argento had both committed and witnessed multiple homicides, so the interview took all day and part of the next. Both Sheriff Rokus and his deputy were arrested at work for a host of crimes, including assault under the color of authority, conspiracy, and filing a false police report. Citing ties to the community, the sheriff was released on a $500,000 bond.

Argento wasn't briefed on these things by some DOJ lackey or liaison. The governor himself called him at his hotel with updates. Told him that after what he'd done to help Julie, he was family.

"Thanks," Argento said at the end of every phone call. "I appreciate your time."

"Two sides to this thing, criminal and civil," Wakefield said during their last call. "The criminal end will start with the Rocker County Sheriff's Department and end at Whitehall with the feds. Our DOJ team will be joined by the American Correctional Association, the Joint Commission. We will spare no expense."

"I've seen large government agencies fail to get results before. I used to work for a large government agency."

"My daughter is involved. They're not sending the B-team."

"All right."

"The civil side will be a circus. Multiple plaintiffs, with Rocker County and Whitehall as defendants plus the State Department of Corrections for training issues. I can't advise you on the civil suit. I work for one of the potentially involved parties. But you should know your options."

"I'm not going to sue," Argento said.

"You were beaten and unjustly jailed, and as a result you were subjected to everything that happened at Whitehall. With the amount of money you will realistically see in this legal action, you'd never have to work again."

"I don't work now. The city of Detroit gives me a pension and my truck's paid off. I don't like lawyers. Having to come back here and testify for the criminal end is gonna be enough. Don't want to deal with the civil side, too."

"Then tell me what you do want, Kurt."

"Medical bills would be nice."

"Done. What else?"

"The SWAT cop who shot that con on the roof who was about to brain me with the hammer. I'd like his name and work address. I owe him a bottle of whatever he drinks."

"Done."

"I want to know that Derrick Coates's family is going to be taken care of."

"I knew Derrick. I mourn him. He was everything you'd want a trooper to be. I will see to it personally."

"That's it," Argento said.

"Before we go, I need to tell you something. I have an idea what kind of man you are. And if I were you, after what Sheriff Rokus did, I'd want payback. Don't do it. You'll go right back to jail, and this time it will be for real."

"Don't worry. My time in lockup has reformed me."

"You are a pretty interesting guy," Wakefield said.

"I'm from Detroit," Argento said. It would always explain everything.

The incident at Whitehall was on every news station and in every paper. Argento didn't pay much attention. He didn't care. Despite what he'd said to the governor, he was preoccupied with his desire to take Sheriff Rokus apart at the seams. It burned in him. Even being on crutches with a bad back and a mending leg, he could so easily picture it, hurting the man who hurt him. The rush of energy released. The images danced in front of him, bewitchingly. What he had to do, or rather, what he had to stop himself from doing required that he be a better person than he was. Rokus would answer for what he had done, but Argento had to convince himself Rokus wouldn't answer to him. He had to keep control. It was the last thing he had left. And he believed Emily was watching him. It helped that he suspected Rokus wouldn't do especially well in prison. There'd be too many guys he'd put in there for all the wrong reasons.

But then there was Hudson. Rokus had his dog killed. And when Argento thought of Hudson, he naturally thought of Emily. The three of them had been a family. So with Hudson gone, it felt like Emily was being taken away from him a second time.

The governor had advised him against confronting Rokus. It was sound advice.

Argento decided not to take it.

When Argento sat in the chair next to Sheriff Rokus at Louie's Smoke House, it was 4:30 and the weekend crowd had not yet arrived. Louie's was dark and cool inside, with blue-tiled tables and country music strumming in the background. Behind the bar were colored placards of Jesus, Mary, and Busch beer.

The lawman was at the bar alone and out of uniform, wearing a University of Missouri basketball jersey and blue jeans secured by an oversized belt buckle. He was nursing a longneck and eating from a basket of curly fries. There were no deputies around. He stared at Argento, face rigid. And rose to leave.

"Stay," Argento said.

Rokus sat back down.

"You told me where you'd be. Every Friday night. Louie's, for the rib special. I remembered the name."

The bartender eyed the two men curiously. "You all right, Sheriff?"

Rokus nodded, looking straight ahead. He looked older somehow, the skin under his eyes bunched with wrinkles Argento hadn't noticed before. Too old to be wearing a Mizzou team jersey.

"Fair would be me busting you up the way you did me," continued Argento. "But my wife wouldn't want that. And I don't need to. You're going to lose your job, your pension, and you're going to prison—although not the same one you put me in, because they're still hosing the brains off the floors."

"I've been meaning to reach out," Rokus said. His posture was slumped, his voice thin. He wasn't the same man who'd sent Argento downriver while spitting sunflower seeds. But just hearing the sheriff's voice rekindled all of Argento's hostility.

"Your boy Micah reached out for you. But I'm told they haven't been able to put that murder-for-hire charge on you yet and you don't have to worry about his testimony. I left him at the bottom of an elevator shaft."

"This was about my brother. He's family. I know you understand that." Rokus spoke quietly, like he was in church, still looking straight ahead.

"My dog was family," Argento replied. He felt the slow simmer of anger picking up heat. He visualized taking the longneck in front of the sheriff and smashing it over his skull. It had been a mistake coming here. He was going to hurt this man. Not in self-defense, but because Rokus deserved it. Because Argento wanted to. Because it would feel good. He was about to go to jail for real, like the governor had predicted. His hands curled into fists.

"Your dog," Rokus said, as if a memory had just jolted him awake. "Hudson."

Rokus gave the faintest of nods to the bartender, who stepped back and opened a door behind him to an office. Argento heard a rustle, then the pad of footsteps.

Hudson came around the bar.

When he saw Argento, Hudson accelerated and came up on his rear legs to greet him, his distinctive curled tail pumping furiously. The impact sent a painful spasm through Argento's battered torso, pain that was worth every second of the reunion. Argento took a knee and pressed his face to his dog's. Felt the rage pour out of him as if from a spigot, replaced by gratitude and relief. Then he checked Hudson's eyes, his ears, his coat. He looked well-fed, his large black tongue hanging out of his mouth as he barked in elation at seeing his pack. Argento scratched Hudson's belly and fought back a crest of tears. He wasn't going to cry. Not here, not in front of this man.

"Just told you he got put down to make you mad," Rokus said. "I ain't gonna do that. I like dogs. I took good care of him."

"I'm taking him back."

"He wouldn't do nothing I said anyway."

"That's because he's a good boy." Argento stood, using the bar stool to help himself up. Hudson remained at his feet, looking up at him, tail still wagging. It was time for Argento to go. Every minute he stayed would up the chances Hudson's return to him would be revealed as a trap or mirage and he would lose him a second time. Every minute he stayed increased the chances that he would disintegrate Rokus's face with a right cross, already the hardest punch in his life not to throw.

"We're cops," Rokus said. Argento wasn't even sure he was talking to him or why he said it. Every trace of swagger the sheriff had shown at the police station was gone, replaced by a kind of muted acceptance.

"I'm not anymore. Not sure you ever were."

Rokus shook his head, as if he could shake away this turn of events, shake away Argento, make life go back to the way it was. The stark reversal of fortune reminded Argento of something he'd read. That there is so little we have that is safe. So little we have that is ours. Rokus would soon be learning that, too. The feeling he'd be having right around now was the screws tightening. He'd fucked with the wrong Lutheran.

"Welcome to hell, shitbird," Argento said. He left the smokehouse and picked up his crutches outside the door where he'd left them.

Back at his truck, Argento put Hudson in the front seat, closed his eyes, and put his forehead to his dog's. Felt his warmth. Heard his heartbeat.

"Hi, pal," he said into Hud's ear. "I'm sorry. I'm back."

Hudson licked his face and whined.

"I'm back," Argento whispered again. Then he opened his eyes and looked around. The coast was clear.

Now it was okay to cry.

CHAPTER 51

It was a well-heeled crowd at the Wakefield wedding. The guests looked like people with comfortable lives. Pricy suits and surgically plumped lips, well-preserved foreheads, and bodies no doubt shaped by personal trainers. Summertime and the living was easy. Security was as tight as Argento had imagined it would be. His ID was double-checked and he had to go through a metal detector, which meant he had to temporarily hand his crutches to a waiting attendant. When the governor's daughter was getting married, wedding crashers wouldn't do.

He'd been staying at the hotel outside of St. Louis for the last few weeks, doing the exercises the physical therapist had given him so he could avoid surgery. His back, knee, and hamstring were improving, although he still walked slowly with a hitch in his gait and needed the crutches for any appreciable distance. Thus far he'd avoided infection in his stab wounds with a regular change of dressing and faithful antibiotic use. He could now raise his arms above his shoulders without an inordinate amount of pain. Progress. He took Hudson on walks to parks around town, watching him chase birds he had no hope of catching, and spent a half day in East St. Louis to see if it was as bad as he'd heard. It was, but he found a good soul food restaurant on Bunkum Road called Sherry J's Homestyle Cooking and had an early dinner. Treated himself to two helpings of peach cobbler. He figured he'd earned them. He was spending more time in Missouri than he'd planned, but he had made a promise to Julie and intended to honor it.

Jefferson City, the site of the wedding, was a two-hour drive from his hotel. He didn't want to leave Hudson alone that long, so he brought him. His was the only aging pickup with mud flaps in the parking lot of the banquet center. The cars were mostly Mercedeses and BMWs and one Aston Martin DBS V12. James Bond's ride. He did see a beat-up Mitsubishi Mirage with oxidized paint on the quarter panels that he guessed belonged to one of Julie's grad school friends. He'd parked near it in solidarity, a tree-shaded spot for Hudson. It was unseasonably cool for late July, so he kept Hud in the car with the windows down. He wouldn't stay long.

When he got on the reception grounds, he made sure she saw him.

She cut through the crowd and stopped in front of him. "I want to give you a hug, but is that, ah, something you do?"

"Bring it in," he said, and she did, embracing him but gently, in deference to his still-battered appearance and to her own broken rib.

"I wasn't sure you'd show." In her wedding white, she looked fresh, energetic, luminous. As if what had happened to her at Whitehall had actually happened to someone else. She had taken everything that place had thrown at her and still radiated good health and cheer.

"Moved some things around."

"And you're in a suit."

"It's a rental," Argento said. "I don't own much clothing with collars. You get your waffles and coffee with whole milk?"

"Had 'em this morning. How are you healing up?"

"I'm getting there." An elegant-looking Asian woman with a head-turning figure wearing a sleek summer dress walked past them. She could have easily been a magazine cover model. "Nice crowd here.

From the looks of things, I might be the only guest who got shanked in the mouth in state prison."

"No," Julie said, "there's a couple others. I sat you at the same table so you'd have something to talk about."

Argento smiled and his mouth instantly ached. "Take it easy on the funnies. Hurts my face. How are you?"

The luminosity faded, just for a moment. "People have been asking me what it was like, being in there. I can't explain it. I can't even begin to."

"Even if you could, they wouldn't understand."

"I couldn't sleep the first few nights. Just stayed up looking at my bedroom door to see if anyone was going to break in. I'm seeing a counselor."

"Makes sense. Something awful happened to you. That doesn't mean there's anything wrong with you."

A waiter in a dark suit passed by with a tray of crab cakes. Julie took one and pounded it down.

"My Lord, I'm so hungry. They forget to tell you brides don't really get to eat at their own weddings."

"Put some of those cakes in your pockets for later."

Julie looked down and grinned. "Kinda bullshit these dresses don't come with pockets."

"So has any of this given you clarity on what you want to do now?"

"For starters, I'd like to avoid prison riots. But I've been giving what you told me some thought. I'm thinking about applying to the St. Louis police academy. I'm not completely sold on it, but it sounds a lot better to me than more law school or Washington, DC."

"How about that."

"Don't tell my dad. I don't want it to ruin his day."

"Might make him proud. He seems like a law-and-order guy."

They looked at each other. Julie's brow creased and the corner of her mouth trembled. She wiped her eyes.

"I'm already emotional right now with the wedding, but seeing you makes me want to cry."

"Is it the hole in my face?"

"No. It's because I am grateful to be alive. To marry the person I love. To pursue a career that's important. But I'm worried about you. Because you have to live with the loss of those things. I'm afraid you're going to be lonely. That you're going to be sad."

Another waiter came by. Julie didn't even glance at the tray. She was focused on Argento to the exclusion of everything else. She put her hand on his forearm. "I know you're not asking for advice. But I'm going to tell you the same thing you told me when we were on the top floor of Whitehall."

"What's that?"

"Be who you're supposed to be."

"I will," Argento said.

"I would have liked to have met Emily. I bet you were a good husband to her."

"I had to do some things in that prison that I thought would make you believe the opposite."

"I think it's more obvious than you realize."

"I tried hard. Maybe that counts for something."

The buzz of wedding activity heightened around them. Someone was pulling on her arm. There was someone else to see. He'd been to a few weddings before. The bride was always in high demand.

"Been a hell of a ride," he said.

"Yes it has."

"Go work the room. I'm going to find your man, tell him how lucky he is."

"I'll miss you, Kurt. You're like the strange, I don't know, violent uncle I never had."

Argento thought that over. Then he said, "You're like the crotch-kicking niece *I* never had."

She smiled hugely and then hugged him again. This time there was more force to it. "Be good to yourself," she said and began walking away.

"Julie."

She turned.

"You saved my life," he said quietly. "I thank you for that. I'm going to try and do something good with it."

Her eyes were very bright when she said, "You're welcome," and stepped back into the wedding throng.

Argento searched the crowd for Eric, whose picture he'd seen in the wedding announcement. He found him near the head table talking to someone's grandmother, looking relaxed in a tuxedo. He had cut the ponytail. Maybe she'd said something to him. He didn't need to tell Eric he was a lucky man. Argento was sure he already knew.

He stopped in the bathroom to clean up and examined himself in the mirror. He looked awful. It wasn't just the facial laceration. It was the bruising that left his face a sickly yellowish-green. Like someone who had just washed ashore. He had made the drive here, but he didn't see himself seated at the reception next to some couple talking about how their son was first team singles at Rutgers. He had nothing against rich people. He had known a few in his day and there didn't seem to be a higher percentage of boring assholes among the rich than any other group. But he felt no need to join them. He said he'd come to the wedding. He hadn't said he'd stay.

It was about two thousand miles to the Pacific. He hadn't found what he was looking for in Rocker, Missouri. If you don't find what you want in one town, you go to the next. The trip took him three days. Through Nebraska, southern Wyoming, Utah, Nevada, and then California. He stopped at roadside diners and stayed in budget hotels where he and Hudson slept next to each other, his hand nestled in his dog's fur, a third of his family back at his side.

It was early afternoon when he saw the blue-green swell of the ocean. He drove south on Highway 1 until he saw signs that said

Montara State Beach. He pulled into the lot and got Hudson out on a leash. He took his crutches, although he wasn't sure he needed them anymore.

He and Hudson followed the path to the water, past a three-story bathhouse, where two men in tight T-shirts were drinking bottled beer and smoking cigarettes while they watched what little action was brewing. The beach was about half full. Argento let Hudson splash around at the water's edge and then they sat in the sand, away from people. The teens on the beach, with their loud conversations and pronounced makeup, were trying to look old and the middle-aged folks in their ill-fitting swimsuits were trying to look young. He didn't spend much time watching them. The ocean was in front of him and he could look at water all day. He wasn't sure why. There was something cleansing about just being around it. He'd had to kill men in Whitehall. Maybe he could wash some of that off him here. But he didn't regret what he'd done. He could square his actions in a court of law and before God.

Emily would have the right thing to say at a time like this. Or she'd know to say nothing at all. She knew *him*. Knew his faults, his sins, and loved him anyway. She said it was because when he saw something wrong, he tried to fix it. She had brought him joy and balance. She was his refuge when he didn't even know he needed one.

"We made it, Hud," Argento said, scratching his dog behind the ears. Now they just had to figure out what was next. Van Dyne had talked to him about his calling. But if he wasn't DPD anymore, what was he?

Argento had walked away from his own life but he could go back. Not to the job, but to the city. Detroit was his home. As far as making a living, he was good with tools. There was always construction or fixing cars. For now, he had a truck, his dog back, and an open road. For now, he had no life but this. Argento was a pragmatic sort, and he knew that as soon as he thought he'd turned a corner, the sadness would return. Grief has a way of waiting for you. He wanted peace and he wasn't sure where he could find it. But he carried Emily's memory with him, and if he could keep doing that, maybe he would not be lost. And helping Julie and the others could be the start of something. Police officer or not, perhaps that was what he was put on this earth to do. When he was finished up on the sixth floor of Whitehall, Julie Wakefield had forced him to go on.

He wasn't going to waste that second chance.

Argento wasn't sure if Julie would join the St. Louis PD or if it had been an impulse thought. But the prospect of her filling the job he'd vacated made him feel oddly satisfied. She'd be as worthy a candidate as any. She was already more than battle-tested.

He heard the sound of glass breaking behind him and turned. The two guys in tight T-shirts on the top level of the bathhouse were trying to drop their beer bottles into a trash can on the beach level and missing badly, the bottles shattering on the concrete island below. A mother walking her young child nearby yanked her out of harm's way.

"Watch it, please," she snapped, checking her daughter to see if she'd been cut by the shards.

"Fuck you," one of the guys said.

"I said please."

"And I said fuck you."

Argento rose to his feet and propped the crutches under each arm. "Cool it, fellas," he called up to them.

"Fuck you too, gimp," the other guy said. Both men were drunk. They each dropped another beer bottle that broke a good six feet from the trash can.

Argento was still injured. He could easily let it be. But it didn't matter that the job was behind him. He despised criminals and would not tolerate bullies. He wouldn't let them get their way. He would not adapt to them. They would adapt to him. This is what he did. This is who he was.

And he'd be the same way tomorrow.

Argento crutched over to the side of the bathhouse. He was at probably 60 percent capacity. More than enough to handle two sloshed townies. He'd ask them to leave first. He'd be polite. Polite but firm. Whether they fought was up to them.

But Argento found himself hoping they would.

He tossed the crutches aside and tied off Hudson's leash. "Be right back," he said.

And went up the stairs.

ACKNOWLEDGMENTS

As a cop, I've spent numerous hours in county jail booking prisoners and interrogating suspects, but I haven't spent much time in state prison (once someone is there, the job of the police is largely over). So I enlisted plenty of help in writing this book. Many thanks to James L'Etoile, former prison warden and current first-rate crime author, for answering my many questions. A tip of the hat to CDC Lt. Samuel Robinson for connecting me with a pre-COVID tour of San Quentin and Sgt. Robert Gardea for leading it. The staff at San Quentin does thoughtful, important work both to secure public safety and to better the lives of their inmates, some of whom have achieved positive, lasting change in their lives and show genuine remorse for the crimes they've committed. My fictional prison in these pages is poorly run, short-staffed, and chaotic. It is not like San Quentin. My departures from actual prison design and protocols are my own to suit the purposes of this story. Any mistakes are mine.

I have relied heavily on a talented squad of beta-readers whose skill would rival that of any metro SWAT team. Thank you to Brent Ewig, Andy Tantillo, Bill Mesce Jr., and Mark Roeda for your wise feedback. You guys bring it.

Thanks to Jim Thomsen, the most noir guy I know, for his coverage edit and words of encouragement.

Author and all-around good guy Nick Petrie offered me advice along the way on matters of writing, agents, promotion, and publishing. Same goes for author Doug Brunt, who pointed me in the right direction on several occasions. These are two established and busy writers who were generous with their time. Thanks, gentlemen.

A nod to SFPD lieutenant and fellow writer Dan Silver, former city paramedic, who assisted me with medic terminology and field practices.

Thanks to Albert Won, family friend, doctor, and my daughter's youth basketball coach, for answering my medical questions, including the physiology of one man tearing another man's ear off with his bare hand. He took this question completely in stride, like there was nothing unusual about it, almost like he was expecting it. Good stuff outta you, Dr. Won.

Thank you to my incandescent wife, Jennifer, and my two daughters, who allowed me to write this book without (many) interruptions. Love you turkeys.

And a thousand thanks to my splendid literary agent, Caitlin Blasdell of Liza Dawson Associates, who rolled up her sleeves, helped me polish my novel, found it a home, and acted as my guide from there. I imagine her with a lamp in one hand and a sword in the other, navigating a steep winding road as I carefully step behind her. It's 2024 and I'm not sure why there's a sword, but it's my image, not yours. I have already started a document called Caitlin's Words of Wisdom, and it could soon become a book in itself.

And finally, thank you to my undaunted editor, Kirsiah Depp, and the top-flight editing and design (that cover catch your eye like it did mine?) team at Grand Central for their ongoing wisdom and expertise. You all made this book better. I am fortunate to be on your team.

ABOUT THE AUTHOR

Adam Plantinga is a patrol sergeant with the San Francisco Police Department whose first two nonfiction books—*400 Things Cops Know* and *Police Craft*—have become his calling cards to the world of thriller writers. *400 Things* was nominated for an Agatha and was deemed "the new Bible for crime writers" by the *Wall Street Journal*.